Renno took the longbow from Beth's hand and gave her the musket. "Try to lower the odds by one with this," he told her.

She put a hand on his arm to stop him, but he was gone, running across the sand toward the dune line and his enemies. Two muskets fired. One ball kicked up sand just behind Renno as he zigzagged. Another snipped at his hair, making a little smacking sound. He dived and rolled and came up with his tomahawk in hand.

He heard Beth's musket bark and glanced quickly behind him to see another Frenchman fall. The musket that had dropped from the dead man's hands had been aimed at Renno's back.

"You!" Lemaître called from the protection of a dune. "I surrender. Do you hear me? I fight no more."

Renno looked back toward Beth. She had reloaded and had the musket pointed toward the sound of the French captain's voice.

"Come out, then," Renno ordered, moving silently toward the dune, his tomahawk ready.

Lemaître extended his left hand toward the white Indian.

"Watch out, Renno!" Beth cried, even as she fired.

The White Indian Series
Ask your bookseller for the books you have missed

The White Indian Series
Book XX

SACHEM'S
SON

Donald Clayton Porter

 Created by the producers of
The Holts: An American Dynasty,
The First Americans, and **The Australians.**

Book Creations Inc., Canaan, NY • Lyle Kenyon Engel, Founder

BANTAM BOOKS
NEW YORK • TORONTO • LONDON • SYDNEY • AUCKLAND

SACHEM'S SON

*A Bantam Book / published by arrangement with
Book Creations, Inc.*

PRINTING HISTORY

Bantam edition / December 1990

*Produced by Book Creations, Inc.
Lyle Kenyon Engel, Founder*

ISBN 0-553-28805-9

Published simultaneously in the United States and Canada

Bantam Books are published by Bantam Books, a division of Bantam Doubleday Dell Publishing Group, Inc. Its trademark, consisting of the words "Bantam Books" and the portrayal of a rooster, is
Registered in U.S. Patent and Trademark Office and in other
countries. Marca Registrada. Bantam Books, 666 Fifth Avenue,
New York, New York 10103.

PRINTED IN THE UNITED STATES OF AMERICA

OPM   0 9 8 7 6 5 4 3 2 1

SACHEM'S
SON

Prologue

For three days he had purified himself by fasting; with each dawn the attack of the enemy seemed imminent. After one day of mental and physical preparation he had been honed to a peak of readiness, every sense alert, every muscle humming with health and youthful power. Three days of communing with the spirits, however, while cleansing his body and soul through self-denial, had left him tense, uneasy, and light-headed. He could not understand the delay. The Chief-Who-Never-Sleeps, the American general Anthony Wayne, had been seeking battle for months, for years. The Ohio tribes, three thousand strong, were massed in a labyrinth of fallen trees before Wayne's position, and still the army of the white man did nothing but demonstrate.

When the grandly uniformed American Legion finally marched with great precision and discipline into the smokes and deadly musket fire from the well-concealed Indians, cold steel gleamed at the tip of the soldiers' muskets. To the Indian, the long knives were unmanly and terrible weapons.

The young Shawnee warrior Tecumseh had chosen his position carefully: In order to use his bayonet, the legion soldier first had to contend with the men hidden within the twisted, entangled labyrinth of the storm-felled trees. Tangled brush and jagged, broken limbs made it impossible for the bayonets of the American Legion to reach Tecumseh. He killed. He selected his targets carefully, for his supply of musket balls was limited. Beside him his brother, Tenskwatawa the Prophet, who spoke with the Master of Life, also made his mark with the strength of his arm and the accuracy of his bow.

A storm of sound numbed Tecumseh's ears: the thunder of musketry, the shrill screams of dying men, the shouts of the well-drilled legionnaires as they surged forward, pushing the full strength of the Ohio tribes before the awful steel of their bayonets.

Surrounded, Tecumseh and the Prophet concealed themselves and took the opportunity to shoot from ambush into the confusion of swirling gun smoke. The two Shawnee brothers were among the few who continued to fight after the American Legion had penetrated the natural abatis. Most of the warriors of the Ohio tribes fled in panic and, emerging from the fallen timbers, ran directly into the field of fire of General Wayne's cavalry. Those who survived sought the promised protection of a nearby British fort only to be locked out and forced to face the merciless offensive of the victorious American Legion.

Tecumseh watched the rout from the timbers, creeping from his place of concealment to see the shame and hopelessness of it. Tears ran down his face. His brother closed his eyes to avoid witnessing the disgraceful retreat.

Never had the Indian fought under a more capable leader, for the Miami war chief Little Turtle had been a wise general who had chosen his ground well. The catastrophic defeat could not be blamed on Little Turtle, Tecumseh thought as he watched the slaughter of those who ran blindly to escape the steel of the legion. Nor could the fault be placed on the individual Indian warrior. Under circumstances of his own choosing, the Indian was as brave as any soldier who had ever taken the field.

The shouts and screams of battle moved away from the fallen timbers. Tecumseh opened his mouth to explain the defeat to the Prophet, then decided that it was unnecessary to speak, for they had discussed the basic difference between the Indian and the white hordes before. The Indian warrior, as fearless as he was, did not have the iron discipline of the white soldier. No Indian warrior could ever be convinced to march stupidly into the muzzles of three thousand rifles. For a while the warriors hidden among the fallen trees had fought well, but when they faced the cold steel of a bayonet charge, their ingrained dread of the long knives and their lack of mass discipline had resulted in vanquishment.

Thus it was that the dream to establish an Indian nation north of the Ohio died on that warm day, 20 August 1794, in a storm-tangled woodland near the Maumee River. The vision of Little Turtle and the hopes of thousands died on the long knives of the American Legion.

On a narrow stretch of open ground bounded by the river, the Indian dead lay strewn. No human scavengers prowled among the dead. The legion, holding its discipline, was still in pursuit of the survivors. Only a small group of mounted soldiers remained on the field near the river, silently surveying the forms of the fallen. One of them was not dressed in the uniform of the Americans but wore the war regalia of a sachem of the Seneca nation. Tecumseh recognized the Seneca as much from the proud set of his shoulders as from his bronzed face and blazing blue eyes.

"Renno of the Seneca," he said, half in salute, half in explanation to Tenskwatawa the Prophet. "Again he fights with the Americans."

Tenskwatawa muttered a Shawnee curse.

"And again the Seneca sachem is on the winning side," Tecumseh said. "Will it be ever so?"

"The spirits tell me—" Tenskwatawa began.

"The spirits have told you many things," Tecumseh said sharply. "The spirits told you that we would win a great victory here. And now—"

"The Master of Life told me," Tenskwatawa said, his voice low and firm, "that victory will come when all tribes fight side by side as brothers. Here that was not true, for only a few tribes faced the white man's steel."

Tecumseh laughed. "And who is to be the man who, like Hiawatha of the Iroquois, carries the message? Long ago the Iroquois were only five tribes. Is the new Hiawatha to travel the length and breadth of this great land to speak to hundreds of chiefs and their tribes?"

"Only thus can victory come," the Prophet responded.

"The Seneca Renno tells all that the path of the future follows the white man's road. Perhaps he is right."

"This is Tecumseh who speaks?"

"The words come from my mouth, but not from my heart." Tecumseh sighed. "There will come a time when we will meet, the Seneca and I, and then perhaps it will be this that will decide." He put his hand on his tomahawk. "Words have but a short life and are easily brought into being. In the end the spirits decide what is true."

"If words could convince the Seneca and others like him that they are wrong," Tenskwatawa said, "we would be many. In the South the Creek are strong, and to the west along the Father of Waters there are many tribes. It is you who was given the gift of the golden tongue, my brother. You will be the new Hiawatha. It will be you who will use your wise words to convince all the tribes and all those like the Seneca Renno that we must stand together. You will tell all those who have the blood that we must fight side by side as brothers or be hunted into oblivion by these teeming whites."

Tecumseh did not want to admit that his brother's words wakened pride tinged with righteous anger in his breast, then combined those emotions into a sense of purpose that threatened to consume him. "Come," he said, "we must leave this place of disaster and shame. But let us not forget what happened here. It will be a lesson burned into our minds like a brand. "We must convince all the tribes that it is death to face the white hordes in disunion."

They had to make their way through scattered Kentucky mounted militia, but that was not difficult because the Kentuckians had become separated in the dense woodlands west of the battlefield. When the brothers were safely into the dense forests to the west, they rested. Tenskwatawa treated the slight wound on Tecumseh's upper arm caused by a musket ball. The tall trees sighed with a night wind around their fireless camp, and the vastness of the forest seemed to belie the constant threat of white expansionism. As Tecumseh tried to sleep, however, his ears rang with the remembered thunder of the legion's guns, and his dreams were troubled.

He was twenty-six years old. He had been fighting against white encroachment into the lands of his people all his life, and he had lost a father and brothers to the struggle. His remaining brother, slightly younger, conversed with the Master of Life and received orders and revelations. The Prophet was certain that the Master of Life had given Tecumseh a sacred mission. The way would be long, and it would take years of his life to accomplish the mission. There was left only the need to make a beginning.

Chapter I

"When Renno and I were young men," said El-i-chi, senior warrior and shaman of the southern Seneca, "we traveled far away to a land of blowing sands and waterless wastes."

Toshabe, mother of two warriors and the warrior woman, Ena, laughed. Her strong younger son looked at her in question.

"It is only because you still seem quite young to me, my son," Toshabe explained.

"My mother herself is young," El-i-chi said.

"Ah. When one counts over fifty winters—"

"One is still young as long as one can laugh," Renno said. He sat between his eleven-year-old boy, Little Hawk, and nine-year-old Renna, his pale-haired daughter, who with every passing day looked more like her late mother, Emily.

"Tell how my father killed the mountain cat in the waterless lands," Renna said.

"We must consider the request of our guest," El-i-chi said, nodding at a tall, gangling white man who wore dusty black and whose lank, black hair hung to his shoulders.

"You are most considerate," said Reverend Waith Pennywhistle. "I would be interested, of course, in hearing of any feat of daring performed by my gracious host." He made a little bow toward Renno, sachem of the Seneca. "At another time, perhaps, I can hear the stories of the wild Apache of the far West."

Pennywhistle had come to the Seneca village riding a moth-eaten mule; he wore a black hat pulled low over his burning eyes and carried a Bible in his hand. He had been invited to stay because he told a thundering good tale based on the heroes and kings of the Old Covenant and because of a promise that Renno had made to his dead wife, Emily. The son that Emily had borne him and the daughter who had been given life only days before the death of her mother would, he had promised, know the words of the white man's Bible, would hear the preachings about the God-With-Three-Heads.

"The Apache storytellers speak of the coyote," El-i-chi said, "as a cunning animal who was envious of the owl in the beginning because the owl was the one who had arrows."

"Yes," said Little Hawk, leaning forward in anticipation of the retelling of a story he had come to love.

"And not only did the owl have arrows, he had a magic club with which he killed men."

"Oooooo," breathed Renna.

El-i-chi made a scary face at Renna and went on in a low, growling voice, "And then he ate them!"

"Ugh," Renna said.

"He sang *woo hwoo woo*," El-i-chi said. "*Woo hwoo woo*. And when the coyote came to listen, the owl said that he was hungry and looking for men in the low pass of the mountains below. Coyote said that he, too, was hungry and asked Owl to allow him to eat men. Owl sang *woo hwoo woo* and thought about it and said that only one could eat man and that it would be decided by the spirits. The one who could vomit human flesh—"

"Ugh," Renna groaned.

"Be quiet, Renna," Little Hawk whispered. "You've heard all this before."

"—would kill and eat men. Owl said that both of them must close their eyes. Owl closed his eyes, but Coyote did not. He watched Owl, and when Owl began to vomit human flesh, Coyote caught it in his hands and substituted his own vomit in front of Owl so that when Owl opened his eyes, he saw only the grasshoppers that had been vomited up by Coyote. 'Where did I drink in grasshoppers?' Owl asked. Coyote showed the human flesh he had stolen from Owl. In his triumph Coyote ran all around Owl and bragged about his speed. He said that because he could run fast, he was to be the one who would kill and eat people. But Owl ran faster and outran Coyote. Coyote said, 'Those legs of yours, Owl, are too long. If they were shorter, you could run much faster. Close your eyes and I will fix your legs for you.' "

"Owl was sort of dumb in the beginning," Renna explained to everyone.

"So Coyote broke Owl's legs and cut them off, leaving them very short so that Owl could only waddle along. Then, running circles around Owl, he stole Owl's arrows, leaving Owl the magic club. Owl threw the club and hit Coyote, and the club returned to Owl's hand. But Coyote, by cutting off Owl's legs, had stolen some of Owl's magic. When Owl threw the club again, Coyote said, 'Where your club falls, there it will lie.' And the club would not go back to Owl's hand. Owl, without his arrows and without his magic club, slunk away and hid. Coyote used Owl's arrows to kill men, and that is how Coyote became an eater of meat."

"Charming story," said Reverend Pennywhistle. "But, I fear, the product of a primitive mind. We know, don't we, that God made the animals and gave them their characteristics, and then He gave dominion over the animals to His masterpiece of Creation, man."

Little Hawk was quite respectful of his mother's God, but he was not at all convinced that the white man had captured God and enclosed Him between the black covers of the Bible. He had reached an age at which he could read the Book himself, and he found it to be a puzzling mixture of meaningless lists of names and accounts of burned animal sacrifices, which in the mind of a Seneca represented a waste of good food. There were some rousing stories hidden away, especially in the chronicles of the kings, but all in all Little Hawk found that the presentation of God in the Bible was confusing. He could understand Jesus a bit better than the God of the Old Bible, for Jesus, like his father and his uncle El-i-chi, could speak with the spirits and cast out devils. A boy of eleven didn't spend too much time thinking about such things, but at night when his father, obedient to the wishes of the long-dead mother, reminded him to say his prayers, he alternated between talking to Jesus, the Son of God, and talking to the Master of Life, the Supreme Being of his father and the Seneca. It was not beyond possibility, he thought, that his mother's God and his father's God shared one face and were, in fact, one and the same.

He had voiced his views to the black-clad preacher. The white man's face had turned almost purple, and the man had emitted a great burst of indignation. Little Hawk had listened carefully, thinking that the preacher's thundering words lacked something, for they did not explain how—if indeed the traditional gods of the Seneca were false gods—they had given gifts to his father such as the magic ax, with which Renno had killed many Chickasaw, and the spirit knife, which had been carved by lightning from a ledge of flint.

"When you shout," he had told Pennywhistle, "my ears ache."

Waith Pennywhistle was vaguely Lutheran and somewhat Baptist. He held no seminary degree. He told his Seneca hosts that his ordination had come direct from God while he was plowing a rocky field on the eastern side of the Great Smoky Mountains. God had appeared to him, saying, "Go, my son, and carry my dread words of warning to the heathen beyond the blue hills."

Since God's word was not to be denied, he had left the hardscrabble farm the next morning, accompanied by one woeful hound dog who did not live to cross the passes that led to the Tennessee Territory and the first of the Cherokee villages southeast of Knoxville. When the old dog, Pennywhistle's last link to his past life, was killed by a bear, the reverend took it as a sign from the Lord that he was meant to be alone, like John the Baptist, the voice of one crying in the wilderness.

The self-appointed evangelist had marched into the land of the Cherokee at a time when the white man's relentless drive to swallow up Indian lands was momentarily slowed by the conquest of the Northwest Territory. In the year 1795, an uneasy peace existed in that vast area west of the mountains and east of the Mississippi—a peace broken with unpredictable irregularity by encroaching white men and young warriors who scorned the teachings of peace by such sachems and chiefs as Renno of the Seneca and Rusog of the Cherokee.

The Seneca had come to the South after the War of American Independence under the leadership of Renno's

father, the great sachem Ghonkaba. Renno's village cojoined
the village of his brother-by-marriage, the principal Cherokee chief, Rusog. Although Rusog's heart held a great
reservoir of resentment and hatred for the white intrud-
ers, he was a wise man forced by events to agree with
Renno that it was self-destructive to fight the white man,
whose numbers rivaled those of the birds in the sky. All
over the far-flung hunting grounds of the Cherokee Nation, men were pitted in a constant pattern of confrontation, battle, and death; but in Rusog's area of influence,
there was peace.

Before the coming of the white man, the great Cherokee Nation had covered large portions of the areas that
would become the states of Virginia, Kentucky, North
Carolina, Tennessee, South Carolina, Georgia, Alabama,
and Mississippi. In pre-Columbian times the ferocious
warriors of the Cherokee had conquered many tribes and
repelled others who sought to infringe upon Cherokee
hunting grounds—among them the fierce Seneca of the
League of the Iroquois. In the time of Rusog the grandeur
of the Cherokee was diminished, and the threat to Cherokee autonomy came not from other Indian tribes but from
the continual pressure of the white man's western expansion.

Pennywhistle's presence in the Seneca village had not
been welcomed by all. El-i-chi's wife, Ah-wa-o, the Rose,
and Ena, onetime warrior maiden who was now the mother
of the active twins Ho-ya and We-yo, were open in their
contempt for the teachings of the white missionaries.

"Why is it," Ena demanded of Reverend Pennywhistle
on the first night of his stay in the village, "that the first
thing a white missionary wants to do is change that which
is traditional with our people?"

Pennywhistle had been preaching that a wife should
be subservient to her husband, using quotes from the
Bible to emphasize the superiority of men. Such so-called
teachings did not sit well with a woman of the Seneca.

In all tribes of the League of the Ho-de-no-sau-nee

there existed a semimatriarchy where women exercised the power to name sachems, among other things. Among the Cherokee a woman had many rights as well. For example, if a husband displeased a woman, she had only to pack her husband's things in a sack and set them outside the door to the lodge and she was rid of him, legally divorced. Remarriages were common, and there was a certain amount of sexual freedom for all Indian women. Most tribes, including the Cherokee, had laws regarding adultery but were lax in enforcing them unless the offending woman became too blatant in her excesses. In such cases she could be taken by up to thirty men on the theory that if she were given what she craved in such excess, she would be satisfied once and for all and would behave rationally in future sexual matters.

Ironically, Pennywhistle was to be a witness to an example of the power of women in the Seneca tribe during his stay.

Little Hawk was large for his age. At eleven he showed signs of one day being taller than his father. His three-quarters of white blood made him a throwback to his paternal great-great-grandfather, the original Renno. The shape of the man-to-be was evident in Little Hawk's lithe form, in his blond, flowing hair, and in his clear, hard-edged blue eyes. Already he could bend a warrior's bow, although he could not quite draw the English longbow that was one of his father's favorite weapons. In a day he could cover many miles at the warrior's pace, and being a true son of his father, he found great pleasure in pushing himself to greater efforts, leaving behind all the other warriors-to-be, who accepted his leadership without question. To run was his pleasure. He loved to run until pain was a blinding, all-devouring ache, and then to run harder until the magic happened, and the lungs seemed to become enlarged and the muscles gained new life. The feel of the wind in his face became a reward, and the long miles passed under feet that were suddenly made light, as if with wings.

On a day when the great thunderheads soared upward in vast, white columns and the squirrels skittered up and down the huge tree trunks in pursuit of romance, Little Hawk ran lightly down a well-traveled trail that led toward the east. His flying feet seemed hardly to touch the ground. The sound of his passage was a soft fall of foot, so there was no forewarning to the animals of the forest. A young deer leaped in panic and crashed into the brush as Little Hawk burst into a small glade. Two amorous squirrels paused in their heated activity to chatter the alarm.

The trail climbed the side of a ridge and opened into a grassy meadow. Larks soared around the running boy. A crow called out a warning to all its kind and flew higher for safety. Where a crystal rill sparkled down the slope of the meadow, Little Hawk paused, fell to his stomach, and drank deeply, then laughed aloud with the sheer pleasure of being strong and young and alive. He threw his arms out and looked upward to the blue sky pillared with the tall clouds. He thought a prayer of thanksgiving, addressing it to God in whatever form, and then he was on his feet and wondering whether or not to run on up the slope to the top of the ridge before turning back toward the village. As he stood in indecision, his chest moving with his deep inhalations, he spotted a figure emerging from the upslope trees into the meadow. His heart thudded. He had not seen his grandfather in over three years, but he recognized Roy Johnson immediately.

Johnson was a tall man, thinned and toughened by life on the frontier. When Little Hawk ran toward him, Roy grinned, his heart filling, his eyes misting. Little Hawk whooped a greeting and threw himself into Roy's arms with a force that sent both tumbling to the grassy earth.

"Hoc-sote'," Little Hawk said in Seneca. "I thank thee that thou art well, Grandfather."

"Grown a bit, have we?" Roy asked, grinning, coming to his knees to clasp the boy to his breast for a moment before pushing him to arm's length. "By God, you beautiful boy, I can see both your father and your mother in you."

Little Hawk jumped to his feet and extended a hand, which Roy took. Roy came to his feet wearily. "Didn't expect a reception way out here."

"Something led me in this direction," Little Hawk explained.

Roy nodded, accepting the statement. He had learned long ago that Little Hawk's father had a special relationship with the spirits. It was not inconceivable that the son might also be gifted with some of Renno's surprising, seemingly clairvoyant insight.

"We were concerned about you, Hoc-sote'," Little Hawk said as he matched Roy's long strides. "My father and my uncle returned months ago."

"Well, I stuck around for a while, boy," Roy said with a sigh. "Stayed too long, maybe. Stayed until I had a bellyful of Anthony Wayne's war."

Roy still looked weary and trailworn after reaching the village, after embracing Renno and El-i-chi, after greeting Toshabe and Ha-ace and Rusog and Ena and all the others, and after holding Renna in his arms to see his Emily reincarnated.

"They lost more than a battle," he told Renno and El-i-chi after Renna had crawled into a bed in Ha-ace's longhouse and the fire had burned low to illuminate the faces of the adults and a sleepy but curious Little Hawk with a coppery glow. "The Ohio Indians were humiliated, deserted by their ally the British, and deprived of everything that mattered to them—land, pride, tradition. It's only a matter of time before all the lands north of the Ohio are gobbled up."

"And will that satisfy the white men?" Rusog asked.

"What do you think, my friend?" Roy asked, disgusted.

"I think the white man will not be satisfied," Rusog said, "until he has cut down the trees all the way to the ocean that is said to exist in the West, until he has killed every deer and buffalo, until he has driven the Indian into that western sea."

Roy was silent.

"You were at the final councils?" Renno asked.

"I was there," Roy said. "You've read the Treaty of Greenville, I reckon."

"We have," El-i-chi answered grimly.

"Way it reads," Roy said, "the tribes gave up a lot of land but kept some. Way it's really working out, it might as well have read that they gave up all lands." He shrugged. "Well, Little Turtle tried. He was a good man." He looked up at Renno. "Now there's another one in the wilderness. Not even a chief, they say, but acting like a great war chief. Name's Tecumseh. Has a brother called the Prophet, Tenskwatawa. Together they're going to give some trouble up there. They let Anthony Wayne know how they felt by refusing to attend the council that produced the Treaty of Greenville. Tecumseh said in advance that there could be only one result of treatying with the white man, and that was loss of Indian land. They're out in the Indiana Territory now. You know that Anthony's aide, William Henry Harrison, was appointed governor up there?"

Renno nodded.

"Tecumseh and the Prophet have sworn to oppose the governor's rule of the territory to their last breath. And Tecumseh is preaching union of all the remaining Indian tribes."

"A futile dream," Rusog remarked.

"Yeah," Roy agreed, "but you'll hear from them nevertheless. This Tenskwatawa speaks to God, gets his orders straight from the top."

El-i-chi felt a chill, for he remembered another who

was in touch with the spirits—the late Hodano, who drew power from the ultimate source of evil.

"Will white man and Indian fight forever?" Little Hawk asked.

Roy looked toward Renno, leaving it to the sachem to answer. Renno shrugged. Although he was concerned about the constant friction along the frontiers between Indian lands and the settled white areas, he had long since made up his mind as to what direction he would travel and the kind of advice he would give his tribe and his friends. He saw no need to repeat himself. Instead he looked at his son and said, "There are not enough Indians to fight forever." Then, to show that he had been joking, if rather darkly, he added, "There are men of goodwill on both sides. It is up to us to see that they—not those who preach war—are heard."

There was a long silence. Roy broke it. "I haven't seen Ah-wa-o."

El-i-chi looked quickly toward his mother. "Ah-wa-o tends the boys," he said. "A lively pair."

"I'll bet," Roy said. El-i-chi was speaking of his own son, Gao, and Renno's son by the dead An-da, Ta-na-wun-da, called Ta-na.

Renno shifted uncomfortably, deeply worried. Roy had touched on a problem that persisted like a festering sore, for El-i-chi and Ah-wa-o had broken Seneca marriage traditions that prohibited the union of brother and sister. The fact that they were not related by blood but by the marriage of El-i-chi's mother to Ah-wa-o's father did not negate the ancient taboo against incest. By running away to become one in a marriage ceremony self-administered by El-i-chi, the two had flaunted the body of tribal laws. El-i-chi and Ah-wa-o had compounded their insult by returning to the tribe with a lively, healthy son, Gao. His rompings with his cousin Ta-na were a daily reminder that the brother of the sachem had long escaped judgment, much less the censure or punishment that was due.

The defiance of law was viewed by many as being all the more serious because El-i-chi was the shaman of the tribe, heir to the magic powers of all the shamans back into prehistory. Since their return from the war in the Northwest Territory, Renno had used his authority as sachem to postpone a final decision regarding his brother and El-i-chi's pretty young wife. "If it were another," the old women were fond of saying, "the sachem would have called a council of the matrons moons ago."

Old ones counted on their fingers the years that had passed since El-i-chi and Ah-wa-o had fled to make their illicit union in the wilderness. Gao was, after all, three years old, having been born while both brothers were away fighting Anthony Wayne's war in the Northwest.

Renno knew that in postponing a council of women to consider punishment for his brother, he had created resentment among certain elements of the tribe and outright animus in some of the older women, who saw his actions as questioning the authority of the matrons. The enforcement of tribal traditions lay in the hands of the older women. Renno realized that he would have to call a council of the matrons soon.

Roy Johnson hunted with his grandson and smiled with pride when Little Hawk crossed the spoor of a yearling buck and tracked it to a glade where he put an arrow directly into the animal's heart. The man swam in the creek below the village with Little Hawk and Renna, who was adamant that she was not to be sent away to the swimming hole of the women. Soon Roy began to feel stronger, rejuvenated. He had been away from his grandchildren for too long a time. He had let his sadness after the death of his wife, Nora, send him into the wilderness and had allowed his wanderings to carry him far to the north, where he had spent years scouting for Mad Anthony Wayne. Now he was home. Home was not the log cabin in Knoxville where he'd lived with Nora during the months that his daughter, Emily, had been falling in love with a white Indian. Home was there with the boy Little Hawk, whose full name was Os-sweh-ga-da-ga-ah Ne-wa-ah, and with the pale-haired little girl whose flashing eyes had the power to coax Granddaddy into all forms of indulgence.

When the visiting evangelist learned that there was to be a council of matrons to determine a question of tribal law, he asked Renno's permission to be an observer. Renno informed Pennywhistle that permission would have to come from the chief matron, Toshabe. With some chagrin the preacher approached Toshabe.

"You may watch," Toshabe told him. "You may not speak or address yourself to any question during the council, for what your Bible says has no bearing on the tribal customs of the Seneca."

Pennywhistle, having agreed, was guided to a spot at the rear of the council longhouse, where he sat uncomfortably on the dirt floor and berated himself for not having had the foresight to bring a blanket to soften the ground, as had most of the women.

It was the duty of the sachem to open the council. Renno appeared only after all the matrons were in the longhouse and seated, some humming a tribal chant. The white Indian was dressed in the traditional garb of a Seneca sachem, his face paint that of a Seneca messenger.

The morning sun came through a smoke hole in the roof of the longhouse to light Renno's face. For long moments he faced the matrons in silence, bringing a little smile to the face of his sister, Ena. He was giving the matrons his sternest look, in effect daring them to go against his will. When he spoke he used the tones of a Seneca orator, his voice carrying through and beyond the walls of the longhouse.

"Since my father, the sachem Ghonkaba, decided that he and his would fight against the English in the white man's war, we have traveled far," he began. "We have left

the snows and the dark forests of our homelands to join
our Cherokee brothers in this good place. I, who can
count thirty-one winters, have traveled even farther. I
have seen much of the United States. I have fought with
and against white men and the people of many tribes. I
have observed the customs of many peoples, some from
those nations that are called civilized by the white man. I
have wondered at the decisions and way of life of these
so-called civilized peoples—the English, the Spanish, and
the French. I have traveled over the great sea to see how
ex-slaves live in Jamaica, and I have walked among the
black tribes in Africa."

He paused and noted with satisfaction that he had the
attention of all.

"In my travels among many peoples and many nations
I have observed that each tribe, each nation, has its laws,
and this is as it should be. That laws differ from people to
people is also as it should be, for the needs of one nation
are the bane of another. But never have I traveled among
a people who condoned the marriage of brother and sister."

A buzz of talk swept through the longhouse, then
faded into a tense silence when the sachem continued.

"It is known to all peoples, from the halls of the
English to the dark jungles of Africa, that weakness, defor-
mity, madness, and decay come from the union of brother
and sister, be they man or domesticated animal. And this
is as it should be." He lifted his head. "Who does not
agree with what I have said?"

There was only silence.

"And so you, the matrons of our tribe, have come
here to consider a violation of one of our strongest taboos.
I am sure that in your wisdom—a wisdom that is the
culmination of centuries of Seneca life going back into the
time of the spirits—you will make the proper decision in
this particular case."

Renno felt that he had a slight advantage, for he knew
the weakness of his adversary, the tribe's matrons. In spite

of their determination to mete out the most severe punishment to El-i-chi and Ah-wa-o, he thought he could sway this gathering because their weakness was based on fear.

The women of the tribe—indeed, the tribe as a whole—felt displaced. There was a general apprehension that the Seneca would be swallowed in the overwhelming numbers of their Cherokee cousins. This dread of tribal extinction magnified the matrons' desire to cling to each facet of Seneca tradition.

Renno knew full well that the matrons had the power to enforce their will in matters of traditional law. He himself had once been judged by them, specifically by the chief matron, Toshabe, and had been approved as sachem in an ancient rite that was the domain of the matrons and the matrons alone. And now he knew that he had to use the weakness of the women to make them understand that on occasion it was necessary to stretch, if not disregard, some of the laws. Reasonable change was not evil.

His speech went on and on until Pennywhistle, his legs cramping, moaned softly and massaged his calves. Renno spoke with a passion that riveted the eyes of the women to his face. He praised El-i-chi as a most gifted Seneca shaman, then offered a stirring recounting of El-i-chi's battles with the evil Hodano. He reminded the matrons that one of the most honored of all Seneca shamans, old Casno, had considered El-i-chi to be a worthy heir.

"My brother's blood comes from greatness," he said. "From our father, Ghonkaba, he has taken courage. From our grandfather Ja-gonh, he has taken truth, and from our great-grandfather Renno, honor."

He spoke of Ah-wa-o and of her staunchness in the midst of peril. He saw tears in many an eye, and he felt confident.

"Our laws were made by the wise ones of old to preserve the purity of the tribe," he continued. "But I am sure that you, in your wisdom and love, will agree that it

would be in the interest of the tribe to consider the union
between my brother and his little Rose to be in the best
tradition, for there is no blood shared by them—only the
tie of marriage binding our mother and Ah-wa-o's father,
the mighty warrior Ha-ace the Panther."

He stood in silence for a long moment. "I submit to
you that our small tribe cannot afford to lose a young
couple with such promise as El-i-chi and Ah-wa-o. I ask
you to suspend the laws of incest in this case so that our
diminished tribe will not lose a shaman and warrior, a
mother, and future warriors and mothers that have come
and will come from the loins of El-i-chi. And now, mothers, sisters, I leave you to your deliberations."

His back was straight and proud as he turned and left
the council longhouse.

Chapter II

The council of matrons continued past the noon hour and into the afternoon before the women began to come out of the large community longhouse to restore their energies with food. El-i-chi and Ah-wa-o, as if to show their disdain for the proceedings, had taken Gao and Ta-na into the forest to pick fall berries. Renno, still wearing the regalia of a Seneca sachem, sat in front of the longhouse he had shared with Emily and watched his daughter stringing beads to make a decorative headband.

There was a smell of autumn in the air. High, feathery bands of clouds pointed eastward to indicate that there would be a weather change. Renno looked up as the first of the matrons began to emerge into the clean, brilliant sunlight, lifting hands to shade their eyes. His mother and Ena walked together across the village square toward Toshabe's longhouse. He nodded in greeting as the two women passed without speaking.

Toshabe's silence told him that there had been no decision by the matrons, and it would therefore be improper for her to discuss what had transpired in the council with any male, even the sachem of the tribe. Ena, however, looked back over her shoulder and winked. Renno grinned quickly and winked back. Ena's wink told him that things were not going too badly.

"I had thought to make this pattern like the one Se-quo-i designed," Renna said in English. "I am having trouble, though. Would you walk with me to Se-quo-i's lodge so I might ask him where I have gone wrong?"

Renno tried not to show his fond amusement. There were times when Renna sounded so grown-up, so precise in her language. The brief time that Renna and Little Hawk had spent with Beth Huntington had touched their speech with a trace of Beth's aristocratic English accent. At other times Renna reminded him of Ena as a young girl—braids and skinned knees and the ability to outrun, outclimb, outjump, and outwrestle any boy her age and many older than she.

"I would be pleased to escort such a beautiful young lady on such an important errand," Renno said, rising and taking Renna's hand. She giggled and, lifting her chin, walked beside him, a pale-haired princess inspecting her kingdom.

An accident had left the Cherokee Se-quo-i with a permanent limp, but if he still considered the shortening of his leg to be a handicap, he hid it well. When the matter at hand was to his liking, he could keep up with any man with two good legs, and if not, he merely let the work lie and went about his business, which was diverse. No man questioned Se-quo-i's decisions, for he had proved his prowess as a warrior in battle and at Renno's side. If Se-quo-i wanted to dabble in experimental agriculture, no man laughed. He had worked metals, pounding forge-heated iron into deadly weapons in the smithy behind his cabin, and he had created delicate jewelry through the art of the silversmith. He had tried his hand at painting, and he had accumulated an impressive library. He kept volu-minous notes in English on all his efforts. When Renno and Renna approached his cabin, built with mud-chinked logs and a split-shingle roof in the style of the whites, he was doing nothing. He sat on the front porch, a pipe giving off the good smell of well-cured tobacco, watching the world begin that wondrous process of preparing itself for winter storage. A butterfly had perched on the arm of his rocking chair. He motioned Renna to silence as she loosed her father's hand and ran up the steps.

"Mr. Butterfly has a long way to go," he said, urging her closer. "And he has asked permission to use the arm of my chair as a temporary resting place."

Renna extended a finger.

"If you touch him, you will displace the golden dust that covers him, and he will become ill," Se-quo-i warned. "He is one of those delicate things in nature that asks only to be looked at."

"He is so beautiful," Renna said. "I wish that we could do him in beads."

Se-quo-i raised one eyebrow. "Perhaps we can."

The butterfly spread its wings, lifted, flitted past Se-quo-i's nose, and was gone.

"I have forgotten how the pattern goes," Renna said, showing Se-quo-i the headband she had been making.

"This looks very nice," he complimented. "Ah. Here is where you missed. We will have to take only a few beads off, and that will take only a minute."

Renno, smiling musingly as the small fair head and the dark, adult one bent close together over the work, looked around at the Cherokee village. It was a picture of prosperity and peace. Ears of corn had been hung to dry. Jerky baked in the warm sun. There was the lodge of Ena and her husband, Rusog. There was the old-styled lodge of a senior warrior who had fought at Rusog's side in the Chickasaw war. A small group of young boys rushed from the edge of the woodlands and raced among the lodges, only to disappear among the trees, trailing shrill, fierce war cries.

Se-quo-i soon had Renna's beading corrected, and she was working eagerly to finish the piece. Se-quo-i limped to stand beside Renno. "So this is the day of decision," he said.

Renno nodded.

"If the matter were being decided by men," Se-quo-i remarked, "I would have no concern. But with women—"

Renno chuckled.

"Still," Se-quo-i said, "Ena thinks like a man, and Toshabe is no fool."

"We can only wait and trust that wisdom, not resentment and envy, guides the matrons," Renno said.

Se-quo-i took a deep breath and held it. "The air smells of rain. There will be a chill after the storm moves through."

Renno felt no need to comment. His friendship with the Cherokee was based on many things: on having fought side by side, on having traveled together, on mutual respect. A silence between them was never awkward. He gazed into the distance, and when he spoke, his voice was low, full of concern. It was not the first time that he had asked Se-quo-i for his opinion on vital matters. He knew that Se-quo-i, well educated in the culture of the Indian and in the white man's written lore, would give careful consideration before answering.

"What must I do, old friend, if the matrons vote to exile the man who is more than my brother, who is my friend, my right hand, and a good portion of my heart?"

Se-quo-i sighed. "It is fruitless to borrow trouble."

"But if the vote goes against us?"

"Then you must exercise your authority as sachem and tell the matrons that your tribe is not large enough to discard a warrior as valuable as El-i-chi and a woman with as many childbearing years ahead of her as Ah-wa-o."

"And so I cut the thread that binds the tribe," Renno said. "And so I discard tradition and law."

"No, only that part of law and tradition that is in blind error," Se-quo-i responded. "That is one of our problems—and I speak of the entire Indian people. We are too rigidly governed by customs whose origins date back in antiquity. You yourself, Renno, have said many times that we must change, that we must learn to live the way the white man lives. By the spirits, man, you call for a change much more fundamental than making a sensible exception to the marriage laws."

"You are using very big words," Renna said, causing Se-quo-i to smile. "Why does the language of the white men have so many big words?"

"Continue your work, and do not interrupt the conversation of your elders," Renno said in Spanish to remind Renna that there were many white languages, as there were many Indian languages. He winked at Se-quo-i and said, "The changes I recommend will be forced upon the Indian sooner or later. This is a large and rich land, and it would seem that there should be room for all—for the white man's fields and towns and for the Indian's hunting ground. But in the end the wild places will be cleared and plowed. The deer and the buffalo will give way to domestic cattle and the settlers' mules. I simply recognize that this will happen and advise that the Indian anticipate the

change and live with it, rather than fighting it to the
death." He grinned at Se-quo-i. "The matrons would say
that I speak of the distant future. The matter of El-i-chi
and Ah-wa-o is of immediate concern. The matrons have
the authority to decide. Have you ever known any individual or group who, once having been assigned authority,
was willing to relinquish it without a struggle?"

"I'm finished, Uncle Se-quo-i," Renna said.

Se-quo-i examined the headband. "That is excellent
work." He slipped it over Renna's pale hair and positioned
it. "A perfect fit, too."

"Of course," Renna replied. "I fitted it before I beaded
it."

"Good thinking," Se-quo-i said.

"We can go now, Father," Renna said, "if you're
ready."

"Come back sometime when you can stay longer,"
Se-quo-i invited, laughing. Then, as they walked away, he
called out, "I've sent my sister's boy into Knoxville, and
he is due back. He should be carrying some books that
I've been eager to get. If you see him, please hurry him
along."

"Uncle Se-quo-i reads a lot of books, doesn't he?"
Renna asked.

"Yes."

"Perhaps you can ask him if I might borrow one," she
said. "I've read mine so many times. And I have read the
first three books of the New Testament. The Bible is slow
reading, isn't it? Would you ask Se-quo-i, please, if he has
a book that would be easier for me?"

Renno felt a little surge of guilt. He knew that if
Emily had lived, there would be books in the longhouse.
And there had been books in Beth's house in Wilmington,
which Renna had been encouraged to read during her stay
there.

He had not thought of Beth in a long time. He could

envision her face, her flame-colored hair. He could remember the way she smiled and how she had looked the last time that they had lain together as man and wife on a lonely shore in far England. Yes, either Beth or Emily would have seen to it that both Renna and Little Hawk had suitable books and the loving instruction required to read and understand them.

"I will speak with Se-quo-i," he said. "And I will go into Knoxville to buy books for you and for your brother."

"Please don't tell Little Hawk that I suggested books for *him*," she said quickly. "He'll pull my braids and tell me to mind my own business."

"Well, we won't have that," Renno said.

They walked on in silence, Renno's thoughts turning darkly to the past. Three times he had loved. Emily, dearest of all, perhaps because she had been his first love. Beth. An-da. There were times when he felt that he had failed all three women. Had he not been far away when it was time for Emily to give birth to Renna, she would not have gone into Knoxville to have the baby. The fever that had killed Emily was a white man's disease, unknown among Indians who lived a healthy life in the great wilderness. And with Beth—had he erred in leaving her too often for too long? Had he been content to stay with her in Wilmington, perhaps she would never have returned to England.

But it was the death of An-da, so young, such a perfect Seneca wife, that weighed most heavily on his conscience. He had left her alone in a strange place to be lured by her possessed brother into the clutches of the evil Hodano, and her death had been a horror from which he would never be free.

He walked with Renna to his mother's lodge. Ha-ace had just returned from a successful hunt. Ena and Toshabe were cutting venison for drying. Ha-ace, who had been sitting with the visitor Waith Pennywhistle, came to his

feet to give his sachem the warrior's greeting. He then
lifted Renna high to toss her in the air and make her
giggle.

"I thought you would be back in council," Renno said
to his mother.

"As senior matron," Waith Pennywhistle said, "your
mother used her authority to postpone the decision."

Renno did not miss the look of displeasure that Toshabe
directed at the white man. Pennywhistle presumed too
much when he gave out any information about what had
happened in the council, but that consideration was secondary to the sudden concern that Renno felt. If Toshabe
had deemed it necessary to extend the work of the council, she must have been reasonably sure that the decision
was going against El-i-chi and Ah-wa-o. Melancholy filled
him. El-i-chi, always quick to anger, would probably accept punishment for himself—but if any blame were directed toward his little Rose . . . In El-i-chi's mind a man
was responsible for his woman, and if he ever heard that
some matrons questioned the morality of his self-administered
marriage or considered Ah-wa-o to be a dishonored woman,
he would seek out the husbands of those who had insulted
his little Rose. Such conflict within the tribe had to be
avoided at all costs. Renno suddenly wanted to be alone,
to run into the light wind that was coming from a bank of
low clouds that had appeared in the northwest, to stretch
his muscles, and to expand his lungs.

Toshabe recognized the look on his face. She shared
his fears because she knew her younger son well. She
moved to stand directly in front of the seated evangelist.

"When I gave you permission to observe a council of
matrons," she said, her voice strong, "that meant that you
were to be silent both during the council and after."

Pennywhistle, not accustomed to being upbraided by
an Indian woman, flushed with quick anger. But, very
wisely—for Renno's blue eyes had gone cold as they fas-

tened onto his—he said, "I beg your pardon. I admit that I erred in mentioning that you had acted to, in effect, table the desire of the others to—"

"Enough!" Ha-ace interrupted gruffly. "You are a guest in my house, and it grieves me to be forced to speak to you in this manner. But from now into the future you will not speak of what was said in the council house. In no manner will you speak of it."

Renno released his quick anger toward the preacher. "No harm has been done, Mr. Pennywhistle. We mere men must remember, however, that the matrons guard their prerogatives jealously. As long as the matter is still unresolved, no man of the tribe is entitled to know what was said, in part or in whole."

"I understand," Pennywhistle replied. "I am grateful to you, Toshabe, for allowing me to attend the council, and I assure you that I will make no further mention of the proceedings to anyone."

"Thank you," Toshabe said. She turned to Renno. "Go ahead. There is no need for you to stay here."

He smiled, a bit startled that she could read him so well.

"Go," Toshabe urged. "If in your wanderings you encounter a young doe and can take time from your crashing through the forest to kill it, I will make a stew of it with corn and squash."

Renno was coming out of his longhouse, the English crossbow on his shoulder, when he heard his name called respectfully. Se-quo-i's nephew approached, bearing a well-wrapped but worn package and, in his other hand, a letter.

"They said in Knoxville that the letter is for you," the boy told him.

"Your uncle awaits you eagerly," Renno said, taking the envelope. "Hurry to him with his books."

The boy smiled. "I value my hide too much to do otherwise." He was off at a trot.

Renno's first reaction when he saw the handwriting on the face of the sealed packet was, *No. Not this time.* For the distinctive, hurried hand of President George Washington was familiar to him, and in the past, letters from Washington had called him away from home.

He went into the longhouse, sat where the light from a window illuminated the letter, and began to read. Washington was inviting a few Indians who were proven and true friends of the United States to come to Philadelphia in the early winter of 1796 to observe the election and installation of a new president:

> The man to take my place, at long last, will most probably be either Thomas Jefferson or John Adams. It is my desire to leave my successor as well connected with sources of support and information among our Indian brothers as I have been during the long years of war and during my tenure in the office of the presidency. I am especially desirous, my old friend, of presenting you to the next man to hold this office.

There was more, but Renno put the letter down to enjoy his feeling of relief: There was no urgency in Washington's request. He had almost a year to decide whether or not to go to Philadelphia. In the past he had seldom been able to spend a long period of time with his children, and he wanted to do so now. His longhouse was often filled with childish laughter and more confusion than he could rationally credit to his two "big" offspring and the two small boys who called themselves brothers, Gao and Ta-na.

When he took up the letter again, he found that Washington was asking his advice on a section of a speech that he was preparing, which was to be his farewell to public service. The section of the speech that had been copied for Renno's consideration concerned cooperation and peace between the United States and the various Indian tribes. There were some very solid promises of perpetual land tenure for the Indian, and a promise from George Washington meant more than the promise of any other man of Renno's acquaintance.

While he read the proposed comments on the Indian problem, Renno forgot his desire to seek the solitude of the forest. He began his answer to the president, giving it serious thought, writing and rewriting his belief that Washington's promises regarding Indian land and Indian rights were fair and just. He concluded the letter by stating that he would withhold a decision about coming to Philadelphia pending the outcome of important tribal affairs.

By evening El-i-chi and Ah-wa-o had returned from their outing in the forest. Coincidentally, the shaman had provided the young doe that Toshabe had requested. The stew smelled delicious as it simmered over the cookfire in Toshabe's lodge, the aroma sending out persuasive tendrils to bring Little Hawk in from the woods. He had bathed in the creek, so his clothing was damp and he smelled cleanly of the outdoors.

"I am pleased to see that you're using the large pot, Grandmother," Little Hawk said.

"I raised two sons," Toshabe told him. "I learned that if anyone else is to get a bite, I must use the big pot every time my grandson eats in this house."

At the first opportunity El-i-chi caught Renno's eye, and the two brothers left the smoky longhouse to stand some distance away.

"At least," El-i-chi said, "there was no delegation of irate women to meet us and drive us out of the village with whips."

"There has been no decision," Renno informed him. "The preacher let it slip that our mother insisted on a postponement."

El-i-chi turned away, lifted his face to the skies, and was silent for a long time before saying, "Then the majority of the matrons were against us. Otherwise she would have allowed a vote."

Before Renno could answer, a cough heralded the approach of the white preacher. "I pray that I am not intruding."

"Your stay in our village has been interesting for you, I trust," El-i-chi said.

"Very," Pennywhistle replied. "I fear, however, that I have incurred the wrath of your good mother in letting out a tidbit of information about the council."

"Be glad that my mother is a tolerant woman," El-i-chi said. "Others would have lifted your hair for divulging such a confidence."

"You can't be serious," Pennywhistle scoffed.

"Reverend," El-i-chi said, the tone of his voice indicating to Renno that his brother was out to pull the leg of the preacher, "what does an Indian warrior fear most? What terrifies him more than facing a boar alone and without weapons? What does he dread more than death or mutilation?"

"I have no idea," Pennywhistle said.

"He fears being captured in battle," El-i-chi answered, "for captured warriors are turned over to the victors' women."

"I see," Pennywhistle said, looking around uneasily.

"For it is the women who have refined the most exquisite tortures," El-i-chi continued. "With fire and knives and unending pain the skilled women of almost any Indian tribe can keep a man alive and screaming—praying and begging for death—for days."

Pennywhistle swallowed.

"But you can thank God," El-i-chi said, "that we Seneca are civilized."

"Ah, yes." Pennywhistle cleared his throat. "In talking with your children, Sachem," he remarked to Renno, "I find that they have a smattering of biblical knowledge. Very commendable."

"From their mother," Renno said. "And I encourage them to read the Bible."

"And you, ah, Mr. El-i-chi? Do you believe in God?"

"Yes," El-i-chi responded simply, not interested in debating the matter with the preacher.

"Then your problems are solved," Pennywhistle declared. He looked around carefully before continuing. "Since I have already violated a confidence, perhaps God—if not your mother—will forgive me for saying this: It seems to me that the principal objection of some of the matrons was the manner of your marriage to your Ah-wa-o—"

"They questioned the rightness of our union?" El-i-chi asked, his face darkening.

"So," Pennywhistle went on, "I think that the entire affair could be defused if you and your, uh, wife, would consent to a marriage ceremony under the law of this territory and the laws of God. I will be most happy to perform the rite. Then no one can say that you are not morally and legally united in holy wedlock."

"Who said that we are not?" El-i-chi demanded, moving to thrust his face into Pennywhistle's.

Renno knew that his brother's blood was up. Any man or any woman who had dared to question the honor and purity of Ah-wa-o was a fool. He knew that he had to do something quickly, before El-i-chi seized the skinny white man by the throat and shook out details of the heated words that had been spoken in council.

At just the proper time Ena emerged from Toshabe's longhouse, raised her voice, and called out for the family's young children, running down the list of names: Ho-ya,

We-yo, Gao, Ta-na. Then she joined her brothers and the white visitor. Renno said, "Ena, you have come just in time to hear Reverend Pennywhistle tell El-i-chi the words that were spoken in council."

When Ena saw Renno's wink, she came to glare at Pennywhistle as if he were something rank and detestable. "You have been warned, Preacher," she grated. She looked at Renno. "What has he revealed?"

"Nothing specific, so far," Renno answered.

"Hold this man here, Brother," Ena said. "Give me time to gather the matrons." She walked briskly away and disappeared around the corner of the longhouse.

"I say," Pennywhistle sputtered, "you did me no favor, Sachem."

"Nor did I intend to," Renno replied grimly.

"Leave this one to me," El-i-chi said.

Renno turned his stern face to Pennywhistle. "I think, Preacher, that you might have just enough time to saddle that mule of yours and, by riding hard and fast, put enough distance between you and this village before my sister can arouse the more bloodthirsty of the matrons."

Renno seized El-i-chi's arm as the preacher turned and ran. El-i-chi's muscles were taut, and for a moment it seemed that he would resist his brother's restraint. Then he sighed. "Well done, Brother," he said. "And you are right, of course."

Renno risked one comment as they went toward their mother's longhouse. "The white man's command of our language was not complete. Perhaps he misunderstood some of the things he heard."

"For the sake of those who said them, I pray that he did," El-i-chi said as they walked through the door. "Otherwise I might be tempted to pay them a visit and let my knife do the talking."

Toshabe looked up in question when her two sons entered without the white man. Before she could ask,

Renno said in French, the language of Toshabe's white
father, "There will be one less guest for dinner, Mother.
Reverend Pennywhistle remembered urgent business
elsewhere."

Winter came early to the Cherokee lands, prompting
Roy Johnson to cut short his visit. Snow fell in early
November, and skim ice lined the banks of the streams.
The hare and the squirrel, the deer, the opossum, the
raccoon, and the bear sported thick coats of new fur. The
harvest had been good, as had the hunting. The affairs of
the change of seasons from autumn to winter, then to
spring, occupied the minds of the matrons for the most
part, leaving only the most resentful to mutter against the
principal matron's refusal to reconvene the council so that
El-i-chi and Ah-wa-o could be properly punished.

Renna had decided that she was going to be more the
sister to Ta-na, and she spent much time that winter
preparing nice things for her little brother to eat—making
double portions, of course, because anything that Ta-na
got, Gao had to have in equal amount. Ta-na tolerated
Renna, for she wasn't *quite* as much a pain in the neck as
most girls.

Preparations began for the major celebration of the
Seneca, the festival of the new beginning.

During the month of Diagona—the second moon after the winter solstice—the young warrior Little Hawk, a
member of the False Face Society, prepared a mask woven
of braided corn husks. Ena helped him in its construction.
During the time of the festival, when old fires were scattered and new fires made, during the rites of cleansing
and prayer and solemn ritual dancing interspersed with
dances, games, and clowning for fun, Little Hawk performed the duty of frightening away evil spirits. He thrust
his false face into every nook and cranny of the village and
dashed with other young warriors among the winter trees,
daring the evil spirits to come out and confront them.

To the surprise of no one, the Master of Life won
again, overcoming the spirits of cold and evil. The prize of
the battle was spring as the days became gradually longer.
Little Hawk, who preferred physical activities to intellectual ones, was chagrined to find several new books, on
loan from Se-quo-i and purchased at the general store in
Knoxville, in his father's longhouse.

On a day when, with one last, frigid blast, winter
reminded the world that it had not been totally defeated,
Renna curled up on her father's lap before the fire. Together they read one of Se-quo-i's books. When they had
finished, the girl looked up at her father and sighed happily. "You said that if you had your way you would never
go away again," she said to him. "And you have kept your
word. Thank you, Father."

Renno was touched.

Roy Johnson returned on a windy March day with the
news that statehood seemed to be assured for the territory
of Tennessee.

"It comes too late," he grumbled. "The state's name
should be Franklin."

"My concern is this," El-i-chi said. "What effect will
statehood have on us and on the Cherokee?"

"Well, El-i-chi, that's a good question," Roy said.
"I've been in Knoxville. A few people remembered me
there and made me a delegate to the convention to draft a
state constitution. We stuck pretty close to the constitution of North Carolina in writing ours because North Carolina's is a pretty good one, except for the lack of a provision
protecting the rights of the Indian. I put in my ideas on
that subject, and I may have made an impression. Here's
what I think we ought to do, Renno: You and Rusog might
come up to Knoxville with me. It's almost sure that Congress will approve Tennessee statehood pretty quick now,
and before that happens, we should have a few provisions
in writing from the territorial governor."

Renno nodded, thinking that everything seemed to conspire to take him away from his children. Then he brightened, for there was no need for a separation. He would take Renna and Little Hawk with him.

Both children had long since outgrown the clothing given to them by Beth during their last stay in Wilmington. That made a shopping excursion necessary upon first arriving in Knoxville, for they were, after all, Emily's children and Roy's grandchildren, and while in the white man's town they should not be objects of curiosity dressed in buckskins and moccasins.

After the shopping was completed, Little Hawk complained bitterly about the discomfort of the hard shoes, but Renna was pleased, acting very much the little lady in her frilly dresses. Seeing them dressed as white children, hearing their language touched ever so slightly with Beth's English accent as they used words with a precision matched by only a few whites there on the frontier, Renno was once again reminded how his offspring were squarely astraddle the invisible fence that separated white and Indian societies.

Renno had met William Blount, governor of the territory of Tennessee, in Philadelphia when Blount had been a North Carolina delegate to the Constitutional Convention. George Washington had introduced them.

Renno remembered Blount as a plain man who spoke in simple phrases, and he had been described by Washington as being honest and sincere. Although Renno had not had occasion to speak with Blount since the North Carolinean had come to Tennessee Territory, he knew that Blount had been, if not a good governor, at least a man of temperance and fairness. When Blount had secured the appointment as territorial governor from George Washington in 1790, the wilderness had been on the verge of war, with the frontiersmen ready to take up arms in protest of the federal government's pacific Indian policy. Blount had handled the potential hostility with tact, firmness, and political adroitness. As a result, he was looked upon by the Cherokee and by Renno as a less dangerous man to the aspirations of the Indian than John Sevier, an old Indian fighter who was almost guaranteed to take Blount's place as governor once statehood was confirmed by Congress in Philadelphia.

Blount was not a fancy dresser. He wore a gray waistcoat with a bleached linen shirt. His hair was styled in the manner of George Washington's but unpowdered, of course—such affectations did not belong to life on the frontier. He rose to greet the three men, shook Rusog's hand first, then Renno's, and only then did he greet Roy Johnson with familiar amiability.

"Sit, gentlemen, sit," he urged jovially. "I'm honored to meet at last the two chiefs most responsible for defeating the Spanish-Chickasaw conspiracy to take Tennessee lands. And you, Sachem," he said, nodding toward Renno, "Colonel Johnson tells me that you fought well in the service of General Anthony Wayne."

Neither Rusog nor Renno spoke, deeming it immodest to comment on the governor's praise.

Blount's gaze kept returning to Renno's face. He squinted in thought. "But I know you, Sachem," he said finally. He sat up straighter in his chair. "Indeed I do, and now I remember where I met you." He did not elaborate, but his change in attitude was evident. From the moment he remembered having been presented to Renno—not vice versa—by George Washington, his tone of voice was more respectful.

"The information you were able to give me about Beth Huntington when we met before, Governor, was quite helpful." Renno was not inexperienced in dealing with men who held public power. He had found over the years that he could disconcert most white men by assuming the almost effete accent of the British upper class.

Blount, who had gradually adapted to the often harsh speech of the frontier, looked at the buckskin-clad man with bronze skin and blond hair. It was obvious from his expression that he was wondering why such a man called himself a Seneca. "Colonel Johnson has briefed me on the purpose of your call," Blount said. "I will listen with interest to what you have to say, but first let me say, gentlemen, that I consider the Cherokee Nation to be a valuable part of this territory, and I pray that the enlightened policy of chiefs such as you will allow the Cherokee to take his rightful place in our new state."

Rusog's face was frozen, but Renno knew that the governor's words had not set well with his brother-in-law.

"However," Blount added quickly, "you must know that the lands that will become the state of Tennessee do not infringe on the hunting grounds of the Cherokee. Cherokee lands have been, uh, reserved."

"It is well," Rusog said in careful English, "that you recognize that the land is Cherokee. I do not grant to you the right to make any decisions regarding the land of the Cherokee, but if that is your way of saying that the land belongs to us, then I will accept your having 'reserved' it." He put a rich contempt into his pronunciation of the word *reserved*.

"Well," Roy Johnson soothed, "I think it's just that you would word it differently, Rusog."

"Yes," Blount agreed. "I assure you, Chief Rusog, Sachem Renno, that the state of Tennessee will make no claims on the land that belongs to the Cherokee Nation."

"You are known as a man of honor," Renno said. "We accept your assurances and assure you in return that the Seneca and that portion of the Cherokee Nation that follows chief Rusog will continue to live in peace with its white neighbors."

Blount beamed. "Good, good. Now that that's settled—" He pulled a bottle from his desk and passed it to Roy,

who took a deep swig, smacked his lips, wiped his mouth
on the back of his hand, and handed the bottle to Renno.
Renno touched the bottle to his lips but did not drink. He
saw Rusog do the same. Passing the bottle was, for some
white men, the equivalent of passing the pipe among the
Indians, and the customs of the host were to be honored.

Having discovered that the sachem of the Seneca who
had left the tribe's northern homelands to join the Cherokee was the same odd, white Indian who was a personal
friend of George Washington's had set William Blount to
doing some serious elementary sums. It was almost assured that he would be going to Philadelphia as one of the
two senators from the new state of Tennessee. He would
be at a great disadvantage in that sophisticated capital city.
The eastern power elite looked upon frontiersmen as being
only slightly more civilized than wild Indians. He would
be a stranger in Philadelphia, and as the old saying went,
he had few fish to fry there.

William Blount did not consider himself to be a devi-
ous man, and he would have immediately called out any
man who questioned his honor and his honesty. He had
been in public service since 1776 when he entered the
army of revolutionary North Carolina to act as paymaster
for various units throughout the war. His fellows had
honored him several times by electing him to office. He
had been four times a member of North Carolina's House
of Commons, twice a member of that state's senate. He
went north in 1782 as a member of Congress and was a
delegate to the Constitutional Convention.

In general, Blount was a contented man, but there
were two things—one of them deeply buried into his
memory—that burdened his otherwise serene life. First
and foremost was his constant concern about his considerable investments in western lands. He had begun buying
large tracts in the unsettled areas beyond the mountains

before he had moved to Tennessee Territory, and his office as territorial governor had given him greater scope for speculation. He saw no conflict between his land holdings and his office; in fact, one of his considerations for having come to the West was to be in a position to better supervise his land dealings.

The object in western land dealings was simple: One bought cheap and sold quickly, taking whatever profit might be possible at the moment. Selling lands to a hopeful settler contributed to the growth of the nation, and if those lands were situated in dangerous areas where a settler might lose his scalp . . . well, that was the risk that Americans had been taking since the first white man stepped ashore on the continent.

The second thing that soured Blount's generally pleasant outlook on life took place when he was a relatively young man: He lost the North Carolina senatorial election in the late 1780s, and he had never been willing to admit that he had reached an end to his achievements in public life. That blight on his personal honor and ambition was about to be erased. He was, at long last, going to be a player on the national stage, a United States senator, and bedamned to those ungrateful people of his native state who had refused to elect him to that office.

He owned a million acres of land that was legally within "The Territory of the United States South of the River Ohio" but called most commonly the Southwest, or Tennessee, Territory. His wife, Mary, had cried bitterly when he told her that he was going to move the family from their comfortable home in North Carolina to the western frontier. Mary Grainger Blount had come from a distinguished North Carolina family. But after his senatorial defeat, he felt he had only one choice—to leave North Carolina and rebuild his fortunes in the volatile West. To quiet his wife's tears he had promised her that he would make the name Blount mean as much in the West as had the name of her prestigious father meant in North Carolina.

As he sat at his desk and smiled pleasantly while his
guests performed the ritual lifting of the bottle, William
Blount was a typical man of his time: ambitious, eager for
wealth, and patriotic, but not necessarily blindly loyal to
the government in Philadelphia. Like most frontiersmen
he looked upon the federal government as something that
operated at a distance with a purpose that was not always
in line with the needs of the Tennessee Territory. He
fancied himself to be a worthwhile man who had given
good service to his country, a decent man who went to
church with his family every Sunday, an honest businessman who took advantage of opportunity and used his
experience to drive a hard bargain, and a politician of
some skill. And he was thinking as businessman and as
politician when he spoke to Roy.

"Let's have a look at that grandson of yours, Roy," he
said. He was going to need every friend he could muster
in Philadelphia, and sitting before him was an old personal
friend of George Washington's. The president wasn't going
to hang around Philadelphia after he left office, but he
would always be the man who, in the mind of the world
and many Americans, *was* the United States. Washington
would be called upon by many for opinion, advice, and
backing. Having a tenuous connection to a man as powerful and as respected as George Washington would be
better than having no connection at all. Now, if the son of
this white Indian didn't turn out to be a surly savage,
there just might be some gain to be had out of this
meeting with the Seneca and the Cherokee.

Roy went to the door and called to Little Hawk, who
had been waiting in an anteroom. The boy looked handsome in tight trousers, frilled shirt, vest, and a short
jacket. His hair had been trimmed so that it looked neat
when it was gathered and tied in the back.

During the state constitutional convention Blount had
had several chats with Colonel Roy Johnson, and being a

good grandfather, Roy had bragged about his grandchildren. As far as he was concerned, Little Hawk was the
smartest boy who'd ever lived.

Blount tested one of Roy's statements, that his grandson was a good linguist, by greeting Little Hawk in Spanish. He smiled with genuine pleasure when the boy
answered in perfect Castilian. "Your grandfather says that
you speak a smattering of French as well," Blount said.

Little Hawk answered in that language, adding, in
English, "I have tried to learn more French, but my
grandmother, who is half French, says that she has forgotten. And my father does not speak French as well as he
speaks Spanish."

"Impressive," Blount said. "How many Indian dialects?"

Little Hawk looked at Renno. Renno said, "Seneca, of
course. The dialects of the other tribes of the League of
the Iroquois. If one speaks Seneca, Cherokee comes easily. He's heard Choctaw, Creek, and Chickasaw enough to
understand them and make do in communication with
common words and signs."

"Very commendable," Blount said. He leaned back.
The boy made a good impression indeed. "Sachem, it is
my decision—and, believe me, it's going to make a lot of
people as mad as a wet hen—that your son will go to
Philadelphia with me."

Little Hawk looked at his father quickly and opened
his mouth as if to protest. Renno motioned him to remain
silent.

"Each senator may bring a page to the office," Blount
explained. "The practice is intended to give a particular
kind of education to a group of outstanding young boys—in
effect, to train the leaders of tomorrow in the caldron of
political action. Senate pages earn a salary, are required to
attend school classes, and serve a genuine purpose in
running errands."

"By golly," Roy enthused, "it sounds like a wonderful
opportunity to me, Renno."

Blount tilted the bottle for one last, small dram, and put it away.

"Governor," Renno said, "my son and I are greatly honored by your offer. I ask you, sir, that you give me a chance to talk with Little Hawk before we give you our decision."

"Certainly," Blount agreed expansively, although he was a bit miffed. He'd just offered one of the patronage plums of his office to the son of an Indian. It was either stupidity or ingratitude when the father said he had to think about it before accepting the great honor.

In the end, the decision had been left to Little Hawk. During the return trip from Knoxville neither Rusog nor Renno had mentioned William Blount's offer to take the boy to Philadelphia city with him. Renna knew nothing about it. Both father and son knew that the matter was lying heavily on each other's mind, but the time to discuss it had not come.

Chapter III

As soon as the travelers returned to their Seneca-Cherokee village, Renna began excitedly to tell Toshabe and Ena all about her stay in Knoxville, about having meals in a boardinghouse where none of the food was as good as her grandmother's cooking, and about the wonderful things that her father had bought her. She had to show each item separately, modeling the dresses.

Toshabe felt emotion constrict her heart. It was an old sadness that she had first felt when her son married Emily Johnson, a white woman. From the day of Little

47

Hawk's birth Toshabe had not been free of the worry that someday she would see her grandchildren leave their homeland to seek their future among the whites. Since Emily's death Toshabe had watched Renno's concern about his promises to his dead wife grow. Now that Little Hawk had spoken to her alone, telling her that William Blount had offered him a very important position in the government and that to take the offer would mean furthering his education in the white man's written widsom, her anxiety was as great as the boy's.

Toshabe knew from the first moment she heard Little Hawk's words what the decision would be. And, having watched her granddaughter pose prettily in frills and gingham, she had the feeling that she would lose more than the presence of her grandson in her longhouse for an indefinite period of time. She offered no opinion, however, and waited for Renno to broach the subject.

The cookpots were filled with fresh goodness in the days of early summer, but Little Hawk felt no regret when his father took down his English crossbow and his musket, strapped the Spanish stiletto to his waist, and said, "Bring your bow and a full quiver of arrows. Tell your grandmother that we're going hunting."

"How long will I say that we will be gone?" Little Hawk asked.

"Until we return," Renno answered.

Little Hawk hid a glad smile. For the first time, he was to be taken by his father on a hunt that would range far. His heart filled with happiness as he ran out of the longhouse. Boys did not ordinarily go on long hunts with an adult. He told Toshabe that he and his father would be gone on the hunt until they returned. Toshabe prepared trail rations—fresh meat for the first day, and jerky, parched corn, and nut balls for the days that would follow.

Renno began the warrior's pace at the edge of the village. Little Hawk trotted easily beside him, checking the sky for a hint of the weather to come during the next two to three days. He saw nothing to diminish his pleasure at entering the great forests with his father.

A boy knows when his father's eyes see him with pride. Little Hawk's chest was filled almost to bursting by the way Renno looked at him when they paused at a fresh-running stream to drink and splash water over their perspiring bodies. And then they were off again, running together, father and son, the son as tall as his father's shoulder. By nightfall they were miles from the village, moving toward the pristine hunting grounds that lay to the southwest.

During the first day and the next, Renno made no attempt to take game for food. When they made camp for the night, the setting was a beautiful one. Little Hawk laid freshly cut branches under an overhang beside a rocky stream. Huge cottonwoods towered over them, and as the sun sank and twilight came, squirrels skittered around the trees, finding their way to their nests.

Little Hawk gathered dry wood and started the fire. He opened his pack, chewed on jerky, and offered the food to his father. Renno, sitting cross-legged near the fire, shook his head. There was an odd look in his eyes, a look that told Little Hawk that it would be best to remain silent. So he chewed jerky and then treated himself to one of the deliciously sweet Cherokee nut balls. Still his father had not spoken nor moved. He sat like a bronzed statue, not even blinking, gazing slightly upward as if waiting for the sky to fill with the stars that came with darkness.

Little Hawk spread his blanket over the fresh pine boughs and, like a dog making a sleeping place in a grassy field, snuggled into his bed, then dozed. . . .

The sachem's son was awakened by Renno's soft chant of an ancient appeal to the Master of Life. A thrill that was close to fear ran through him. To know from the tales over the campfires that his father was on a familiar basis with

the spirits of the ancestors was acceptable when the teller
of the tale was, perhaps, his uncle El-i-chi and when his
entire family and many friends were around him. In the
darkness of the starry night Little Hawk felt almost as if he
were alone, for Renno's voice rose and fell as if coming to
him from a distance. The soft sound lost itself in the night.
From far away came the challenging scream of a wildcat
on the hunt. He slept.

When he awoke it was dawn. The summer sun was
lighting the tops of the cottonwood trees, and the squirrels
were about their business of finding breakfast. His father
sat in the same position, legs crossed, head inclined so
that his eyes stared unblinkingly toward the lower sky.
Little Hawk crept out of his bed and went to the stream
for a drink and a wash, detoured into the near bushes,
then came back to walk directly in front of Renno. It was
as if the boy did not exist.

It was a strange day for Little Hawk. He ate. He
hunted. He killed a yearling dear and butchered out a
haunch of meat while wondering if Renno would repri-
mand him for wasting so much, for two men could not eat
an entire deer before the meat spoiled. He did not disturb
Renno's meditations at all as he built the fire, roasted
cubes of venison, ate his fill, and washed it down with cold
water from the stream.

With the coming of night he was beginning to be
concerned. He thought that it would have been impossible to remain seated and gazing into the distance for a
night and a day. When he assumed the cross-legged position beside Renno for an hour, trying his best to share his
father's meditation, or prayer, or whatever it was, his legs
began to feel numb almost immediately, so he had to get
up and limp around.

He ate rewarmed venison, watched night come, heard
the call of a hunting owl from across the stream, and
offered food to his father. Renno seemed not to hear. He
was whispering ancient words. Awed and a bit frightened,

Little Hawk drew back the food he had offered and secured it on a tree at a height to discourage raids by the
small nocturnal animals. He was preparing to go to his rest
when Renno broke his chanting to say, "Beside me, my
son."

He sat, legs crossed. The dying scream of a rabbit
told him that the owl had killed. He envisioned the bird
snug in its favorite tree, tearing at the tender, bleeding
flesh. He shivered. His father's voice had risen and now
was chanting strongly. There were no other sounds. It was
as if the spirits had told the world to hush, to listen to the
old, rhythmic words that came musically from Renno's
lips.

There came a silence so deep that Little Hawk could
hear the blood surging through his veins. And into that
hush came a voice that was soft, sweet, and familiar.

"Mother," Little Hawk whispered, and a longing for
her threatened to overwhelm him.

She was singing. The song was a lullaby, one that
Little Hawk had heard from the time of his birth. His eyes
filled, but the tears would not flow. He knew a bittersweet
agony as the song faded, and there was a stir of movement
in the darkness beyond the flickering fire.

"Oh, Mother," he whispered as he saw her pale hands
and fair hair gleaming as if they had captured sunlight
from a far place.

The manitou's face was hidden in her alabaster hands.
She was weeping.

"Speak, manitou," Renno said. "Tell me that your
sorrow is not for our son."

The spirit lowered its hands, and there was the dear
face, contorted in anguish, eyes reddened by many tears.

"No, no," Renno pleaded as the manitou receded into
the distance and was gone.

"Mother . . ." Little Hawk croaked.

With a suddenness that caused Little Hawk to cry
out, another manitou filled the night, glowing with an

eerie presence, a Seneca sachem in full war regalia, face painted frighteningly, head shaved, only a scalp lock as evidence of the blackness of hair.

"Ghonka!" Renno said.

The fearsome old warrior's eyes softened. "The blood of my son has done well." His voice was harsh, the words forced explosively from his lips. Ghonka, sachem of the Seneca, who had replaced a dead son with the surviving boy baby of a slaughtered settler family, rested his fierce eyes on Little Hawk's wide-eyed face, grunted in approval, and spoke directly to the boy. "The fault will not be yours," he said. "You are of the blood of Renno. The shame will not be yours. Remember that always, and you will walk with honor." The manitou shook his head sadly and then was gone.

"Father?" Little Hawk gulped. If shame were to come, he wanted to know what to expect and how to fight it.

Renno was chanting again. There was a feeling of magic in the air, as if the night were filled with orenda. He chanted his pleas for more information, and she was back.

"My son, my son," the manitou said, sobbing. "Ah, the woe that will be yours."

"Not him," Renno entreated. "Manitou, say that sorrow will not be the lot of my son."

"The anguish of ages, of generations, will be yours," the manitou said, looking directly at Little Hawk. "Ah, my son, my son."

"Give it to me," Renno implored, his hands held outward. "Let me bear this burden for him."

The manitou turned to face Renno. "No," she whispered. "Tell me, manitou, what must I do? What can I do to lighten my son's load?"

"Your promises have already pointed the way," the manitou said. One lovely hand reached out and almost touched Little Hawk's blond hair.

"There is another question, manitou," Renno whispered.

But the pale-haired spirit of Emily was gone. Little Hawk sat motionless, stunned. In a nearby tree the owl was hooting contentedly with his belly full, and there was a whir of insects. Something small rattled dry brush near the camp. Both father and son tensed as another manitou materialized in the flickering firelight.

"This is my great-grandfather's manitou," Renno whispered to Little Hawk. "When you become a man, you will look like this bronzed, straight, proud sachem who stands before us."

"Unlike you, I had no brother," said the manitou.

There was a quality to the voice that filled Little Hawk with awe and pride to know that he was of the blood of such a man.

"Brothers are to be separated only by choice," said the spirit of the original white Indian, Renno.

And then there was only the night, the sleepy mutterings of the owl, and a hint of a breeze that would become brisk with the morning.

Renno shook himself as if coming awake. He looked down at his son's face, tear-stained and pale.

"What does it all mean?" Little Hawk asked.

"What I must do is clear to me now," Renno said.

"But *she* cried for me," Little Hawk said with a shiver.

"I feel that she wept for something in the distant future," Renno said. "But whatever comes, I will be with you."

"I am not afraid," Little Hawk said. "For the great Ghonka said that I will walk with honor."

"Yes."

"I can think of only a few things that would make me sad," the boy said. "To lose one that I love—"

Renno could not speak. He wanted to hold his son to his breast, but that was not the way of a Seneca warrior. He wanted to take his little family and his brother's family and go far away to the west, to find a valley untouched by

the white man, and to live as his ancestors had lived
before the coming of the white man. The woe that was to
come to Little Hawk was not to be his fault, and he would
walk with honor. . . . That meant that the manitou had
not been referring to something as simple as death.

"We will be together," Renno said, clasping his son's
shoulder.

A Creek war party made up of young warriors still in
their teens had been traveling north for a matter of two
weeks, creeping through Choctaw lands without announcing their presence, although at times it took great will-
power not to count coup on unsuspecting Choctaw hunters.
With the Creek was John Chisholm, a white man dressed
in frontier buckskin and carrying a long rifle. Chisholm was
sandy haired, and his pale English skin responded to the
sun by turning bright pink. He spoke fluent Creek, and
although he did not presume to give advice to the ambitious young Creek warriors, he was consulted about his
choice of direction after the party had crossed the Tennessee. He pointed northeast.

John Chisholm had soldiered for the king during the
American colonists' rebellion against the Crown. When
the festivities had ended in disaster, which, he felt, had
been brought on by the ineptitude of British officers and
by apathy at home, Chisholm had seen no future in returning to England with his unit. He would have had
limited choices there: to stay in the army and be killed in
one of the wars that England seemed to attract as carrion
attracted flies, or to do the work of a lackey in a society
that gave no opportunity for advancement to a man of his
station in life, which was low by English standards. He
had chosen to seek his fortune in the new nation and had
gravitated, as did many deserters from the defeated British forces, to the frontier.

In the years since the surrender at Yorktown, Chisholm had been an innkeeper and small merchant, thief

and beggar, all without notable success. He had found his niche as a self-appointed emissary to the Creek, where he eked out an existence by trading until, by good fortune, he had encountered men who were in need of services that only a fellow such as he could provide. When he had first met Zachariah Cox, John Chisholm quickly realized that he had found a man with whom he saw eye to eye, a man who had one goal and one goal only—to make a lot of money out of Southwest Territory lands, regardless of the consequences. Cox had re-formed the troubled Yazoo Company, which had corrupted the Georgia legislature to "purchase" lands—Indian lands—extending all the way from the Mississippi to the big bend of the Tennessee at Muscle Shoals. In Chisholm, the land speculator had a man who knew the frontier and who had contact with the Indians and with the half-wild white men who lived among them.

Now, at Cox's behest, John Chisholm was traveling through Cherokee lands, having left Choctaw territory behind, to meet another man interested in the vast territory around Muscle Shoals. That man was Waith Pennywhistle.

Soon Chisholm would have to take his leave of the young warriors. He would do so with regret, for the war party afforded protection in a strange land, and he himself took no great pleasure in killing. He had done his share, he supposed, having killed men in line of duty as a soldier and having killed others, mostly Indians, to keep his scalp during his years on the southwest frontier. He didn't particularly object to the idea that young men such as the Creek warriors had to kill other young men in order to be recognized as adults. In fact, he had a personal interest in seeing the inexperienced Creek become adept at killing—an interest that was rooted in his early years on the frontier, when he'd been captured by Spanish troops. A period of torment in the Spanish dungeons at Pensacola had left Chisholm with a burning hatred for all things Spanish. Now, by the grace of a God who understood the need for

vengeance, he was being given an opportunity to strike a
blow that would, if properly administered, be felt all the
way across the wide ocean in Madrid. Accomplishing his
purpose would require the weapons and courage of thousands of men like the young Creek warriors.

Running Foot, the leader of the small war party, was
son to one of the Creek chiefs who was to be a vital
constituent in Chisholm's future plans. The eldest warrior
at sixteen summers, Running Foot was the first to cross
the spoor of a Cherokee hunting party. By that time they
had traveled deep into Cherokee territory and were moving slowly and with great caution.

Chisholm took a look at the spoor and said, "A man
and a boy moving fast."

But Running Foot's eyes held the look of blood. The
man and the boy had passed only a short while before.

"Not much coup to be had there." Chisholm removed
his hat, pushed back his sweat-dampened sandy hair, and
sighed. "I will leave you here, then, my brother."

"If that is your wish," Running Foot said. "May you
have a safe journey."

"And you, Running Foot."

"If you have need for us, we will wait at the bend of
the river."

"No," Chisholm said. "I may continue on to the east
toward Knoxville. The spirits of your ancestors be with you."

Chisholm struck out toward the northeast. From the
top of a ridge he could see the foothills of the Great
Smoky Mountains rising ahead of him. Within a day's
march he would encounter the first of the southernmost
Cherokee villages, where he would be greeted in friendship and passed along toward Knoxville with best wishes.

The eastern sky was pinked by the coming day when
Renno and Little Hawk wakened from their few hours'
sleep.

"There is meat," the boy said.

"You hunted well." Renno watched as his son built up the fire and warmed the venison. They ate heartily, then drank deeply.

"She . . . the one who—"

"The spirit of your mother?" Renno asked.

Little Hawk nodded. "She said that your promises already pointed the way. Do you know what . . . she meant?"

"My promises to her were to see that Renna and you were educated with the white man's books and that you knew the white man's God."

"Oh." Little Hawk pondered. "Then I am to go to Philadelphia."

"Does that please you?"

"I think so," Little Hawk replied. "I knew that I was meant to leave the village, at least for a time. I've been trying to imagine what I would do when we get back home, and I can't think of anything. Oh, I could hunt near the village and kill rabbits and squirrels for the cookpot, but after killing the deer yesterday, there is no honor in such hunting. I could swim with the other boys my age, but that makes me feel as if I am wasting time or opportunity—" He spread his hands and laughed. "Or something."

"You saw the manitou."

"Yes."

"Not everyone has that gift."

Little Hawk laughed uneasily. "I'm not sure I'm grateful."

"At every crisis of my life I have asked guidance from the manitou," Renno said, "and they have never left my side or betrayed me. I can ask only that you have that same advantage."

"When you go to the Place across the River," Little Hawk said, "which I pray will be many, many years from now, please don't come back and scare me the way old Ghonka did."

Was his remark that funny? Was Renno's laughter out of all proportion to his son's comment? It didn't matter. When at last their hilarity was under control, they walked side by side, then broke into the warrior's pace. The morning breeze cooled their perspiring bodies. They ran into the wind, legs pumping. A second wind came to both at about the same time until, at the top of a ridge, Renno pulled up.

"Why do we stop?" Little Hawk asked.

"I thought you might be ready to rest."

Little Hawk grinned. "Don't blame it on me."

"Sprout," Renno said, laughing, tugging at Little Hawk's ear, "are you hinting that you think you can outlast me?"

"It was not I who stopped," Little Hawk said, giggling.

"So," Renno said. He pointed down the slope. "Here the trail splits. To the south it is more direct. There the path goes down into the swale and straight up the side of the next hill. To the north it meanders along the slope, and the climb up the hill is more gentle. Which would you choose if you were in a race?"

"The distances are roughly equal?"

"Yes."

"But the trail to the south would be harder?"

"Yes."

"Then I will take the trail to the north," Little Hawk said. "My mother didn't give birth to a fool. Your legs are longer. I will need all the advantage I can get."

"Go, then. I'll even give you a head start."

The young Creek warrior Running Foot had been leading the war party by some fifty yards. He had not followed the tracks of the boy and the man when he had crossed them, for John Chisholm had said, and rightly, there was little honor in killing such a pair. The Creek were, he knew, deep into Cherokee hunting grounds. To blunder into a large group of Cherokee would be fatal. He

had paused at the stream that ran through the swale
between two heavily wooded hills and had just satisfied
his thirst when he heard a rattle in the brush above him.
He leaped for concealment. His rapid movements startled
a blue jay. Soon he heard the sound of running feet. The
one who came was being very reckless, announcing his
coming with hasty, careless steps. Perhaps he would win a
Cherokee scalp this day.

Running Foot took his bow from his shoulder, nocked
an arrow, and waited.

Little Hawk ran with the wind at his back, pounding
down the trail, skirting huge, shadowy trees. He was
careless of noise. A small rock rolled away from contact
with his flying feet and crashed down into the swale. He
did hear the warning cry of the jay and caught a glimpse of
blue through the green branches of the trees along the
stream. He was nearing the water, running full tilt. His
eyes darted swiftly to take in an impression that a deer
had drunk from his side of the stream, leaving deep tracks
in the sand. On the far side of the water a flash of something brought him to a halt, his feet sliding on the damp
sand. He ran backward, away from the stream and toward
the cover of the trees, his left hand swinging his bow from
his shoulder, his right reaching for an arrow. His eyes
searched frantically for the source of the very fresh hand-
print at the water's edge on the other side of the little
stream. He knew that the man who had made that print
was nearby, because disturbed sand still clouded the shal-
low water.

Little Hawk saw the movement of leaves across the
stream and threw himself to one side onto his belly. An
iron-tipped arrow sang its deadly way past his ear as he
fell, then rolled into the cover of a large cottonwood tree.
He snaked his way into brush, found a place where he
could see the stream, and watched a young warrior in
Creek war paint emerge cautiously, fitting another arrow

to his bow. The Creek turned his head, cupped his mouth
with his hand, and made the sound of a mourning dove,
three times quickly, paused, then cooed once more.

For one fear-filled moment Little Hawk considered
shouting for his father's help, but he knew that Renno was
at least a quarter of a mile away on the southern branch of
the trail. There would be no help—not with this warrior—
and if he hesitated until the Creek's companions joined
him, having heard the signal of the dove, there would be
no chance of escape. He drew his bow and centered the
sharp tip of the arrow on the Creek's torso at the point
where the lower ribs came together. The Creek was a
perfect target, arrogant from knowing that there was only
a boy facing him. The kill would be easy. But then Little
Hawk remembered the stern, frightening face of old Ghonka
and recalled the words that the manitou had thundered:
"Walk with honor."

His heart pounding, Little Hawk eased his way from
concealment and stepped into the open trail. "Here, Creek!"
he called.

The warrior's head jerked around, and before he could
protest or evade death, the barbed tip of Little Hawk's
arrow pierced the warrior's skin and penetrated into his
heart. He fell heavily, his head in the water.

Little Hawk felt odd for a moment, but this was not
the first warrior he had killed. He was again fully alert,
listening for the other Creek. From the woods across the
stream he heard the call of a dove, three times quickly,
then once more. For a heady moment he considered
facing the remaining Creek alone, but he had no way of
knowing how many opposed him. He moved to the stream
and ran toward the south. Soon he reached the trail and
saw sign that Renno had crossed. He raised his head and
gave the call that a scouting crow sends back to his flock
when danger is spotted. "Caw, caw, caw, caw." He waited.

The call came back. "Caw." Pause. "Caw, caw."

Again he waited but heard nothing until Renno emerged from the upslope brush, moving swiftly.

"Creek," Little Hawk whispered.

Renno, asking no questions, merely raised his eyebrows. Little Hawk pointed upstream. Renno motioned Little Hawk to stay behind. Little Hawk shook his head violently and led the way upstream. The dead Creek lay where he had fallen. Renno saw the body, looked at Little Hawk, and nodded approval. Little Hawk motioned him to be still.

"The others have not seen him," he whispered. Then he made the call of a dove in the rhythm that the Creek had used. He was answered immediately.

Renno pointed, indicating the position Little Hawk was to take, and chose a place of his own behind a large tree, where he readied his musket and the English crossbow.

When the war party burst out onto the open bank of the stream to see the corpse, Renno was saddened. They were only boys, two of them not much older than Little Hawk, the other three as tall as warriors but reedy with the slimness of late boyhood. One of them was talking excitedly while the others looked around, fear in their eyes.

Renno used a hand signal to tell Little Hawk to hold his fire. He stepped into the open. "Creek boys," he called.

Five faces jerked toward the sound of his voice, and all five began to turn their bows toward him.

"Go home," Renno commanded. "Here you will find only death."

The boy of quickest response was ready to loose an arrow at Renno when Little Hawk's bolt took him at that most fatal spot in the chest.

Renno did not move. "Go," he urged. "Return to your mothers."

The surviving four scampered back into the trees for cover.

"I tell you for the last time," Renno called after them. "Leave this land. Go home. When you have reached manhood, then come if you must."

His answer was a Creek war cry, shrill, wavering, fading. He looked at Little Hawk sadly. "Has it come to this, that Renno must kill boys?" The language was Seneca. He was Seneca now, for the faint sounds from the forest told him that the Creek boys were circling to the attack.

"Then a boy will kill them," Little Hawk declared.

"We fight together. They are young and foolish, but their arrows are as deadly as arrows fired by a senior warrior. They will come two by two from opposite sides. Shield your torso behind a tree and wait for a killing shot."

The wait was not long. Renno heard the Creek before he could see their movement. He was well concealed, with Little Hawk at his back facing south. He saw a flicker of movement and readied his musket. Although the young Creek had come into Cherokee lands to kill—and they would have killed indiscriminately, from ambush if necessary, for their one purpose was to accumulate coup, to take scalps back to the Creek Nation to prove their manhood—Renno felt only regret.

Behind him he heard the deadly *zing* of a loosed arrow, followed by a sharp cry of surprise and pain. Little Hawk was again successful. Two boys in front of Renno leaped to the offensive, crying out their rage. They died quickly, one with a musket ball in his forehead and the other with a stout arrow buried to the hilt in his torso.

The sachem turned around. Little Hawk was gone. Renno called his name. One Creek killed by Little Hawk's arrow meant that only one attacker was still alive. Renno cast for Little Hawk's track and followed it at a trot. The trail led up the gentle slope among the trees. Renno had run only a few yards when he heard the triumphant war whoop of a Seneca warrior. He came into a small clearing to find Little Hawk on his knees, sawing at the hair of the last Creek. He waited patiently while his son scalped the Creek who had died by his hand.

Little Hawk faced his father with his hands wet with blood. Four scalps dangled from his fingers.

There was no more sadness in Renno. He was Seneca. He and his son had defended their lands, and if the invaders were mere boys, they had come with death for the Cherokee as their goal. There was no guilt, only pride, for before him stood a Seneca warrior—thin, erect, only a boy . . . but a boy who was blooded, a boy who had fought so well that his father's heart was large for him.

Renno bent, dipped his finger into Creek blood, and made downward slash marks on Little Hawk's cheeks. Then, in silence, he put his hands on his son's shoulders.

More than half the women of the Seneca village had gathered outside Toshabe and Ha-ace's longhouse. When Toshabe emerged, she knew by their grim expressions that those who were bitter in their hearts had chosen the time of Renno's absence from the village to make their final demands for justice in the case of El-i-chi and his Ah-wa-o. She listened quietly and nodded. The council of matrons was reconvened within the hour, and this time there was no possibility of delaying the verdict.

A few of the women—about one-fourth of them, mostly those who were old enough to have made the trek from the far North, who remembered Ghonkaba, the great sachem—were loyal to Toshabe's wishes and spoke their convictions that it would be wrong and foolish to punish two young people for their love when there was full opportunity to interpret the law in their favor. Three-quarters of the women, however, insisted that the law was the law and no one was above it.

One by one those who were against exempting El-i-chi's marriage from the laws spoke, their repetitive rea-

soning soaring on thin, female voices through the smoke
hole. The principal spokeswoman for the exile of El-i-chi
and Ah-wa-o was a stoutly built matron called O-gas-ah,
wife of O-o-za, who had the blood of sachems. O-o-za had
come south with the group of Seneca led by Tor-yo-ne,
who had once aspired to be sachem in Renno's absence.
O-o-za was an impressive warrior who had seen not quite
forty summers and who had proven his worth in battle.
Toshabe thought that it was O-gas-ah's ambition speaking
more than O-o-za's, but whatever the reason, O-gas-ah's
oratory was well delivered, her words sharp and verging
on insult for the entire Bear Clan. Her voice rose to
compete with the low, continuous rumble of thunder and
the rising howl of wind around the longhouse.

"The punishment, then," O-gas-ah said with obvious
satisfaction, "is that El-i-chi, son of Ghonkaba and Toshabe,
and the woman called Ah-wa-o are to be lashed out of the
village to become as of the dead, never to return."

Ena, her blood rising to her cheeks, rose and faced
O-gas-ah. "I make a humble request, O-gas-ah, that you
be the first one to apply the lash."

"That will be my duty," O-gas-ah agreed.

"I long for that moment," Ena said. There was a chill
in her voice that made the other woman cringe. "For if
you touch Ah-wa-o, El-i-chi will kill you. If he does not,
then I will kill you."

A sudden darkness quieted the gathering. Even
O-gas-ah was still. The wind stopped. In the silence Toshabe
could hear Ena's breathing, her chest heaving with her
anger.

"Daughter," Toshabe said, "the council of matrons
has made its decision."

"That is as it is," Ena said. She took a step toward
O-gas-ah. "But I still long to see this one apply the first
lash."

"There will be no lashing," Toshabe said.

O-gas-ah started to protest, but she was silenced by a

low, bass bellowing that came from vast distances and grew with frightening intensity. The light failed, and the darkness of night came into the longhouse. There was a cry of fear from one woman. Thunder crashed, and lightning burned quick images into the eyes of those who saw a form at the center of the longhouse, in the space that had been occupied by the speaker. It was a black bear, the totem of Renno and El-i-chi's clan. The bear's head touched the roof of the longhouse, and his challenging roar blended with the thunder.

"El-i-chi is Seneca!" Ena shouted triumphantly. "Who can deny this sign from the manitous?"

Women moaned in fear and awe as the bear roared once more and struck out at empty air with one powerful paw. Lightning reflected from the cruel, sharp claws, and then the vision vanished.

"The shaman is Seneca!" a woman cried out. "He must not be cast out from among us!"

"We have voted to uphold the law," O-gas-ah shouted. "We risk the disapproval of the manitous if we waver from our duty."

Now the roar of the storm was all consuming. With a sharp crack the council longhouse roof lifted and swirled away on the gale-force winds. Rain lashed the village, but none fell inside the longhouse, even though the matrons were exposed to the storm. Fearfully, everyone turned her face to the sky, which was pitch black, lashed by wind, and slashed by continuous bolts of lightning. And to each in her turn there appeared the image of a stern Seneca warrior, a different manitou for each individual—a father, a dead husband, a grandfather—all standing with crossed arms and disapproving looks, and the voices of these manitous came on the thunder, pronouncing, *"The shaman is Seneca."*

With screams of terror the matrons fought to leave the longhouse and, outside, bent into the force of the storm. The sky continued to bellow, and the white bolts of lightning seemed to be directly overhead as the women scattered to the safety of their own dwellings.

Then the skies cleared as swiftly as they had darkened. Toshabe sent young girls to summon the matrons. They came to the roofless council longhouse to sit in silence and apprehension.

O-gas-ah spoke. "We have voted to abide by the laws," she said.

With a stern look Toshabe grated, "Yes, you have agreed to uphold the law."

"The law is clear," O-gas-ah insisted. "Those who offend in this matter are to be lashed out of the tribe."

"Will we now bring certain death into our diminished tribe by being vindictive?" Toshabe asked. "It is just possible—I doubt it, but it is possible—that my son El-i-chi would submit his own back for a ritual lashing. But as I live and breathe, I swear to you that blood will flow if anyone—male or female—touches his little Rose."

"I say that as well," Ena agreed.

"There will be no lashing," another matron asserted. "The shaman is Seneca. Did you not hear the voice of the storm say as much?"

O-gas-ah heard murmurs of assent from many of the matrons. She shook her head and smiled. "You heard the voice of the storm, and that was all you heard. Now there is only the matter of telling the exiles of our decision."

But several women rose together. One by one they stated that they had heard more than just wind and thunder, and they had seen more than lightning.

"One of the fierce, whirling storms of summer passed near our village," O-gas-ah scoffed. "My husband has seen its track of fallen trees. That is what you heard. The whirling storm leaped over our village, taking only the roof of this longhouse. It is true that the shaman is Seneca, but how shall we interpret that statement? I say that makes him doubly responsible for his actions: A shaman holds a position of great responsibility. He, even more than others, should honor our laws."

Ena pushed O-gas-ah aside and glared at her as if daring her to object. "Let me tell you this," Ena said. "What O-gas-ah proposes will split us into two factions that will soon be swallowed by the Cherokee sea that surrounds us. You say that we must observe the traditions in order to preserve our tribal identity. What you are proposing will create the very situation that you fear most, for if El-i-chi and Ah-wa-o are rejected, my husband and I will welcome them as Cherokee, and many others will follow them. You will lose not just one or two warriors, for Renno will never abide by such a decision. You will lose many—entire families."

"Ena speaks a truth that we cannot deny," said an older woman. "Perhaps there is a middle ground. The shaman is Seneca. The manitous have said it on the wind of the storm. El-i-chi must be our shaman; indeed, he is the only one who was trained by Casno, the only one who has the powers. But it is well-known—" She paused, leered, and chuckled. "It is known to all women that men have little choice in matters of love. Let us place the blame where it belongs. The woman who led him into defying tribal law will be shunned by all. Ah-wa-o will be considered a nonperson in our village. From today onward, no one will speak to her on the threat of punishment. Is this not a way to avoid the trouble that was described so well by Ena?"

Toshabe knew that El-i-chi would never accept such a decision. Her son was not a man to blame his actions on a woman. Her son would be more ready to fight to prevent insult to his little Rose than to himself.

It was Ena who spoke. "You are foolish and empty-headed," she told the women.

"Daughter . . ." Toshabe said warningly.

So, there in the roofless council longhouse, they voted. There would be no lashings, no exile. El-i-chi would be shaman. Ah-wa-o would be isolated by silence; she would become invisible to all.

"Neither I nor my mother will accept your stupidity," Ena stormed.

"No one is above the law," O-gas-ah said.

"My mother will speak to her daughter Ah-wa-o. I will speak to my sister, Ah-wa-o, as will my husband and my children. May the manitous protect anyone who tries to *punish* me or mine."

El-i-chi had not waited for the formal decision of the council. His belongings were few. Much of his life had been lived on the march. He had his weapons and the paraphernalia of a Seneca shaman. Since his union with Ah-wa-o, he had accumulated cooking utensils, blankets, and warm robes of hide for his wife and his son. One packhorse would carry all the family's possessions. Gao and Ta-na would walk with Ah-wa-o and him.

"Surely we will not leave before Renno returns," Ah-wa-o said tearfully as El-i-chi finished loading the horse.

"By doing so," El-i-chi said, "we will help to keep peace among our people. My brother will not agree to this punishment."

"You do not know that it is to be exile," said Ha-ace the Panther, glowering to think that it could come to this, that one of the tribe's most valuable warriors was to be driven out.

"I counted noses when the matrons appeared in the square before your house," El-i-chi said. "We will go, Ha-ace."

"What about Ta-na?" asked Ena. "Renno may want the boy to stay here."

"Ta-na and Gao are as brothers. Ah-wa-o has been like a mother to him. I cannot separate Ta-na from them now and cause my wife and son even more pain. When my brother returns, tell him that I travel to the east. The boys will know the way of the white man. Tell him that I will send word."

Ta-na and Gao were looking forward to the adventure. "Do we go all the way to the mountains?" Gao asked.

"And beyond," El-i-chi said. He seized Ha-ace's arms in the warrior's clasp. "You are father and friend, Ha-ace. I could ask no better protection for my mother than you."

"We will grieve in your absence," Ha-ace said.

Chapter IV

When John Chisholm first saw Waith Pennywhistle, he thought there had been some mistake. The Bible-quoting Pennywhistle did not seem to be at all the sort of man necessary for the job at hand. In the central square of a Cherokee village, with an amused audience of Indians, Pennywhistle hailed the Englishman as "Brother Chisholm" and heaped prayers and blessings upon his head. Later, in the privacy of a lodge, however, he put aside his Bible, and his sand-colored eyes seemed to become more piercing.

70

"So, Brother Chisholm," he said without a trace of the cornpone, country accent he had affected, "how go your efforts among the Creek?"

Chisholm was still unconvinced. Pennywhistle was just too lanky, too awkward looking, too much the hayseed. "Let me say only that the enterprise will not founder for lack of achievement on my end," he said.

"Let *us* say," Pennywhistle responded, his voice hardening, "that I did not ask out of my own curiosity."

"My reports are to be made directly to our principal," Chisholm retorted.

"Our principal is not presently available to you," the preacher replied.

"Has he left for Philadelphia yet?"

"That is a distinct possibility."

"Then I must go to Philadelphia."

"I have no authority to give you orders," Pennywhistle said.

"No, Pennywhistle, indeed you do not."

"I will make this suggestion: Go back and continue your work among the Creek."

Chisholm gave the preacher a thin smile. "I have done my job, 'Brother' Pennywhistle. But I don't see any preparation for war among these people."

The meeting between the two unlikely conspirators was taking place far to the south of Knoxville in the lands of the Chickamauga Cherokee. Pennywhistle, after his unsuccessful visit to the village of Chief Rusog, had decided to begin his efforts with the remnants of the Cherokee groups who had first encountered white settlers around 1763. Subsequent white expansionism had forced the Chickamauga to give up their lands on the eastern and northern boundaries of the Southwest Territory. Under the warlike chief Dragging Canoe they moved to the south. During the American Revolution, Dragging Canoe had led raids on white border settlements while siding with the British. In 1794 a good portion of the Chickamauga Cherokee had moved to Arkansas to become known as the western Cherokee.

It was among those Chickamauga who had remained in the Southwest Territory that Waith Pennywhistle hoped to recruit his first confederates for the plan in which both he and John Chisholm were deeply involved. Already he was near success because the Chickamauga had more reason than most to hate the white man and to fear the further expansion of the United States.

The preacher's pale eyes were the only indication that Chisholm's remark had penetrated. With a slow smile he picked up John Chisholm's musket. He showed his teeth in a challenging grin as he placed his hands close together on the weapon's heavy octagonal barrel. His cold, pale eyes did not blink as he slowly bent the musket barrel until the tip of the muzzle touched the stock.

Chisholm felt a chill of apprehension. Such strength was unnatural in one so thin and frail looking. He tried to hide his reaction, but a slight curl of Pennywhistle's lips told him that his effort had not been successful.

"Brother Chisholm," Pennywhistle said softly, "I wonder if it wouldn't be in the best interest of everyone concerned if you would drop your unbecoming belligerency toward me." The smile widened. "I am, after all, just a poor servant of God doing what he thinks is right. Our principal has directed me to determine the extent of your success among our Creek brothers to the south. If I do not bring this information to him, he will be displeased with me. It makes me very edgy to consider such a possibility."

Chisholm looked at the bent rifle barrel, then shrugged. He had one hand on the handle of his Georgia toothpick, a knife with a wide, sturdy blade of six-inch length. "I would not want either our principal or a fellow laborer in the vineyards to be unhappy," he said. "I think the attitude of the Creek leaders can be summed up quite easily. They ask merely, what's in it for the Creek? They would as lief take Spanish scalps as American or British scalps, but as it happens, the Spanish are their main source of arms and trade goods."

"Arms will be brought to them aboard British ships when they are our allies," Pennywhistle answered.

"Into Flroida ports?" Chisholm asked. "Or into New Orleans? Isn't that putting the cart before the horse? Alexander McGillivray is not a fool, and the other Creek chiefs listen to him. If I tell him he's got to drive the Spanish out of New Orleans before we can give him arms and trade goods, what do you think he's going to say?"

"McGillivray is not ignorant of world politics," Pennywhistle said. "Tell him that war is coming between Great Britain and Spain. Tell him that Spain is senile, tired, and weak and cannot stand alone against her old enemy on the British Islands. Spain will turn to France for an alliance, and France will demand a price: Spain's possessions in Florida and Louisiana. McGillivray has been to England, and he has hobnobbed with powerful men. He knows what it would mean to have to face the soldiers of a young and vigorous and very greedy France. He will agree that it would be preferable to have friends on his northern and western borders rather than bloody-minded young revolutionary soldiers from Paris."

Pennywhistle paused, his icy eyes holding Chisholm's. "The army that will move down the Mississippi will carry Kentucky long rifles and field cannon. It will consist of the best fighting men on this continent—the men of the southwestern frontier. There will also be Cherokee warriors, well armed, with this army. We will sweep the Spanish ahead of us down the river, destroying their forts as we move. This army, unlike that of the French, will have no designs on Creek lands but would make treaties to live in peace side by side with the Creek Nation. The new nation will control the mouth of the Mississippi, so free trade can move up and down the river. Prosperity will come not only to the new nation through this trade but to the friendly Creek."

"The Creek have heard such talk before," Chisholm said. "Once before an army was to move down the Mississippi to expel the Spanish and establish a new government on the Yazoo."

"There was no war between Spain and England at that time. There will be now."

"So we are asking the Creek to trade Spanish possession of the mouth of the river for British possession? The Creek will remember how the British deserted the Ohio tribes, their allies, after the Battle of Fallen Timbers, leaving the defeated Indians to the mercy of Wayne's legionnaires."

Pennywhistle sighed. "I realize, sir, that you are playing devil's advocate. The difference, again, is this: England will be occupied in fighting a war with Spain and in keeping an eye on the unpredictable revolutionaries in France. England's participation in this affair will be to provide arms by sea and to recognize quickly the new American nation when it is declared by the leaders of the white army coming down the river. All future dealings between the Creek and the lands that lie to their west and north along the Mississippi will be with this new government, not with England. It will be in the best interests of both the Creek and the new nation to be firmly allied against incursions from Georgia, from the Spanish lands in Mexico, or from the west, and from the new state of Tennessee to the north."

"Has the time come when I can use the name of our principals in my talks with the Creek?" Chisholm asked. "After all, Senator Blount established a reputation of fairness in his dealings with the Cherokee. And the Creek chiefs will be impressed to know that men like John Sevier will be lending their military experience to the effort."

"Not just yet," Pennywhistle said, looking around uneasily. "Don't even whisper those names, especially Blount's. He is the key to it all, you see, for it is his prestige that convinces the British that our plan is viable. To have it become known prematurely that he is involved would be disastrous."

Chisholm looked gloomy. "You leave me little information with which to convince McGillivray and the other chiefs."

"Our principal has great confidence in you and, not incidentally, in your ability to rally a few fighting Englishmen to our cause from the English settlement at Natchez."

Chisholm smiled. "That last is easy. It takes only a bit of ready gold."

John Chisholm took his leave, but not before he had insisted that Pennywhistle replace his ruined musket. He would travel as quickly as possible back to the Creek lands and gather a few of the more doubtful chiefs for a jaunt to the capital of the United States. There, Chisholm knew from experience, the chiefs would be wined and dined by the government. The gala reception given to them would be so condescending, so transparently self-serving, however, that the duplicity of the United States would be evident. A few words from a friend—himself—and perhaps a sincere promise or two from old Blount, and the Creek would be ready to join in the war against the Spanish territories.

When Renno returned to the village after his time in the forest with Little Hawk, he knew immediately that something was amiss. Knots of people, women and warriors, stood in the streets. Men returned his greetings but seemed reluctant to meet his eyes. The women stared at him openly, faces blank.

He saw little Renna coming from a distance, her sturdy legs pumping, her skirt lifting with her running strides. He halted, a smile of pleasure coming to his face, and held out his hands to catch her. But she halted before leaping into his arms. "Uncle El-i-chi and Aunt Ah-wa-o

are gone," she said, tears filling her eyes. "The matrons
made them leave."

Renno felt a sliding, cold sensation in his heart. His
face was a frozen mask as he let his eyes sweep the village
square, taking in the face of each person in turn. Now,
under the challenge of his gaze, the eyes of the women
fell. Warriors stirred uneasily.

Ena had approached in time to hear Renna's last words.
"There was some confusion, Brother," she said.

Renno put first things first. He would ask questions
about the vote of the matrons later. "When did they
leave?"

"Only hours ago." She pointed toward the east and
the trail toward Knoxville.

"They took Ta-na," Renna said in a constricted voice.
"And Cousin Gao."

Grimly Renno removed the crossbow from his shoulder and handed it with his arrows and musket to Little
Hawk.

Ena put her hand on Renno's arm. "I've seen my
brother's face before battle. I know the look in your eyes
now. In the past that anger meant death for enemies of
the tribe. It grieves me to know that the actions of our
own people have roused such emotions in my sachem.
Before you go after El-i-chi, you must know the decision
of the matrons."

He listened in silence as she told of the storm, the
appearance of the totem of the clan, the fear of the women,
and the "cowardly" way that the matrons decided to deny
the obvious will of the manitous by leaving El-i-chi uncen-
sured while punishing Ah-wa-o.

"Our brother does not know that the women put the
entire blame on the little Rose," Ena said. "He left before
the storm lifted the roof from the longhouse."

"I think it best that he does not know," Renno decided. "Tell Ha-ace that I require a full council of pine
trees, the tribal elders, and senior warriors when I return."

"I will go with you," Little Hawk offered.

Renno, shaking his head silently, put his hand on his son's shoulder. Little Hawk, sensing his father's anguish, did not dispute the decision.

The white Indian left the village armed with only his tomahawk and the Spanish stiletto. He started running with the long, easy strides of a distance runner, built the pace until he was near the limit of his endurance, and held it while his body cried out and his lungs pumped desperately. By punishing his body he was easing his fierce anger because, rightly or wrongly, the decision regarding El-i-chi had been made by his people under the laws of the tribe.

He settled into a loose-limbed pace that allowed his pumping heart to slow and gave his lungs time to take in adequate oxygen. El-i-chi's tracks were on the trail: a man and woman, two boys, one packhorse. Becuase of Gao and Ta-na's short legs, El-i-chi's pace would be leisurely.

He overtook them when the sun was only midway down the western sky. They had paused by a stream to refresh themselves. When Renno came upon them, El-i-chi's musket was aimed and at the ready. He lowered the weapon when he saw Renno. At first there were no words except eager greetings from the two small boys. Renno fell to his stomach and drank from the stream, then splashed water into his face and over his sweat-drenched hair.

"Is it his advanced age that makes my brother breathe so hard? Has my brother's pace been made slower by a few steps?" El-i-chi asked with a wry grin. "I expected you to overtake us an hour ago."

Renno's chest was still pumping. He laughed, shook his head, and sent droplets of cold water to spray Gao and Ta-na. The two boys yelped and jumped back.

"This is a good place to camp for the night," Renno said.

"I had hoped to put a few more miles between my

family and those who were once my people," El-i-chi said
bitterly.

"My brother must have pity on this old man," Renno
said, "and not make the distance I must travel any greater."

El-i-chi's face was grim as he switched from Seneca to
English. "It's done, Renno. Whatever the matrons decided, it was done under the law, and there's no undoing
it."

Renno formed his answer carefully. He knew his brother's scorching temper and knew that El-i-chi would not
accept the severe criticism of Ah-wa-o. "The battle is not
lost as long as one warrior remains alive," he said. "Make
your camp. Let the boys swim. Let Ah-wa-o rest. I will
return to the village but will rejoin you again at midmorn-
ing, regardless of whether or not the decision of the matrons stands."

El-i-chi nodded. "The sachem and the shaman of a
tribe have responsibilities. But do our people not have a
responsibility, too, to be loyal to their leaders? Whatever
you decide, I will accept."

Renno stayed long enough to watch his son and Gao
splashing, naked and unconcerned, in the stream. He set
out at the warrior's pace and alternated it with spurts of
harder running to reach the village at dusk. Fires were
burning in front of the council house.

Ha-ace met him at the edge of the village. "It is as
you requested, Sachem," he said. "I have only to sound
the signal."

"My father, my friend, thank you," Renno said, clasping Ha-ace's arms. "First I will take time to eat and
freshen myself."

Toshabe came to his longhouse while he was drying
himself from a hasty and incomplete basin bath. He drew
on fresh buckskins and thanked her for the food she had
brought.

"I assume that not all of them voted against, Mother,"
he said. "Please find the leaders among the matrons who

voted to punish Ah-wa-o and, by punishing her, my brother. You know them."

"Yes," she said.

"Have them at the council."

Toshabe nodded. He could see by her eyes that there was fear in her heart, fear that she was going to lose much more than her younger son and his family, for Toshabe knew well the bonds that existed between Renno and El-i-chi—ties stronger than blood, greater than sibling love.

The roofless council longhouse was crowded. Renno was not dressed in the formal regalia of a Seneca sachem. He looked more the frontiersman in buckskins and moccasins, with his hair still wet from his bath and brushed back severely. But his manner was that of a sachem, and his words and voice sounded out in the tradition of the finest Seneca oratory.

"From the time of the great Ghonka, those of my blood have served the needs of the tribe as the times and events dictated," he began. "The names of the sachems of my blood carry honor—Renno, Ja-gonh, Ghonkaba."

His eyes searched the faces of the seated gathering. "And now there are those among us who would strip honor from a name that belongs with the others. I speak of my brother, the shaman and senior warrior El-i-chi. I speak of a young Seneca maiden who loved with honor, my sister Ah-wa-o. You have decided to punish the Rose, but did you not consider that in punishing her, you also give pain to my brother?"

His voice lowered. "And did you consider, matrons, mothers and sisters of the Seneca, that your judgment against the Rose would, in effect, mean exile to my brother? For no Seneca warrior of honor would allow his wife to be treated thusly."

"There was a choice," said a female voice. "They could have stayed and accepted the punishment."

Renno recognized the woman O-gas-ah, wife of O-o-za.

"Tradition was defied," Renno allowed. "There is no disputing that. Once before I spoke to the matrons, telling you that in our reduced numbers we are vulnerable, reminding you that we are far from the main body of the Seneca in our northern homelands. I asked you to weigh the value of a warrior and our shaman against one ancient law that applies rather doubtfully in this case and to agree with me that this exception to the traditions would be in the interest of our tride as a whole. You did not agree."

He let his eyes sweep the gathering. There was accusation in his gaze. "And the matrons, even after having seen signs from the manitous—"

"How did we know," O-gas-ah interrupted, "that the shaman himself had not sent the so-called visions?"

Renno felt his anger rise in a white-hot flare. He closed his eyes and beseeched the manitous to put the right words into his mouth. He would not lose his temper; nor would he beg. Neither was in his nature. His mind had been made up before he entered the council longhouse. He would not ask the matrons to alter the decision. By their silence, the warriors of the tribe had agreed with the judgment. But he was only human. He had given the tribe his best efforts and his unquestioned loyalty. The heavy responsibilities of being sachem, thrust upon him when he was quite young by the untimely death of his father, had been borne without complaint. Yet there was a point beyond which no man could go.

"Is it proper for a people to question the actions of a sachem? Is it desirable that a tribe voice its beliefs and keep its leaders uninformed of the tribe's state of mind? In the past you have exercised that right. Once, in my absence, many of you were ready to accept Tor-yo-ne as sachem."

There was an uneasy stir among the people.

"I hold no grudge. I know only sorrow that it was Tor-yo-ne's actions that led to the death of my wife An-da. Tor-yo-ne had the blood of sachems in his veins, and had it come to a selection by the senior matrons, he would have seemed to be a qualified candidate for sachem."

He lowered his head and thundered, "But only in the absence of Renno. Only in the absence of El-i-chi, who also has the blood of Renno, Ja-gonh, and Ghonkaba, and who was and is more qualified than any other man among you to be leader of this people who came to the South. You have insulted not only a shaman, not only a senior warrior whose strong arm would be useful in the event of trouble, but you have exiled a man well qualified to be sachem should something happen to me."

"Sachem," ventured a soft female voice, "not all of us voted against them."

"But enough did," Renno responded hotly. "I am here to give you what you apparently want. You wanted Tor-yo-ne to be sachem in my absence, but he was flawed. His weakness was his downfall and the cause of the death of a woman I loved. I could not allow you to choose Tor-yo-ne, but now I will give you what you want—a new sachem."

He was giving them a chance to change the unwise decision against El-i-chi and Ah-wa-o. A few women were showing signs of distress. The majority of the women and the men remained silent, their faces closed.

So be it, he thought.

"I will not, however, allow the council of matrons to make the same kind of mistake that it would have made had the women picked Tor-yo-ne the Weak." He stalked three paces forward, looked directly down into the face of O-gas-ah. "There are those among you who think that O-o-za would be sachem."

A few women said, "Aye, yes." Others, including some warriors, said, "No, no."

Renno moved to look down into the face of O-o-za. "You will not be sachem, O-o-za."

"That is for the matrons to decide," a woman objected.

Renno lifted his arm. He had no weapons, of course

—no weapons were allowed at council. He flexed his arm. "This says that O-o-za will not be sachem," he said.

"Bring back El-i-chi!" a warrior called out. "We must not lose our sachem."

"By insulting my brother, you also offended me," Renno said. He lowered his head. "My heart aches. I am Seneca. I have lived for and fought for the Seneca. And now it is the same Seneca, my people, who would separate me forever from my brother. There comes a point where duty palls and one's own soul requires service. That time is now."

There was a chorus of protest.

"I have a duty to my children, too," Renno continued. "And so I will join my brother in exile and give you what you ask—a new shaman and a new sachem. Matrons, choose wisely, for I will return and negate any unwise decision with the sharp blade of my tomahawk in the names of the great Renno, Ja-gonh, and Ghonkaba."

Renno turned and started for the door. Several warriors sprang up to touch his arm and to beg him to reconsider. He shook his head but returned the warrior's clasp to men with whom he had faced the Chickasaw and other enemies. Then there was Toshabe standing beside the door.

"I understand," she said. "You could do no less, for loyalty to a brother is the greatest tie of all."

Renno nodded.

"Stay for a few minutes," Toshabe requested.

He stood beside the door while his mother walked to stand before the council. She lifted her hands. "My son is no longer sachem. We refused to alter tradition and accept the union of El-i-chi and Ah-wa-o, but we will depart from tradition now. It is usual for the senior matrons of the tribe to meet in privacy to consider the selection of a new sachem, but we all know that sachems are self-chosen by blood and by personal strength. The vote of the women merely acknowledges the natural ability of the selected sachem. My son has said that your husband, O-gas-ah, will not be sachem, although you so obviously wish him to become our leader."

"Renno has no right," O-gas-ah protested.

"He has made the power of his arm and the sharpness of his blade his right," Toshabe said. "And now I, who was wife to Ghonkaba, tell you this: For the first time in generations we will be led by one who does not have the blood of Renno, the first white Indian, but he will be allied to the family of Ghonkaba." She paused and motioned to Ena. "Stand by me, Daughter," she said. Ena came to her side. "These two matrons say that Ha-ace the Panther will be sachem until the time comes when my son can forgive and come back to take his proper place. Those who are my friends will agree. Those who do not agree will be given opportunity to fight for the sachem of their choice or to leave the village with the man of their choice."

There was a strained silence for long moments. Toshabe was advocating bloodshed within the tribe, a return to the evil days before Dekanawidah, He-Who-Was-Holy, kindled the Fire of Great Peace that halted warfare within the tribes of the Iroquois. To emphasize the seriousness of the situation, the pine trees, the wise men of the tribe, the senior warriors who had come south with Ghonkaba, all began to stand one by one. And one by one the older women, the senior matrons, rose to take their place beside Toshabe and Ena. The count was obviously in Toshabe's favor.

Perhaps, Renno thought, they were beginning to realize the consequences of having disavowed El-i-chi and wanted no further disruption of their lives.

But then the tribe was pushed back to the brink of violence or, at best, a serious division.

"I will be heard!" O-gas-ah cried out.

"Speak," Toshabe said.

"This is all very clever, Toshabe," O-gas-ah said. "By threatening to split the tribe, even to spill blood, you and your older son hope to obtain a pardon for the sins of El-i-chi and Ah-wa-o. I say that we made the right decision under the law. I, for one, will never agree to reverse it. Under that condition I accept the warrior Ha-ace as sachem and pledge my allegiance to him."

"That is just," a female voice said, and the opinion was seconded by a chorus of voices.

And so it was done.

Renna had gone from Ena's arms to the warm, familiar, beloved embrace of her grandmother. Her face was wet with tears, and forgetting her manners, she wiped her nose on the back of her hand.

"Renna," Little Hawk said sternly, "Seneca women do not weep."

"Are the women of our mother's people allowed to weep when they are sad?" Renna asked.

"I suppose so," Little Hawk conceded.

"Then for this time I am white," Renna said with a sob. She hugged Toshabe, and for a moment Toshabe looked as if she was going to prove Little Hawk a liar.

Alone and in small groups the men of the tribe had approached Renno, asking him to change his mind. "Give the matrons time," they told him. "They will see the error that they made."

He said the name of each warrior, shared the warrior's clasp, and exchanged memories with those among his people who had stood at his side more than once.

"Follow Ha-ace," he urged them. "Listen to the wise council of our brother Rusog, for your fate is bound to that of the Cherokee."

Renno could not travel quite as lightly as El-i-chi. Two packhorses were required for Renna's clothing, the dolls that had been made for her by her grandmother Johnson, books, the cooking utensils that would be used on the trail, a store of travel rations, Little Hawk's lesser

amount of possessions, blankets, and Renno's extra buckskins freshly cleaned by Toshabe and Ena. They left not
long after the sun rose. Little Hawk explained his sniffling
by saying that he was getting a touch of congestion. Renna's
eyes were wet.

"When next we see you two," Toshabe said, "you will
be a proper lady and a distinguished gentleman."

"I am Seneca," Little Hawk protested.

"Be Seneca, for that is your heart," Ena approved.
"But be able to live in the white world, for that is the
future."

"We have gone away before," Renno consoled. "We
have always returned."

"I pray to the manitous that it will be the same this
time," Toshabe said.

Word of the sachem's departure had spread. When
Renno and his children arrived at El-i-chi's camp on the
stream, other Seneca were there before them. El-i-chi,
having heard everything pertinent from the gathering,
met Renno with a face that showed true fury. The young
warrior's eyes were bright with anger.

"I have prayed to the manitous," El-i-chi said, his
hand on his tomahawk, "to relieve me of the honor and
manhood that prevents me from killing women. They
refuse me that prayer, but perhaps they will grant me the
right to kill a few of the men who were silent as their
wives condemned Ah-wa-o."

"We will not shed the blood of our brothers," Renno
said. "Not even in such a just cause. I am with you, little
brother."

Renno had not called El-i-chi his little brother in
years. El-i-chi smiled grimly. "You will leave them because of me?"

"And the Rose, and my son, and your son."

Tears sprang into El-i-chi's eyes. He reached for
Renno's arms, and then, forgetting the warrior's clasp,
drew Renno to his breast and held him there for a long

moment. When he broke the embrace his face was flushed with embarrassment. Renno laughed and struck him lightly in his hard-muscled belly.

"I smell food," Renno said.

Rusog, who had been oddly absent at the leave-taking in the village, had killed a young deer and brought it to El-i-chi's encampment. Ah-wa-o was roasting fresh meat. Se-quo-i was there with gifts—carved toys for Ta-na and Gao, and a book for Renna and Little Hawk. Throughout the day others came, including Ena and her twins and warriors from both the Seneca and the Cherokee villages.

Rusog and Renno walked alone at a short distance from the camp. "I cannot believe that it ends here," Rusog said.

"There will be no end to our friendship," Renno promised.

"Come back to us," Rusog said.

"My heart will be always with you," Renno said.

Se-quo-i's farewell was as simple. He limped to Renno's side and seized the white Indian's arms. "Perhaps I should go with you," he said. "Among the scholars in the cities of the United States, there must be one who could help me in this wickedly frustrating project to which I keep returning."

Renno knew that Se-quo-i was speaking of his efforts to isolate all the different sounds in the Cherokee language, the first step toward forming a Cherokee alphabet. "You are needed here, my friend," he said. "Your wisdom and your patience will be required in the future." He chuckled. "I suspect that if you narrowed your sights a bit, you might make progress on your project."

Se-quo-i joined him in laughter. "You know me too well, Sachem. It is true that just when I feel that I am making progress, something more interesting comes along, something that demands some investigation."

"Be content, friend," Renno said. "Live in peace and prosperity."

*   *   *

The exiles had a friendly escort all the way to Knoxville. Rusog and Ena were among those who accompanied them, so that there was always a gaggle of children underfoot. In Knoxville final farewells were made. Rusog and Ena, having secured the merchandise that had been the excuse for their having come to the town, were gone. Roy Johnson's old log cabin was crowded with four adults and four children. Roy took the opportunity to spoil his own grandchildren, without neglecting Gao, with sweets and small gifts.

Renno, Roy, and El-i-chi sat on the front porch of the cabin and watched the raucous celebration that began when word reached Knoxville that the Congress had made Tennessee the sixteenth state of the Union.

Roy spat tobacco juice. "Well, things go on changing, don't they? When Nora and I came out here, a man was lucky just to hold on to his hair. Now here we are, all civilized, a full-fledged state in the United States of America. We got stagecoaches running betwixt Knoxville and Nashville. We've got almost regular mail service with the East. Darned if we aren't even plagued with the beginnings of some of the things we left civilization to be rid of—white trash moving in, stealing just like they do back East. West of town are two brothers, name of Harp, who live in the woods with their women and make their living stealing hogs. First thing you know, we'll have to build prisons for the likes of Micajah and Wiley Harp, and we'll be pushing a road, maybe even one of those railroads, over the mountains so a man can travel to the old states without having to go shank's mare."

The new senator, William Blount, had already left for Philadelphia, but he'd left a letter with Roy reaffirming his desire to have Little Hawk become a Senate page. For some reason that Renno didn't understand, he postponed his own trip to Philadelphia. He, El-i-chi, and Roy went off into the woods to have one final, rambling, forget-what-day-it-is hunt. The heat of summer closed down over Knoxville.

Now and then, during the lazy days in which the three men did a lot of porch sitting and Roy talked a lot about politics with passersby, someone would speak of future plans. Roy offered to become civilized, hire a widow he knew to keep his house, and make a home for Renna while Renno accompanied Little Hawk to Philadelphia.

"Oh, no you don't, Grandfather," Renna said quickly. "Father promised that he'd take me to see the president and all the ladies dressed in fine clothes."

"Well, we wouldn't want to deprive such a sophisticated little lady of that, would we?" Roy teased.

The older man, in spite of his outward jocularity, was worried. From what he could gather, neither Renno nor El-i-chi had taken time to think the situation through. El-i-chi figured that he'd become a scout with the U.S. Army, but at the moment there was no war on the horizon and the fine army that Mad Anthony Wayne had built to defeat the Indian tribes of the Ohio was rusting away from inaction. Renno seemed to have no plans beyond granting George Washington's request that he be in Philadelphia to meet the man who would succeed Washington as president.

Roy also was aware that neither Renno nor El-i-chi had a lot of money. When Roy asked about it, Renno admitted that he had brought the last of the money that had come from the gold of the ancients, gold that he, El-i-chi, and the Huntingtons had brought back from the ghost mountain beyond the lands of the Apache.

"That won't last long in Philadelphia," Roy warned. "Now, me, I'm going to earn a few coins by playing soldier. I'm going to be a big dog in the state militia."

"That's good," Renno said.

"Comes from having friends." Roy grinned. "The new governor of this brand-new state of Tenn-o-by-God-see, old John Sevier, and I fought a few Indians together in the early days. So what I'm saying, Renno, is that what with Knoxville becoming right civilized, with schools and everything, why not bring Renna back here and let her live with me and get her education?"

"Roy," Renno said, "I am not ready to make such a decision."

"I understand," Roy said, his eyes softening. "I love you like a son, Renno, and I can imagine the turmoil you're feeling, having left your people and knowing that you're going to be separated from Little Hawk and Ta-na for a long time." He put his hand on the white Indian's shoulder. "Well, the offer will remain open. And there'll always be a place here for you, too."

Chapter V

For weeks the white Indian had felt disoriented. For the first time in his life he was alienated from his Seneca. On many occasions he had traveled away from the tribe, but always he had known that his home was there waiting for him, and many times his expeditions had been on behalf of the tribe. True, his journey now to Philadelphia had purpose, but it bore no real meaning for the Seneca. In the past when he had answered a summons from George Washington, Renno had been acting as a representative of his tribe—or at least that portion of the

Seneca that had followed his father to the South. Now Renno represented only himself and his children. Not even El-i-chi was at his side, having been left behind at an army training camp on Virginia's western frontier, where, in spite of the defeat of the tribes of the Ohio at Fallen Timbers, a man could still lose his hair if he traveled alone in the wilderness.

Renno and his children had spent a few days with El-i-chi and his family and Ta-na, seeing them settled into a log cabin and meeting the young officers, two of whom had been with Wayne in the Ohio lands and who had known both Renno and El-i-chi as valued scouts. The younger men of the officers' mess had wondered why their commander was seated with two buckskin-clad frontiersmen as bronzed as Indians. When the captain in command had described how Renno and another scout named Roy Johnson had held off "about a thousand redskins," however, the young soldiers gathered around and listened.

Renno had told anecdotes of Wayne's campaign as readily as the veteran officers, exchanged "remember old so-and-sos," and laughed as loudly as the white officers at old jokes. Then there had come the game of "where is old so-and-so?" A few men whom Renno remembered were still with Wayne in Pennsylvania. William Henry Harrison, who had been an aide to Anthony Wayne, was now governor of the Indiana Territory.

"El-i-chi," the young commanding officer had said, "you might find more exciting employment out west with Harrison. No Indian wars are going on right now, but there'll be one if Tecumseh has his way."

"I think that this time I will fight white men," El-i-chi had said. "I'll have more incentive to kill."

That remark had earned general laughter. Renno had raised an eyebrow at El-i-chi to show his brother that he knew the shaman hadn't been joking.

"Well, you might not have to wait around too long if the Frenchies keep acting up," the captain had said.

Since Ta-na was happy with El-i-chi's family, Renno decided to leave him there, playing with Gao and being cared for by the gentle Ah-wa-o.

As Renno's journey toward Philadelphia with Little Hawk and Renna had continued, there had seemed to be more people everywhere: more farms, more new houses in the towns.

"Truly," Little Hawk had said, "the whites multiply like the gnats of summer."

And then they entered odorous, raucous, populous Philadelphia, where thousands of inhabitants were crowded into an area that would not have provided a decent range for one doe deer before the forests had been cleared away.

The city had changed since Renno had last visited the capital of the United States. Hovels and shacks ringed it, and the streets were dirty. Peddlers with farm wagons and pushcarts cried out their wares to him as he walked toward the governmental complex, holding Renna's hand and being forced to call out now and then to keep Little Hawk's wandering attention. The boy gawked at the taller buildings while Renna examined the clothing and hairstyles of the women who passed in handsome vehicles and looked down their noses at the plebeian mobs on the boardwalks and streets.

Near the ornate house that had been the executive mansion during the presidency of George Washington, six soldiers in the striking uniforms of the new army filled the boardwalk, three abreast. Little Hawk, who was leading, was shoved unceremoniously into the muddy street. Renno hoisted Renna into his arms and stepped down into the dirt, giving the soldiers a mock bow.

"Taught ya some manners out in the wilderness, eh?" asked one of the soldiers with a laugh as he eyed Renno's buckskin clothes.

Little Hawk reached for his knife. Renno put a firm hand on his son's arm and shook his head with a grin. "Poor quality scalps," he said. "Not seasoned in battle."

"But they wear the uniform of the American Legion," Little Hawk pointed out.

"If they had fought with Anthony Wayne they would have fought beside men dressed in buckskin," Renno said. "We will not shed such innocent young blood on the streets of George Washington's city."

"Manners," Little Hawk spat out. "They had none."

"If you are to live among them, my fierce warrior, you must learn patience and tolerance. Think of how William Blount's face would look as he tried to explain to the Senate why his page took scalps not a hundred yards from the presidential mansion."

"It is going to be more difficult to live among these white men than I had believed," Little Hawk said.

"Is Uncle El-i-chi going to scout for men like that?" Renna asked in disbelief.

"They're not all like that," the white Indian said.

The mention of El-i-chi reminded Renno again of the weight of sadness that was in his breast.

The three travelers halted in front of the presidential mansion. Smartly uniformed soldiers stood guard, although their presence was ceremonial. No danger could threaten the man who was the father of his country in his own capital city, in his own home. Renno approached a guard and handed him the letter he'd received from George Washington. The young man looked properly blank as he fumbled the letter open and recognized the signature.

"Yes, sir?" he asked.

"Please take this letter to the general," Renno requested, "and give him this message: that I will return when I have found lodgings."

They had walked not half a block when the young soldier appeared behind them, running, his boots making loud thuds on the boards of the walk. "The general bids you come to him, sir," he said.

Renno had not wanted to impose his children on

Washington's hospitality, but he obeyed the summons. George Washington met them in an anteroom. He looked older than Renno remembered, with lines of age or fatigue around his eyes. His face was set sternly, as if his teeth were still hurting him. But his half smile was as much of a smile as was ever seen on his face, and his clasp of Renno's arms was full of genuine regard.

Renna made a polished curtsy. Little Hawk blushed and nodded. Washington narrowed his eyes at them and said, "Yes, my friend, I can see you in both of them. But you, child"—he leaned toward Renna—"you must look like your mother, who obviously was quite beautiful."

"Thank you, sir," Renna said. "Yes, my mother was very beautiful."

"Renno, you will, of course, be my guest. God knows there's enough room in this house. Since it is a working house, we'll put the children with the servants, if you have no objection—"

Renno's face was impassive when he said, "My son has his own place in Philadelphia. My daughter is not a servant. I will find a place where she can be with me."

Washington looked distressed. "I beg your pardon, old friend," he said. "I meant only—" He shrugged. "Well, that's what comes of growing old and cranky. I will have to admit that I was selfishly thinking of my own peace of mind, fearful of being disturbed by the sound of childish shouts and laughter. Forgive me. Perhaps the sound of children at play would put new life in this old house." He rang a bell, and a man in livery entered the room. "My guest will have the blue room. His daughter in the room next to his."

"Yes, sir," the servant said, bowing his way out. "I'll just take your, uh, packs to the blue room, sir."

Quickly enough Little Hawk and Renna were bundled off with a serving girl not much older than Little

Hawk. Washington quietly seated himself in a comfortable chair, his booted feet on a hassock, while Renno read a print of the published speech that was being called Washington's Farewell Address, which the president had handed him for evaluation.

At last Renno looked up, his face troubled. "But you took out all references to permanent tenure for the Indian's lands."

"Renno, the memory of the Indian atrocities in the Northwest Territory are still fresh, as, indeed, are the memories of such men as Joseph Brant during the War for Independence. On the advice of several men whose opinions I value—Mr. Alexander Hamilton among them—I removed the section of the speech that you refer to, lest it be considered inflammatory in the newer states, where settlers still face Indian hostilities. I assure you, however, that the promises are just as secure as if they had been included."

"Sir, a promise from George Washington is more than a promise," Renno said. "The words will not carry the same weight coming from another man."

"I appreciate your concern, Sachem," Washington said stiffly, "but this nation is more than one man. There will be a continuity established when another man lives in this house and holds the title of president. His word will also be good. If this nation is to survive, the promise of its chief executive must be as solid as if cast in bronze." He rose.

"There will be a few people in for dinner tonight, Renno. You'll know most of them. Now, if you'll excuse me, the Senate is still trying to get some work out of me before I'm retired to my little farm in Virginia. There will be time later for talk."

Later that same day Little Hawk was installed in a cozy, private attic room in the house that had been rented by William Blount for his stay in Philadelphia. Renno was relieved when Blount advanced the money to buy the clothing that Little Hawk needed, for his own stash of coin was diminishing. He gave in to extravagance in buying Renna two new dresses and all the little accessories needed by a very feminine ten-year-old. He was pleased when, the next night, she appeared in one of the new frocks at dinner at Blount's house and acted very grown-up.

During dinner Senator Blount told Renno that Little Hawk was going to work out well as a page. "The Senate clerk has a problem with it, Renno," Blount admitted. "He's a man without imagination and claims that Little Hawk is not a proper name."

Little Hawk laughed. "So I told him, Father, that my name was Hawk Harper."

"What would he have said," Renna asked, "if you had given him your Seneca name, Os-sweh-ga-da-ga-ah Ne-wa-ah?"

"I believe he would have turned pale in frustration," Little Hawk replied. "At any rate I have a name for my stay in this white man's place—an honorable name, the name of my great-great-grandfather's white father."

"It will serve the purpose," Blount agreed. "At any rate, Renno, be assured that your son will be properly looked after. I'm sure that his experience in the Senate will stand him in good stead in the future. I have heard that you advise all the Indian nations to become closer to the United States and to move as quickly as possible toward living cooperatively with white society. It's too bad that we don't have more people such as you in positions of responsibility."

"You state my position rightly, Senator, but most Indians feel that it's too bad that the white man can't be satisfied with the land he has already taken," Renno said frankly. "I believe that we Indians must adapt to your ways. Unfortunately, there is something in the makeup of the European that abhors empty spaces. Empty land must be filled with farms and houses, settled with grazing domestic cattle, and divided by fences. Ownership of land is a foreign idea to the Indian. To protect his survival, he will have to change his ancient style of life and cease to rely on the hunt for a major portion of his food. Actually, the Cherokee—and by association my own tribe—are farther along the road toward assimilation into white society than most, for agriculture is a very important part of our life-style. We have only to begin to raise cattle, sheep, and hogs, and we will be white men with red skins."

Blount studied Renno's face carefully for a moment. "Do I detect bitterness?"

"Naturally there is some. As a boy I ranged the northeastern woodlands. I killed ducks and geese when they were needed for our cookpots, along with passenger pigeons, deer, of course, and the small game that is the usual target for boys—rabbit, squirrel, and turkey. As a young lad I could travel for hundreds of miles in any direction and be in my own country, the land of the League of the Iroquois. Tell me, how far do those lands extend now? And how far will they extend ten years from now? Fifty years from now?"

"Yes, I see what you mean," Blount said. "If you had the opportunity, would you be interested in moving your people to new lands, lands that would be yours and yours alone in perpetuity?"

"As long as waters run and grass grows?" Renno asked with a laugh. "I have read some treaties of that sort." He looked thoughtful. "The idea has occurred to me. My brother and I have traveled far to the southwest, into the deserts, where water—or the lack of it—means life or death. I have looked to the northwest, far off, and wondered if there would not be a valley rich in game somewhere there before one runs into the western sea, which would make a suitable home for a small tribe."

"I was thinking of something a bit closer," Blount said vaguely. He shook his head, as if waking from a nap. "But now is not the time to speak of dreams, not with my lovely wife's best dessert about to appear—peach cobbler with lots of cinnamon."

Blount had gathered from Little Hawk that departure from the Seneca in the South had not been totally peaceful, that there was now bad blood between the sachem and his people. Blount's reports from Pennywhistle had told him that there was very little likelihood of convincing Rusog's Cherokee and the neighboring Seneca to join in the great adventure of seizing all the Spanish lands along the Mississippi River, the eastern Gulf of Mexico, and at New Orleans. If, however, the sachem of the Seneca was unhappy with his people, perhaps he would be interested in joining the great crusade. Renno was an influential man, Blount knew, among both whites and Indians. Not too many men—and no other Indian that Blount knew of—had been a houseguest of Washington's. The senator decided to tread easily, though. He had solid access to Renno through Little Hawk. He would approach Renno on the subject with great care.

Never had Renna spent so much time with her father. They were together constantly. The girl had become a great favorite with the staff of Washington's house, and she could charm the cook out of choice tidbits at any time of the day or evening. In the rush of activity that centered around the election of a new president, the convening of the electoral college, and speculation as to which of the front-runners would be the winner, Renno saw little of George Washington. Renna and he walked the streets of the city, attended a musical concert, which, Renna said, was "pretty but too long." They spent pleasant evenings in the Blount house, where Little Hawk complained not about his job as page but about the great load of study that was being thrust upon him in the pages' school. He got no sympathy from his father.

There was much talk about the election. The main contenders represented opposite poles of political philosophy in the young republic. John Adams, revolutionary, diplomat, and vice-president under George Washington for eight years, was considered by members of the Federalist Party as the legitimate successor to Washington. Standing in Adams's way was the brilliant Virginian Thomas Jefferson.

The opposing views of the two main candidates could have filled books. Simply put, Adams stood for a powerful, all-pervasive federal establishment. The patrician Jefferson, a man who prized freedom, believed that any rights not retained by the individual freeman should reside in the state governments, not in Philadelphia.

Adams knew that he faced a tough political battle against Jefferson. Adams sincerely believed himself to be more deserving. After all, he had been elected to Congress in 1774, a full year before Tom Jefferson held a national office. Moreover, Adams had served his nation abroad for nearly twice as long as Jefferson, and he had put in eight long, boring years being almost invisible as vice-president. His only excitement in that office was in casting a few tie-breaking votes as presiding officer of the Senate.

"I refuse to countenance being vice-president under Tom Jefferson," he told his wife.

Abigail Adams smiled and patted his hand. "Don't concern yourself. I have known that you would be president from the day that Martha Washington hinted that her husband was to retire at the end of his second term."

"Before I would continue as vice-president," Adams said flatly, "I would resign and seek election to the House of Representatives."

"That will not be necessary," Abigail assured him.

"But if some dark-horse Federalist such as Alexander Hamilton or John Jay siphons off just a few votes, the office will be Jefferson's," Adams said glumly.

"Your support is solid in the North," Abigail reminded her husband. "That will be enough."

But it was in the South, oddly enough, that John Adams won election as the second president of the United States. He defeated Jefferson seventy-one electoral votes to sixty-eight by virtue of nine southern votes, winning all the votes from Maryland and one crucial vote each in Virginia—Jefferson's own state—and in North Carolina.

In February, acting as presiding officer of the Senate, John Adams had the pleasure of reading the results of the balloting of the electoral college, thus breaking the news of his election in his own voice.

Adams had described himself as short, thick, and fat. That was not the only contrast between the first and second presidents. Washington, tall at six feet four inches, was an outgoing, physical man, graceful in his movements, always active, seldom contemplative. Adams was a loner, a brooder. On occasion he could be quite caustic, even about his predecessor. He had said, "The history of our revolution will state that Dr. Franklin's electrical rod smote the earth, and out sprang General Washington, electricized by Franklin's rod, ready to join the good doctor in conducting all policy, negotiations, legislatures, and the war itself."

Thomas Jefferson, vice-president elect in a political system that allowed one man to be elected president while his most talented political enemy was ensconced in office as the number-two man in the country, hid his disappointment well. On a visit to his old friend Washington, he said moodily, "One would have thought that his 'Discourses on Davila' would have lost him the election, especially in areas where the masses remember the kings and emperors of the old nations."

Jefferson was speaking of a series of essays written by John Adams in 1790, in which he argued that an American aristocracy was inevitable and that hereditary monarchy would be necessary as a check on the abuses of the privileged class. "Hereditary monarchy," he had written, "is attended by fewer evils than having a republican chief executive. Hereditary monarchy is the true answer, and the only one."

Even as vice-president Adams had told friends, "Our ship must ultimately land on that shore," meaning that a king would one day replace the office of the presidency.

"Yesterday's newspapers," George Washington now said to Jefferson in full explanation of why those essays had had no impact on Adams's election.

"And a semiliterate public," Jefferson agreed.

Christmas had been a time of good food, goodwill, and good conversation for Renno, lifting his spirits for the first time in long weeks. He had Christmas Eve dinner with the Washingtons, spent Christmas Day with his two children, and dressed for a small but formal reception at the Blount house. Good cheer was so abundant that even Mrs. Blount could not help but guess that her husband had sweetened the contents of the punch bowl with a full half-gallon of good Tennessee whiskey.

Most of those present were connected in some way with the frontier, either as lawmakers from such states as Georgia and Pennsylvania or as traders, merchants, or land speculators doing business in western areas.

Renna had been allowed to attend the reception. She was dressed in her finest, her pale hair falling loosely to her shoulders. She had spoken politely with several of the guests when another group of people arrived. Hers were not the only curious pair of eyes that examined two well-

dressed young men as they handed hats, capes, and canes
to a servant.

"He might have been the king of France but for the
Revolution," said a woman standing near Renna.

Renna wanted to ask questions, but she didn't care to
seem presumptuous beyond her years. She strolled through
the milling people, following the two young men. William
Blount introduced them to her father. She wasn't near
enough to hear all the senator's words, but she did hear
the name of the taller of the two young men.

"Louis Philippe, duc d'Orléans, may I present a man
from my neck of the woods, the Seneca Chief Renno,"
Blount said.

"I am charmed," Louis Philippe said. "But are not
the Seneca a northern tribe?"

"You are correct, sir," Renno answered.

Renna moved close to her father's side. The one
called Louis Philippe was handsome—but, ah, the other
one, the younger one. Never had she seen a young man's
face so open, so fair. She had not heard his name, nor
would she ask, lest her question give her away and reveal that her eyes could not get enough of the young
Frenchman.

"I have studied my geography," Louis Philippe said
with a laugh, "but I am confused."

"Sir," Renno said, "it's a long story. I understand that
you are to tour the states of Kentucky and Tennessee?"

"That is my plan. I plan a leisurely tour of the United
States. I could, in fact, be here for years."

"Then I invite you to visit our Seneca village," Renno
said. "It would be convenient for you to do so if you
should find yourself in the vicinity of Knoxville."

"*Merci*," Louis Philippe said. "I shall remember your
invitation with gratitude."

"This is my daughter, Renna," Renno said, putting
his hand on her shoulder and bringing her forward. "And

my son," he said, nodding toward Little Hawk, who was
approaching at that moment. There were greetings around,
some small talk, and then the two sons of a royal French
house were swallowed up by an admiring gaggle of ladies
of varying ages. Renna knew she would remember the
meeting as one of those treasured moments in life, not
unlike seeing the first butterfly of spring after a particularly severe winter.

The weather had turned for the worse, necessitating
that Renno purchase warmer clothing for Renna and for
himself. He had been presented to the president-elect by
Washington, and for half an hour John Adams had asked
cold, only faintly pertinent questions about the situation in
the new state of Tennessee and on the southwest frontier.
It had been obvious that Adams's interest was elsewhere,
in spite of Washington's description of Renno as an important Seneca sachem and a true friend of the United States.
Renno had the sinking feeling that the era of his influence
and value to the young government was ending.

He discovered, in a three-way conversation among
himself, Washington, and Vice-President Elect Thomas
Jefferson, that the Virginian remembered him well from
the time Renno had been in Philadelphia prior to the
Battle of Fallen Timbers and still had his finger on the
pulse of the frontier.

"Mr. Jefferson is still the dreamer, Renno," Washington said. "But don't laugh at his dreams, for as sure as the
sun will rise tomorrow, he'll be president someday."

"I wish I shared your confidence, General," Jefferson
said.

But Jefferson's talk was warm and enthusiastic about
the prospects of a great nation stretching from sea to sea.
He was quite frank in his appraisal of John Adams. "I
think you'll find Mr. Adams to be a virtual stranger to the
needs and aspirations of the people of the frontier, just as

he was for many years a stranger to America herself. Perhaps, sir, you would be kind enough to keep in touch with me during the coming four years. The least two old friends can do for each other is to share information."

"It will be my privilege," Renno agreed.

"By the way, Thomas," Washington said, "Renno's son, a lad by the name of Harper, is a page for the Tennessee delegation in your Senate. I'm sure Renno will be appreciative if you'd keep an eye on him."

"That will be *my* pleasure," Jefferson said.

Chapter VI

The new year was born on the breath of a winter storm that sheathed the city in a film of crystal-clear ice, then settled several inches of powdered snow atop the ice. Those who were forced by necessity to venture into the stinging wind and the lingering snow flurries tucked their collars tightly to their necks, covered their ears with a variety of furs, clothes, hats, scarves, and rags, and hunched shoulders against the biting, blustering wind. Pedestrians shuffled along carefully lest the slippery undercoating of ice be, literally, their downfall. Death by freezing came to

the old and the weak in the miserable hovels that had
sprung up by the hundreds on the outskirts of the city. In
an effort to combat the all-pervading, persistent cold, fires
were built too high and too hot, and they spread to consume entire edifices as the fire department fought to un-
freeze their hoses. When the firemen were able to pump
water, frozen cataracts formed even while the fires burned
on.

Renna, of course, simply had to get out into the cold
to try out the ice skates that had been given to her as a
Christmas present by Senator Blount and his pleasant
wife. The girl looked like a small princess, dressed in an
ermine hat and mittens, rabbit coat, sturdy woolens, and
generous cotton garments.

"I can hardly move," she complained.

"But you are not cold," Renno pointed out. He was
wishing for a bearskin robe instead of the greatcoat that
had taken an unwelcome bite out of his decreasing funds.
His feet felt cramped inside woolen hose and leather
boots.

The skating pond was not crowded. Only three other
brave souls had dared to venture out in the diminishing
storm—one a bareheaded youth of perhaps thirteen years
who was very accomplished on ice skates. Renna donned
her own skates and began her time on the ice by falling
repeatedly, with her ankles turning inward. The boy came
gliding toward the spot where Renno was holding Renna
up. He braked to an abrupt stop, sending shaved ice flying
before his blades, and offered his services.

"I have a sister just your age," the boy said.

"I'm almost eleven," Renna told him.

"My name is Philip," the boy said, standing proudly,
looking Renno directly in the eyes. He had black hair that
curled tightly to his scalp. He was a handsome lad, straight
of nose. His breath issued in a white cloud from smiling,
full lips. His dark eyes smiled, too. "Philip Woods."

"I'm Renna. This is my father."

Renno extended his hand. Philip Woods whipped off his mitten and took the hand in a good grip. "I know you, sir," he said. "You're Renno, chief of the Seneca."

"You have the advantage, young sir," Renno said, favorably impressed.

"My father has pointed you out to me. He knew you when you were scouting for General Wayne."

"Your father being Colonel Philip Woods?"

"Yes, sir."

"I am honored to meet the colonel's son," Renno said.

"Thank you. The honor is mine," the boy responded. "With your permission, sir, I'll show your daughter the rudiments of ice skating."

"With my blessings," Renno said.

With the adaptability of the young reinforced by her natural coordination, Renna was soon moving around the pond under her own power, if a bit stiffly. The voices of the two young ones rang out on the cold, brittle air. Laughter exploded from them in white, fluffy clouds. Renno felt oddly saddened without knowing why until, as he walked briskly up and down the bank of the pond to keep the blood circulating in his feet, he had a revelation: Renna's self-confidence and poise often made her seem older. He laughed at himself. His fatherly concern was premature. Renna was, after all, only ten. She was entirely too young for this handsome boy to be counted as her first suitor.

He halted his pacing and turned to face the pond. Philip Woods had taken Renna's arm and was guiding her along in a swooping waltz. With his steadying arm linked in hers, she became grace in motion. Philip was just a head taller, and his dark costume contrasted to the gleaming white of her ermine hat and rabbit coat.

Renno's heart filled. The two young people made a charming picture. From a distance it was not evident that Renna was only a child. He knew that the time would come when she would be a woman, and young men would appreciate her feminine beauty.

"Ah, Emily," he whispered to the darkened, cold skies of Pennsylvania. "We will both need your guidance."

His thoughts were heavy. To school Renna in white society would increase the chance that she would fall in love with someone like Philip Woods. To take her back to the wilderness would certainly assure that she would be courted by young Seneca and Cherokee warriors in a few short years. She would be eleven in September. Already there were signs of her development as a woman. Seneca maidens often blossomed early, loved young, and bore children before their sixteenth year.

What did he want for her, this pale-haired daughter who looked more like her mother with each passing year? Emily had chosen to be a Seneca wife, but the difference between the life of an early white settler in a new territory and the life of a Seneca in his longhouse had not been great. When Emily had moved from the Johnsons' rustic log cabin to Renno's longhouse, her adjustment had been easy. Renna, on the other hand, had known the comforts and refinements of an English-type household with Beth Huntington in Wilmington, North Carolina. She had lived in the splendor of the presidential mansion for months. Could she be content keeping and cleaning the longhouse of some stalwart young Seneca warrior, kneeling on a fur spread over the dirt floor to cook venison stew in a blackened, cast-iron kettle?

He shook his head. Thank the manitous he had time before he had to face such problems. In the meantime, there were many decisions to be made, including that regarding Renna's future education. He paced along the bank of the pond, making a trail in the snow, and watched as Philip Woods, holding on to Renna's hands, taught her to skate backward.

The two young ones approached, Renna's mittened hand tucked under Philip's arm. They stopped together.

"You may tell me I am very good." Renna smiled proudly.

"You are very good," Renno agreed. "And I am very cold."

"Sir," Philip said, "I skate here every day. May Renna join me tomorrow?"

"Yes, please," Renna requested, "Philip is a very good instructor, and I do love skating."

"Perhaps," Renno said.

"Excellent," Philip said. "I'll come by the presidential mansion at one, Renna."

"I'll be watching for you," Renna told him.

The next day was bright. The passing storm had scoured the sky to a pristine blue, and the brilliant winter sun gave an illusion of warmth that was soon dispelled as Renno walked to the pond to see his daughter swooping across the ice as if she'd been skating forever, guided by the strong arm of young Woods. He watched for a few minutes. They were, he told himself, just children. They were skating in the heart of the capital city of the United States, only a half mile from the governmental buildings.

Renna waved. He motioned to her. Philip guided her over. "I'm going for a walk," he told them. "Philip, don't keep her out too long."

"No, sir," Philip said. "Another hour." He laughed. "When ice begins to form at the end of our noses, I'll take her back to the presidential mansion, sir."

"Very well," Renno agreed.

"By the way, sir," Philip said, "I told my father about meeting you. He said that he'd like very much to see you. He begs you to call on him at your convenience. He's working on the staff of the new secretary of war."

Renno told the son that he'd accept Colonel Woods's invitation soon.

The city was beginning to come alive after the snow-and ice storm. Walks had been shoveled; the streets had been pounded into mush by horse-drawn vehicles and riders. The aroma of fresh bread wafted appetizingly from a bakery. Small boys manned snow forts and engaged in spirited snowball battles.

Renno walked swiftly, feeling the good stretch of muscles that had been too long inactive. He smelled water, and when he saw the tall masts of ships rising over the warehouse buildings, he made his way down an alley to the waterfront. The broad Delaware River Bay made Philadelphia a fine port. Although the city did not front on the sea, the commerce of a nation came and went from Philadelphia's docks. There were several oceangoing vessels in the bay. One of them was being unloaded at an icy quay. The lines of the ship were very familiar to Renno. He walked toward her and saw the name *Seneca Warrior* on her prow. She'd been named for him, that ship. Visions of the woman who had chosen the name, the flame-haired Beth Huntington, came to him.

Renno spotted Billy the Pequot, one of the last of his tribe, standing at the rail of the *Warrior* and watching the stevedores carry bales down the gangplank. The short, blocky Pequot, once the finest harpooner of the American whaling fleet, saw the white Indian at about the same time, did a double take, leaped from the rail to the dock, and ran to meet him, arms open to seize Renno. No mere arm clasp would do for Billy. This reunion required a full hug, shouted greetings, and then questions that went unanswered because Billy didn't give Renno time to answer.

"Listen to me!" Billy cried out. "I sound like a woman." He grinned broadly and clasped Renno's arms. "But, by God, we are well met, old friend."

"Well met, indeed," Renno agreed enthusiastically. "What was your last port of call?"

"Kingston," Billy answered.

Renno waved a hand at the *Warrior*'s riggings. Ropes were frayed, spliced, and worn. A roughly furled sail showed ragged edges, tattered by winds. "Difficult passage?"

"Four days off the Cape of Storms," Billy said, "fighting to keep from being swept onto the shoals." He shrugged. "But she's a stout ship."

"When were you last in Wilmington?"

"Four months ago."

"How is my cousin Nathan Ridley?"

"He's well," Billy said. "What brings you to Philadelphia?" Before Renno could answer, Billy seized his arm. "But let's get out of this blasted cold. I'm fresh from tropical waters, and my blood's thin."

He led Renno to a waterfront pub. A fire crackled in a huge fireplace. Hot buttered rum was brought for Billy, while Renno requested hot tea. Then there was the opportunity for comparing notes on all that had happened since they had last been together aboard the *Seneca Warrior*. Billy shook his head and grinned as Renno described El-i-chi's new position as a senior scout for the U.S. Army. They exchanged memories of the long, arduous trip to the Bight of Benin and drank a toast to the big black man from Jamaica, Mingo. Renno nodded when Billy expressed hope that Mingo was in good health and content in the bosom of his family in that odd land of the cockpits far to the south.

It was a full hour and several servings of hot buttered rum later before Billy cleared his throat, looked at Renno uncertainly, and said, "I was in England in the summer."

"Ah," Renno said.

"She came to port to examine the ship."

"So."

"Lord Beaumont was with her."

"And how is William?"

"In fine fettle. Right proud of his children. Two of them—one the son and heir. He looks like his uncle."

Billy was referring to Adan Bartolome, brother of the lovely Spanish woman whom William Huntington had taken back to England as his bride after the journey to the arid western lands of the Apache.

Renno had been resisting the urge to ask questions about Beth. Then he told himself that he was being stupid; it was natural for him to be curious about her. "And Beth?"

"Lord, Renno, she's more beautiful than ever."

"I imagine so." She was a few years more mature.

"A queen," Billy said with awe. "That red hair piled up like a fountain of hot lava—"

"She was well?"

"Oh, quite well. Said the ship looked great. That was the truth—old Billy sees to that." He tried to suppress a hiccup. "And speaking of the ship—"

"I take it that the Huntington Shipping Company thrives," Renno said.

"Doing well," Billy confirmed. "Three ships. They stay busy. Good men running them. Moses Tarpley and Adan are good skippers, but they can't hold a candle to the old Pequot."

Billy was more than slightly drunk. The Pequot couldn't handle the white man's potent beverages.

"The *Warrior* shows a bigger profit than the other two ships," Billy continued proudly. "She's in and out of ports faster. No wasted time in loading and unloading, and she doesn't loaf along at sea, mind you. All sails set, mate. Tight to the wind."

"So it's back to Wilmington now?"

"We have a couple of days' work to do here," Billy said, "but I want to leave this damnable cold behind as soon as I can. I want to get her back on the good old Cape Fear, where winter is not quite as unreasonable as it is here, and give her a good going-over. We'll have to replace most of the rigging and give her a new suit of sails. She's due to be careened, as well, because she's got more hair on her bottom than a grizzly bear." He finished his rum. "What about you?"

Renno had been asking himself the same question. He thought constantly of home, but he wasn't ready to go back to his people, who had turned against his brother and, therefore, against him. He did know that he had had his fill of Philadelphia. But the question of Renna's future was still unresolved. Little Hawk seemed to have settled in well with the Blounts and was excited about his work as a Senate page, if not about the pages' school.

School. Renna was ten. She had been helping Little Hawk with his schoolwork. She was bright, but Renno could take no credit for her appetite for books. She was mainly self-taught, aside from the few months she had spent with Beth and selected tutors in Wilmington. And she had benefited, mainly in being urged to read and in being loaned the materials, from being Se-quo-i's favorite Seneca youngster.

Wilmington might provide the answer. He had made the four-hundred-mile trek along the east-west length of North Carolina several times. It was an easier trip than the journey from Philadelphia to Tennessee. Sooner or later he would be going home; he knew that he could not desert his people forever, in spite of his disappointment in them. In the meantime, Renna could be getting some schooling in Wilmington. He and his daughter would be welcome to stay with Nathan Ridley, who had his own fine children, sensible values, and a wholesome atmosphere.

In truth, he admitted to himself that his decision had something to do with the way his ten-year-old daughter hung on to the arm of the handsome young son of Colonel Woods. Renno was not quite ready for her to start looking at boys with her eyes wide and with that pretty little smile on her lips.

If he had not been, in effect, a displaced person in the white man's bustling city, such a decision would not have been made without fasting and praying for a message from the manitous; but he had been in Philadelphia for a long time. He had not heard the Seneca language spoken in weeks. He heard the chaos of the streets instead of the familiar sounds of the wilderness. He was homesick, and Wilmington was closer to home. Forests began across the Cape Fear from Wilmington.

"Billy, have you room for two passengers to Wilmington?"

"Only if you're one of them," Billy answered.

George Washington wore a tight-lipped smile as he watched the president-elect arrive in his new carriage. Thomas Jefferson's expression, as he stood beside Washington, was a failed attempt at serenity. Washington was among the few men who suspected the depth of his fellow Virginian's disappointment that on 4 March 1797 it was John Adams and not Jefferson who would take the oath of office as the nation's chief executive.

The men who had framed the Constitution had created the office of vice-president as an afterthought. The late Roger Sherman of Connecticut had said, "If the vice-president did not preside over the deliberations of the Senate, he would be without employment." The vice-presidency, Thomas Jefferson believed, had been created for men like Adams. He himself disdained the office so much that he had considered taking the oath of office in his home at Monticello, postponing a trip to Philadelphia until Congress assembled again; but his natural wisdom had prevailed, and he was in Philadelphia on Inauguration Day. He was now the man who would stand in waiting. That, in the end, was the prime legitimate function of the vice-president—to wait, to be on hand to provide an orderly succession to the office of the presidency in the event of tragedy. It was not a position that was to Tom Jefferson's liking.

John Adams wore a pearl-colored suit. His hair was powdered to perfection. An ornate sword strapped to his side accentuated the shortness and stoutness of his stature. For once his wife, Abigail, was with him. She did not like Philadelphia and spent her time at Peacefield, the Adams's farm.

"King Adams," Thomas Jefferson muttered under his breath to Washington.

Neither Virginia aristocrat had ever experienced the belittling, grinding strain of having to make do on an inadequate income. Both were a bit amused that John Adams had rushed out after the election to seek credit against his new $25,000 a year salary. The resplendent carriage that carried him to his inauguration was his first major purchase.

The ceremony was a simple one. The oath of office was administered. Before the little gathering was dispersed, Washington found opportunity to whisper in John Adams's ear.

"Ah, John," he said. "I am fairly out, and you are fairly in. See which of us will be happier."

For eight years as vice-president, John Adams had endured obscurity, neglect, and loneliness. The transition to that office had not been an easy one. Prior to being elected vice-president, he had enjoyed power, fame, honor, and prestige. His had been a significant voice prior to and during the glorious War for Independence; and he had represented his nation abroad for ten years, from 1778, when he sailed for France to negotiate an end to the war, to 17 June 1788 when, to his surprise, he had been greeted in Boston Harbor by a thundering salute of cannons, the clanging of church bells, and Governor John Hancock himself standing at the foot of the gangplank of the British ship *Lucretia*.

He and Abigail had paid a large sum of money, six hundred pounds, for a new house situated on eighty-three fertile acres near Quincy, Massachusetts. It would have taken a skilled artisan a decade to earn that much money, and the expenditure left Adams low on capital. For the first time in nearly a decade, all three of the Adams's sons, John Quincy the eldest among them, were with their parents.

It was at Peacefield that Adams had decided that the only federal office worthy of his efforts would be the vice-presidency. He had the doubtful support of James Madison, who said, "John Adams is the person most likely to relish the unprofitable dignity of the vice-presidency." In spite of his service to his country, his election had not been assured. Among the names that were advanced by various groups of supporters were those of Governor John Hancock, John Jay, General Henry Knox, and New York Governor George Clinton.

Adams had the support of New England in that first U.S. presidential election, with its huge block of electoral votes, and he was regarded as a man of integrity. For a few heady months the possibility existed that Adams might actually garner as many electoral votes as George Washington, thus throwing the election into the House of Representatives. The voting procedure mandated by the Constitution called for each elector to cast two ballots—to advance two names—without designation as to office. The individual with the majority of votes would become president; the runner-up would be vice-president. Frightened by the possibility that the Father of the Country might be humiliated by the machinations of the New Englanders, Alexander Hamilton and other political leaders began to fight to take votes from Adams. They were, from Adams's viewpoint, almost too successful, for although Washington was unanimously elected president, having gotten one vote from all sixty-nine electors, Adams managed only thirty-four. Since the other votes were split among ten others—including Hancock, Jay, and John Rutledge of South Carolina—Adams had the job.

From the beginning of his term as vice-president, he had been melancholy, deeply hurt to know that fewer than half the electors had wanted him for the post. Not even a hero's send-off in Boston could erase what he felt was a stain on his character. He disembarked in New York City— the capital had not yet been moved to Philadelphia—before George Washington's arrival and was sworn in during a simple ceremony at Federal Hall, the former City Hall. A few members of the Senate were there to hear him deliver what Pennsylvania Senator William Maclay described as a dull and uninspiring inaugural address.

Ah, but the greeting that had been given to George Washington! His passage from Mount Vernon, which he left reluctantly, to New York was described as one continuous ovation. Each town along the way had greeted his carriage with cannons and church bells. Governor Thomas Mifflin of Pennsylvania, who had been one of his officers during the war, awaited him at the Pennsylvania border. Troops of cavalry escorted Washington into Philadelphia, and he was given a splendid white horse, which he rode past thousands of people who shouted, "Long live the father of his people!"

Where he had stood on the shores of the Delaware River one cold and stormy Christmas night agonizing over whether to risk a crossing of the river amid floating ice floes to attack Trenton—a decision that had dramatically altered the progress of the war—the women of the town had erected an arch of laurel and evergreen. Girls in white gowns strewed his path with flowers and sang an ode composed in his honor.

At Elizabethtown, New Jersey, he had boarded a barge manned by thirteen master pilots, all dressed in white uniforms. The bay was thick with boats, and the air was filled with music from the bands aboard the largest craft. Troops fired salutes from the shore. A Spanish man-of-war ran up the flags of several nations, and the crew lined the yardarms and stood at attention beside the ship's cannons. Fireworks lit the night sky. Thousands cheered. The parade from Washington's house on Cherry Street to the new Federal Building was led by American soldiers in their fanciest dress uniforms. Scotch infantrymen in kilts marched to the wail of bagpipes.

In the Senate chamber John Adams had waited. "Sir," he had said, "the Senate and the House of Representatives are ready to attend you to take the oath required by the Constitution, which will be administered by the chancellor of the state of New York."

"I am ready to proceed," Washington had said.

Ah, how well John Adams remembered that gaudy day in April of 1789! Now he himself was president, but he could still see in his mind's eye the tall, poised Washington standing between two pillars on a balcony overlooking Broad and Wall streets, where an immense crowd had gathered. Baron Friedrich von Steuben, who had taught close-order drill to the ragged Continentals at frozen Valley Forge, had smiled as Washington repeated the words:

"I do solemnly swear that I will faithfully execute the office of the president of the United States and will to the best of my ability preserve, protect, and defend the Constitution of the United States."

The words were the same when John Adams delivered them in a firm voice on 4 March 1797, but where were the crowds to shout "Long Live John Adams, president of the United States," as they'd shouted for George Washington?

Nevertheless, he had Abigail at his side, and he *was* president. No longer would men mock him, call him the "Duke of Braintree" or "His Rotundity" simply because, as newly elected vice-president, he had believed that the office of the presidency should have some dignity and had suggested that George Washington be called "His Highness, the President of the United States of America, and Protector of the Right of the Same."

Lord, lord, how they had laughed. And, he had to admit, he had been a bit carried away when he had

suggested calling the president "His Most Benign Highness," but not "superlatively ridiculous," as the autocratic
Jefferson had stated.

Adams and Washington had not been friends. Adams
had determined early on that the president would lean on
Alexander Hamilton, his brilliant secretary of the treasury;
upon Thomas Jefferson, his secretary of state; and upon
Henry Knox, his secretary of war, for advice. In spite of
ten years' experience representing the United States
abroad—including having been minister to Great Britain—
the vice-president had played no role in facing the various
crises of foreign policy that had arisen during the eight
years of Washington's presidency. He had not even been
consulted before John Jay was sent to London in 1794, an
event that resulted in the Jay Treaty and made an enemy
of a once-staunch ally, France. Nor had Adams been consulted about the several vital decisions that were made
during those years regarding the policy of the United
States toward the Indian tribes.

The man who was now president, although by no
means a small-minded man, was human. He could not
help but remember that for eight years George Washington had been indifferent to him, that Alexander Hamilton
had treated him as a potential rival for leadership of the
Federalist Party after Washington retired to Mount Vernon, that Thomas Jefferson had pointedly ignored him in
spite of the fact that they had been warm friends while
serving together in France in 1784–85.

Adams was human enough to have been influenced
by the events of the eight years of his vice-presidency and
had been squeezed by the financial strain of supporting
two residences on the vice-president's salary of $5,000.
With Abigail in Massachusetts, he had lodged alone in
Philadelphia after the capital had been moved from New
York, renting rooms at the Fraunces Tavern on Fourth
Street. His letters to his wife had depicted him as being a
bitter man. He had talked of resigning the office and had

written to his absent wife, "I want my wife to hover over and about me. I want my horse, my farm, my long walks, and more than all, the bosom of my friends."

And yet he never lost sight of the hope that the vice-presidency was a stepping stone to the office he coveted most, the presidency. In pursuit of that goal he toned down his attempts to establish an American nobility. He abandoned his powdered wig. He put his regal sword away, and he kept up his contacts with those New Englanders who believed as he did—and as Alexander Hamilton also believed—that the federal government had the power to enact any law necessary for the benefit of the people.

Adams and his fellow Federalists drew that belief from the clause in the Constitution that read: ". . . to provide for the common defense and general welfare of the United States." New Englanders wanted a strong central government to protect their manufacturing trade and their jobs. Thomas Jefferson, James Madison, and others maintained that there were no "implied powers" given to the federal government by the Constitution, that unless definitely assigned, all powers belonged to the individual states and, ultimately, to the individual.

Thus, Adams, the newly elected president, was to oversee the development of the two-party system, which pitted the urban interests of the East against the free-wheeling westerners, southern planters, small farmers, and others of more independent nature. Because such people were generally in favor of freedom for all and sympathized with the French in their efforts to form a republic, they were called Republicans. The rivalry between the Federalists and the Republicans was to be bitter, and domestic political considerations would, by their intensity, draw attention from the very real dangers that were forming for the young nation on the international front.

In his inaugural address the second president of the

United States declared a policy of peace for all nations. Even as he spoke, French corsairs were beginning to prey on lightly defended American merchant vessels. For decades the main danger to American commerce on the high seas had come from British ships. After the ratification of the Jay Treaty with Great Britain, which was considered by the French to be a direct insult, an odd state of affairs was to begin to develop, a situation in which American vessels were often happy to see the previously hated British flag and dismayed when an approaching ship ran up the tricolor of Republican France.

"Perhaps Adams can keep the peace," Thomas Jefferson said doubtfully later, at a dinner at which both George Washington and Renno were saying good-bye to Philadelphia. "But the French say that the Jay Treaty was an open betrayal of France, and they blame Adams and his Federalists for the insult. And to face such a situation, he appointed an incompetent, Charles Pinckney, to succeed an able man, James Monroe, as American minister in France."

"That's not very kind, Thomas," Martha Washington said with a smile, knowing full well that her husband agreed with his fellow Virginian.

"All I can say is this," Jefferson replied. "God help us all if, as we suspect, France has her eyes on the Spanish holdings in North America."

Charles C. Pinckney, who replaced the sophisticated James Monroe as American minister in Paris, had begun the job confident that he was equal in tact and knowledge to Mr. Monroe. But after several months, Pinckney was no longer so certain. He was being deliberately snubbed, and since he was the official representative of the United States, his country was being insulted.

For weeks he had been trying to see various members of the French governing body, the Directory, but

without success. He was spending a lot of time in anterooms, waiting . . . waiting. . . .

Revolutionary France was a turmoil of intrigue, confusion, and danger. Pinckney felt that the French Republic had been bathed in blood long enough and thoroughly
enough to satisfy even the most sanguine, but blood still
flowed both within France and abroad. A ragtag army of
thirty thousand Frenchmen under Napoléon Bonaparte
had conquered all of Italy, and when mighty Austria had
come to Italy's aid, Bonaparte had defeated her in four
straight battles, the last at Rivoli during the siege of Mantua.

Wars and rumors of wars were the current French
delight. An English fleet had observed the little general's
Italian campaign . . . a French fleet had refitted in Spain
. . . the British had abandoned Corsica, leaving it for
Napoléon's occupation. God only knew what was going to
happen in France and in Europe as a whole as the bloody-
minded young French Republic flexed its muscles.

It was Pinckney's job to see to it that European
events had no adverse effects on another young republic,
the United States; but much of the time he felt helpless
before the unfolding events. The fate of nations, Pinckney
felt, seemed to have been placed in the hands of a former
French army corporal who, as a hero of the people and
France's most famous general, was unbeatable.

In the meantime, a familiar player on the diplomatic
and political scene had sailed across the Atlantic from
temporary exile in the United States. Pinckney wondered
if, perhaps, he might gain some information about what
was likely to happen in Paris in the coming years if he had
a chat with this fellow, Maurice de Talleyrand. Back in
Paris at his old post at the Institut National, Talleyrand
seemed to have as many political lives as a cat. He had
been reported as saying that France needed new colonies,
and he had hinted that some of those colonies should be
the Spanish possessions in the southeast portion of North
America.

At the moment, however, Talleyrand was out of power and would most likely stay out of favor as long as the membership of the Directory was stable. Pinckney decided not to seek an audience with Talleyrand at that time but to continue his efforts to see the elusive members of the Directory. If France did pressure its weaker ally, Spain, into ceding Spanish lands in America to France, the consequences to the United States would be highly unpredictable, at best.

And so it was that in the late winter of 1796–97, the chief diplomat of the United States in Paris spent his time waiting in drafty anterooms, being told repeatedly that this or that member of the French government was unavailable. He wrote numerous notes and letters, explaining again and again that the Jay Treaty, which ended the belligerency between the United States and Great Britain, had not been directed against France. In reality, however, Pinckney realized that the treaty had freed England to turn a hostile face across the Channel and toward the coast of France. Pinckney's extended olive branch of peace began slowly to wilt as the early months of 1797 passed.

The attitude of the French nation reflected the continued successes of the invincible French army, which had now humbled Austria and, as a result, had added the southern Netherlands to the growing French Empire. And the feeling of destiny, of invincibility, extended to the captains of French warships and privateers at sea.

"Must we?" Renna asked when Renno told her that they were to take ship for Wilmington. "I've just begun to feel at home here, Father."

"Wouldn't you like to go home, perhaps in the spring?"

She shrugged. "I will be eager to see my grandmother and Aunt Ena and all the rest." Her face was glum. "But Little Hawk won't be there. Neither will Ta-na and Gao."

"One day Ta-na and Gao will return."

"One day," she said.

She skated with Philip that afternoon, knowing that it was to be her last time on skates. Somehow she could not see herself skating on the frozen creek near the Seneca village. She felt as if she were being ripped directly down the middle. She was dressed in furs in Philadelphia, just as she would have been dressed in furs had she been at home in the Cherokee country—but, ah, what a difference. Here the fur was tailored to fit her slim young body; there the fur would have been draped over her, a warm bag of deerskin or bearskin. Here the mittens of white ermine were stylish; there they would have brought snickers from the other young ones and odd looks from the older ones. Here she spoke with the accent of upper-class England, the accent of the woman who had been her stepmother for a short time; there she would be speaking Cherokee or Seneca, except, perhaps, when talking with her father.

And here was Philip. That was the main reason she was feeling as if she were being torn into two separate Rennas. She was too young to be thinking seriously about love, but that didn't make the feeling that had been growing in her any less powerful. She loved the way he smiled at her, the way he was so kind as he instructed her on a fine point of skating. She loved the way his dark hair curled close to his scalp and the dark sparkle of his eyes.

"When I leave here, I will never see you again," she told him. He brought her to a halt. They'd been skating side by side.

"Then don't leave," he said.

"I have to go with my father."

"Yes," he said. "Not soon, though, right?"

The tears came to her eyes and rolled down her cheeks. He wiped her face with his mittened hand. "Oh, no," he said. "How soon?"

"Tomorrow."

"Oh." There was hurt and sadness in the one word.

"Yes."

He sighed.

"We're going south, to Wilmington, North Carolina. I'll be given some schooling there for the rest of the winter. Then, in the spring, we'll probably go back to the Southwest Territory."

"But that's so bloody far away," he protested. He brightened. "Look, your brother is staying in Philadelphia, isn't he?"

"Yes."

"Then your father will be coming back to see him, won't he? If he comes, he'll surely bring you."

"It's a long, long trip," she said.

"I know. Mother and I were with Father out in the Indiana Territory. You don't realize just how big this country is until you start crossing it, do you?"

The weather had worsened again. Snow was spitting down from low-hanging clouds, and there was a wind that seemed to be bringing the cold all the way down from Canada. They were, for the moment, alone on the pond. He bent and kissed the tears from her cheeks. His lips were chapped and rough but sweetly warm.

"Don't cry. I will not let too much time pass without seeing you."

"You're thirteen years old," she said. "What can you do?"

"In less than three years I'll be sixteen. You'll be thirteen." He laughed. "Still too young to get married, but old enough to be kissed, I'll bet."

"You're naughty."

"So will you stop crying?"

"I have."

"Good. If you're leaving tomorrow, we'll have to get busy if you're going to learn how to skate backward alone."

                    *   *   *

When he left her at the gate of the presidential mansion, she stood in the blowing snow and looked at his back as he walked away.

His last words had been, "If you don't come back to Philadelphia before my father's duties take us elsewhere, I will find you when I am sixteen. I promise you that."

Three years. Three years were an eternity, and she was being foolish, for she was only ten and she was Seneca, and Philip Woods was white. As the daughter of a wise and practical man, Renna was a practical-minded girl. She told herself that it would be best to forget Philip—or, if not forget him, to put the memory of the days spent skating with him off to one side in her mind, a pleasant memento of her stay in Philadelphia to examine and fondle now and then, but not to be taken seriously.

Chapter VII

The *Seneca Warrior* maneuvered down the Delaware
River and into the Atlantic Ocean under skies of pale,
wintry blue. The favoring wind, Billy the Pequot said,
indicated a weather change. The sun meekly slipped down
behind the fading land, and the dark winter night swallowed the small ship. The restless sea weighed it with
tentative tossings and heavings, got its measure, and with
the fiery red dawn, began to show white, surly teeth.

The sun made a token appearance just above the
horizon, then swam upward into dark, brooding clouds.

The *Warrior* ran southeastward to distance herself from
the coast. Billy had resolved to go farther to sea, if it was
necessary, to buck the invisible but tremendously powerful current of the Gulf Stream. He did not want to get
caught with the "graveyard of the Atlantic" at Cape Hat-
teras on his lee.

The northeaster that had greeted the ship soon after
she'd left the Delaware River roared on for four days and
nights, but the *Warrior* was a stout ship. She did wallow a
bit on the plunging seas, and the motion began to affect
Renna. At the table with her father, Billy, and the ship's
first mate, she toyed with her food. Neither Renno nor
Billy had mentioned her growing queasiness, hoping that
it would pass. Billy had a theory that if old salts would
keep silent about seasickness, not nearly as many landlub-
bers would suffer that most miserable of all nonfatal ail-
ments. But when Renna pushed her untouched bowl away
in disgust and wiped her forehead with her scarf, Billy
knew that she was becoming nauseous.

"Not hungry, Princess?" Billy asked.

Renna crossed her eyes, stuck out her tongue, and
said, "Blah."

"I think it's bed for you, young lady," Renno said.

"Yes, please," she whispered, and for a time she was
a little girl again, content to lie snugly in her father's arms,
to be carried to the cabin she shared with him, and to be
lovingly tucked in and covered to the chin with feather
comforters.

"Better?" he asked.

"A little." She managed a smile. "You know, Father,
I once thought that you could do anything."

"But I can," Renno said with a smile.

"I thought that if I said, 'Father, would you please
move the moon for me?' you'd simply do it."

"And now you're growing up, and you realize that I
am only a man?"

"No," she whispered, making a face as the ship leaped,

rolled, and dived. "I still think you can do anything, and so I ask you to please make this miserable ship stay still."

He laughed. "I can do better than that. I can give you an instant cure for the sickness you feel."

"By the manitous," she said forcefully in Seneca, "do it."

"Simple," he said. "All you have to do is find a huge cottonwood tree and sit under it."

She moaned in real anguish and rolled away from him. "You're terrible," she said.

He put his hand on her shoulder.

"Sorry. Billy told that joke to your uncle El-i-chi, and I couldn't resist. Your discomfort will pass."

"Since you have never lied to me, my reason tells me to believe you," she said. "Even if my stomach does not."

"Try to sleep. I'll be here."

She found his hand and squeezed it with both of her small, soft ones. "When I was little and a bad dream would awaken me, you always seemed to know. You'd be there, bending over me, whispering to me that everything was all right. How did you know? Did I cry out and waken you?"

"I don't know," Renno said. He pulled a chair to the side of the bunk. "Your mother was . . . not there. You were mine, mine to love, to tend, to care for." He was touched to know that her memories were of the times he was with her, not of the times when duty took him away.

"Well, I think I'll keep you, as opposed to breaking in another father," she murmured.

"Sleep."

"Ummm," she said, snuggling into the soft bed, moving her shoulder under his hand.

By morning the winds had shifted and the sea had changed. The steep, white-toothed waves became long, green rollers that gave the ship a rocking-chair motion. Renna walked the deck dressed snugly in her rabbit fur.

Billy kept the *Warrior* inshore of the northward river of warmer water that was the Gulf Stream. The weather held. At one time they could see land to the west and watch white water shoot high into the air as the long swells smashed down onto sandy shoals. The Cape of Storms was showing a benign face, and for the remainder of the trip the *Warrior* skirted the lower North Carolina banks to enter the sheltered waters of the Cape Fear River without further strain.

It was an odd feeling for Renno to come back to Wilmington by water. He could see the Huntington house on the bluffs overlooking Cape Fear. The memories of his time with Beth flooded back vividly. There was no sign of life around the house. Billy said that it was partially closed up, looked after by the wife of an employee of the shipping company.

No one met them at the wharves. Both Adan Bartolome and Moses Tarpley were at sea with their ships. The young man left in charge of the shore facilities was a stranger, but quite courteous, especially when Captain Billy made it clear that Renno and his daughter were friends of the Huntingtons'. Renno left their packs in the office and walked up the familiar paths to Front Street, then turned south past the Huntington house.

"It was a very nice house, wasn't it?" Renna asked.

"It was."

"It was nice having a mother."

He felt an inner pain.

"I'm sorry," she said. "That was not meant as a criticism."

"I know. No offense taken."

She looked up at him. "Do you miss her?"

"I miss your mother," he answered.

"I know, but she's been dead such a long time. You loved Beth. I could tell."

"Could you, now."

She giggled. "At first it made me angry to see you looking at her so—"

"And how did I look at her?"

She spoke in Seneca. "With moon eyes."

"Speaking of moon eyes, I saw a pair of ten-year-old moon eyes in the presence of a certain young man in Philadelphia."

She blushed intensely. "You did not!"

"Did too," he teased.

"Did not!" she said, sounding like a little girl. "You did not!"

Nate Ridley was in the front garden of his family's house on Front Street, along with two of his three children. James, now seventeen, was in Boston. Some sort of game was under way, but it stopped immediately when Nate saw Renno and came rushing out the gate to greet him with open arms. The warm welcome was seconded by Nate's wife, Peggy. Renna was a bit older than the elder Ridley girl, but they seemed to get along from first glance and soon disappeared into the attic rooms where the children slept.

"You are well met, Cousin," Nate boomed as his wife, Peggy, left them to check on the progress of the evening meal. "I'm sick and tired of eating pork. As soon as you're rested, I'm going to drag you off into the woods and impose upon your hunting skills to put some good, lean venison on the table in this house."

For the first time in months Renno felt pleasant anticipation. "Cousin," he said, "if a hunt is in the offing, I'm rested enough." He raised one hand. "I ask only that you and Peggy help me to find suitable tutors for my daughter and an economical place to stay. I plan to spend the remainder of the winter here."

"Peggy will do much of the tutoring," Nate offered. "The arithmetic teacher comes twice a week, and she'll handle your Renna along with our girls. And as for a place to stay, I can't think of any place more economical than here. I insist that you be our guest for as long as you wish—winter, summer, fall . . ."

The cold of Philadelphia, the formality of living in the presidential mansion, and the endless succession of dinners and meetings seemed far behind Renno.

"Cousin," Renno said, "you put me ever more deeply in your debt."

"There is no debt between us," Nathan said. "There is never a debt between cousins who are also fast friends."

Tennessee Senator William Blount was disappointed when he was told by his page that the sachem Renno had left Philadelphia. Blount had never gotten around to having the talk he intended with Renno and had never had the opportunity to sound out Renno's feelings about the possibility of driving the Spaniards out of their Mississippi lands. Life, however, was busy for a new senator in Philadelphia. The international scene was becoming unpredictable, and there was much discussion and speculation about French intentions toward the United States. In addition, Blount had to keep up with his land holdings in the Southwest Territory and to find time now and again to meet clandestinely with intermediaries who assured him that Great Britain was still vitally interested in his enterprise.

Much to Blount's chagrin, his plans to sell frontier lands sight unseen to the rich and powerful men of England and France had been stillborn, leaving him—a former governor of the Southwest Territory and a United States senator—so deeply in debt that he was constantly being hounded by his creditors. It was an embarrassing predicament.

John Chisholm came to Philadelphia in the company of a half-dozen Creek chieftains of varying importance, men who ate like horses and drank to excess if given the opportunity. Chisholm assured Blount that the entire Creek

Nation would turn out to drive the hated Spanish from the continent and that not only the chiefs who were being regaled in Philadelphia but the others, including the so-called king of the Creek, Alexander McGillivray, would sign the necessary treaties to assure the existence of the new nation. Chisholm reported that Reverend Waith Pennywhistle had been partially successful with the southern Cherokee and that John Sevier was eager to see the formation of an army of tough, woods-wise frontiersmen armed with long rifles and ready to sweep the Spanish from their Mississippi forts on the way to New Orleans.

For a time Blount was intrigued and dreamed of even greater coups and glory, for Chisholm hinted that he had gained the interest of the very powerful Aaron Burr, whose name he mentioned in a cautious whisper. There was one thing that Blount feared more than any other: that the United States would get wind of his plan before he was able to implement it and would move to block a presence on the Mississippi that would be friendly to the British. But with a man of Burr's influence and power on his side, the danger of interference from the United States would be greatly reduced.

He instructed Chisholm to proceed with his talks with Aaron Burr, to tell Mr. Burr everything he wanted to know, and to arrange a meeting with Burr if possible. Chisholm said that Burr would, of course, be circumspect in becoming a member of such a conspiracy and would, most probably, limit his contacts with the group to the one man with whom he had already spoken, namely John Chisholm.

In spite of the strain of his financial crisis, Blount was finding the social life of Philadelphia to be pleasant. While it was true that he was living beyond his means in the luxurious house that he had leased, that didn't lessen his enjoyment in it. He generously included his page in the dinners Mary and he hosted for political personages, telling the boy he called Hawk that it would further his education to listen to the discourses of the learned representatives and senators who made up the majority of Blount's guests. Blount knew that it didn't do him any harm to have others feel that he was truly a humanitarian, having an Indian boy as a page. And he knew that it didn't harm the Indians' cause to be represented by a lad of Little Hawk's poise and education. Blount used the boy as an example of how the Indian, given time and education, could become a valuable citizen of the United States. And Blount never lost sight of the fact that Little Hawk was the son of a man who could be very useful to him as an ally.

The daily sessions of the Senate began with a prayer to the God of his mother, and Little Hawk had no problem in bowing his head and silently adding his own prayers to those of the chaplain. Some days there was little to do. As the pages waited in a special room to be summoned for messenger duty by their principals, they whiled away the long hours in various activities. One group, led by the pages from New York State, gambled with dice. Others talked in quiet voices about their homes; the younger boys, especially, were often homesick. Little Hawk, who was having a little difficulty with his schoolwork, spent the time in study and took what was, at first, mostly good-natured teasing about being a bookworm.

He had introduced himself to the other pages as Hawk Harper, but it very quickly became known that he was part Indian. Some of the boys were curious and asked friendly questions, showing disbelief when Little Hawk told how he had killed deer with a bow and arrow. He learned to understate his stories, not daring to reveal that he had killed not only deer but men and had taken scalps with his own hands and knife. The eastern boys, he found, were ignorant about life on the western frontier. They felt that all the Indians of any importance had been killed by Anthony Wayne in the Northwest Territory.

Since Little Hawk was in Philadelphia to learn from

books and to become acquainted with the white man's way
of thinking and living, he felt no need to establish his
identity as a Seneca with details that would have upset
some tender stomachs. He listened a lot. He teased back
with the boys who were good-natured and ignored the
sometimes abusive verbal thrusts of taunters such as the
pages from New York State. He was not concerned about
physical abuse. He was sturdy, large for his age, and
muscled by his life in the wilderness. Only a few pages
were taller than he, the two New York boys among them.

The pages from New York, Cadwallader Sloughter
and Peter Colden, were bulky Dutch boys, sandy haired
and blue eyed. Both were on the verge of phasing out as
pages because of their age, and both frequently let it be
known that of all the pages they had been at the Senate
longest. Sloughter was especially quick to use physical
violence to overrule any doubt about his leadership of the
pages, although, like all bullies, he tended to teach his
"lessons" to boys who were younger and smaller than he.
Peter Colden had a slight speech defect in that he could
not pronounce the letter *r*. Water, from Colden's lips,
became "wat-to." Representative became "wepwesentative."
Colden was not as easily roused to violence as Cad
Sloughter, but woe be any boy who mocked his speech
impediment.

From the first time that Little Hawk appeared in the
pages' room and introduced himself, Sloughter and Colden
had watched him warily. Each of the New York boys
outweighed Little Hawk, and Cad Sloughter stood half a
hand taller. They were also broader. But Little Hawk,
aware that he was being sized up belligerently, measured
each potential adversary and saw that both were meaty
instead of muscular and that Colden's movements were
slow.

Considering the fact that circumstances threw a group
of boys from different backgrounds together in close prox-
imity for many hours each day, things went surprisingly

well. There had been only one minor fistfight between
two of the younger boys . . . until Thomas Jefferson came
to the page room and asked for Little Hawk by name. To
be singled out by the vice-president, the president of the
Senate, for a special errand was an honor. In the past such
choice assignments had gone to Peter Colden and Cad
Sloughter because of their seniority.

Colden, who was a bit slow-witted, wanted to remedy
the situation immediately. Sloughter put a beefy hand on
his friend's shoulder and said, "Maybe it was just a courtesy to a new page. Let's not go off half-cocked."

Colden satisfied himself by putting a dead rat in
Little Hawk's lunch basket. The rat had been well mauled
by a cat and was a bloody, sodden, sad little bundle. It lay
directly atop a dish of bread pudding. Little Hawk showed
no reaction when he lifted the cloth that covered his
midday snack and saw the dead rat. The well-wrapped
bread and cheese that was the main portion of the meal
were untouched by the bloody, wet body. He ate while
reading his daily Bible lesson and became aware of Peter
Colden's steady gaze. Thus Little Hawk learned that it
was Colden who had deprived him of his dessert.

He remembered words spoken to him by his father
before Renno had left Philadelphia: "You are the representative of the Seneca," Renno had said, "but you represent all Indians as well. I do not ask you, my son, to
submerge your honor in this obligation. I ask you to
consider your actions well."

He had withstood teasing before and had accepted it
in good grace. He had shrugged off a few belittling comments. He finished his bread and cheese and washed
them down with water from a bucket on a table beside the
washbasin.

"Hey, Indian," Peter Colden called, "didn't yo-ah
missus send you any dessoit today?"

Little Hawk turned and fastened his steel blue eyes
on Colden's. He picked up his lunch basket, walked to

stand directly in front of the New Yorker, took the dish of bread pudding out of the basket—dumping the rat—and extended it toward Colden. "Well, Peter," he said, "I wasn't really hungry, but Mrs. Blount makes real tasty bread pudding. Here, it's yours."

Colden sneered. "I don't eat Injuns' lefto-vos."

"Just thought I'd offer," Little Hawk said, smiling into Colden's slightly uneasy gaze. After long seconds he turned and walked away.

Little Hawk was not deliberately unfriendly, but he quickly established the reputation of being a loner. His persistence in study soon allowed him to catch up with other boys in the tutored classes in reading, writing, history, and arithmetic; but his habit of reading or studying while waiting in the pages' room, instead of joining in the talk or the gaming, caused many to look on him as being odd. No one could understand why this fellow from a new state that supposedly had more bears than people had the attention of the president of the Senate. Thomas Jefferson called upon Little Hawk's service once more, then again, and that was too much for Cad Sloughter and Peter Colden. They didn't stop to think that they were totally helpless to punish the individual who had created the situation, the vice-president himself. They knew only that their leadership and prestige were being eroded by having special attention directed toward a backwoods Indian.

Even in the coldest days of late winter, Little Hawk made a point of going outside at least once during the working day. A vacant lot near the legislative building became his private exercise yard. He had tamped down a pathway around the perimeter of the lot, which he used to stretch his legs by running carefully on the packed snow. He had just begun to run on a day when the lowering clouds threatened snow. Peter Colden stepped out onto the dirty slush that had thawed and refrozen. His way blocked, Little Hawk came to a halt and stared at Colden's sneering face.

"You wun weal fast," Colden said.

"So," Little Hawk said, using a tone that he'd heard from his father many times.

"Whea-evo you wun, I'll catch you," Colden threatened.

Little Hawk smiled. "Why, Peter," he said, "I'm not wunning fwom you at all, but if you think you need exercise, I'll lead you in a chase."

Colden's face darkened. "You making fun of me?"

"Not a'tall. If I gave you that impression, Peter, I apologize."

Colden, puzzled, turned to look back at his friend. Cad Sloughter was standing in the shadow of the next building, his hands in his coat pockets, his shoulders hunched against the cold. "Cad," Colden called, "you can't insult this one." He turned back to Little Hawk. "When you go home does yo-ah moth-o wun out and bite you on the ankle?"

Little Hawk knew that he'd been given the ultimate insult: His mother had been called a dog and he, the son of a dog. He showed his teeth in a mirthless grin and remembered what his father had said about patience and tolerance.

Cad came to stand beside Peter. "Guess you can't insult a Tennessee hillbilly Injun," he said. "Listen, Chief Buffalo Droppings, we've taken about all we can stomach of you. Next time Mr. Jefferson sends for you, you send word to him that you're unavailable. You understand what I'm saying?"

"Perfectly," Little Hawk said coldly, holding himself back with great difficulty.

"See how easy it is?" Cad asked, grinning at Peter. "You just have to speak his language." He placed his hand on Little Hawk's shoulder, not realizing how near he came to being kneed in the groin. Fortunately he did not squeeze or push. He just set his hand on Little Hawk's shoulder and said, "Just you remember. You don't work for Mr. Jefferson anymore, boy."

Dinner at the Blount house was a private affair that night, just Blount and his wife, two of his children, and Little Hawk. When the women had left the table, Little Hawk waited until Blount had lit a cigar and was contentedly blowing smoke toward the ceiling.

"Senator," Little Hawk said, "I need a word with you, sir."

"Speak," Blount said, waving the cigar.

"Sir, I know that you think I'm doing some good here in Philadelphia, being the token Indian and all—"

"Don't belittle yourself, boy," Blount said quickly.

Little Hawk flushed. "I had no such intention." He smiled wryly. "Perhaps I intended to belittle my position here, which has become untenable."

"How so?" Blount asked, becoming more attentive, impressed by Little Hawk's seriousness.

"I know that I must behave well, in a gentlemanly manner for the sake of my tribe and for all other Indians. I have reached a point, sir, where that will no longer be possible."

"I think you'd better explain," Blount said.

"Perhaps it would be best, sir, if I simply resign and go back to my home."

"You're talking serious matters, boy. Give me a chance to help you. I can't give you advice if I don't know your problem."

Little Hawk sighed and began.

Blount listened, his face darkening as he heard how Sloughter and Colden had given Little Hawk the ultimatum to decline errands assigned by Thomas Jefferson. Then he slapped the table and leaned forward.

"Sounds to me, son, as if these eastern fops are trying to tie a rattle to the tail of a good old Tennessee boy."

"Yes, sir."

"Think you can handle 'em?'"

"Not if I have to act like a gentleman," Little Hawk replied.

Blount nodded. "Just don't scalp 'em, son."

Little Hawk's eyes widened. "Let me be sure I understand you, sir. You're telling me that I don't have to turn the other cheek with these fellows?"

"Do what you have to do," Blount said, "to maintain your dignity." He smiled lopsidedly. "I don't have to tell you no weapons, do I?"

"For this task, no weapons will be needed," Little Hawk said.

He did not have to wait long. The very next afternoon he was summoned by the president of the Senate to run papers to the president's house—some bill that was ready to be presented for the president's signature. It was a double honor, to serve the vice-president and to deliver an important sheaf of papers into the hands of John Adams himself. Little Hawk was pleased when President Adams greeted him by name and inquired about his welfare. He handed the chief executive the papers and stood tall.

"You look very much like your father," Adams said.

"Thank you, sir," Little Hawk replied. He left with a feeling of pride. He was glad that William Blount had given him permission to defend himself, for he believed that it was a true honor to be able to work for such men as Jefferson and President Adams. It did not seem odd to Little Hawk that both men were acquaintances of his father's. Jefferson and Adams were powerful men, great leaders, and their people were many; but Renno, too, was a great leader and although his people were few, the Seneca were not to be dismissed.

So it was that he was feeling proud and pleased with his life when he checked back into the pages' room to find that the Senate had adjourned for the day and that the room was empty except for four pages: Cadwallader

Sloughter, Peter Colden, and two of their cronies, the pages from Pennsylvania.

"Well, looky here," Cad said. "Chief Buffalo Droppings is back."

"Whe-o you been, boy?" Peter Colden asked. "You been wunning for the vice-pwesident again?"

"No more," Little Hawk said. "We played that game once, gentlemen. We will not play it again."

One of the Pennsylvania boys moved toward Little Hawk. "Cad," he said, "this Injun has a smart mouth. Want me to close it for you?"

"Well, we do delegate small jobs now and then," Cad said. Peter Colden laughed.

The Pennsylvania boy lifted his fists into a fighting stance. "But you told me, Peter, that this one doesn't fight," he said.

"This is not your affair," Little Hawk told him.

"It talks," the Pennsylvania page taunted. He turned, motioning to his fellow page. "It talks. Come here and listen."

Little Hawk faced the two Pennsylvanians. One was not quite as tall as he; the other was bigger but younger. He knew that he should have been facing the instigators. "This has nothing to do with you," he told them. "Let the New Yorkers do their own work."

"But it's our concern, too," said one of the Pennsylvanians. "We're to be senior when Peter and Cad go home next year."

"So be it," Little Hawk said. "You have made the choice." He waited until the larger boy tensed, stuck his tongue out the corner of his mouth in deep concentration, and began a blow with his right hand that traveled all the way from behind his shoulder. Little Hawk ducked easily under the haymaker and kicked the boy hard in the shin, then lifted his knee into his attacker's genitals. There was a hoarse scream as the boy started to fall; but before he hit the floor the second page was engulfed in a whirling storm

as Little Hawk buried one fist into his stomach and, as he
bent, lifted his face with an uppercut to the nose. Blood
splattered. The second Pennsylvania page sat down, cup-
ping his nose and gasping for breath.

Little Hawk turned in time to see Colden and Sloughter
advancing toward him. Their eyes were wide, their mouths
open in surprise. The destruction of the Pennsylvania
pages had taken no more than ten seconds—not enough
time for the two New Yorkers to aid their friends.

"Now we come down to it," Little Hawk said.

"I'm gonna kill you," Cad Sloughter seethed, jerking
a knife from his pocket and whipping it open. It wasn't a
huge knife, but Little Hawk knew that it was sharp, for
he'd seen Sloughter honing it on his boot many times.
Little Hawk danced away, leaping to attack the unarmed
and slower Colden, kicking him in the back of the knee
with his boot. Colden's leg collapsed, and as he went
down, Little Hawk came around, aimed a kick at him, and
connected. Colden's nose sprayed blood, then he fell limply
and lay still.

Sloughter advanced relentlessly in a half crouch, the
knife-fighter's stance, with the knife held low, the sharp
side of the blade upward. Little Hawk moved so that he
had the entire room behind him in which to maneuver.
He whipped off his jacket and wrapped it around his arm,
holding the padded arm in front of him.

"Cad," he said, his voice calm but cold, "I'll hurt you
less if you'll put away the knife."

Sloughter's answer came in the form of curses. He
attacked, bringing the knife up from down low. Little
Hawk sidestepped, and as Sloughter tried to whirl to
follow him he punched the big boy hard in the left kidney.
Sloughter cried out in pain and retreated. Then, with a
cry of rage, he charged.

Little Hawk stepped to one side and extended his
leg. Sloughter tripped and fell onto a table, smashing the
legs, and crashed to the floor with the sound of breaking

wood. Little Hawk kicked the side of Sloughter's head.
The dazed New Yorker struggled to his feet. Little Hawk
let Cad advance and watched the New Yorker's confidence
return. The young Seneca skipped away from the knife to
land a kick behind Sloughter's knee. Sloughter was on one
knee on the floor, the knife sagging in his hand, when
Little Hawk moved in and landed the side of his boot
directly in Sloughter's face.

When the Senate sergeant at arms burst through the
doorway, the scene that greeted him was a bloody one:
One of the Pennsylvania boys was in a fetal position on the
floor, holding his genitals tenderly with both hands. The
other Pennsylvanian was drooling blood from his mouth
and nose onto the rug. Peter Colden lay unconscious, his
face a mess, while Cad Sloughter was on his hands and
knees with blood running freely from his face.

"By all that's holy!" The sergeant at arms gasped.
"Are you trying to kill them, you savage?"

Little Hawk backed away. Here was a grown man,
armed. Little Hawk knew him to be an ex-soldier, a
noncommissioned officer in Anthony Wayne's American
Legion, a veteran of Fallen Timbers.

"I did not start this fight," Little Hawk said.

"He tried to kill me," sobbed the younger Pennsylvania page. "I don't know what he used, but he hit me with
something—"

"Where's the weapon, Indian?" demanded the sergeant at arms, lifting a bludgeon from his belt and advancing on Little Hawk.

"He tried to use a knife on me," Cad Sloughter said,
grasping. He pointed to his own knife lying on the floor.
"There."

"All right, savage," the man said, moving toward
Little Hawk. "Will you come along peaceful, or do I have
to soften your skull a bit?"

"You are making a mistake," Little Hawk said.

"Not me. The mistake was in letting a savage like you

into these hallowed halls." The ex-soldier lifted his hand to swing the bludgeon. Little Hawk, his heart pounding, moved forward under the swinging arm, seized it, and put his weight on it in a wrestling trick that he'd learned in his many bouts with Seneca and Cherokee boys. The sergeant at arms was catapulted over Little Hawk's shoulder, to land heavily on his back. He began to make horrid, strangling sounds, for the fall had knocked the breath from his lungs. Little Hawk took that opportunity to head for the door, only to have his way blocked by one of the senators from Virginia. He saw William Blount's face peering over the senator's shoulder.

Blount pushed forward as the sergeant at arms regained his breath. "Hold that boy," the sergeant croaked. "Don't let him get away!"

"I don't see him trying to get away, Sergeant," Blount said. He looked around. "My God, Hawk. I told you no blood."

"No, you said no weapons," Little Hawk reminded.

The defeated pages hurled accusations at Little Hawk, demanding that he be arrested. The sergeant at arms struggled to his feet and advanced on Little Hawk, bludgeon ready.

"Hold," Blount ordered.

"I'm going to show this little—"

"Strike that boy, Sergeant, and I'll have you jailed," Blount warned.

"Look what this savage has done!" the sergeant shouted. "He's the one who should be jailed."

"That is not for you to decide," Blount told him. "Well, Little Hawk?"

"Others started it," Little Hawk explained, his blood still running hot. "I merely finished it."

"He had a knife!" Cad Sloughter shouted.

"Senator," Little Hawk said, "you will find that the knife belongs to Cad himself. Ask any of the pages. He sits in the pages' room, honing it."

"Liar!" Cad shouted, still trying to stem the flow of blood from his nose.

"I think, sir," said the senator from Virginia, "that we should get medical attention for these boys. Then we'll sort out the question of who is to be punished."

The four pages who had been bloodied by Little Hawk's lightning attacks stuck to their story that the young Seneca had started the fight deliberately, that he had stolen Cad Sloughter's knife, and that he had used it to threaten all of them. The sergeant at arms, meanwhile, shamed by having been defeated by a mere boy, slanted his statements against Little Hawk and described him as a troublemaker from the beginning.

The dispute was heard by the vice-president and a panel of distinguished senators. William Blount spoke, saying that Little Hawk had reported persecutions against his person by the pages from New York. "Since this was a boyish dispute," Blount said, "I deemed it best to let the boys settle it themselves."

Jefferson looked puzzled. "Senator Blount, am I to understand that you expected one boy, Little Hawk, to stand against two—perhaps more—who were larger than he?"

"I did, sir," Blount said. "You see, I knew the boy."

"Apparently you were correct in your assessment," Jefferson said.

"Mr. Jefferson," said the New York senator who had appointed Cad Sloughter as his page, "are you condoning this Indian massacre that has taken place under the very roof of the legislative house?"

"I will hear what Little Hawk has to say," Jefferson said. "Boy, did you have weapons?"

"I did not, sir."

"How do you account for the damage that was done, then, to no fewer than four opponents?"

"Sir, I told Cad that if he'd put down the knife, I

would not have to hurt him as badly. You see, sir, you don't dare take a chance against a blade. When you're facing a fellow with a knife, you have to put him down quickly or risk having steel in your belly."

"I see," Jefferson said. "And the others?"

"Perhaps I was a bit rough on the Pennsylvania fellows," Little Hawk said, "but I had to put them out of action because Peter and Cad were coming at me."

"Li-o!" Colden shouted.

"He's calling me a liar," Little Hawk translated.

"I will not have my pages savaged by this renegade from the frontier," the New York senator shouted.

"Mr. Jefferson, my colleagues of the Senate," Blount said, "allow me to take the blame for this affair. After all, I told this boy that he was free to defend himself against the bullying of others, who, incidentally, threatened him with physical harm if he continued to run errands for you, Mr. Jefferson."

"I don't understand," Jefferson said.

"It seems, sir, that among the pages it is considered to be a great honor to be called for an errand by the president of the Senate. In fact, the senior pages are usually called for such duty. When you asked for Little Hawk by name . . ." Blount paused.

"This I did not know," Jefferson said. "Traditions are established rather quickly in our new republic. In that case, I, too, must take some of the blame." He turned to the New York senators. "I take it, gentlemen, that there is no lasting damage to your pages or to the boys from Pennsylvania."

"It will be weeks before the bruises are healed," grumbled one of the senators.

"As I see it," Jefferson said, "this page from Tennessee was taunted because he was from the frontier and because he has Indian blood. From what I can determine he was patient with his tormentors. I must say, gentlemen, that in such a position I myself would not have endured their taunts and insults as stoically as did this young lad for so long. I am going to recommend that no punitive action be taken against the page from Tennessee. And I am going to end this competition for the doubtful honor of serving the president of the Senate by—with your permission, Senator Blount—naming Little Hawk as my assigned page during this session of Congress." He stood. "Now, that ends the matter, gentlemen, does it not?"

The affair that became known as Little Hawk's Revenge was the talk of Philadelphia and began to spread out into the nation. The violence of it grew with the telling until Little Hawk became a six foot four inch Cherokee or Creek or Choctaw warrior, his victims numbered up to one dozen, and the entire legislative building was drenched in blood.

There was some bitterness because Thomas Jefferson had taken the word of Little Hawk and William Blount against the word of five others. Although Blount was an affable, outgoing man, he did have the frontiersman's disdain for what he liked to call the "effete East," and he had thus not endeared himself to senators from Massachusetts, New York, Connecticut, Pennsylvania, and New Jersey prior to the Little Hawk affair, and that incident made him new enemies. There would come a time in the Senate when Blount would desperately need friends. He would find few.

In Seneca society a man could gain orenda, or spiritual strength, by surviving combat with powerful foes, for the higher the quality of the enemies, the greater the victorious warrior. Little Hawk took no great pleasure in the caliber of his enemies in the pages' room. Whereas he had once chosen to be a loner, now he had no choice. Those who did not side with the battered pages were frightened of Little Hawk. The sachem's son, however,

was content. Often he was present when Thomas Jefferson
was discussing questions of national policy with senators
and others. He recognized in the Virginian a wisdom and
an intellectual curiosity that he had encountered in only
one other man previously—the Cherokee Se-quo-i.

As winter retreated, then attacked once more, Little
Hawk felt homesick. The celebration of the new beginning
had probably been held in his village. He missed his
grandmother, his aunt Ena. He missed Renna and his
father and the little ones, his half brother, Ta-na, and the
cousins.

He heard that the defeated pages had sworn vengeance. But as the forces of good, which operated in the
land of the whites as well as in the lands of the Indians,
pushed winter once more into the depths of the earth, he
saw no sign of trouble from Sloughter and Colden or from
anyone else.

Chapter VIII

The *Seneca Warrior*, heavy with a cargo of naval stores, dipped her bow gently to light seas as she sailed southwestward in the Long Bay. It was a good season to sail southern waters. The weather was fair, and the destination was a relatively close one, the port of Nassau in the Bahamas. Governor Lord Dunsmore, former Crown governor of New York and Virginia, would pay good British gold for the turpentine and tar and the long, straight pine spars that were lashed securely to the *Warrior*'s deck.

Billy the Pequot, captain, had tried to interest his old

friend Renno in making the short trip with him. The white
Indian, however, had been absorbed in helping his daughter learn the multiplication tables and struggle with the
often puzzling and sometimes delightfully idiosyncratic
spelling of English words. Seeing Renno in a domestic
setting had surprised Billy, but the white Indian had
seemed quite content. Renna and he were living with
Nate Ridley and his family. Renno, as usual, was in demand as a dinner guest, for it was well-known in Wilmington that he had been one of Mad Anthony Wayne's chief
scouts, that he was a personal friend of George Washington's, and that he had experienced adventures in many
exotic locales.

Billy was pleased to be back at sea after a winter of
inactivity during which the ship had been careened, her
bottom freed of all oceanic hair and parasitic shellfish, her
wormy boards replaced, and in general, her function and
appearance improved. The old girl was feeling her oats
now that she had a clean bottom and was skipping along
nicely before the moderate wind. When the ship had
reached a point to the south of Charleston, Billy turned
his helm toward the southeast. Soon the rougher waters of
the Gulf Stream were making the *Warrior* dance. He had
to shorten sail during a period of frisky squalls, and then
he was sailing again under velvety blue skies with the
islands of the Bahamas no more than two days away.

Billy noted the time when a lookout called out, "Sail,
ho!" He used his glass and picked up the tip of the sail just
on the horizon. During the next several hours he noted
that the course of the stranger was converging on his. He
kept checking the sail with his glass. He was in what was
considered to be British waters, but that did not necessarily mean that those waters were one hundred percent safe.
There was always one dispute or another going on between the European powers, and the United States was
sometimes caught in the middle. Since the United States
did not possess a powerful navy to punish transgressors

against its merchant marine, it was always best to beware of every sail. He ordered an alteration of course and watched the stranger closely. He saw her take the same tack.

"Let's hope she's just nosy," he told Lawrence Warren, his young first mate. "But stand ready to alert the gunners."

Heavy as she was, the *Warrior* had no hope of outrunning the following ship. She was close enough now to make out her riggings. She was a man-of-war for sure, bulky but strongly powered by a veritable forest of sails. She flew no flag that Billy could see, and that made him nervous. Just to be certain that the intruder's intentions were clear, he altered course once more, only to see the faster man-of-war follow.

Billy did some rapid calculations. He was much too far from the northern islands of the Bahamas to find shelter. He scanned the horizon, hoping to see other sails—a British ship of the line, ideally—but the sea was empty except for the bulky warship that was now closing very rapidly.

"Mr. Warren," Billy told his first mate, "you may man the guns."

All too soon he saw a puff of smoke blossom from the side of the warship. A cannonball splashed down in front of the *Warrior*. Even as another puff of smoke was formed, Billy saw the French tricolor being run up. He looked to his mast top to be sure that the Stars and Stripes was in place. The flag of the United States was there—large, clearly visible, and fluttering in the breeze. The French captain couldn't help but know the nationality of the ship at which he was firing warning shots; he was deliberately attacking a ship of the United States. So, Billy thought, the rumors that had been flitting around among sailors were true: The French had gone belligerent at sea.

The *Warrior* was outgunned. She was not as fast as the French ship. Billy considered trying to lighten his ship

by tossing the pine spars overboard, but the huge, heavy
tree trunks were difficult to handle even with dockside
facilities. He had two choices: He could fight, with the
certain knowledge that the *Warrior* was no match for the
warship, or he could strike his colors and surrender and
trust to the mercy of the Frenchmen. In view of the
bloody recent history of France, that last was not to his
liking; but it seemed to be more sensible than having the
Warrior pounded to splinters by the French ship's superior cannons.

The second cannonshot splashed water over the *Warrior*'s rail.

"Permission to open fire!" First Mate Warren bellowed.

"No, sir, do not open fire!" Billy shouted in response.
He motioned for Warren to approach him. "We can't fight
her, Mr. Warren."

"I fear not, sir," the first mate agreed. "She's got us
outgunned ten to one, and with heavier guns."

"Bring down the colors, Mr. Warren," Billy said sadly.
"Fly a white flag, if you please."

"Aye, aye," Warren said, springing into action.

Billy felt a pang of bitter regret as he watched the
Stars and Stripes come fluttering down the lanyard to be
replaced by a white flag of surrender. He put his glass on
the French commander, who was so close that Billy could
distinguish facial features. An ornately dressed man stood
on the bridge with a glass in hand. As Billy watched he
waved a hand imperiously, and a full broadside thundered
out from the French ship.

"God help us," the first mate whispered.

Shot crashed into the rigging. The mainmast was
struck solidly. There was a crack of wood, and the *Warrior*
rocked, stricken, as her weight of spars, rigging, and canvas came cascading down toward the deck in a tangled
mass. There was a scream of agony. Out of the corner of
his eye Billy saw a man go into the sea from the rigging.

The *Warrior* slowed and began to wallow as another broadside smashed into her.

"My God, sir!" Warren screamed. "He's trying to sink us."

"Mr. Warren, please tell the gunners to fire at will," Billy ordered.

The *Warrior*'s guns responded immediately, their throats bellowing sound and spitting shot into the warship's rigging. Billy saw to his satisfaction that the *Warrior* was not going to go down without leaving a few marks on her attacker. A spar went on the enemy ship, but most of her sails were still intact, enabling the attacker to maneuver for another broadside. The man-of-war was so close that Billy saw his own shot bounce off the stout wooden hull and watched the *Warrior*'s grapeshot and shrapnel sweep the French ship's deck, leaving men dead and wounded.

And then Billy's world ended as the guns of the warship thundered from just over a hundred feet away. He felt as if he'd been kicked in the chest by a mule. He sat down forcefully. The deck began to tilt, and then he knew only blackness.

First Mate Lawrence Warren saw two of the *Warrior*'s guns explode at almost the same instant. The oddly shaped, sodden pieces that landed at his feet were, he realized, pieces of human anatomy. The ship was sinking. Men lay dead all over her decks. Captain Billy was down, his chest bloody.

Warren reached out and snagged two running seamen. "The longboats, men! The boats!" he yelled. The two seamen jerked out of his grasp and disappeared over the rail. Smoke billowed up to hide the entire scene from Warren's eyes. He bent, seized the captain under his arms, and dragged him amidship, where three men were launching a longboat. They helped him lay the captain down in the bottom of the boat.

"Tell the others that we are abandoning ship," Warren told a seaman. His order was ignored. The man jumped into the longboat. Warren looked behind him. He could see nothing through the smoke. His feet were wet—the *Warrior* was going down by the head. Another broadside from the warship rattled through what was left of her rigging, and Warren felt death brush past him. He leaped down into the longboat just as it pulled away from the sinking ship. The smoke hid them from the French ship until they were a thousand yards away. The *Warrior* had disappeared.

"What if they come after us, Mr. Warren?" asked a young seaman.

The warship had sailors in the rigging trying to repair the damage done by the *Seneca Warrior's* guns.

"I reckon they'll do just about what they damned well please," Warren replied, praying silently that the French captain would be satisfied with having sunk the *Warrior*.

Apparently the captain was satisfied, for after a while he sailed away slowly, not yet able to mount a full suit of sails. The *Seneca Warrior* had left her mark, but the *Warrior's* captain could not appreciate that fact.

"The cap'n's dead, Mr. Warren," a seaman said quietly.

"May God have mercy on his soul," Warren intoned.

"Being an Indian, did he believe in God?" the young seaman asked.

"We'll have to consign his body to the deep," another man said. "God only knows how long we'll be in this boat."

Lawrence Warren covered Billy's face with a small piece of canvas. "Not just yet," he said. "I figure we're not too far from the northern Bahamas. The captain didn't want to be buried at sea."

"How do you know that, Mr. Warren?"

"It came up in conversation once," Warren replied. "Something about the belief of his tribe. If a man was to make it to the other side—to the Indian heaven or whatever—he needed to be buried in the soil of his own country."

"I doubt that'll happen," said a seaman, "seeing as how we're a few watery leagues from the North American continent."

"We'll wait awhile," Warren told him.

A British ship picked up the survivors of the *Seneca Warrior* before nightfall. The sails of the French man-of-war that had sunk the *Warrior* had just disappeared over the horizon toward the north.

To the surprise of Lawrence Warren, one of the first faces he saw as he climbed over the rail of the British ship was that of Moses Tarpley, captain of the Huntington ship *Seneca Chieftain. Chieftain*, too, had run afoul of a French corsair as she was returning from Jamaica with a cargo of rum. Tarpley's crew had been more fortunate in that the ship and her cargo had been taken as a prize, but her crew had been put ashore on an uninhabited Bahamas island.

The captain of the British man-of-war offered a burial-at-sea ceremony for the dead captain of the Seneca Warrior, then listened with respect as Warren explained that it would be a good thing if the body could be sewn into canvas and sealed into a wooden casket, where it could be kept until the ship reached land.

"I'm afraid not," the Royal Navy lieutenant said. "You see, we're heading for Montréal."

Warren nodded sadly. Billy the Pequot would have to be buried at sea, after all. Then he brightened. "We're headed for Wilmington, which is on your way."

"Then there is one possibility. . . ." the lieutenant suggested. He summoned the ship's doctor and spoke to him in low tones for a time. Then he approached Warren. "There is a way, sir, that we can get your captain's body to the United States without, uh, without—" He could not put into words what would happen to a dead body in tropical heat. He went on to explain his idea. Warren consented and expressed his thanks.

Several members of the British ship's crew and most of her officers watched as men brought a huge wine cask up from the hold, then opened its lid. Since there was no reason to waste the wine, ship's regulations were relaxed, and a ration of wine was given to the entire crew. Then the body of Billy the Pequot was submerged in the remaining wine, and the lid of the wine cask was resealed. The Pequot was going home.

To have a British ship of the line visit the port of Wilmington was an event that had not occurred since Lord Cornwallis had occupied the city prior to his last march northward toward Yorktown. By the time the impressively gunned ship was tied up to a wharf, half the town had gathered along the waterfront. There was general puzzlement when a ship's davit offloaded a huge wine cask. But then the surviving members of the crews of the two lost Huntington ships began to come ashore. Soon there were cries of glad greeting followed by wails of anguish as the news of the *Warrior*'s terrible losses spread.

Renno and Nate Ridley arrived after the survivors were already ashore. Adan Bartolome and Moses Tarpley were in the office of the Huntington Shipping Company with a young ship's officer whom Renno did not know. After seeing Renno and Nate through the thin glass of the office window, Adan jumped to his feet and threw open the door.

"It's war with France," Adan said grimly. "There's bad news, Renno."

Renno listened with an impassive face as Tarpley described his encounter with a French vessel with superior guns.

"Thank God your crew is safe," Nate said.

"The *Seneca Warrior* did not fare as well," Adan said. "Renno . . . Billy the Pequot is dead."

"The British captain was kind enough to help us bring him home," the young first mate said.

Renno felt a sudden hollowness. He listened as Lawrence Warren described the merciless attack by the French warship. Renno's hand went reflexively toward the handle of his tomahawk, only to find that it was not there. He was wearing a fine suit of clothing—dark pantaloons, red vest, white linen, and coat to match, and his only weapon was the Spanish stiletto that was snugged under his vest. He felt the need to strike out but was helpless to do so.

Later Renno stood staring down at the top of the wine cask. He said a prayer to his manitous, to the Master of Life who was recognized in various forms by every Indian tribe he'd ever encountered. The Pequot Nation had long since been scattered or exterminated, for their land had lain directly in the path of the white man's conquest—on the Long Island near New York City and to the north on the mainland—but he knew that Billy had been a devout man, trusting in the Master of Life and doing his best to abide by the traditions of his ancestors even as he plied his profession among the whites. One of the keystones of Billy's belief had been that a Pequot had to be buried in the soil of his homeland if he were to be assured swift passage to the Place across the River.

Adan stood beside Renno.

"We must take him home," Renno said.

"Yes, I know," Adan agreed.

Two Huntington ships remained, the newest of the oceangoing traders, the *Huntington Pride*, and a small coastal sloop, the *Seneca Glory*. The names of the two vessels were indicative of past events between Renno and Beth Huntington, for the *Glory* had been purchased during the time when Beth was his wife, when she was naming all of her ships in honor of Renno. The *Pride* had been acquired to replace an older ship after Renno had told Beth good-bye in England.

As it happened, the *Seneca Glory* was scheduled for a trip to Philadelphia, New York, and Boston. The *Pride* was being loaded for her semiannual Atlantic crossing to England. Renno questioned the wisdom of putting the last major Huntington ship at risk.

"The cargo has been contracted," Adan explained. "To refuse it would open us to litigation from the shippers. As you can imagine, there's not much enthusiasm about going to sea at the moment, so it would be impossible to find a substitute ship. Moreover, we are in business to carry cargo, and if we don't do it, then it wouldn't matter whether we had ships or not."

"My thoughts will be with you, my friend," Renno said.

"I appreciate that," Adan said, "but I'd rather have your good right arm in case the Frenchies try something."

Renno laughed. "I've *been* to England."

"And you've lost nothing there?" Adan looked at him searchingly for a moment, then, clearing his throat, continued. "Listen, old friend, I saw you together—you and Beth. You belong together. I see her every time I cross to the old country, and she never fails to inquire about you."

"We are of different peoples," Renno said.

"Sure, I know that. So were my sister, Estrela, and William Huntington. But they're doing all right—apparently trying to populate their area of old England with pretty little Spanish-English children. Come with me. Visit Beth."

For a tantalizing moment Renno was swayed. Just thinking of the flame-haired beauty filled him with loneliness. The forces of evil had, of late, been depleting his world of those he loved—An-da and Billy dead, El-i-chi separated from him by circumstances, Little Hawk at a great distance. Beth had been an important part of his life; her arrival had been foretold by the manitous, and their time together had been happy . . . as long as they were in his country, in his wilderness. This realization sobered him, for if he went to England with Adan he would, once

again, be on her soil, competing with men such as the
English dandy she had apparently chosen in preference to
him while he was away in Africa.

"Please give both Beth and William my kindest re-
gards," Renno said. "And sail under the protection of the
manitous, my friend."

The Ridleys offered to keep Renna with them during
Renno's absence, but the white Indian decided to bring
her to New York. Renna was delighted to escape her
studies and to accompany her father. The accommodations
aboard the small sloop were cramped, but it was summer,
so the Atlantic slumbered peacefully under fair skies and
balmy breezes, and the passage north past the Cape of
Storms was uneventful. The little *Seneca Glory* delivered
cargo at New York and then at Boston before her acting
captain, Lawrence Warren, found anchorage in Long Island Sound.

Renno and Warren went ashore in a longboat. It was
a glorious day. Fluffy white summer clouds decorated the
blue vault of sky. There was a breeze from the sound to
offset June's warmth. The white man's civilization now
occupied the land where the Pequot once lived. There
were neat farmhouses and well-cultivated fields. The men
landed near a house that overlooked the water and were
greeted by two curious young boys who led Renno and
Warren to the field where their father was plowing.

After an exchange of pleasantries Renno explained the
mission of the little sloop. The farmer was sympathetic.
He pointed to a partially wooded knoll. "Ye be welcome to
bury the poor man there, for there lie his people. Some
say I'm daft not to put it under the plow. But I said to
myself, 'Rafe, the Good Lord would frown on plowing up
a graveyard, even if it is only heathen Injuns.' "

The entire crew of the sloop accompanied the wine
cask to the little knoll. There was no lack of volunteer
labor to dig the oddly shaped grave—deep, short, and

wide. The farmer and his family were there, too, the
children gaping with wonder and just a little fearful to
know that inside the dripping wine cask was a man's body.

As captain of the ship, Lawrence Warren read portions of the burial ceremony from the Book of Common
Prayer. Renno stood at the head of the wide, short grave
and looked down at the cask, which had sprung leaks
during its trip ashore and up the rise. He spoke in Seneca,
chanting the song of the dead. Renna joined him, and a
respectful silence settled over the others. The unfamiliar
droning chant caused one of the farmer's little girls to
move close to her mother for security.

When the grave had been filled, Warren sent the
crew back to the boats while he stood indecisively, watching Renno. Renno was motionless, standing at the head of
the grave, his gaze lost in the distance.

"Well . . ." Warren said.

"Go," Renno urged. "I will join you soon."

"Yes, well," Warren said. "Come with me, Renna?"

"I'll stay with my father."

She sat on a fallen log and watched her sire, who had
not moved. He stood with his hands at his sides, his head
tilted so that his staring eyes were pointed to the fluffy
clouds on the eastern horizon. The sun's movement seemed
to accelerate as it neared the tree line to the west, and
then twilight came. Renno began another hymn to the
dead. When Renna trilled the woman's part of the song,
he motioned her to join him. She stood by his side, his
hand warm on her shoulder, as he said good-bye to a
friend and prayed to the manitous to make the Pequot's
journey to the place of his ancestors quick and pleasant.

And then Renno was silent for a while before beginning a different sort of chant.

Oddly enough, Renna did not tire, although the twilight faded and darkness came before the rising of a moon
that lit the little grove with a warm, silvery light. She was
not familiar with the chants that her father was voicing,

but they were beautiful, poetic, and pious. She was only mildly surprised when a different kind of light flickered in the moonglow. Renno lowered his voice to a whisper as a figure materialized directly over the Pequot's grave. Renna reached for her father's hand as the form became clear: An Indian warrior in odd dress, wearing his hair in a way that was unfamiliar to her, stood in midair and extended one hand as if in blessing.

Renno nodded his respect to the manitou of the Pequot.

"Honor be to you who brought the child of our people to his homeland," the manitou intoned.

Renna shivered and held on to her father with both hands, and then the ghostly figure was gone. She looked up at Renno's face, hopeful that it was now time to go back to the ship; but he did not move. There was movement in the air over the grave, and Renna held her breath as another manitou materialized. She sighed, for the woman standing before them was young and beautiful, an Indian maiden in her full glory.

"Ah-wen-ga," Renno whispered. "Grandmother."

"She's beautiful," Renna whispered.

The manitou smiled and looked directly at Renna. Then the dark eyes shifted, and her words were in French, for Renno's ears only. "Hear me." The voice seemed to come from far away. "Those who once seized me are in turmoil. To you, my grandson—" The voice began to fade. "Danger . . . change . . ."

The silver moonlight was warm and reassuring, and there seemed to be no more spirits about. Renna, still clinging tightly to Renno's hand, breathed, "That was my great-grandmother. . . ."

"As a young girl, as she was when she was kidnapped by the French and taken to the old country."

"Why?"

"Because she was beautiful," he said. "Because she was beautiful enough for a king."

"Yes," she said, "but my great-grandfather Ja-gonh went after her and rescued her."

"You remember."

"Yes, but what did she say? Why did she speak in French?"

Renno smiled reassuringly. "The French are at war with others and are still unsettled after their revolution," he said. "I think that the manitou was warning me to expect danger from a French source."

"Oh," Renna said. "Well, *you* can handle that, I'm sure."

Chapter IX

Estrela, Lady Beaumont, was feeding the latest addition to the Huntington clan. She sat in a massive rocking chair in front of a huge fireplace and held a lace shawl decorously over the red, laboring mouth of her son to prevent any exposure of her richly swollen, blue-veined breast. Her sister-by-marriage, Beth Huntington, had just arrived from London and had not yet changed from her travel clothes. Her flame-colored hair, although it had been protected by a hat, was damp. Her thick, blue skirt was made heavy by absorbed moisture. A raw autumn

storm sent sheets of windblown rain against the windows
of Beaumont Hall. The heat of a blazing fire was welcome.
Beth stood with her back to the fireplace, a musing smile
on her face as she watched the domestic scene.

"He's a healthy little lad, eh?" Beth asked idly. "Are
you and my brother intending to have more little Huntingtons?"

Estrela and Beth had been close friends since the
perilous days of traveling together in the far west of America, after William Huntington had risked so much to rescue Estrela from Apache captivity.

"It seems, dear Beth," Estrela answered dryly, "that
I have to do duty for the both of us."

Beth frowned. "If you are to start that tune, I shall
leave you to sing it alone while I go to my room to change
clothing."

"Yes," Estrela said, "before you catch your death."

"First I want one look at his nibs," Beth said, bending, lifting the shawl to see the baby's flushed face. She
laughed as Estrela flushed in embarrassment and tried to
jerk the shawl covering back in place. "Oh, heavens,
Estrela," Beth said. "You act as if I had never seen you
bathing stark naked in the Rio Grande."

"That was a long time ago," Estrela protested.

"And now you're a proper English lady."

"I would like to think so," Estrela replied. She looked
at Beth through long, black lashes, her dark eyes penetrat-
ing. "Not for me to preach, but I do believe that others
should also consider the benefits."

"Hush," Beth said, but there was no harshness in her
tone. "Now I *will* go up to my room."

Estrela watched her go, a mature woman at the height
of her beauty, stately, always poised, the object of adora-
tion of several men, the mistress of one. And that liaison
was what bothered Estrela, not because of the moral question of Beth's spending so much time with Sir Joffre Jowett, but because of the waste of it. Estrela knew the

wonder of love and reveled in the fulfillment of bearing the children of the man she adored; because she loved Beth with all her heart, she wished the same happiness for her.

Once Beth had been happy. Estrela had watched her fall in love with Renno during that long, dangerous expedition to and from the Mountain of Gold in the arid lands of the Apache and the long-dead pueblo builders. That it had been a strong love was evidenced by the fact that Beth had left her ancestral home in England to enter the world of business as a shipowner in Wilmington, North Carolina. She had seemingly sought any excuse simply to be on the same continent with Renno. And Estrela had witnessed the romance's end, had seen Beth become involved in the sophisticated social life surrounding the royal court in London and begin to waver in her love during the time that Renno was feared to be lost in darkest Africa.

Estrela was disposed to be a romantic, and it was sad to her to remember how the two of them—Beth and the bronzed, light-haired American—had looked together upon Renno's return from Africa, how they had clung to each other's presence even while pretending that their love was no longer of importance.

"What fools they are," Estrela had told William at the time. "If it were you who was sachem of the Seneca, I would go with you anywhere. They love each other. You can see that, can't you?"

Beth always enjoyed coming home to Beaumont Hall. It held good memories of her spendthrift, gambling, but always jolly father. There on Beaumont's grounds her father had taught her the basics of archery—a skill she had mastered to the point of besting William, much to his chagrin. There in the woods and fields she had hunted with her father, learning how to ride a spirited mount and handle firearms. Those three talents had been put to use in far-off America.

Only a few people knew that she had killed men in that faraway, savage land. To see her dressed in her London finery, dancing lightly at the royal court, was to see nothing more than a spectacularly beautiful daughter of old England, flame-haired like Good Queen Bess herself. Only a few knew that Beth had traveled widely in the American wilderness not only with her brother but with several Indians. Among those who knew was Sir Joffre Jowett, powdered and prim, always impeccably dressed, one of the richest and most influential men in England.

When Joffre went into her bed and held her in his arms, it added to his passion to imagine that the beautiful woman whom he adored had just returned from bloodily using her crossbow to kill dozens of hapless American savages. It gave him a shivery sense of power to possess such a deceptively fragile engine of destruction. It was also exciting to him to imagine his mistress in the arms of the savage Renno, he of the cold blue eyes. Jowett often fantasized about the two of them alone in the endless wilderness, Beth's white teeth tearing into a half-cooked hunk of venison, her green eyes locked on the Seneca's blue eyes until, bellies full, the two rolled in lustful abandon on the leafy floor of the forest.

Beth, too, often found herself reliving those times that now seemed to be so far in the past. She had known two men in her life, both of them without benefit of a formal, Christian ceremony or the blessing of the bureaucracy. With Renno she had felt married, for they had performed the Seneca marriage ceremony. With Joffre? She was thinking of him as she stripped away her sodden clothing and stepped gratefully into a steaming tub prepared by Estrela's maids. Joffre often proposed marriage, at times becoming quite insistent about it.

"Damme, Beth," he had said only last night in London, "I have my reputation to consider, you know."

Remembering, she chuckled. She sank into the deliciously hot water and was beginning to lather her smooth skin with a perfumed soap that William had imported from France for Estrela.

His reputation! After all, she didn't exactly revel in the knowledge that she was the subject of whispers. She rationalized away her guilt by telling herself that if every woman who accepted a man other than her legal husband into her bed were to be banished, London would be a dull place, and the female population of the court would be decimated.

She tried to put everything out of her mind save the sensual pleasure of the hot bath and the fragrance of the perfumed soap. And, in doing so, she stopped all movement, her head lowered, her mouth sagged into an uncharacteristic laxness. A sense of tedium, of emptiness suddenly overwhelmed her. This had happened before, and it was becoming more frequent. Without warning the foundation seemed to fall out from under her life, leaving her suspended in nothingness. At such a time she could identify with "the Preacher" in Ecclesiastes, who had written: "Vanity of vanities, all is vanity. What profit hath a man of all his labor which he taketh under the sun? The sun also ariseth, and the sun goeth down."

Her eyes were *not* satisfied with seeing, and her ears were filled not with hearing but with meaningless babble. She was, at such times, like the sea, unfilled although all the rivers ran forever into it. Like the Preacher, she had made her great works—not gardens and orchards and pools of water, but a tidy little shipping business that, thanks to favoritism early on from the king—a favor for which she had to acknowledge Joffre's aid—had thrived. She had piled up her little store of silver and gold, as the Preacher had done, and: "I looked on all the works that my hands had wrought, and on the labor that I had labored to do: and, behold, all was vanity and vexation of spirit, and there was no profit under the sun."

The Preacher had sought salvation in wisdom, only to

realize that the wisest man and the greatest fool come to a
common end, death.

Beth often sought relief from her own personal tor-
ments in the words of the Preacher, although she had to
admit that she was selective in her choice of the Preacher's words. Two, she agreed, are better than one, and if
two lie together, then they have heat. One could not be
warm alone. She lost herself in memories and wept a bit,
the tears disappearing into the soapy bathwater, and felt
grateful that no one was there to see. In the end God
would bring her into judgment "with every secret thing,
whether it be good, or whether it be evil."

From her despair came both defiance and shame. She
was willing to be judged on her love for Renno, for in her
mind and conscience, the simple wilderness ceremony she
had undergone to become Renno's wife before their first
lovemaking had just as much validity as if they had been
joined in so-called holy matrimony in Westminster Abbey.
As for the affair with Joffre? She could only plead human
weakness and quote the Preacher's words: "Two are better
than one."

The gowns she kept at Beaumont Hall were not the
latest fashions, but her beauty did not suffer when she
donned a royal blue creation in good Scottish wool. As she
was putting the last touches to her hair, she heard vague
sounds of commotion from below. She swept from her
room to hear loud, cheery male shouts of greeting. Her
curiosity aroused, her malaise conquered for the moment,
she hurried down the steps, for she had recognized both
beloved voices.

Her brother, William, was standing in front of the
fireplace. A dripping Adan Bartolome was bending down
to admire the baby in Estrela's arms.

"Adan!" Beth called as she entered the room. "How
wonderful to see you."

It took awhile to conclude the rituals of greetings, for
each of Estrela and William's offspring had to be pre-

sented to their uncle in turn. And then Adan was taken
away by William to be dried out and to don fresh clothing.
So it was not until after dinner, with the family seated in
the great dining hall, all the children present in honor of
their uncle's visit, that Beth had a chance to talk with the
man she had put in charge of her American holdings.
Estrela had gone off with the nanny to help prepare her
brood for bed. William leaned on the mantel of the fireplace. Beth was escorted to a comfortable chair by Adan.
He stood beside William, warming his backside and his
hands.

"Beth," Adan began, "I fear that I have nothing but
bad news for you."

"Then let us hear it," Beth said, "so we can put it
aside and enjoy our visit."

"You know there's an undeclared war at sea between
France and the United States," Adan began.

Beth nodded, and one of her hands went to her throat
as she waited for Adan to continue. Her quick concern was
not for her ships; it was for the men who manned them,
her friends Billy the Pequot and stolid old Moses Tarpley.
"Please," she said. "Tell me quickly."

"Both the *Warrior* and the *Chieftain* are gone," Adan
said. "Billy was killed."

Beth's expression spoke for her.

"Billy's body was brought home," Adan said. "Renno
took him to New York, so he could be buried in what had
been his homeland."

Beth's face burned at the mention of Renno's name.
"Renno?"

"He's in Wilmington, living as a white man."

Unreasoning anger made her flush more brightly. If
he had only consented to do so before it had been too late
. . . but no, nothing would do for him then but to go back
to the wilderness, to his people.

"He has Renna with him," Adan continued. "She's
being educated by Nate Ridley's wife and by the same

tutors who teach Ridley's daughters. Little Hawk is in
Philadelphia working as a page for a senator from the new
state of Tennessee."

Beth had a million questions, but she could not get
her constricted throat to open. She felt as if the room had
suddenly become smaller, closer. When she could speak,
she whispered, "And Moses?"

"Safe. We lost quite a few crewmen, however."

"Ah, poor men. Poor Billy," Beth said. She had to
hear it all in detail, how the Pequot had been brought
home in a huge wine cask, the alcohol making it possible
to keep him unburied until he had reached his homeland.

Estrela had returned. "I don't understand," she said.
"France and the United States were allies. Lafayette is a
national hero."

"It's the blasted French Revolution," William said.

Adan nodded. "At first almost every American was on
the side of the common people in France. Renno told me
that frontiersmen were especially in sympathy with the
French Revolution because they know the meaning of true
freedom and value that commodity above all. It's the
excesses of the Revolution that have alienated many
Americans—too much blood, too much senseless killing.
Americans don't want anything to do with royalty or a
peerage, but I guess every American thinks that he's going
to improve his lot someday, that he might even be rich.
So when the Jacobins began to kill all the aristocracy, all
the people in the United States began to wonder how it
would feel if—assuming that their dreams for success come
true—the masses rose up and began to kill all the rich
people in America."

"And now the French are seizing and destroying American ships at sea," William said. "Will the United States
declare war?"

"Hard to say," Adan replied. "We stopped allowing
the French to bring captured English ships into American

ports for refitting, and Congress has refused to pay the American war debt to France in one lump sum."

"The French wanted payment in one sum to buy more armaments for their continual wars of conquest," William explained.

"I suppose it would be an understatement to say that the alliance based on the friendship of men like Lafayette is getting frayed around the edges," Adan said.

"You shall stay in England," Beth told him. "I will not have another friend killed in this senseless affair."

"No sailing, no profits," Adan pointed out. "Because of the risk, cargos are bringing good money in the United States."

"No matter," Beth said flatly.

Adan laughed. "I fear that it matters to me. You may be as rich as you want to be, Beth, but you know me: I've spent it as quickly as it has come in."

"William," Beth said, "speak to him. Tell him—"

"Tell him what?" William asked. "Tell him that he's to give up his work, cast aside his livelihood because of the danger represented by French ships?"

"Adan," Estrela said, "for me? For the sake of your nephews and nieces who love you?"

Adan glowered. "Both of you are putting unfair pressure on me. A man does what he must do, and I have a cargo of manufactured goods to take to Wilmington. My lading does not represent mere money. It is needed. Farmers and plantation owners need the tools my ship carries. A large portion of my cargo is made up of armaments and munitions for the North Carolina militia, which would be a part of the American army in the event that this undeclared war expands."

"I don't think we need fear a French invasion of the United States," William remarked. "Right now Napoléon has his hands full trying to digest Italy, and there are rumors out of the Continent that he has plans for an adventure farther afield, but most certainly not as far afield as the New World."

"Nevertheless," Adan said, "there is more at stake aboard the *Pride* than money."

Beth rose and walked with long, purposeful strides to stand before Adan and William defiantly. "Then if you're to risk your life—and my ship, incidentally—I will go with you."

"You'll do no such thing," William said automatically, only to see his sister's green eyes flare.

"Beth, please," Estrela pleaded. "One lunatic in the family is enough. Has my brother's madness infected you?"

"I will need to purchase new ships," Beth said.

"That would be done best here in England," William said.

"On the contrary," Beth corrected. "With the threat at sea, I warrant that many shipowners in the United States would welcome a reasonable cash offer. Is that not true, Adan?"

Adan reluctantly agreed. William blustered without making an impression on Beth's adamant stand that her business demanded that she go to the United States.

Later, as Beth was preparing for bed in her room, she heard a light tap from the hallway. She pulled a dressing gown over her shoulders and opened the door.

"May I come in?" It was Estrela, her long, ebony hair braided for the night. She was wearing a woolly nightgown that covered her from chin to floor. Beth stood aside, then closed the door behind her sister-in-law. Estrela turned. "I'm pleased for you, even though I fear for your safety."

"Thank you. I'm glad that at least one of my relatives doesn't think I am a feckless, empty-headed woman."

Estrela looked at Beth with a sweet little smile. "But it is not just to buy ships that you will risk a late-fall crossing and the threat of the French, is it?"

"I'm sure I don't know what you mean," Beth said frostily.

"Don't you?" Estrela took Beth's hand. "I saw your face when Adan mentioned that Renno is in Wilmington."

"He may be gone by the time we arrive."

"But he may not. Adan told us that Renno has had a misunderstanding with his tribe and that he is in Wilmington to fulfill a promise he made to the mother of his children, to see that they are educated." She smiled and kissed Beth on the cheek. "He'll be there, Beth, dear. He *will* be there. I think that God, and perhaps Renno's manitous, have arranged it."

Without warning Beth burst into tears.

"Oh, my dear," Estrela said, clasping her close. "Oh, my dear sister."

Beth controlled herself with an effort. Her voice was choked with emotion and made indistinct by her sobs. "I feel so . . . empty."

"I know, dear, I know."

"I had thought that I no longer cared."

"But you obviously do."

Beth used a lacy kerchief to dry her eyes and cheeks. "For a moment I thought I saw him there," she said. "He was dressed in a plain, dark suit, an everyday type of thing, with white lace at his throat, and he had trimmed his hair. When he saw me, he smiled." She became quiet, and her eyes stared into an unseen distance. She went pale and grasped both of Estrela's hands in hers. "Do I feel this way only because Adan said he was living as a white man?"

"Only you can determine that."

"Perhaps he will not want me."

"He will."

Beth groaned. "Perhaps he has found another."

"No. He is alone with Renna in Wilmington, living with his cousin."

"All right—suppose that he still does love me. What will I do if, in the future, he wants to return to his people?"

Estrela's voice was firm. "You made that decision once. Were you right?"

"Oh, my God, no," Beth uttered, and the weeping began again as, for a moment, she felt a return of the dreariness that had been growing in her for years. "I was wrong. I was so wrong."

"Then thank the good Lord for giving you another chance," Estrela said.

"If, indeed, He has," Beth said. "I have not respected His commandments."

"He will forgive," Estrela told her.

Charles-Maurice de Talleyrand-Périgord, prince et duc de Bénévent, patted an eminent revolutionary munitions maker on the back and escorted him from the office of the foreign minister. The munitions maker left with the assurance that the minister would do everything in his power to see that the French army favored his products when it came time to rearm for an important foreign venture. For this assurance the man had left behind a considerable sum in gold.

Talleyrand, as he was known, he of the multiple political lives, had little faith in the latest French regime. He had heard the deadly, stomach-turning drop of the blade of the guillotine too often and had seen too many of his former peers lose favor as the bloody Revolution continued to evolve. The fall of two of the members of the Directory had allowed his return to the office of the foreign ministry. By agreeing to what he secretly felt was a totally insane adventure, he had secured the friendship of the famous general Napoléon.

In his position of power Talleyrand was free to demand compensation in return for favors, as he had with the munitions maker. His accounts in London and in Hamburg grew steadily, approaching the healthy sum of three hundred million francs. If he himself became the target of a coup d'état, he had several options for a quick exit from Paris, a speedy escape from France. Once safely away, he had the wherewithal to live splendidly while the Revolution continued to feed upon itself.

For weeks the foreign minister had been refusing to see the American minister to France, Charles C. Pinckney of South Carolina. Privately, Talleyrand was too much the realist to think that such tactics were worthy of the representative of a great nation; in fact, he had not even been upset by the Jay Treaty, which other Frenchmen called an insult. He believed that the only worthy enemy of France lay across the English Channel. The sea war that was being conducted against the United States was, in Talleyrand's mind, unwise, for if things worked out France would become neighbor to the United States after taking over Spain's holdings along the Mississippi and in Florida. Always the cautious opportunist, however, Talleyrand did not voice his opinion that it was unwise to antagonize a new ally.

It was only when two other important Americans arrived in Paris to reinforce Pinckney's efforts that Talleyrand began to realize that the United States was becoming desperate to straighten out the dispute with France. War, he felt, was very close, but France did not have the assets needed to fight a land war on the other side of the Atlantic. He alone could do little to stop the actions of French ships at sea, for in spite of his title, foreign policy was largely under the control of the Directory; but he could, perhaps, ease the situation while adding to his fund for a comfortable life in exile. After letting the three Americans cool their heels in his anteroom for weeks, he sent word to John Marshall, the chief American negotiator, that a conference had been arranged.

Thus, Charles Pinckney, John Marshall, and Elbridge Gerry met with three of Talleyrand's agents: the messieurs Hottingeur, Bellamy, and Hauteval.

After formal greetings had been exchanged, Pinckney

asked when he and his associates might expect to meet
with the foreign minister himself.

A Frenchman cleared his throat, then said, "The price
for seeing Minister Talleyrand, monsieur, is two hundred
fifty thousand dollars."

The Americans, being diplomats, did not allow their
disgust to show.

"The terms you describe—you speak with the authority
and knowledge of the French government?" John Marshall
asked.

"*Oui, monsieur*," the agent replied. "And if the cor-
rupt Americans are truly interested in keeping the friendship of France and in ending the war on the seas, there is
an additional fee."

Charles Pinckney's face began to flush with anger.
"And what, sir, might that be?"

"Ten million dollars as a loan—and quickly."

John Marshall raised his eyebrows. "And the method
of repayment, should the United States decide to accept
your terms?"

The French agent smiled smugly and shrugged.

Pinckney leaped to his feet and shouted, "It is no, no;
not a sixpence for bribery!" Without saying good-bye, he
stormed from the meeting room, Marshall and Gerry at
his heels. Once outside on the street, he drew some
calming breaths, then said, "I am the product of a fiery
society. My state's army, under the leadership of such
men as the Swamp Fox, Francis Marion, pushed a large
British army into siege positions at Charleston. I'll be
damned if I'd give in to Talleyrand's demands! And that's
exactly what I'll put in my communiqué to Philadelphia
about this whole sordid affair."

Charles Pinckney did not have to wait in an anteroom
in the presidential mansion in Philadelphia. Upon his
arrival, following his uncomfortable trip across the Atlantic, he was ushered into John Adams's office immediately.

Greetings and polite inquiries concluded, Adams leaned on his desk.

"You know, Mr. Pinckney, that the newspapers are quoting Washington's old advice against making alliances with any nation."

"I had a chance to read a few items before coming here," Pinckney said.

"One can't believe everything one reads in the newspapers," Adams said. "Did you see what one enterprising young man did with your 'not a sixpence for bribery' statement?"

"No, sir, I did not. But I see that the newspapers are calling the French agents X, Y, and Z, as I did in my missives to you."

"Yes, well, you are quoted as having said, 'Millions for defense, but not one cent for tribute.'"

Pinckney smiled. "It has a certain ring, sir."

"Washington sees an alliance, however informal, with our old enemy, England. I have to admit he has a point, what with Royal Navy ships escorting our merchantmen in the Caribbean, off the coast of Europe, and even in home waters. Meanwhile, England is extending credit for small arms, cannons, and munitions."

"Sir, we'll need England's help if it comes to full war with France," Pinckney said.

"Now, you and I both know, Mr. Pinckney, that there will be no land war with France. Oh, they might get Louisiana and maybe Florida as a price for their alliance with Spain, but they can't possibly put enough troops on this continent to challenge not only the United States but the British in Canada and the Caribbean." Adams rose and paced the office stiffly, his hands behind his back, his portly body looking as if it were trying to burst out of the bonds of its clothing.

"We are both aware, Mr. Pinckney, that your mission to Paris was a failure." He raised his hand quickly. "I know, I know, the failure is not yours so much as it is simply a product of the arrogance of Talleyrand and the indifference of the Directory." He laughed bitterly. "I wonder what they will think if they ever are told that we were *willing* to pay them their ten million?"

"Perhaps it's not too late," Pinckney said. "Mr. Gerry is still in Paris. Perhaps he can somehow get to Talleyrand without paying the bribe."

"No," Adams said. "It's too late for that. Talleyrand's greed has awakened even the most sluggish men in Congress. Your brave statement has become a rallying cry that you're going to hear repeated until you're sick of it. The whole country is agitated. We're going to have to fight a naval war with a nation that by history, by treaty, and by its actions has been our best friend." He halted by his desk and picked up a newspaper, which he handed to Pinckney. He had drawn a circle around one particular editorial in which a learned newspaperman was warning that American homes were being threatened with fire, plunder, and pillage. The writer shrilled that "your wives and sweethearts face ravishment and assassination by horrid, outlandish, sansculottish Frenchmen."

Pinckney snorted and put the newspaper back on Adams's desk.

"I have no choice," Adams said. "I must go public with the full details of the X,Y,Z Affair. I'm breaking off commercial relations with France, and I'm going to ask the Senate to repeal the French-American treaties."

"That will mark the first time that our nation has ever unilaterally revoked a solemn treaty," Pinckney warned.

"Not so," Adams said. "It will be the first time we've broken a treaty with a *white* nation."

When Beth Huntington set sail from England aboard her last large ship, the *Huntington Pride*, the weather was beautiful. The sun blessed them, and favorable winds steered them northward for the crossing. On chill but sunny days Beth strolled the deck with Adan while the world approached crises on several fronts. Ahead of them French picaroons from the West Indies ranged up and down the Atlantic coast of the United States, seizing or sinking American ships within sight of land.

Renno attended a meeting of shipowners and cargo agents with Nate Ridley. Wilmington ships had been hit hard by the undeclared war. Beth Huntington's ships were not the only ones lost, and there was malcontent among merchants and traders who had had cargo aboard the missing ships. Shipping agents urged owners to arm their vessels.

"With what?" Nate Ridley demanded in disgust. "Do you realize that there's not a single cannon foundry in the entire South?"

An agent, whose income depended on his acting as a go-between for shipper and carrier, tried to instill some optimism by stating that the government in Philadelphia was in the process of creating a Navy Department and building fighting ships.

Nate stood up, removed his tricornered hat, and looked around at the gathering of worried men. "Sure the government is talking about ships to fight the French pirates, but so far it's just talk. We certainly haven't heard the boom of U.S. naval cannon off the shores of North Carolina, have we? We have two choices, gentlemen: We can keep our ships in the Cape Fear, or we can send them out, not knowing whether we'll ever see them, and the men aboard them, again. I, for one, will keep my ships in the river."

Renno knew that Congress had authorized the building of six new frigates four years past but had never provided the funds needed to begin construction. He had to agree that so far the federal government was doing nothing but talking about the loss of American merchantmen and American lives.

Captain Jean Claude Lamaître had spent thirty of his thirty-nine years at sea. He was a dedicated Loyalist of the

Republic because the sharp blade of the Revolution had
removed several senior men who had stood between him
and a command. Lamaître was a man of the people, having advanced through the ranks of the French navy on his
loyalty to his superiors, his hard work, his eagerness to
please, and a sense of seamanship that seems to be inbred
in a very few men.

Once the blade of the guillotine had made him captain of the thirty-gun *Sans Doute*, he underwent a change
of personal philosophy that puzzled his underlings but was
not displayed to those good Revolutionists who had given
him a ship, because he took the *Sans Doute* as far away as
he could as quickly as possible from France and the blades
of the Jacobins. He had been refitting and reprovisioning
at St. Domingue, on the isle of Haiti, since leaving France,
and he had begun to build up nice holdings there with his
share of the spoils from the American ships taken by *Sans
Doute*.

From Haiti Lamaître could range the entire Caribbean northward to the coast of Spanish Florida and the
United States. He had been fortunate in his voyages; he
had convinced his crew that it was much better to damage
an American ship just enough to stop her, thus making it
possible for *Sans Doute* to assume her cargo if it had value
or to take the captured vessel back to Haiti as a prize if the
distance was not too great. If a vessel were captured
reasonably intact and Haiti was not within easy reach,
there was a market of sorts for captured ships in the ports
of Spanish Florida.

Lamaître now had a private fleet, the newest of which
was a former American merchantman named *Seneca Chieftain*. He had it armed, manned, and put to sea under
trusted subordinates. The Revolutionists in France knew
nothing of this private fleet and were sent just enough of
the spoils from *Sans Doute*'s raids to keep them satisfied.

Jean Claude Lamaître was a solid man of five feet ten
inches. His hard torso narrowed sleekly under the sash of

fashionably cut uniform trousers that were in need of a
wash. One of his little idiosyncrasies was an abhorrence of
the stickiness that came when saltwater dried on his skin.
Since fresh water aboard ship was always at a premium,
Jean Claude resorted to a time-honored practice of the
hated and now mostly expired French noble class—the
liberal use of perfume in lieu of baths.

So it was that from a distance Captain Lamaître made
quite a splashy picture. He, with his sweeping mustache,
his sharp nose, his broad forehead, and his keen, gray
eyes, could have served as a patriotic model for the French
fighting sea captain. If his lack of personal fastidiousness
made it slightly less romantic to be near him . . . well,
only hardened ship's officers and the occasional seaman
ever stood at his side on the vessel's command deck.

The *Sans Doute* was making her way northward past
the Windward Islands, all eyes alert for British men-of-
war, when the *Huntington Pride* ran into the tail end of a
late season *huracán* moving up the Atlantic east of Ber-
muda. The storm slowed the *Pride* just enough to put her
offshore from the southern tip of North Carolina just as
the *Sans Doute* took up her station astride the eastern
approach to the Cape Fear River.

Chapter X

The *Huntington Pride* sailed directly under Jean Claude Lamaître's guns in the night. The French ship, lying athwart the direct route to the Cape Fear River, had been without lights during the hours of darkness so that she was not seen until dawn came in a splendid red burst of glory. There she was, the heavily gunned picaroon ship, waiting.

Adan ordered all sails to be hoisted and tacked away from the French ship, but the big war vessel billowed up what seemed to be acres of canvas and began to close the distance rapidly.

Beth came on deck to watch the frantic preparations of the crew. Men brandished cutlasses. Others manned the *Pride*'s small battery of guns.

"We're so near the river," Beth said to Adan. "Is there no chance of outdistancing them?"

"I'm afraid not," he responded. "Nor can we fight them."

Beth looked up, shocked. "But we must fight."

"Beth, count the gunports. Look at the size of that ship. She'll have a crew of well over two hundred; we have only thirty."

A shot came winging to splash in front of the *Pride*. The puff of smoke from the French ship's cannon had not totally dissipated before another shot came dangerously close to the tip of the mainmast.

"Do what you think you must do," Beth said. "Best to lose the ship than to sacrifice lives." She gave a quick prayer of thanks to God that she had listened to William and Estrela when they advised her not to risk her business capital in the form of gold and silver to a lightly armed merchant ship in such times. Even after losing the *Huntington Pride* she would not be bankrupt, for she had been a smart manager and had accumulated a small fortune during the good days when she enjoyed a virtual monopoly in trade between U.S. ports and the British Caribbean Islands.

"Strike the colors," Adan ordered. "Lower sails and heave to."

There was no grumbling among the crew when Adan ordered surrender. The pattern of the undeclared war at sea had been established: Those men who put up no resistance would be set ashore at the first opportunity— most often on an uninhabited island of the Bahamas, where rescue was never too long delayed. Most of the seamen considered that infinitely preferable to dying with honor, only to have the ship seized or destroyed in spite of their sacrifice.

Shouting, grinning Frenchmen came swinging across
into the *Pride*'s rigging, and soon the crew of Beth Huntington's ship was clumped on the foredeck surrounded by
its captors. Jean Claude Lamaître leaped the distance
between the two ships, landing lightly just below the steps
to the quarterdeck, where Adan stood with Beth at his
side. For a moment, Lamaître was stunned by Beth's
flame-haired beauty. Then, quickly, he doffed his feath-
ered hat, made an elegant bow, and introduced himself.

"Captain," Adan said, "as you can see, we offer no
resistance. I ask your permission to disembark my crew
and passengers into longboats."

"Ah, but Captain," Lamaître protested, "it will be a
long and arduous ordeal to reach shore in small boats."

"On the contrary," Adan said. "We can make the
North Carolina coast in no more than twenty-four hours."

"As you please, sir," Lamaître said, nodding. "Now,
if I may see your manifests?"

Lamaître was obviously pleased to learn that the ship
carried manufactured goods. The tools and weapons would
find a ready market, in exchange for Spanish gold, in
Florida. He thanked Adan profusely.

Meanwhile, the *Pride*'s officers were loading the longboats. Not all the crew could be accommodated. There
had been a call for volunteers to stay aboard the French
ship to be put ashore in the Bahamas, and, rather surprisingly, Beth thought, enough men elected to stay to allow
the rest to be seated in the available boats.

It was a magnificent day at sea. The red morning sky
had faded to a blue so deep and perfect that the sea itself
reflected the beauty far down into translucent depths.
There was only a slight breeze. The sun was pleasantly
warm. Beth slipped into her cabin and packed a small
canvas bag with a change of clothing, some soap, her hair-
brush, and a vial of sweet oil to prevent damage to her fair
skin from the sun. When she emerged onto the deck,
Adan was still standing next to the French captain. Three

of the longboats were standing off; the fourth waited at the *Pride*'s side.

"I'm ready, Adan," Beth said.

Adan's face showed that he was agitated. He opened his mouth and spread his hands.

"I'm so sorry, mademoiselle," Jean Claude Lamaître said. "I should have saved you the trouble of packing a bag."

"Just what do you mean?" she asked.

"I would not dream of allowing so beautiful a lady as you to suffer the hardships of a long trip in so small a boat," Lamaître said. "You will be my honored guest aboard this ship."

Beth felt a tremor of fear but concealed it well. "How thoughtful of you," she said, "especially in view of the fact that it is, after all, my ship."

Lamaître smiled. "One must not resist inevitable change. At least, mademoiselle, you will be comfortable in your own cabin."

Adan moved to stand beside Beth, took both her hands in his, and whispered, "Put down your bag and wait for my move. We're going over the rail. Once we're in the water, maybe he won't bother to come after you."

Her heart gave a bump. She leaned down and placed the bag on the deck. Adan turned to face Lamaître. "My appreciation, sir, not for your act of piracy but for your generosity in not harming any of my crew."

"I wish you a pleasant voyage," Lamaître said.

Adan turned, took two steps, broke into a run, and gathered Beth into his arms. He was nearing the rail when, with a move of surprising swiftness, Lamaître struck him across the head with the flat of his cutlass blade. Adan faltered, fought to stay on his feet, and was overcome by blackness.

Beth stumbled, caught herself at the rail, and considered leaping over. The longboat was just below. But Lamaître was quickly at her side, taking her arm in a firm grip. She was immersed in his overpowering scent. The odor of his long-unwashed body mixed sickeningly with heavy perfume.

Adan felt hands lift him, then hand him down to his men in the longboat. He could see, but only dimly. Then, slowly, his vision cleared. He struggled into a sitting position on the bottom of the boat. His men were already pulling the oars lustily, putting distance between them and the French. He felt a surge of dizziness and dropped his head between his knees to stabilize himself. Then he looked up to see Beth standing beside the ornately dressed French pirate. Adan despaired, but there was nothing he could do.

"Did you hear what the Frenchie said, sir?" asked a seaman.

"No," Adan answered.

"Heard him give the orders to his crew, I did. 'We're off for Floridee,' he said. I heard him clear. Said, 'Mr. Mate, set course for St. Augustine.' "

Adan put a hand to his head. His fingers came away bloody, but despite a bit of nausea and a severe headache, he was feeling stronger.

"Reckon I wouldn't mind being in that Frenchie's bunk during that voyage to Floridee," another seaman joked.

"Enough!" Adan snapped, his voice shaking with anger.

The longboats were equipped with thin spars and small sails. The winds were favorable. Rather than try to negotiate the river, Adan guided them to the beach opposite Wilmington. Fishermen ferried them across the sound, and they rode into Wilmington on salt wagons.

General Roy Johnson of the Tennessee militia sat with his feet up on his desk, looking out a window that gave him a distorted view of a Knoxville street. His new enjoyment—a cigar—had gone out. Now and then he used his tongue to shift the sodden butt to the other corner of his mouth. He heard footsteps in the hallway outside his office, looked up, and sighed when the steps went on past his door. He took the cigar from his mouth and spat into a newly polished brass cuspidor.

It had taken only a few months as a desk officer to convince Roy that his real talents did not lie in administration, although, as far as he knew, there'd been no complaints. Governor John Sevier had given him a promotion along with a hint that he might be back in an active field command sooner than he suspected. Roy, however, thought it more likely that the old Indian fighter who had been governor of the prospective state of Franklin and who was now governor of Tennessee was becoming a bit vague.

Roy had been following the news out of Philadelphia as best he could in a frontier state where newspapers from the East were weeks old by the time they reached Knoxville. It seemed that a patriotic fever was sweeping the nation, and old war-horse that he was, Roy could hear in his mind the sounds of battle, the hoarse yells of conflict, the moans of the wounded and the dying, and the shouting of the captains.

But in his office in Knoxville, where he was in charge of just about everything that had to do with the militia except when to call them out—that being the governor's prerogative—the sounds were only echoes of the past. The way Roy saw it, the only way he would have any excitement as a general in the Tennessee militia would be if the French moved into Louisiana and got ambitious about coming north up the Mississippi. There was, he believed, more likelihood of a Second Coming. It looked as if the Frenchies' best general, that fellow named Bonaparte, was preparing for an invasion of England, and if that were the case, France would have bitten off more than it could chew in Europe, much less on a continent an ocean away.

But maybe the folks in Philadelphia knew more about the situation than he. After all, George Washington had agreed to come out of his retirement and to leave his beloved Mount Vernon if a real emergency arose, meaning a French invasion of the North American continent. Old George had shaken up a few people by insisting that he would leave his farm only when it became necessary and that his second-in-command would be Alexander Hamilton. This last didn't sit too well, of course, in certain quarters in Philadelphia, especially in John Adams's presidential mansion.

Congress, Roy read, was at last moving to do something about the loss of American ships at sea. New frigates were being put into action. The names had a certain ring to them, Roy felt: the *United States*, the *Constitution*, and the *Constellation*. In addition, Congress had voted to expand the provisional army of fifty thousand men with an additional army of ten thousand troops. To encourage enlistments, a private soldier's pay had been raised from four dollars to six dollars a month, in spite of arguments on the floor of Congress that such riches put into the hands of the common soldier would do nothing but encourage drunkenness.

Yes, things were happening over to the east across the mountains, and in spite of John Sevier's hints that there might be some action, Roy felt as if events were leaving him behind. El-i-chi was with the army. The last time Roy had heard of him, he was a chief scout in western Virginia, helping to train a unit in wilderness lore. Roy wondered why El-i-chi hadn't gone to join up with the army in Indiana Territory, where there were constant rumors of unrest fomented by a firebrand named Tecumseh, the newest advocate of a united Indian war against the white man.

A fly buzzed around Roy's unlighted cigar. He brushed it away lazily. If he rode north through Kentucky and crossed the Ohio, he could be in Indiana Territory before the snows. He knew the land, for he'd made that journey once before. There wasn't anything like Mad Anthony

Wayne's war going on, but Roy knew the governor of the Indiana Territory, William Henry Harrison, from the time they both had worked for Wayne. With things fairly quiet in the Southwest Territory, Harrison's Indiana lands were the front lines of the continued confrontation with the Indians. Maybe, he thought, El-i-chi stayed in Virginia because those units of the army that were training there wouldn't be too far away if Tecumseh and his brother, the one who spoke with the Master of Life on a first-name basis, repeated Little Turtle's feat of getting several Indian tribes to fight together as they had at Fallen Timbers.

Roy didn't make up his mind right away. He called in his aide, an eager young lieutenant, and told him that he would be out of the office for a few days.

"Sir, in case the governor asks—"

"Tell him I've gone on a personal reconnoiter."

"May I tell him exactly where, sir?"

"Nope," Roy said, letting his booted feet fall heavily to the floor. He tossed the cigar butt into the cuspidor and stalked out of the office.

Within an hour he was dressed in comfortable buckskins and moccasins and was riding toward Renno's village. He knew that neither Renno nor his grandchildren would be there, and that gave him a hint of melancholy that was, however, quickly dispelled by the pleasure of being in the open on an inspiringly beautiful early autumn day. He shaded his eyes with one hand and looked up as a V of Canadian geese flew overhead. Only last fall Little Hawk had taken a goose in the traditional manner, swimming underwater to seize the bird's legs. It made Roy grin just to think of his grandson, and he felt lonely. If he got as far as Virginia, he might ride on up to Philadelphia to see the boy.

When he reached the village, he rode directly to the longhouse of Ha-ace and Toshabe. The Panther greeted him with a warrior's clasp and evident pleasure, then escorted him inside, where Toshabe stuffed him with a

beautifully seasoned stew and the first sweet, tasty pump-
kin pudding of the year. During the meal Ena and Rusog
came in with Ho-ya and We-yo, the twins. The eight-year-
old boy and girl were served generous portions of the
sweet pudding.

To that time no one had mentioned those who were
absent. Roy asked, "Have you heard from any of them?"
He did not have to mention names.

"I have had one letter from my younger son," Toshabe
replied. "He reported that he and his family were doing
well in Virginia."

"And Renno?"

Toshabe shook her head.

"We have had two letters from Little Hawk," Ena
said.

"Yes, I, too, have heard from the sophisticated master
Hawk Harper," Roy said with a proud smile. "He's becoming quite the gentleman in Philadelphia."

"I hope that he does not forget how to draw a bow,"
Ena remarked grimly.

"I'd doubt that," Roy said. "He's his father's son."

Ena fixed Roy with her large, green eyes. "I know
Renno is our greatest warrior. He is my brother, and like
you, I love him. I would kill anyone else who said this,
but now he is gone once more and dissension grows among
the Seneca. This Renno of ours has, in the past, taken on
the problems of the white man as if they were his own.
Once he left us for well over a year, and the young
warriors tried to elect a new chief. You know the tragedy
that resulted. Now there is another attempt under way to
wrest the leadership of our people away from the bloodline of the great Renno."

"Well, I guess Ha-ace can handle that," Roy ventured.

While the Panther nodded grimly, Rusog said, "If my
brother Ha-ace requires the blade of my weapon—" He
brandished his well-honed tomahawk.

"That's just what I mean," Ena said. "It has almost

come to that, Roy. First the matrons turned against El-i-chi and Ah-wa-o. Now, largely because of the sharp but convincing tongue of O-gas-ah, there are many who want O-o-za to be sachem. This cannot be. Renno himself promised to come back if that happened."

"It will not be necessary to wait for Renno," Ha-ace said.

"So," Toshabe said, spreading her hands.

"There's a real threat of bloodshed?" Roy asked.

"Very real," Ena answered. "O-o-za, you see, listens to a white preacher who calls himself Waith Pennywhistle. And O-o-za has led a delegation of young warriors to counsel with the Chickamauga Cherokee. O-o-za would lead our young men to war in the South against the Spanish."

"I've heard a few rumors to that effect," Roy said. "This white preacher—he's trying to recruit Cherokee warriors to fight the Spaniards?"

Ena nodded. "Cherokee and Seneca. He tells them, through O-o-za, that there will be a great army led by well-armed white men from Kentucky and Tennessee. He promises land in the West, much land, to be the Indians' forever."

For a moment Roy wondered if his old friend Sevier could have been thinking of such a plan when he hinted that Roy might soon see some real action near home. He shook his head. No, a man of Sevier's caliber wouldn't be involved in still another harebrained scheme to seize Spanish territory. George Rogers Clark had been singing that tune for twenty years, and the melody had never been catchy enough to influence men of honor and responsibility.

"I wouldn't mind having a talk with this preacher," Roy muttered.

"He is not among us," Ha-ace said. "I would not advise that you seek him among the Chickamauga."

"No," Roy agreed, grinning. "I don't want to talk to him that badly."

*   *   *

He spent three days with his friends. There was good
food and excellent talk, and then he left them. What he
had heard and seen in the village had helped him make up
his mind. He stopped in Knoxville only long enough to
outfit himself for the trek across the mountains and to
send a letter to John Sevier telling him that the governor
would have to do without his commandant of militia for an
indefinite period of time.

His destination was Virginia, to see El-i-chi. Ena and
the others had convinced him that there was likely to be
bloodshed—the blood of Seneca brothers—in the village.
Ena, having sought out Roy on his last evening in the
village, had said, "Tell my brother El-i-chi when you see
him that many are going to die. Tell him that Ha-ace will
not be safe, for he will defend the honor of our family and
the bloodline of our sachems. Tell him that without the
presence of the tribe's sachem and the tribe's shaman we
will be riven, blooded, and destroyed as many of our
young warriors go off to yet another white man's war."

She had put her hands on Roy's arms and looked him
directly in the eyes. "Tell him this: He left us to avoid
killing, but there is to be killing. Perhaps there would be
less if he were here. I even fear for Ha-ace and Toshabe,
who are strong targets for those who would like to see
O-o-za in power. Tell El-i-chi that he will have support
and that the precious traditions of the tribe as regard his
marriage are now secondary to other, larger considerations."

The attic room that had become home to Little Hawk
in the Blount residence on Chestnut Street in Philadelphia overlooked the side entrance to the house. That
entrance, sheltered from Chestnut Street, became, during
the spring and early summer of 1797, a portal for frequent, mysterious visitors. Little Hawk had come to recognize a few of the men who came calling on William

Blount in the dark of night. Having begun to absorb a bit of political savvy through the things he heard as a page, Little Hawk considered it odd that not once but several times the Honorable Mr. Liston, Great Britain's minister to the United States, crept into the side entrance to the house on Chestnut with his face shadowed by a large hat and his figure draped in a dark, voluminous cloak.

Little Hawk himself had had an opportunity to talk with John Chisholm, who had come to Philadelphia accompanied by several Creek chiefs. Chisholm was a likable man who had become a true frontiersman and, thus, appealed to Little Hawk's natural affinity for westerners. Chisholm had treated Little Hawk with due respect, had questioned him about his Seneca connections, and had said that he knew of Little Hawk's father and admired him. As time went on, one statement that had been made by John Chisholm just before he set sail for England on a mysterious mission for William Blount aroused Little Hawk's curiosity and inspired him to take closer note of the late-night callers. Soon the boy was actively trying to learn specifically upon which course his benefactor had embarked.

"How d'you fancy the city?" John Chisholm had asked.

"I would not want to spend my life in such a place," Little Hawk had responded.

"Ah, yes, laddie," Chisholm had replied, "I do know what you mean. Nor would I spend my days in an ant heap of people. But then perhaps before year's end, lad, we'll both be back in God's country, eh?"

Since Little Hawk's appointment as page would be concurrent with Blount's stint in the Senate, there was little likelihood that he would be back in the western country soon. Blount might make trips, but when the Senate was not in session, Little Hawk was imprisoned in a classroom full-time along with the other hapless pages.

The more he thought about John Chisholm's statement, the more unsettled he became, so that one night, when the most prominent of Blount's visitors in the dark

came to the side door, Little Hawk slipped down the
narrow, steep stairs, crept to the lower floor, and watched
the English minister to the United States enter Blount's
study. The young Seneca made a place for himself behind
a large hall tree, which was festooned with umbrellas,
hats, and capes. From there he could see Liston's legs and
feet through the door, which had been left ajar, and he
could hear quite well.

"There is no word as yet from England?" Blount
asked.

"There has scarcely been time," Liston told him. "I
assure you, Senator, that Great Britain will not desert you
in your memorable enterprise."

Blount's voice held a belligerent tone. "The success of
the entire effort depends upon British frigates being in
place to block the mouth of the Mississippi and the harbor
at Pensacola."

"I'm sure, Senator, that if you maintain your end of
the bargain, my government will not fail you."

"I pray not," Blount said curtly. "For I take the main
risk, Minister."

"I understand," Liston soothed. "Would you be so
kind, Senator, as to go over your plan for me?"

"The attack will consist of three phases," Blount explained. "First, my agents Mitchell and Craig will lead a
force of northwestern volunteers, aided from Canada by
your people, to take the Spanish fort at New Madrid and
the silver mines on the Red River. This first force, in the
guise of traders, will travel down the Ohio. They will
leave a garrison in New Madrid once the fort is taken. The
second force, which I will lead consists of southwesterners—
good fighting men from Tennessee and Kentucky, and our
Indian allies, mainly Choctaw with a few Cherokee. This
second force will be the key element, for our purpose is to
seize New Orleans. The third force, under Chisholm, will
consist of British ex-soldiers from Natchez and the southeast, plus their Creek allies. They will take Pensacola."

"Very good," Liston approved. "Now, let me be sure what you ask of my government: a sum of money to be determined—"

"Correct," Blount said.

"And ships of war to close the Mississippi and to block the harbor at Pensacola. Six frigates, as I remember?"

"That should do the job."

"Florida is to be a British colony."

"Yes," Blount said, "but only if there is quick recognition by the king of the new nation on the Mississippi."

"Each private soldier in your army is to receive a Crown grant for one thousand acres of land. Pensacola and New Orleans are to be declared free ports—"

"That is very important," Blount confirmed. "The majority of the people in Kentucky and Tennessee are farmers. They grow wheat for flour, corn for meal, and tobacco and wool. They also make the finest hickory-smoked hams in the country. They can't sell to their neighbors because their neighbors are producing the same things. There are no towns of any size yet. It's a long and dangerous trek with packhorses to the markets of the East. The trip costs more than the goods will bring. But water transportation is relatively quick and quite economical. The Mississippi is the highway to market for westerners. All the Tennessee and Kentucky farmers ask is that when they arrive at New Orleans, buyers will be waiting on the docks to bid on their goods. They'll welcome a Louisiana under the control of Americans—not Spaniards or, perish the thought, Frenchmen."

"I've heard New Orleans called the Paris of America," Liston said. "I would imagine that a voyage downriver is a very romantic adventure for the frontiersmen."

"They wouldn't put it exactly that way," Blount said wryly, "but it's a part of their lives. Once we've established control, they'll resist any efforts by the federal government to interfere with a river that's wide open to them and markets that are eagerly awaiting their coming.

They'd be afraid that if the politicians in Philadelphia got
their hands on New Orleans they'd muck things up again,
maybe let Napoléon and the Frenchies in after all."
Blount paused and looked keenly at the Englishman. "We'll
need formal assurances from you, in the form of a treaty,
that the Mississippi will be forever open to the people of
the United States."

"And to the people of Great Britain, I might add,"
Liston said. "I see no problems, Senator. No problems at
all."

Little Hawk had no difficulty understanding what he
overheard. He had listened to talk about seizing lands
from the Spanish before. His grandfather Roy Johnson had
spoken of the possibility while discussing the plans of
George Rogers Clark and John Sevier. The boy knew
enough about the international situation to realize that
Spain was at war with England and that the onetime
strongman of Europe was old and weak. For centuries
Spain had been sending the best of its young men off to
the New World, and the rich sources of gold and treasure
had been swiftly drained by the rapacious conquistadores.
Roy Johnson had once said that if Clark and Sevier ever
had formed a proper army of long-rifled frontiersmen to
take the Spanish forts on the Mississippi and the port at
New Orleans, all of New Mexico would then have fallen,
and rebellions would have sprung up throughout South
America demanding independence. In short, Little Hawk
felt that there was a great possibility that this time, considering the leadership of a man of William Blount's influence, the dream of forming a new American nation on the
Mississippi would be fulfilled.

As he sneaked back to his room he felt mixed emotions.
To rid the continent of the Spanish would be desirable.
He had heard his father's stories of Spanish enslavement
and extermination of entire Indian peoples. But would
it be desirable to have a second American nation on
the Mississippi? How would that affect the Indian? Wil-

liam Blount had been a reasonable man when he was Indian commissioner and then governor of the Southwestern Territory; but John Sevier was known to believe that the only good Indian was a dead Indian. That there were people in the United States who felt the same way was not to be denied . . . but then there were men like Thomas Jefferson, who believed in fairness to all, and other good men like his father's old friend George Washington.

He wished that his father were here. He did not know what to do with the knowledge that he'd gained by eavesdropping on William Blount. He felt friendship for Mr. Jefferson, but he felt a form of love mixed with respect and gratitude for William Blount. He knew that Blount was not an evil man—or at least he believed so—but weren't Blount's plans coming close to treason toward the nation he had sworn to uphold when he took the oath of office as senator from Tennessee?

It was a long time before Little Hawk found sleep that night.

In the ensuing days and nights the sachem's son remained alert and spent more evening hours in the hallway outside Blount's home office. His situation became more and more complex as he learned that Blount was heavily in debt, that he had strained all his resources and used all his credit to buy hundreds of thousands of acres in the Southwest Territory. Worse, he had been unsuccessful in selling lands to satisfy his persistent creditors. Little Hawk wondered if Blount's plan to attack Spanish lands was merely a way to ease his financial problems. Or did Blount sincerely fear that Spain would cede Florida and Louisiana to France, putting the mouth of the Mississippi under the control of a nation that was now making war on the United States at sea?

The boy hated himself for becoming a sneak, a spy in the house that had made him welcome, where he was free to roam as he pleased, to raid the kitchen for snacks, and, as he agonized over what he had learned, to read letters stored in Blount's desk drawers. It was one of Blount's letters to his agents in the Southwest Territory that was to bring about his downfall, for the content of Blount's correspondence convinced Little Hawk that his mentor was wrong. Already Blount's agents had enlisted the Chickamauga Cherokee to fight another battle for white men, and according to a missive from Waith Pennywhistle, whom Little Hawk remembered from the Seneca village, many of the Cherokee warriors who called Rusog chief and—this was the final straw—many Seneca warriors under the war chief O-o-za would be in the army that attacked New Orleans.

It was a difficult and traumatic thing to betray a man whom he loved, a man whom he had respected, who had never shown him anything but kindness. Now that Little Hawk had made the decision, he intended to reveal his knowledge of Blount's scheme to the president of the Senate.

       *

On a steaming day in July, Mr. Jefferson looked quite cool and calm as he sat at his desk and listened to debate concerning a tax to be levied on liquor. One senator, given a chance to speak briefly, reminded the chamber that one of the most significant dates in American history, the fourth of July, was coming.

There was no call for pages to run errands. Little Hawk, feeling a drop of sweat run down his neck, wished that Jefferson would call a recess so that he could do his distasteful chore. He saw William Blount yawn, stretch, and rise from his desk, then stroll from the chamber.

Not long after Blount had left, the secretary to President Adams hurried into the Senate chamber and, whispering to Vice-President Jefferson, passed him a letter. A hush settled over the chamber as Jefferson ordered a Senate clerk to read the missive that had been presented to him by the presidential secretary. Little Hawk, half-asleep, came fully alert as the clerk read.

The letter had been written by Senator William Blount to one of his agents, an Indian interpreter named James Carey, who worked in the Cherokee Nation.

There had been rumors of a plot against Spanish lands in North America, but such tales had been flying for years. Finished with his reading of the letter, which detailed Blount's role in the conspiracy, the clerk fell silent.

Exclamations of surprise and shock came from the listening senators. It was terrible to learn that a senator of the United States had entered into a conspiracy with the old enemy, England, to give that nation a new foothold on the continent, so that the young United States would be forced to face British armed might on both their northern and southern borders. Thomas Jefferson, too, was shocked by the letter.

"May I inquire how the president came into possession of this letter?" Thomas Jefferson asked the secretary.

"I think, Mr. Vice-President," the secretary said, "that Mr. Carey deemed Senator Blount's news to be worthy of celebration. He became quite inebriated and began to brag about coming events so that the letter fell into the hands of loyal men."

William Blount came back into the chamber in time to hear a second reading of his letter.

"Senator Blount," Jefferson asked, "did you write this letter?"

Blount's hands were shaking. His face was pale, for with the reading of the letter, he had seen his plans come crashing down. There was to be no immediate relief, Little Hawk knew, from the senator's crushing debts, and his splendid vision of a free Mississippi River and a new nation was dead.

"I did write a letter to Mr. Carey," he responded weakly, "but it would be impossible for me to identify that letter without reference to my notes, which are in my

home. I ask, Mr. Jefferson, that I be given time to consult
my papers."

"Your request is granted," Jefferson said. He pounded
his gavel. "Gentlemen, we were, before this interruption,
discussing certain taxes to be levied on liquor."

There was a buzz of talk in the chamber as Blount
summoned all his poise and walked calmly from the room.

Little Hawk, feeling sympathy for Blount and relief
that he had not been forced to betray his friend, watched
Blount leave. Reluctantly the Senate turned its attention
from the beginning of a juicy scandal to the dull matter of
liquor taxes.

Since William Blount was an anti-Federalist senator,
there was a considerable amount of glee among Federalists as they attacked. On 7 July, Blount came into the
kitchen where Little Hawk was eating breakfast. He sat
opposite the boy and patted him on the hand.

"The jackals are gathering, my boy," he said. "They'll
condemn me today."

Little Hawk could find no words.

"I am sending my family away," Blount continued. "I
have spoken about you with my fellow senator from Tennessee. You are doing well with your education here. My
colleague has agreed to make a place for you. I hope you'll
find that quite satisfactory."

"I think I should go home, Mr. Blount."

"It is not really necessary, my boy. I promised your
father that you'd get schooling here, and that is one promise I can keep. I will pen a letter to your father in Wilmington, explaining the situation to him. I order you to
follow my advice and move in with my fellow senator,
William Cocke, and continue your work and your education. This, I'm sure, is what your father would want as
well."

Little Hawk said, "Yes, sir." He himself would write

to his father that very day, asking permission either to go home or to join Renno and Renna in Wilmington.

Before Blount and Little Hawk could leave for the Senate, constables arrived to seize Blount's trunks, papers, and clothing.

In the Senate session on that July day, Blount was asked to confirm or deny his authorship of the letter. He declined. He listened, grim faced, as his fellow senators voted one by one to expel him from the Senate. Only one man, Henry Tazewell of Virginia, voted against his expulsion, and Tazewell explained that his vote was a protest against what he considered a violation of a technicality of procedure.

A date for an impeachment trial was set. While trying to involve other prominent anti-Federalists, including Thomas Jefferson, in the plot, the Federalists called for Blount's imprisonment. This last didn't fit into Blount's new plans. He was soon riding a fast horse southward, toward home, his friends, and safety in Tennessee.

Little Hawk, left behind, had a new room and plenty to eat, although he was not invited to sit at Senator Cocke's family table. He felt the burden of a new set of problems. Although no one in a position of real responsibility had transferred William Blount's guilt to the page whom he had appointed, there were those who said that the Indian brat who had been brought to Philadelphia by the traitor should have been run out of town with him. Such talk could not help but influence Little Hawk's fellow pages.

Chapter XI

Adan Bartolome rode a salt wagon down Market Street to the corner of Front Street, jumped to the ground while yelling out a word of thanks to the driver, then walked swiftly up the slope toward the area where the finer houses of Wilmington overlooked the Cape Fear River from the bluffs. The day was fading as he passed Beth Huntington's house and hurried on to the Ridley home. The front garden was enclosed by a low stone wall. Renna and the two younger Ridley children were playing there. Renna called out an excited greeting when she saw Adan.

"Your father?" Adan asked.

"He's inside with Uncle Nate," Renna answered. "Did you have a nice voyage, Captain Adan?"

Adan smiled at her absently without answering as he strode up the walk. He pushed past a servant who opened the front door.

Renno and Nate were in the great room. The Ridley home was built in the style of Greek Revival architecture, with huge, graceful columns standing two stories tall. The great room, too, was a full two stories high, from the parquet floor to the ornate plaster ceiling. A specially made cabinet for books stood just inside the room. The largest mirror in Wilmington, perhaps in North Carolina, extended almost to the ceiling and gave Adan a view of himself as his boot heels rang on the wooden floor: His black, wavy hair was matted by salt spray from the long row to the beach in the longboat, and his clothing was wrinkled and soiled.

Renno was sitting with his distant cousin Nate in front of the wide window at the rear of the great room. The window provided a splendid view, overlooking the river. A coastal sloop was making its way upstream toward the dock area, and a fisherman in a small boat had just hooked a big one and was straining to pull the fish in on a hand line. The sun filtered through the trees on the western side of the river. A bank of low clouds was beginning to burn with the dying light of day.

"Well, Adan," Renno said, rising, moving to meet his friend with, first, a white man's handshake and then with the warrior's clasp.

"You have made good time, Captain," Nate said.

Adan didn't know how to begin. He stood facing Renno, and the stricken look in his eyes told Renno that all was not well. "Adan?" he asked.

"I told her that you and Renna were in Wilmington," Adan began, and then could say no more.

"Beth?" Renno said. "She's here?"

Adan shook his head and started to speak but faltered. Renno, feeling sudden dread, put his hands on Adan's shoulders and shook him. "Speak up, man!"

"She is taken," Adan said. "Along with the ship. It's those bedamned Frenchmen. Now they have accounted for three Huntington ships."

Renno's face had become a study in stone, his way of hiding strong emotions. Nate stepped forward, took Adan's arm, and said, "Come, Adan, sit and rest while you tell us what has happened. I'm sure you've been through hell yourself." He called out, and a serving girl came, then bobbed acknowledgment when he told her to bring whiskey. Adan declined a chair. He stood in front of the unlit fireplace, pacing as he told of his decision not to waste lives in fighting the well-armed French warship.

"You acted wisely," Nate affirmed.

"I was thinking that it was war, not piracy," Adan explained. "I expected the Frenchman to conduct himself as a man of honor. I had no idea that he would—"

"You could not have known," Renno consoled. "As Nate said, you acted with wisdom. It would not have been wise to sacrifice lives in a hopeless cause and to risk the life of your principal." He could not, just yet, bring himself to say the name Beth, for inside he was in turmoil.

Adan briefly described his attempt to get Beth off the ship and into the longboat.

"And you definitely heard the captain say that he was going to St. Augustine, in Florida?" Renno asked.

"Not I," Adan answered, "but the men in the boat heard him give the order." He shrugged. "That does not rule out the possibility of deception on his part. Perhaps he deliberately let my men overhear him give a false course for his ship in the event that our longboats encountered a British warship to send in pursuit."

Renno asked questions, and Adan responded with a description of the *Sans Doute* and its captain, then estimated that the ship would have a crew of over two hundred, including the fighting men. It would take perhaps a week for the ship to sail past the Georgia coast and down the Florida peninsula to the mouth of the North River at St. Augustine Inlet if the weather held.

"Renno," Nate said, "I think I know what you're thinking. It would be madness. I regret this as much as you—"

Renno felt a surge of unreasoning resentment. Nate could not possibly know what he was feeling. He wasn't even sure himself about his emotions.

"Surely, in this day and time," Nate said, "no honorable man would force himself on a captive woman. My bet is that sooner or later she'll show up on one of the British islands, none the worse for the adventure."

Renno nodded as if in gratitude, but he did not speak. He turned, walked out of the great room and onto the covered run alongside the servants' quarters and the kitchen. At last he reached the edge of the bluff, where a ponderous stone seawall had been erected to prevent erosion, put one booted foot on the wall, and looked up at the darkening sky. A hint of crimson remained on the horizon, and the evening star was swimming among small, puffy clouds to the southeast.

From the moment he had learned that Beth had been on her way to America, he knew that he would go after her. There would be no need to consult the manitous; indeed, he had already been warned by the spirit of his grandmother—who had also been kidnapped by Frenchmen —that his life would be changed by men of that nation. Yes, he would go.

A sudden moodiness overset him. Waves and surges of memory surrounded him, for once before he had been forced by events to go into Spanish Florida. It was odd how life seemed to repeat itself. He had gone to Florida long ago, when he was barely a man, to seek out another woman, Emily, who had been taken by the white renegade who had killed his father. And now the manitous were sending him into that land of sun and palm trees because, once again, a woman for whom he felt emotion had been taken there against her will.

The epiphany that Beth still had a place in his heart came to him as a surprise. He had mistakenly believed that he had purged the flame-haired Englishwoman from his system and that the fresh, new, young love that he had felt for An-da had once and for all cleansed his heart of the woman who had been unwilling to give up her business and luxuries to be his wife. But now all past knowledge of her was back, and in his mind he remembered her lush body's heats and softnesses, her bravery in times of peril, and her undeniable intelligence. All that aside, however, she had been his friend—as her brother, William, was his friend—and friendship was a strong tie for the Seneca. Whatever followed, he must go to her.

He found Nate and Adan seated in the great room, sipping whiskey from crystal glasses. "I will require the sloop," Renno said.

Adan nodded. "I was afraid of that. I will go with you, of course."

"And I," Nate said.

"I am grateful to you both," Renno said. "You, Cousin, are a family man with responsibilities. I would not expose you to such danger."

"I think I'll run out and marry myself a widow with ten children," Adan said lightly.

Nate thought for a moment. "St. Augustine is the strongest point in all of Florida. The fort would require a fleet to reduce it, and God only knows how many Spanish soldiers are garrisoned there, in addition to the men you'd have to fight from the French ship."

"Beth will not be rescued by superior force," Renno said.

"We'll need about six crewmen to raise the sails," Adan estimated.

"Can you recruit them?" Renno asked. "They will not be required to go ashore. Only I will land."

"And I," Adan said. "You speak Spanish well, Renno, but remember, I *am* Spanish. And Beth is, after all, my sister-by-marriage."

"Thank you, my friend," Renno responded.

"Then you'll need me to stay with the sloop," Nate offered. "I'm no hero and don't care to become one at my age, so I won't beg you to take me into the teeth of the strongest Spanish fort in the New World. But I do think I can help with the sloop."

Renno shook his head. "Cousin, I will be leaving my daughter in your care. I will not cause your wife, Peggy, the torment of grieving for you if things go wrong. I will ask you to promise me, out of our kinship and our friendship, that should it be necessary, you will see that Renna gets home to my sister, Ena, and that Little Hawk, also, will be returned to his home from Philadelphia."

Nate started to protest, but his willingness to take part in the venture faded in the face of Renno's earnest plea. He nodded. "I do so promise, Cousin."

There were more than enough seamen fed up with being intimidated and attacked by the French to man the little sloop that was the last vessel of the Huntington merchant fleet. She left the Cape Fear River with a crew of six, plus Adan and Renno.

The sloop was small and fast. She would be able to outsail any French or Spanish ship she might encounter, but she was not armed.

Renno, however, went well armed. In preparation for the voyage he spent hours honing the blades of his tomahawk and his Spanish stiletto and oiling and cleaning his musket and his brace of pistols. He had only recently restrung the English crossbow and had spent time in Wilmington fashioning true, straight, iron-tipped arrows.

His quiver was packed full, holding more than fifty of the deadly, slim missiles.

The crew suddenly grew to seven when, a few hours away from the Cape Fear into Long Bay, Nate Ridley came up from below.

"I appreciate your concern for me," he told Renno, "but I didn't feel that I could be left out. A man has to take a stand at one time or another, and I guess this was my time."

Their plan was simple: The sloop would creep into St. Augustine Bay in the dark of night. Renno and Adan were to be set ashore to the north of St. Augustine by longboat, and the sloop would put back to sea to wait until the following night, and to repeat that performance at a set time if Renno and Adan had not returned.

The little sloop, the *Seneca Glory*, seemed eager to please as she skipped over moderate seas running in front of a fresh wind. Once, as she romped southward off the lower Georgia coast, a sail was seen on the horizon, but the *Glory* quickly outran the sighting. Adan was using Spanish charts from his brief stint as a pirate, so he had no difficulty in spotting landmarks as the *Glory* closed on the Florida coast and ran parallel to sandy beaches that gave way to riotous greenery. He took the sloop to sea, out of sight of land, when he was sure that they were near the tip of Vilano Island.

The *Glory* tiptoed into the North River in the darkness with a linesman at the bow whispering the soundings, which were quietly passed back to Nate, who stood at the wheel. He was making careful note of the compass readings, for it would be up to him to take the sloop back to sea once Renno and Adan were ashore.

A few lights were visible from the old city—some of them at a height that indicated they shone from the ramparts of the Castillo de San Marcos. In the night the linesman's voice seemed rashly loud and the slap of tiny waves against the hull, a small thunder. The guns of the fort could, within moments of an alert, lay down a hail of fire on the inlet and the river.

At last Renno and Adan waded ashore to a sandy mainland beach on the western side of the river. The *Glory* slipped into the darkness, heading for the sea. Adan swore softly as a relentless attack began—an assault—by voracious mosquitoes, which continued for the remainder of the night and left both Renno and him itching and splotchy from the bites. Since the men were dressed to look like Spanish trappers or settlers, it would not have been a good idea to use the Indian method of discouraging mosquitoes—coating one's exposed skin with mud—so there was nothing for it but to bat away as many as possible and to kill others, leaving bloody spots on the skin. The pair found some relief when Renno cut palmetto fronds to be used as fans to brush the insects away.

At first light they began to move inland through the dense maritime forest. The brush near the bank of the river was an almost impenetrable mass that sloped upward. The top of the growth, however, was smoothed and trimmed as neatly as a hedge by the effect of windblown salt spray. Behind the brush the trees were huge, the going easier. Mounds of oyster shells marked the eating habits of generations of the Indians who had been on the land before the coming of the conquistadores.

After a half mile of tough going Renno and Adan broke out of the dense growth and found themselves on a sandy road, which led toward the south. A mile or two down the road they got their first glimpse of the fort. Its thirty-foot walls towered over the surrounding town. At the junctions of its rectangular bastions, round, dome-topped watchtowers were manned by helmeted Spanish soldiers. Several ships were anchored in the sound before the fort.

"There," Adan said, pointing out the *Huntington Pride* riding at anchor, all sails furled. Lighters were offloading her cargo. Nearby the *Sans Doute* swung to her chains. The deck of the French ship was deserted.

"That's the Frenchman's crew moving the *Pride*'s cargo," Adan said.

"Then there will be few left aboard ship," Renno said. "That will be to our advantage if Beth is still there."

They strolled into the old city as if they were just two good Spanish settlers coming for a visit, talking and gesturing as if in admiration of the neatly constructed homes. Men who lived in the wilderness had to contend with Indians and, to the north, the occasional set-to with Georgia hunters' trespassing into Spanish lands. It was not unusual to see roughly dressed men walking the streets heavily armed, and if anyone thought that it was odd for a Spaniard to carry a quiver of arrows and an English longbow, he did not choose to express his thoughts to a man who was bronzed by the sun, well muscled, and looked as if he knew how to use the weapons he carried.

They walked directly under the guns of the fort. A moat that was a full forty feet wide protected the thick stone walls.

"Let us hope that we don't have to find a way to get in there," Adan said.

Renno led the way to the dock area, where they stood idly watching the boats carrying the *Pride*'s unloaded cargo. Adan nudged Renno and nodded toward a man in fancy dress who was yelling orders in French to the cargo handlers. "Lemaître," he grated. "It wouldn't do for him to see me."

They retreated into the city and found a seaman's cantina. The pair entered the dim, empty room, which stank of old rum and decaying food. A buxom girl with an Indian face served them hot tea and rewarmed fish cakes. Adan flirted with the girl and won shy smiles in return.

"Ah, señorita," Adan said in Spanish, "I know that I am far too late, for with ships in the harbor and so many

Frenchmen around, I am sure that you have countless suitors already."

The girl giggled. "I do not speak French," she said, then giggled again.

"So there is hope?"

"Go on with you," she said. "Leave a poor girl to do her job."

"But the Frenchmen try to speak to you. This I will warrant."

"Oh, they try." She lowered her head and looked at him through thick, dark lashes. "Perhaps it is not always necessary to converse." She held out one hand and rubbed her thumb across the pads of her first two fingers in that age-old gesture that says money.

"Ah," Adan said, glancing at Renno. "The Frenchmen are generous?"

"Well, they are rich, having taken the American ship filled with valuable things."

"And with a greater prize, I have heard," Adan said. "I have heard that the woman is very beautiful."

"So it is said," the girl confirmed. "Beautiful enough to be a guest of the commandant himself."

"So," Adan said, "the Frenchman has already sold the woman?"

"They say it is not like that," the serving girl replied. "They say she was driven through the streets of the town in a splendid carriage, that she entered the commandant's home on the arm of the French captain."

"And now she is a guest in the commandant's home?" Adan asked casually. "Where might a poor farmer find such a splendid establishment?"

The woman laughed. "Do you wish to see the commandant's fine house or the red-haired Englishwoman?"

"I would not turn my eyes away from feminine beauty," Adan answered. "Just as I cannot take my eyes off you."

"If you mean what you say," she flirted, "I will be finished with my work after the evening meal. Before that it is more expensive to lie with me, because my master then must serve clients of the cantina himself." She leaned close. Her breath smelled of onions and unwashed teeth. "In the evening it is better, for in the day I must hurry and get back to my work here."

"Until evening, then," Adan said, turning his head quickly.

The home of Colonel Juan de la Cruz Calvos occupied a choice site overlooking the bay and the entrance to the Matanzas River. It was a neatly whitewashed dwelling with wide verandas that sat on a foundation of ballast stones.

Unlike the Spanish soldiers that Renno had seen guarding forts on the Mississippi, the sentinels at the colonel's house were smartly uniformed, neat, and alert. Without moving his head, one guard watched Renno and Adan saunter past his post, his eyes following them until they turned away.

"Two guards at the front of the house," Renno said. "Probably at least one at the rear."

"And, I would suspect, military aides inside," Adan contributed.

They stood on a street corner and watched the colonel's house. It appeared that he also used his home as his headquarters, for there was a steady stream of visitors, both military and civilian. Since it would be impossible to attempt any rescue before dark, they strolled the streets of the town, determining the best escape route to the north. To the south there was some water traffic on the Matanzas River.

When they were sure that they had memorized the layout of the town, they walked past the impressive fort once more, found the same cantina, had the same fish cakes for an afternoon meal, and stayed to observe as the French sailors began to come into the cantina. The Frenchmen ordered rum and food in Spanish so terrible that the serving girl and her employer had to guess at the sailors' wants, not always guessing rightly. That made for some interesting arguments.

A gruff-voiced Frenchman occupied a table next to Renno and Adan's. He glared at them belligerently. Renno nodded benignly in response. The serving girl came. The Frenchman began to speak to her with broad gestures, telling her in a mixture of French and broken Spanish that he wanted food. The simple girl was both confused and alienated by the harsh tones. She explained patiently that there were only fish cakes and fried bread. The Frenchman threw up his hands, cursed, and looked around helplessly.

"If I may," Renno said in French, "the rum, fish cakes, and fried bread are quite tasty."

"I thank you, sir," the Frenchman said. "Would you be so kind as to tell this wench to bring me whatever she has, so long as I am not poisoned?"

Renno laughed. "One survives in spite of their efforts."

"You are not French, and yet you speak our language well."

"If we are to be allies," Renno said, "we must understand each other."

The Frenchman nodded. The serving maid brought his food, and he pitched in with a will, washing down the fish cakes and fried pone with rum.

"You are from the *Sans Doute*?" Renno asked.

The Frenchman nodded with his mouth full.

"You are to be congratulated on your capture of the American ship."

The man nodded again, then spoke around a mouthful. "It was a rich prize."

"Yes," Renno said, "our poor colony here is always in need of manufactured goods, and the English make good tools and weapons."

"Well, we are. allies, as you say."

"I would like to be a close ally to your captain,"

Renno said with a leer, "so that I might share in his personal prize."

"That one," the Frenchman said. "He will be lucky if she does not scratch out his eyes."

"What will he do with her, this English captive?" Renno asked.

The Frenchman laughed. "I think he will leave her here, with the Spanish colonel." He looked at Renno seriously. "You know, there are times when we French are too civilized, too much the gentlemen, so to speak. Had it been I—" He chuckled. "After all, we are at war. But the captain? Oh, no. When the Englishwoman with her red hair fought him and called him vile names—" He chuckled again. "I know, because I was on watch and heard. When she told him that if he touched her again she would kill him as he slept by pouring hot lead from the shot foundry into his ear, he became the perfect gentleman. I do not think the Spanish colonel will be so sensitive." He made the last word sound like profanity.

"A real English wildcat," Renno said. "Yes, it might take a Spaniard to tame such a one."

The Frenchman fell silent as Renno and Adan ordered more hot tea. Soon the serving girl went around the room lighting candles. The Frenchman finished his meal and arose. He looked down at Renno and grinned. "Too bad you're not high brass or gentlefolk, Spaniard," he said. "If you were, you might catch a glimpse of the English wildcat at the party in the colonel's house tonight."

Renno waited until the Frenchman had departed, then whispered to Adan, "Come, we must find an invitation to the colonel's party."

It was a balmy evening. A Spanish family was out for a stroll. A brace of junior officers met the family, saluted politely, and stepped from the boardwalk to the dirt street.

"That looks like our invitation now," Renno said, nodding after the departing Spanish officers.

Adan and the white Indian lagged behind as the officers walked toward the bay and entered a cantina that looked much like the other but smelled not quite as bad. Adan went in alone and saw that the two officers had ordered rum. He watched for a few minutes as the Spaniards drank quickly and heavily, then paid the barman and started toward the door.

Renno stayed on the other side of the street as the two officers emerged, Adan not far behind them. It had become dark while Renno waited. He crossed the narrow dirt street and fell in a few paces in front of Adan, keeping his eyes on the two officers who sauntered toward the western edge of town. Soon the pair entered a street that was more narrow and darker than the other. From somewhere nearby there was the sound of a guitar and a woman singing plaintively. Now and then there would come a burst of laughter.

Renno motioned to Adan to come forward and join him. They picked the darkest spot in the alley and ran on silent feet to close on the two officers. Renno used the butt of his musket to render his quarry unconscious. Adan simultaneously struck the other officer with the heavy barrel of a pistol.

In the shadows of an unlighted house they stripped the officers and donned their uniforms. Renno had estimated sizes well. His tunic was a bit tight in the chest, but otherwise the clothing fit both of them nicely. They could not risk having the Spaniards revive to give an alarm. To spare Adan, Renno did the deed swiftly, mercilessly, using the well-honed blade of his Spanish stiletto. They dragged the bodies under the porch of the unlighted house. Near the colonel's headquarters Renno found a similar hiding place for his and Adan's muskets, tomahawk, and the longbow, since it would hardly be suitable for a visiting junior officer to enter his commander's residence carrying such weapons.

They waited until the sounds of guitar music and the

rhythmic clicking of the heels of a dancer drifted from inside the colonel's home, accompanied by shouts of approval from the gathering. Then the imposters followed two other officers to the entry and handed their hats and their swords to servants. The establishment looked larger on the inside than it had from outside. From the foyer they walked into a large salon, where the colonel and his lady sat on raised chairs with their guests—both military and civilian, male and female—ranged around the walls of the room, leaving space in the center for a dancer in a red-and-black tunic and tight breeches. A guitar player was bent over his instrument. The dancer posed handsomely, his heels clicking out rhythms on the wide planks of the wooden floor.

Renno took stock of the room quickly, noting the placement of doors and windows. Lamps burned on pedestals along the walls to light the scene. His eyes halted their movement only when they were locked onto the face of the lady sitting beside the colonel. It was Beth. He knew that she saw him, for her green eyes widened, and one hand jerked convulsively before she recovered her poise. To the right of the colonel sat the special guests, Beth's abductor, Captain Jean Claude Lemaître, and his officers.

Renno knew that the longer Adan and he stayed in the room, the greater the risk of discovery. The St. Augustine garrison could not be so large that two strange officers—or two men impersonating officers—could expect to go forever without being questioned. He caught Beth's eye and indicated, with subtle head and eye movements, that she was to move toward the large windows at the southern end of the room. She rose almost immediately. The colonel looked up at her, and two armed men stepped out from behind the high-backed chairs to stay at her side as she walked to the windows and looked out. With a glance at Renno she then went back to her chair, having shown him that she was not free to move about alone.

"I will handle the guards," Renno said to Adan, "and make a way for you through the large window. Take Beth and go to the house where we hid the weapons. I'll hold the soldiers back for a minute or two with my pistols."

Adan nodded. Already he had noticed that Renno and he were getting curious looks from the other officers present.

With a flurry of tappings that sounded almost as loud as gunshots, the dancer concluded his performance, the guitarist struck his closing chords, and there was polite applause. Renno and Adan moved to stand beside the colonel's chair. The attention of the guests was on the side-door entrance, where a female dancer with swirling skirts that ballooned outward over many petticoats came twirling into the room.

Renno said, "Now!" as he moved to club one guard with a pistol and lance the other's heart with his stiletto.

"Sorry, old boy," Adan said as he brought his pistol barrel down hard on the colonel's head.

Renno hoisted one guard and threw him through the window, smashing glass and sashes. Adan and Beth were on the run, but Beth was hampered by her voluminous skirts. Adan lifted her, tossed her through the broken window, then dove after her to catch her while she stumbled but before she fell. He didn't bother to look back as he heard all hell break loose inside the house. One pistol shot rang out, followed by shouts and another shot.

A too brave young lieutenant was the first to die from Renno's pistols. The callow officer rushed toward the broken window, crying out in alarm. He fell to the white Indian's shot. Others, meanwhile, hurried toward the window, only to fall back as Renno raised the other pistol.

"Outside!" shouted Lemaître in Spanish. "Block their escape."

Men ran toward the front door. Two officers rushed Renno. One died with a ball in his heart. The other closed in, trying to slam his fist into Renno's face, only to impale himself on the stiletto, which penetrated between his ribs, then slid out easily to slash the cheek of another brave soldier. Renno, seeing men going out the front door, hurtled out the broken window and landed running. As he raced into the street, he heard the odd song of musket balls passing close by his head as the guards fired.

He ran into the darkness, but the mob pouring from the house was not far behind. He saw faint movement ahead and could only hope that it was Adan and Beth at the house where he had concealed the weapons. His desire was confirmed when a stoutly constructed arrow zipped past him to stop a pursuer in his tracks. He let out a whoop of pure joy, for he knew whose arm had guided that arrow; Beth had proven her worth with a longbow among the Comanche and Apache of the West.

Now Adan's musket blasted. Renno reached the house, seized his own musket, shot to kill, then began to load rapidly. Beth's arrows were more quickly prepared, and their deadly barrage stopped the onslaught toward them until both Renno and Adan could reload.

A bell began to toll, and a bugle blared an alert. From the fort came an answering call.

"They'll have the whole garrison on us," Adan said, panting. "Let's move."

"Just a minute," Beth said. She lifted her heavy skirt and ripped away at her petticoats until a pile of white material lay on the ground. "Now I can run."

They pounded up a street that opened into a little square. This gave access to the grounds of the fort. Soldiers by the dozen were streaming out the entryway.

"We'll have to circle around," Renno said. "We can't go directly north." He took Beth's hand and started toward the west. A squad of soldiers double-timed from a street just ahead of them. They were surrounded: To the east was the water, to the south was the hornet's nest around the colonel's headquarters, to the west and north were soldiers.

"Adan, quickly," Renno urged as he pulled Beth back

toward the colonel's home. No one would expect them to return there.

When they turned the last corner toward their destination, they saw men racing toward the fort. Behind the running men, the street was deserted. The threesome clung to shadows and moved behind the colonel's headquarters to see a sandy beach on the riverbank. Ahead were wooden docks with small boats tied alongside. Renno led Beth and Adan to a longboat, checked to see if the oars were aboard, and helped Beth down. Adan jumped in as Renno chopped the mooring lines with his tomahawk. They pushed the boat from the dock and into the river, then began to row southward. Soon they were out of sight of the town, but they could still hear the commotion from the disturbed garrison.

"We've got them stirred up like an anthill," Adan said, laughing. "Once they've had a chance to count their dead, they won't settle down for a while."

Behind them, in the vicinity of the dock from which they'd taken the boat, a lantern glow appeared. Shouts told them that the boat had been missed. A voice bellowed an order to block the river. It would not be possible, as Renno had planned, to row back past the fort and into the bay. He had only two choices: to leave the boat and go inland or to continue toward the south in the boat. Within a few hours the *Glory* would be sneaking into the bay to the rendezvous point. She would stay until an hour or so before dawn and then put back to sea to return once more, on the following night.

Boats were moving down the river toward them. Men called back and forth in two languages. The crew of the *Sans Doute* had joined in the hunt.

"We will go south for a time," Renno decided. "Then we will leave the boat and circle the city to the west."

"We have just over twenty-four hours to get to the rendezvous," Adan said. "Or it's going to be a long walk home." He pulled his oars in silence for a time. "Renno, one man might be able to make it past the fort on the seaside."

Renno had had the same thought, but as much as he liked and respected Adan, he was reluctant to leave Beth in Adan's care.

"I can swim to the shore of the barrier island from here," Adan said, "and sneak up through the woods."

"You'd have to swim the inlet, too," Renno pointed out.

"Yes," Adan confirmed. "I might not get there before the sloop leaves tonight, but I can be there waiting tomorrow night. Once I'm on board, we'll sail south along the coast until we see your signal."

"So," Renno said, thinking the plan was workable.

Adan removed his boots, tied them together, and slung them around his neck. He eased into the water.

"God go with you," Beth whispered as Adan disappeared in the darkness.

Renno bent to the oars, and Beth slipped onto the forward seat and began to ply the other set of oars. No words had been exchanged between Renno and her. The boats behind them had seemed to be gaining, but now their pursuers' voices slowly faded as the longboat sliced through the dark waters.

Renno had studied Adan's charts of the Florida coast. To the south, at a distance of some ten miles, was another access to the sea—an inlet with the same name as the river, Matanzas—and it, too, was protected by a fort. Matanzas, the place of slaughter. To reach the sea beach, where they would hide until the *Glory* appeared offshore, they would have to sail past Fort Matanzas or land on the inland shore of the barrier island and make their way across its dense jungle of vegetation.

"Rest, now," he told Beth. "They have fallen well behind."

She rested her oars and turned on her seat to face him. There was just enough light from the stars for him to see her outline and the soft glow of her eyes. "Don't ask me how, but I knew that you would come."

"So," he said as he pulled the oars. "The fervent wish of a desperate woman."

"I remember, Renno," she teased back, "that when you feel something strongly and are, perhaps, afraid you'll show emotion, you grunt out that word—*so*." She laughed. "You can't honestly tell me that I'm wrong, can you?"

"So," he said, and laughed with her.

She was silent for a time. "I wouldn't have blamed you if you hadn't come," she said, "but I knew you would. Not that I was in any great danger."

"But a long way from home," he said.

"The French captain was a lamb," she said, "who smelled like a skunk."

"And the Spanish colonel?"

"I hadn't had time to assess his character."

"You had been sold to him," Renno revealed.

He saw her shudder. "I had feared as much, and I felt small and helpless in the colonel's presence. Renno, I prayed that rescue would come, not really daring to hope that it would be you, and then, suddenly, you appeared."

She rested a tentative hand on his hard-muscled arm. "I was a long, long way from home," she acknowledged. "Thank you for coming after me."

"Thank me when we're safely on board the *Glory* and sailing northward," he said.

Chapter XII

The home of William Cocke, the second senator from Tennessee, was not nearly as grand as William Blount's had been. The house was modest in size and in decor, the rooms were few and small. Little Hawk and the one servant, a black slave named Chancy, who served as both cook and maid, occupied the dormer rooms in the attic. Little Hawk's room was a tight, crowded little space just big enough for a narrow bed, a washstand, and a small clothes trunk.

The boy rarely saw Cocke or Cocke's family, for he

took his meals in the kitchen and came and went through the back door, walking to the legislative buildings to work and to attend the school for pages. That he had not been accepted as a part of Cocke's family, as he had been taken in by the Blounts, didn't bother him. Cocke was not a warm man, as William Blount had been; even if Cocke had extended his friendship to the boy from the Seneca Nation, Little Hawk would have been reluctant to return it. He had come to be quite fond of Senator Blount, and he had been sorely disillusioned by Blount's actions. He wasn't certain how the seizure of Spanish territory could be considered treason to the United States, but he was certain that Blount had been wrong in his efforts to convince the Indian tribes to fight his battles for him.

Little Hawk had received letters from home. Toshabe wrote of ordinary, everyday things, but his aunt Ena, who had always considered him to be a solid-minded boy capable of grasping adult concepts, wrote of the rift within the tribe and detailed the efforts of white men to recruit Seneca and Cherokee warriors for an excursion down the Mississippi. The white men who were spreading dissension among his people were undoubtedly agents of William Blount's. He felt that his ex-mentor had betrayed his trust, for, in a way, Blount had represented not only Tennessee but all the western frontier areas, including the lands of the Cherokee and the Seneca. Aunt Ena said nothing about Reverend Waith Pennywhistle in her letters, so Little Hawk assumed that that man had not returned to the Seneca village. Little Hawk decided to be very careful in the future about trusting a white man.

The House of Representatives was beginning impeachment proceedings against Blount, who was by that time back in Tennessee, where he was safe. The citizens of Tennessee would have risen up in arms against the four million citizens of the United States *and* their one million black slaves to prevent the federal government's removal of one of their own, William Blount, for trial in the cor-

rupt and foppish East. Blount's disgrace in Philadelphia
did not put an end to his prestige in Tennessee, nor to his
schemes for land, riches, and glory.

Even though Tennessee was a state of the union, its
people still had the frontier mentality. Their way of thinking
represented a chasm more difficult to span than the sheer
distance separating the western frontier from the East.
About half a million Americans lived beyond the Alleghenies
in Tennessee, Kentucky, and in the rapidly developing
areas along the Ohio River, and it would have been difficult to find one settler who believed that the federal
government in Philadelphia gave fair consideration to a
westerner's problems. For decades frontiersmen had been
left on their own to fight Indians, Spaniards, renegade
Frenchmen, the elements, the wilderness, and the ten-
dency of eastern merchants to pay low for frontier furs and
farm produce and charge high for anything the settlers or
trappers wanted to buy.

It was not fair, but it was human nature for Little
Hawk to be tarred with the same brush that had blackened Blount's reputation in the capital. During those days
the Federalists tried to paint all political opponents as
dark as William Blount, and the eastern press howled for
blood. Men of honor, such as Thomas Jefferson, felt it
highly unlikely that a thirteen-year-old boy would have
been privy to Blount's plans. Unfortunately, not all of
Philadelphia's seventy thousand people, plus visiting elected
legislators, were men of honor. With Blount gone, Little
Hawk had only one protector, Thomas Jefferson, and that
gentleman, having tired of the "office of unprofitable dignity," the vice-presidency, had gone home to Virginia for
an extended visit.

In the pool of Senate pages, juvenile vindictiveness
proved more potent than whatever honor young boys had
developed in their brief life. Because Little Hawk—or
Hawk Harper, as he was known to the pages—had demon-
strated that it was unhealthy to challenge him to fight,

even when he was outnumbered, no physical violence was directed toward him. The malice of the pages who had felt the fury of Little Hawk's defense under attack kept the pot boiling through acts of wanton vandalism—for example, ink spilled over his schoolbooks when he was away from his desk and knife slashes in his coat, which was left hanging in the anteroom of the school.

There were times when he felt terribly alone and longed to follow Blount's example by literally running for the hills, to head for the Smoky Mountains and home. But pride sustained him. He was still the page who was called when the president pro tem of the Senate needed an errand. He was Seneca, and he was his father's son. The sachem had set Little Hawk's goals: to study the white man's books, to live among the white men, and to learn their ways. It would take more than deliberate damage to his personal property and whispered insults behind his back to make him forget his pledge to Renno.

Little Hawk showed his contempt for the petty actions of other pages by ignoring them, by concentrating on his studies, and by being arrogantly aloof as he waited with the others in the page room. He knew that not a single one of them had killed an enemy. Not a single one of them could bring down a deer with a musket, much less with a well-placed arrow. Not a single one of them would be able to survive if he suddenly found himself in the great wilderness. But his disdain for the eastern pages almost cost him his life.

The page room fronted on a busy street that housed a volunteer fire company only a few doors away. Quite often the dull hours of waiting would be enlivened by fire-alarm bells. The alarm was a signal for all pages to pile out onto the wooden sidewalk to watch the volunteers pull the hook-and-ladder wagons, equipped with hats, picks, axes, buckets, whale-oil torches, and racks of ladders.

On an early-winter morning under sullen skies that occasionally spat scattered snowflakes to join a skim of

half-thawed, soiled slush, the fire bell clanged, and the
pages rushed out to line the boardwalk. Little Hawk was
among the last to leave the room. He walked with dignity,
not lowering himself to jostle for position with the other
boys, and he arrived just in time to see the wooden wagon
wheeled out from the firehouse.

"Go, go!" the pages yelled as the men positioned
themselves. Some of the men pushed, others pulled. The
wagon was loaded with water, and it was very heavy, well
over five thousand pounds. It began to roll reluctantly,
then faster as the men put their backs to the work, their
hobnailed boots digging into the slush. Soon they were
breathing hard, their breath making small clouds of steam
in the nippy air.

"You're slow today, O'Malley," one of the pages called
out to a man of obvious rank who was yelling orders as the
second engine was being pulled and pushed from the
firehouse.

A space had opened up in front of Little Hawk. He
stepped to the edge of the wooden walkway. The pumper
wagon, which required sixteen men to operate the hand
pumps, was moving smartly toward a plume of smoke at a
few blocks' distance. The equipment wagon was beginning
to roll as the gathering crowd cheered.

The page standing nearest Little Hawk was not speaking to him when he shouted, "Here he comes. He's right
early today."

He was a man without a name—or at least his name
was not known to Little Hawk and the other pages. He
was a small man of Slavic features, including a bristling
mustache, who delivered coal in the neighborhood in a
big, black dray with high, iron-rimmed wheels. In the
time that Little Hawk had been in Philadelphia he had
watched perhaps a dozen fire alarms, and almost every
time the engines had not gone more than a block before
the little man in the coal wagon, obviously a person fascinated by fires, was rumbling after them.

The coal wagon was pulled by four black horses. The little Slav was perched on the driver's seat, dwarfed by the high wagon, the huge, rumbling wheels, and the straining, lively animals. He snapped his whip over the rumps of the wheelhorses and yelled something in a foreign language. Steam jetted from the nostrils of the horses. As the pages shouted encouragement, the pounding hoofbeats were rhythmic, and the great, iron-rimmed wheels ground down to stone through the slush.

As the lumbering coal wagon neared his position, Little Hawk leaned forward to get a better view. Some of the more timid pages withdrew, for the wheels of the wagon were quite near the wooden walkway. He heard his fellow pages cheering on the driver as the horses' black heads bobbed toward him from twenty feet, then ten feet away. He could see the wide, alert eyes of the horses very well when he was struck solidly and suddenly from the rear, the impact between his shoulder blades. He tried to throw himself to one side as he was impelled into the street directly into the path of the rushing coal wagon; but he had landed hard on his hands and knees in the cold, wet slush, and it was too late for him to scramble back to the boardwalk . . . too late to roll toward the center of the street.

Little Hawk had only a split second to react. He threw himself down onto his back and pointed his feet toward the onrushing horses. As the forefeet of the lead team of blacks clattered past his ear, he reached up to seize the double tree, the wooden shaft connecting the lead horses' harness. Something sharp hit him just below the left eye, but he held on for his life as he was jerked and jolted into motion. He thought that his arms were going to be pulled out of their sockets. His back and buttocks bounced and skidded along the slush-covered street.

The coating of slush on the cobblestones was all that saved Little Hawk from serious injury as he was dragged

down the street. On either side of him hoofbeats rang. His
rump and heels were banged painfully against the cobblestones. He knew that he had to do something lest he lose
his grip on the double tree and be thrown backward
toward the hooves of the wheelhorses and the tall, iron-
cased wheels. He lifted his legs and locked them around
the tongue of the wagon. No longer was he being jounced
against the rough stones. He worked his way to the top of
the tongue, then reached up to seize the harness.

He prayed that the fire buff who seemed so small on
the driver's seat of the big coal hauler had seen him go
directly under the horses. Through the sound of hoofbeats, Little Hawk thought he heard the driver yell at the
horses. It took a while to break the momentum of the
heavy vehicle, during which time slush and pebbles pelted
him in the face. Before the wagon had lost all its forward
momentum, he was standing on the tongue, his hands on
the backs of the horses on either side of him.

When the wagon stopped, he leaped over the back of
the gee-side horse but lost his balance. He landed in the
slush but immediately jumped to his feet and ran back
toward the Senate pages, who were still standing on the
sidewalk. He heard the coal dray's driver yelling at him
and was aware of a constable's shrill whistle, but rage was
burning in him. He had been deliberately pushed into the
path of death, and he felt that he knew who had done the
deed.

Indeed, Peter Colden and Cadwallader Sloughter,
the New Yorkers who had tested Little Hawk's fighting
ability and found it not to their liking, were standing in
the spot from which Little Hawk had been pushed.
Sloughter was laughing, but the laugh froze in his throat
as Little Hawk charged toward him.

He was Seneca, a sachem's son. He had lived by a
code unknown to the two New York pages. He suspected
that it had been Sloughter who had pushed him into the
path of the thundering horses. The fear on Sloughter's face

convinced Little Hawk that he was right. Had he possessed a weapon, the code of the Seneca would have
prevailed, for when a Seneca warrior escaped an attempt
on his life, he was bound to kill his attacker.

Pages scattered, but Sloughter seemed to be para-
lyzed. Peter Colden, beside him, held up his hands as if to
ward off Little Hawk's fierce attack.

Little Hawk threw himself at the two pages from
three paces away, his body becoming a missile of anger.
Sloughter and Colden were carried off the walk by the
impact, and the three boys rolled in the cold, wet slush.
Women screamed, and men shouted. Little Hawk was
atop Sloughter and had the New Yorker's throat under his
hands. He knew where to press his thumbs to crush the
delicate, shell-like larynx. Colden scrambled to his feet
and, yelling for help, fled. Little Hawk applied pressure
with his thumbs. Sloughter tried to scream but could not.
His eyes began to bulge with terror.

In moments one of those who had attacked him would
be dead. The larynx would be crushed. Cadwallader
Sloughter would not die instantly. He would be unable to
breathe; his lungs would spasm, his face would turn purple, and then he would die of air deprivation. The desire
to see it happen was a fiery, roaring need in Little Hawk.
But at the last moment, just before it would have been too
late, he remembered the shame he had felt when William
Blount, whom he had considered to be a fellow westerner,
had been exposed. Blount had brought enough shame to
the state of Tennessee. He himself would not bring shame
to the Seneca by killing a stupid boy, although, by his
code, Sloughter deserved to die. Little Hawk jerked his
hands away, climbed to his feet, glared down on the
gasping, frightened Sloughter, and grated, "No, you are
not worth it."

A heavy hand clamped down on his shoulder, and a
policeman shouted, "What d'ye think yer doin' here?"

Little Hawk jerked out from under the hand, ducked

into the crowd, and ran. Voices were raised behind him.
He skidded into an alley and quickly outdistanced a half-
hearted pursuit by the uniformed policeman. He was wet
and cold. His buttocks and hips were bruised, and he
knew that he was going to be very sore and stiff.

When he was sure that he was not being chased, he
slowed to a trot, moved toward the Cocke house, and
found it deserted save for the black cook, Chancy.

"What happened to you?" Chancy demanded. "You
git out of them wet clothes this instant, you hear?"

"I will," he said. "Listen, Chancy, can you fix me a
sack of food? Some corn bread, apples, whatever you
have."

"You hungry, you git out of them wet clothes and
Chancy'll fix you a meal."

"I've got to go, Chancy," he said. "I've got to go back
home to Tennessee."

"You in trouble, boy?"

"A little."

"Tell me," she said.

"A boy tried to push me in front of a coal wagon," he
said. "I almost killed him. No one saw him push me. They
only saw me attack him."

She nodded. "I got no reason to believe in the white
man's justice. I git the foods ready for you."

He went to his room and packed his money and
weapons, a blanket, and winter clothing. When he came
back down to the kitchen, the cook had a little basket of
food ready for him, and she handed him a hunk of bread
and cheese. "Eat this as you go," she said. "You goin' to
make it back to Tennessee?"

"Yes," he said.

"Long way. You's only a boy."

"I am Seneca, a sachem's son," Little Hawk said
fiercely, and he had never felt more pride in those facts.

For over an hour Renno had rowed steadily, and the

sounds of voices had diminished behind him. The sweeps made liquid noises, and he was breathing hard. He was regretting the period of relative inactivity in Wilmington. The edge had been taken off his usual superb condition, and his body was not accustomed to rowing. He eased off a bit to save his strength for the future. Beth gave a sigh of relief and adjusted to the slower pace.

"Leave off," he told her. "I will do it."

She turned to face him again. "They can't be sure we're continuing down the river," she said.

"No."

To his right was the maritime forest that covered the barrier island from the riverbank to ocean beach. "When we have gone a few more miles," he said, "we will hide the boat in the brush and make our way to the strand."

He rowed in silence. He realized that Beth would have much to say about their past and future relationship but would know that the time was not right for a discussion. Renno had begun to look for a suitable spot to land when the decision was made for him.

"Renno, listen," Beth whispered. He shipped his oars and heard sounds coming from behind them: Multiple oars dipped and lifted . . . a man cleared his throat. The boat was close, too close, and there were none of the excited shoutings and confusion that had marked the initial pursuit. More than one set of oars were at work, and the boat was moving at a speed that Renno and Beth would have been hard put to match, even for a short distance. He dipped his oars and turned toward the shore of the barrier island.

In a short time the bow of the longboat grated on a shell bottom. Renno climbed out, pulled the boat up onto the sand, and helped Beth out. For a moment they stood face to face in a night perfumed by a balmy sea breeze. He could feel the heat of her, the softness of her waist under his hands.

He waited for the multioared boat to pass by. When

the sounds could no longer be heard, Beth helped him
pull their stolen boat across the narrow sand beach and
into the edge of the brush. He cut bushes and concealed
the boat well, then used a leafy branch to wipe out the
V-shaped trail where the boat had been dragged through
the sand.

In the gray light of dawn he looked to the south to see
a longboat turning into the inlet leading to the sea. Ten
men were in the boat—those not rowing held muskets.
Instead of going all the way into the inlet, the boat drifted
while a large man in fancy dress stood and held a glass to
his eye to look seaward.

"That's Lemaître," Beth uttered.

They were standing under an overhanging roof of
brush, so they could not be seen; but when Lemaître
turned the glass back up the river, Renno pulled Beth
farther into the forest. Mosquitoes attacked immediately.
Renno led the way toward the ocean, sometimes having to
use his tomahawk to cut a path through the dense undergrowth. Beth's hair was disheveled. She called a halt while
she ripped a piece from the flounced insets of her skirt to
use as a turban. With her flame-colored hair mostly hidden under the cloth, her classic face and large, green eyes
were emphasized. Perspiration had darkened her gown
between her breasts, at her waist, and under her arms. A
smudge of soil marked her right cheek, but to Renno she
was so beautiful that his breathing was affected. He forced
himself to look away, although her eyes seemed to be
pleading with him.

It was full light, with the sun burning through a layer
of low clouds to the east, when they came to the edge of
the hedgelike waterfront growth. The strand was deserted.
A few hundred yards to the south, white water caught the
sunlight in the entrance to Matanzas Inlet.

"It's going to be a long and uncomfortable day," Renno
predicted.

He busied himself clearing a small circle in the growth,

chopping the low bushes off under the sand so that there would be no sharp stubs protruding. He used the cut brush to weave an impenetrable wall around the little clearing, with a tiny hole left to seaward so that he could occasionally check the ocean. They could not be seen even from a few feet away.

"I can't do anything about the mosquitoes," he apologized as Beth sat down on the sand. "And it's going to be hot."

She surprised herself with the words, "If I am with you, I can bear anything."

He sat down facing her but did not speak. His eyes sought hers for a moment. The communication was there, at least in a glance, but he was unable, at that time, to speak, to react to what she had told him.

"I'm tired," she confessed.

"I'm not surprised," he sympathized. "You should try to sleep before the heat of the day."

She made herself as comfortable as possible on the sand. When she lay on her side her hip created a sensuous curve under her skirt. Her face became serene as sleep overcame her quickly. He leaned toward her and brushed a mosquito from her cheek.

The murmurous rote of the surf lulled him into a state that was not quite sleep, although his eyelids drooped. He lay on his back, using one arm as a pillow, and looked up through the tangled vegetation toward a robin's-egg-blue sky. The increasing heat of the day added to his languor. Did he sleep? Did he dream? In a trancelike state he heard sounds but was not alarmed. . . .

He felt a heaviness, an awareness of blood and terror and senseless carnage. Antique ships lay discarded by a violent storm on a sandy strand. Soldiers in body armor wielded swords, pikes, clubs, and axes against defenseless men, some of whom knelt in prayer or tried to flee or begged for mercy or fought defiantly with bare hands, having given up their weapons in trustful surrender. This vision was so clear to Renno that he experienced the victims' agonized disbelief when fellow Christians began the heinous slaughter. He seemed to hover over a white beach baking in a tropical sun to see the carnage. The weapons and clothing were of a bygone age, and he felt a sense of sadness and disgust for wanton killings that served no real end. . . .

He shook his head, and the vision left him, but for a long moment he could hear the voices of the dying praying in French to sweet Jesus, while one man risked his mortal soul by cursing those who butchered unarmed men.

He checked the sun and was amazed to see that it had scarcely moved during that timeless period. He sat up. Beth slept on, to awaken when perspiration began to bead her forehead.

"You slept well," he said.

"*Ummm.*" She sat up and rearranged the scarf over her hair. "My kingdom not for a horse but for a cup of water," she said. Then, before he could speak, she added, "No, I'm all right. There were times in the desert when we went all day without water. Remember?"

"Yes." Had there been a way, he would have risked much to bring water to her, but there was no water available on the barrier island. They could only hope for an afternoon shower, for he expected to have to wait until after nightfall to find the *Glory* offshore.

"We have had our adventures, haven't we, Renno?"

He smiled. "The Master of Life was watching over us."

"I think He was," she agreed. She was silent for a long time. Once or twice their eyes met before she asked: "Do you remember the last time we were together?"

"Quite well."

"You gave me a history lesson about my own country," she said. "We were at Hastings, where William the

Conqueror and his relatively few Normans changed the course of English history. You said you had seen it. I've thought about that for a long time, and I've done some reading since. The battle was just as you described it to me. How did you know?"

"It's difficult to explain. I did not see it with my eyes but with my mind—a vision from the manitous."

"Your manitous followed you all the way to the English coast?"

He shrugged. "Perhaps."

"Are they with you now?"

"If I were on my home grounds," Renno said, "I would know that every Seneca who has ever faced an enemy would be at my side."

"The manitous don't travel?"

Again he shrugged. "There is a feeling of oddness about this place, this narrow island."

"What feeling?" she coaxed. "What oddness?"

He spoke reluctantly, for he suspected that he might have been dozing when he saw the Spaniards in body armor attack unarmed white men. "As if many men have died here."

"But they have," she told him. "Many men, and perhaps women and children as well. French Huguenots came here in 1564 and established a fort farther up the coast at the mouth of the St. Johns River. A Spanish expedition under Pedro Menéndez de Avilés was sent to destroy the settlement. They killed almost all the garrison of the fort. Jan Ribault, who had founded the settlement, had started back to France with the survivors when their ships were driven ashore by a storm. They surrendered to Menéndez, but he killed them all—not because they were Frenchmen, he said, but because they were not Catholic. That's why they call the inlet Matanzas Inlet. Matanzas—"

"Slaughter," Renno said. He thought: *Sleep well,*

*Frenchmen, and do not blame your God, for it is not He
who commands murder. It is man who kills his fellows in
the name of religion, not God.*

"Yes, I did teach you well," she said with a smile.

"Quite well," he said, trying to clear his mind of the
residue of his vision.

"But why am I talking about something that happened here so long ago," she asked, "when there are other
things on my mind? Do you remember what you said to
me at Hastings after you had described the battle to me?"

"Yes."

"You asked, 'Will you come with me not only to
Wilmington but to my homeland?' And I said that I couldn't,
and it was true. I couldn't at that time because I was
stupid—"

"No," he cut in quickly.

"Confused, then," she said. "You told me that I had
been captured by the enemy, and in a way you were right.
But the enemy was myself and my desire to prove that I
could do anything that a man could do, that I could build a
great fortune in an area where many men had failed. I was
contrasting life at court to life in your village, and in your
village I knew that there would be no great galas where I
could indulge my vanity in a gown that cost more than a
good artisan could earn in England in a year."

"We have not yet built a ballroom," Renno said with
an edge of resentment to his voice, for he was fighting his
urge to take her into his arms. Much had happened since
that last time he had held her in his arms on an English
beach. He had loved and lost An-da. And he had put this
flame-haired Englishwoman out of his heart, only to find
her clamoring at the gates once again. His tone's harshness was not lost on Beth.

"I have worn the fine gowns," she said. "I have
proven, at least to myself, that I can be as effective at
business as any man. Even though I've lost my three large
ships, I am by no means a pauper, nor will I ever have to

call on my brother, William, for financial assistance. And I've discovered how miserable it is to be lonely, Renno."

For a moment he relented. "To be lonely is to be sick in the heart."

"Yes, oh, yes," she said. She lifted her head and looked at him proudly. "So—as you say. So. I have opened myself to you. I was on my way to Wilmington not just to buy more ships. I was coming because Adan had told me that you were there. Now I will say just one more thing, and it will be up to you." Tears formed in her eyes, and she turned her head away. "I beg your forgiveness for not accepting your invitation to go to your home with you to become your proper Seneca wife."

He felt his heart melt. He knelt beside her to clasp her into his arms. She gasped as his lips found hers.

Roy Johnson and El-i-chi, both dressed in buckskins, sat on a split-rail fence in front of El-i-chi's quarters and watched Gao and Ta-na-wun-da playing at soldier. The two boys were of a size and, having had brothers for fathers, bore a strong family resemblance. Ta-na knew that El-i-chi and Ah-wa-o were not his parents, but he called them mother and father because whatever Gao did, Ta-na did, and whatever Ta-na did, so did Gao. El-i-chi treated both of them as his sons and meted out teachings and punishment impartially. Indeed, so close were the boys that when punishment was due to one, pain for the other was usually not far behind.

On a parade field behind the row of log cabins that had been built to serve as quarters for officers, a unit of infantry was marching to the barked commands of a tough old sergeant who had been with Anthony Wayne at Fallen Timbers.

Roy Johnson had been back with the U.S. Army just long enough to be bored. Leading recruits on training marches through the woods wasn't his idea of fun. This modern army, it seemed to Roy, amounted to nothing more than fancy uniforms on boys who had been enticed into enlistment by a generous bounty and the promise of good food. Even with those inducements, the "new" army was only at one-third of the proposed strength.

Although no sansculotte French rogues had invaded hearth and home in the United States, the war fever seemed to grow stronger. Any American who still supported the French Revolution was called a democrat, a mobocrat, or some other kind of rat.

After a time of army living—and the food in this new army was, indeed, pretty good—Roy was about ready to follow the flocks of ducks and geese that flew over the valley toward the south, or to go on up to Philadelphia to see his grandson, from whom he had not had a letter since arriving at the Virginia army post.

Ah-wa-o, as pretty as ever, came to the door of the cabin and called the boys in to wash up for supper and told the men that it would be ready in a few minutes.

"Beef stew," El-i-chi complained.

"Yeah," Roy said.

El-i-chi did not really have to explain, but he did. "Tastes like straw, beef. What I wouldn't give for a good venison roast."

"Know what you mean," Roy said. "But you know how it is, *Lieutenant*. You U.S. Army boys live off the fat of the land."

El-i-chi made a derisive sound with his lips, heaved himself off the fence, stretched, and looked at the sky. "Come on," he said. "If I have to eat the white man's meat that tastes like straw, so do you."

"Thought I'd mosey over to the mess hall. I think they got mutton tonight."

"Ugh." El-i-chi scowled.

"Dammit," Roy said, easing himself down off the fence, "if the Frenchies are going to do something, I wish they'd have at it.

In spite of their complaints, both men ate heartily. After the meal, while Ah-wa-o put the boys to bed in the loft, Roy and El-i-chi drank tea and watched the fire in the open fireplace. Ah-wa-o came back down from the loft. The voices of the two boys were muted, sleepy.

"Winter soon," Roy said. "No French fleet is going to try a winter crossing."

"Roy," El-i-chi said, "you sound to me like a restless man."

"Well, aren't *you*?"

"No," El-i-chi answered frankly. "I'm fairly content, considering the circumstances. The United States has allowed that I'm an officer and a gentleman. They're paying me more for wearing the uniform of a lieutenant than they'd pay me as a scout . . . and all I have to do is see that there's a full complement of scouts available."

"Tell me about *that*," Roy said. "I could make more money trapping and skinning skunks back home."

"Now, when I hired you, Roy," El-i-chi said with a grin, "you didn't complain about the pay."

"Don't you fun me, boy," Roy said. "Have some respect for these gray hairs and remember that I'm a dad-blamed general in the Ten-oh-by-God-see militia."

"Yes, sir, General," El-i-chi said. He winked at Ah-wa-o, who hid a smile behind her hand. "But we don't have any use for Tennessee militia generals in this professional army."

"Provisional army," Roy corrected.

"Same thing," El-i-chi said. "Only very professional fighting men are allowed."

"Bull," Roy said, rising. He walked to the door. "It's getting just a bit too deep in here, so I'm leaving before I have to go put on my hip boots."

He opened the door and almost got hit on the nose by a uniformed private soldier who had been just about to knock. "Mail for the lieutenant," the soldier said.

Roy took the letter and examined the handwriting.

"It's from Ena," he said, handing it to El-i-chi. He closed the door behind him, sat back down, and waited as El-i-chi opened the letter.

"Shall I let you read it first," El-i-chi teased the very curious Roy, "or will it be all right if I just read it out loud?"

"Out loud will be fine," Roy replied, ignoring the barb.

El-i-chi bent to put the letter into the light from the candle on the table. "It's from Ena."

"Told you that," Roy said.

"It begins 'Beloved Brother,' " El-i-chi said.

"Well, go on," Roy urged, as El-i-chi fell silent and went stiff in his chair. He leaned forward. "What's the matter, boy?"

El-i-chi read the rest of the one-page letter in silence, then, rising, handed it to Roy. He paced to the fireplace, then back, his hands clenching.

Roy held a candle with one hand. He had to hold the letter at arm's length, and still the neat handwriting blurred so that it took him awhile to make out the message that was contained in the first sentence after the greeting.

"Beloved Brother," the letter said, "there is no way to ease the shock of telling you that Ha-ace, our father, is dead."

"Oh, damn," Roy said before reading on.

"Ah-wa-o, we will leave at first light," El-i-chi instructed. "We will travel light and fast."

"Yes," Ah-wa-o said, although she did not yet know the reason for her husband's agitation.

"You can't do it like that," Roy said. "You're not just a hired scout now. You're a part of the army. You've accepted a commission."

"You will stay, Roy," El-i-chi said. "You will explain it to them."

"They may not listen," Roy cautioned. "Look, another day, another few days . . . you can resign a commission, El-i-chi. You can make it legal. If you just take off, you're a deserter."

"You will explain," El-i-chi insisted. "Now I must prepare for the trip." He cast a significant look at Ah-wa-o. She would have to be told that her father was dead, and he preferred to do it in privacy.

"And then, too, El-i-chi," Roy said, "if you're interested in traveling fast, maybe you'd better consider this: I'm ready to go home myself. I was getting about as much action in my office in Knoxville as I'm getting here with the provisional army. So I'll stay and explain it to the brass that you had an emergency at home, and then I'll travel along behind you, slow and comfortable, with Ah-wa-o and the boys."

"Thank you, my friend," El-i-chi said. "As always you give wise advice. And now I must prepare."

Roy left, but he was thinking that El-i-chi had more to consider than just getting ready for the trip home. He didn't like what he'd read in Ena's letter, didn't like it at all. He wished that Renno was there to go home with El-i-chi. He was glad that he had not been asked to stay to witness Ah-wa-o's grief.

By the time Ena's letter reached El-i-chi, Ha-ace the Panther, father of Ah-wa-o the Rose, husband to Toshabe, adopted father to Renno, El-i-chi, and Ena, had been dead for over two months. His death had come with a shocking suddenness and in a manner that had further stressed the incipient rift in the Seneca tribe.

Waith Pennywhistle had been in the Cherokee-Seneca village talking with O-o-za and some of the followers of the Seneca who had been giving increasing support to the urgings of his wife, O-gas-ah, to be more aggressive in tribal affairs. Ha-ace had had no patience with those who wanted to go looking for a war between white men, and he had told Toshabe that he was going to O-o-za's longhouse to tell the white preacher that he was no longer welcome

in the village. Ha-ace never arrived at O-o-za's longhouse.
None of the three people there—O-o-za himself; his wife,
O-gas-ah; or Waith Pennywhistle—claimed to have seen
Ha-ace on the night of his death. His body had been found
near midnight by a young couple who had sneaked into
the woods to tryst. Ha-ace the Panther had been murdered by a Cherokee arrow that, judging from its deep
penetration through the heart, had been shot from only a
few feet away.

All those facts were contained in the letter that Ena
wrote to El-i-chi, along with some personal speculation,
and it was the latter that had made Roy Johnson's brow
furrow with worry.

"It is possible," Ena had written, "that somewhere
here exists a Cherokee who hated Ha-ace enough to kill
him, but surely not in my husband's village, where Ha-ace
was loved as a brother. It is possible, too, that this death
came at the hands of a Seneca, for the void left by the
departure of *both* leaders of the tribe had not been suc-
cessfully filled, and there was much enmity. And, too,
there are those who blame the new element that has
begun to surface in the Southwest Territory, white scum
such as the infamous Harp brothers, who began their
introduction to Tennessee by stealing hogs and killing off
their own unwanted babies and then moved on to worse
atrocities. I have written also to Renno in Philadelphia. I
pray to the manitous that one of you appears soon."

Little Hawk had saved most of his salary. When he
left Philadelphia, he carried enough money to buy food
along the way and to purchase a friendly little gray horse
from a farmer not far from the capital.

He rode through some of the most beautiful country
in the eastern United States—the rolling hills of southern
Pennsylvania and the plantation areas of Virginia. The
weather was kind to him. Because he was large for his age,
rode confidently, and avoided towns whenever possible,

no one challenged him. It was not uncommon at all for boys who were old enough to leave home and seek their fortunes.

He had made an excellent purchase in his horse, for it had carried him far and was still eager to get under way each morning. To keep the animal in good condition he had purchased oats and corn at every opportunity, and he never begrudged the animal the time for a bit of good graze when it was available. He had decided that horseback was the only way to travel, but that realization came after the first week or so—it took that long to wear off the soreness of his rump that had been so badly battered by cobblestones while he was being dragged under the coal wagon's horses.

The journey as far as the western Virginia mountains was a pleasant one. From there he followed the trail blazed by Daniel Boone, rode through Kentucky as winter began to make its cold breath felt, and crossed into Tennessee on a day of chill, miserable rain. He decided he would not go through Knoxville. He had been alone on the trail for a long time, and he was young and lonely. If he rode cross-country west of Knoxville to the boundary of Cherokee territory, he would end up quite near home.

Although there were farms and settlements along his route, he traveled most often through virgin forest. He had his bow. He ate mostly small animals, but once he treated himself to a roast of venison from a young deer and carried the carcass to the next farmhouse, where, in exchange for the gift of meat, he was offered a home-cooked meal and a bed for the night. He accepted readily.

"You're a mite young to be out and about so fur by yourself," the farm wife said as she watched Little Hawk do great honors to a bowl of her chicken and dumplings.

"Not really, ma'am," Little Hawk said. "I am Seneca."

"But that won't help you none if you run into them Harp fellers," the farmer warned. "That Wiley and Micajah Harp done stole more pigs and kilt more people than ole

John Watts and his Chickamauga lately. Mean as sun-burned snakes. Were I you, I'd ride from here rat on into Knoxville and take the southern route to your place."

"I appreciate your concern," Little Hawk said. "Per-haps I will."

But once he was out of sight of the home of the friendly settler and his wife, he turned the horse's head toward the south, not toward Knoxville.

Chapter XIII

Adan was able to make good time after having left the longboat. He followed the river to a point near the fort and the inlet and could not resist a chuckle when he observed the activity around the fort and the Spanish colonel's residence-headquarters. The Spaniards were like a swarm of hornets buzzing around in futile fury after their nest had been knocked down. On the bay, lanterns bobbed on a number of boats, and the shouts of the searchers came to him with great clarity across the water. He could afford to wait—the night was only half gone. He made himself as comfortable as possible considering his sodden clothing and the inevitable mosquitoes and waited. One by one the searching boats put back into the St. Augustine docks.

It was Adan's good fortune to have begun his swim across the inlet just as the tide reached dead low. It was a calm night, and there was only a gentle swell moving into the mouth of the inlet. The water was as smooth as glass at the point where Adan was to make his crossing. He started out strongly and, as it became apparent that the distance was greater than it had seemed, blessed the Holy Virgin for the slack tide. As it was, when the tide turned and began to rise, he was just over halfway across, and the building tidal current threatened to carry him away from the shore of the northern barrier island and into the broad waters of the upper bay. He called upon his reserves and swam hard, his lungs burning and his arms and legs feeling more and more like lead.

When his feet finally touched the sandy bottom and he was able to wade ashore on the tip of the island north of the inlet, he fell onto his face in the sand and lay there until he began to get his breath back.

A crescent moon was riding the night sky. The brilliant field of stars was the main source of light. Adan still had to travel a short distance up the island and then swim the river to the mainland rendezvous point. When an early morning feel freshened the air, he pushed himself up, got to his feet, and looked out to sea. In the ghostly light he saw a faint outline that caused his heart to thump. He had waited too long to begin his swim, had taken too long in the crossing. The *Seneca Glory* was entering the inlet, her sails searching for the faint night breezes. She would be past him and into the upper bay leading to the river before he could swim across. If he missed her, he'd have to hole up for an entire day and wait for the next night. He decided on a desperate measure. He waited until the sloop was almost opposite him. He cupped his hands around his mouth and called out, "Nate! Nate Ridley!"

At first he thought that he hadn't been heard; then there was a slapping of rigging and sails, and the *Glory* was angling toward him.

"Where away?" Nate called out from the sloop.

"On the point," Adan responded, then plunged into the water and swam to meet the sloop. Soon he was being hauled aboard, and Nate was busy turning the sloop and tacking into the onshore wind. The course forced upon him by the wind took him toward the southern side of the inlet. He saw lanterns moving on the tip of the barrier island.

"It'll be a near thing," Nate told Adan, who had come to stand beside him at the wheel. "Where's Renno?"

Adan explained the circumstances as Nate nodded grimly. The *Glory* slipped along in near silence, with only an occasional slap of sail and the gurgle of water past her bow. The ship moved closer to the beach. Adan could hear the sound of the Spaniards' voices as they searched the northern tip of the island. He held his breath, then had to breathe, for things seemed to be moving in slow motion. The *Glory* was barely making headway against the incoming tide, and just as it seemed that she was about to go aground on the seaward point of the island, the breeze gusted, shifted to the southwest, and filled the sails, causing the keel to bite in. Now Nate could steer her off the point and into the open sea.

"Do you think they saw us?" he asked Adan as the shore slowly receded behind them.

"Let us pray not," Adan said. "Had they seen us, I think someone would have sounded an alert."

"If they saw us, we can expect company at dawn," Nate said. "And if ships put out in pursuit, it will be next to impossible to sail down the coast to pick up Renno and Beth."

* * *

No air stirred in the little bower that Renno had made. Mercifully, not even the mosquitoes seemed to be able to find their way through the walls of cut brush that he had built up around Beth and himself, or perhaps it was simply too hot for any self-respecting mosquito to ply her sanguine trade. Renno had stripped away his shirt. Beth had opened the collar of her dress.

The heat that continued to build as the sun rose toward the zenith did not prevent Beth and Renno from engaging in animated talk, a continuous exchange—begun by Beth—that was designed to bridge the years of their separation.

At first, as Renno spoke of An-da, Beth's heart twisted in jealous torment, but then she wept softly and held his hand so tightly that there were fingernail marks in his palm as he told of An-da's terrible death and his final encounter with the evil shaman Hodano.

"We will take little Ta-na into our house," she said. "Oh, I long to see him, and I ache to hold Renna in my arms and kiss Little Hawk."

"About Ta-na, we will see," Renno said gently. "He is a brother to little Gao."

And so the exchange continued into the steamy afternoon, a cascade of words that made Renno's throat dry and left him speechless as Beth spoke of her growing disillusionment with her life in the court circles of London, of the shallowness of the man whom she had once intended to marry, Joffre Jowett. She did not tell Renno that she had been bedded by Joffre while Renno was in Africa and afterward, nor did he ask. She felt guilty, but she had the feeling that it wouldn't have mattered to Renno if she had told him. That being the case, it was unnecessary to speak of something that caused her shame and regret; and, if she sensed wrongly that Renno would have shrugged away what she had done while they were separated, great harm was averted by her silence. All that mattered was that they were together now. She was not frightened, not even when Jean Claude Lemaître led a search party of French sailors and Spanish soldiers within fifty feet of their place of concealment. She had confidence that Renno would see her out of Florida.

"Do you know," she said after Lemaître's group was safely in the distance, "I'm rather glad that my ships were taken by the French. Perhaps it was God's way of telling me that I have been a fool, that my place is with you forever. I am yours to command, my love. What we do when we get back to Wilmington is your decision."

Renno still had his doubts. Beth's house in Wilmington was not a mansion by English standards, but it was infinitely more luxurious than his longhouse.

"I'm looking forward to seeing Ena and your mother." She smiled ruefully. "Toshabe never really took to me, you know."

"She did not dislike you."

"No, but she didn't think that I was a proper wife for you." Her mouth formed a determined line. "Well, I'll just have to prove to her that I can be a good Seneca wife, won't I?"

Renno laughed. It was difficult to understand why, but he felt as if he had never been separated from Beth. It was puzzling, for he did not consider himself to be a fickle man. He'd never been a womanizer, although it was true that he had loved and married three women.

As Beth fell silent and dozed, he considered an interesting question. Emily had been his first love, the mother of two of his children. She had come to him from the Place across the River to advise him and to give him courage in time of danger. He knew that she was waiting, that she would be there when his time came to join his ancestors. But what of An-da? Why had her spirit never come to him? She was Seneca, and the Master of Life had promised her, as He had with all Seneca, a spot in that place where the old ones lived. Thus, she would be waiting, too. And in the future Beth would come to her time as well.

He shrugged, got to his knees, and peered out toward the sea. The blue waters sparkled in the afternoon sun. A small surf lifted into white foam and then surged down with a *whoosh* onto the dark strand. He told himself that the Master of Life must have worked out such questions as this long ago. Moreover, he was incapable of dwelling too long on morbid matters. He was a man of action, and this passive waiting was the cause of his wayward thoughts. He turned and looked at Beth. Perhaps she would not long endure life on the frontier. She had said that she was still a rich woman. That was good. At any time, if she tired of life as a Seneca, she could go back to her own.

That thought made his heart heavy. As he examined the flawless skin of her face and watched the rise and fall of her bosom as she breathed, he knew a desire that threatened to consume him.

Into his new reverie, which was decidedly erotic, came distant sounds. Brush crashed under some sort of blade. Searchers were approaching from the river side of the island, and it soon became apparent that they were following the very clear trail that he had made in forcing his way through the dense undergrowth.

It was, he estimated, only two hours to sunset and sheltering darkness. He considered his options. Movement in the jungle of oceanside growth was too difficult to allow them to stay ahead of the searchers and would become impossible as the light failed. There were only two places to go: the woods with its dense undergrowth, or the strand. He peered out again toward the sea. Emptiness. Even if Adan had been successful in meeting the *Glory*, Nate would lie offshore until after dark.

He put his hand over Beth's mouth and woke her gently. Her green eyes went wide, then narrowed as he put his finger to his lips to indicate silence, and took his hand from her lips. *Come*, he mouthed.

* * *

The strand was wide. Wind-rippled dunes lay just outside the hedge of maritime forest. Some past storm tide had risen far above normal and had cut a bank, only three feet high, along the front of the dunes. Renno picked a spot that offered a good field of fire toward the forest, a semicircular cut that also offered them some protection from the flanks. He laid out his weapons—pistols, his musket, the longbow and its quiver of arrows. He left the tomahawk in his belt.

"If they are wise they will circle to the north or south before emerging from the brush," he said.

"This is mine," Beth said, taking the longbow. "You can reload the rifle much faster than I."

"So," he said.

She laughed. "I have a certain feeling of déjà vu."

Renno nodded. Together they had faced enemies before. He knew that she was a master of the longbow, that she would take a toll of the attackers. But as they waited and the sun sank lower, the sea behind them was still empty. He could only guess at the number of men who would come at them from the forest; there had been ten aboard Lemaître's longboat. He chanted a prayer under his breath and searched for an answer from the manitous. He tried to analyze his feelings, but he sensed nothing. He felt, however, that he should speak his thoughts lest he never have another chance after the attack began.

"I pray that you will be content with me, Beth," he said, "for, by the manitous, it saddened me when I left you behind in England. You have been in my thoughts often, and I am grateful to the Master of Life that He has brought you to me again."

"Thank you," she whispered with tears in her eyes.

There was no time for further talk. The solid wall of brush heaved, and the contingent of French sailors and Spanish soldiers began to emerge one by one. Lemaître was the last to appear. His ornate uniform was soaked with perspiration and torn from his trip through the junglelike forest.

Renno had laid several false trails before settling on his current position, and the tracks were clean in the pristine, white sand of the dunes. Two men began to scout cautiously toward the forward edge of the low dunes, muskets at the ready.

"There are ten," Renno whispered. He began to feel more confident that Beth and he would live to see the *Glory* sailing southward to find them, after all.

The men spread out in a long line and advanced toward the water. The two eager ones were still in the lead. "Take the one on the left at your maximum accurate range," Renno instructed softly. Beth nocked an arrow, tested the bow, and waited tensely.

"Now," she whispered, her eyes squinted in concentration. She rose to her knees, and the bowstring sang as she pulled and released in one swift, practiced motion. The arrow winged toward its fleshy target. She had aimed at the man's heart, but the shot went high and pierced the Frenchman's throat, the point lodging in the hollow under the Adam's apple to cut flesh and arteries and to bring instant death as it severed the spinal cord. Before the man fell, Renno's musket spoke, and the other eager one was knocked backward by the force of a ball that pierced his heart.

"Now there are eight," Renno said as the enemy's shouts of consternation and warning slowed the advance.

Lemaître had sought cover behind a low dune. Renno and Beth could hear him urging his men on, telling them that it was their duty to kill those who had brought death to their companions.

It was some time before the enemy began to move forward again. They were more cautious this time, splitting their forces. Lemaître, having seen the smoke from Renno's musket, pointed out the pair's whereabouts to his men and instructed them to take the position from the flanks.

Renno faced south, Beth faced north. Musket balls began to whisper their deadly passage above their heads, but by staying low behind the tidal cut they were safe. To the south one man began to edge toward the water. When he was in a position to see Renno and Beth, he shouted his discovery and motioned to the others. Renno allowed for the long range, aimed the muzzle of his musket high, and the ball fell from its trajectory to smash into a French stomach. The man fell and tried to crawl, crying out in agony. The others backed out of range.

"Seven," Beth said.

Lemaître was haranguing the men in French, calling them women, cowards, and telling them that they were being held at bay by one man and a woman. "Come!" he ordered. "I, Lemaître, will lead you."

And, indeed, he stepped out from his cover and advanced swiftly toward Renno's position. The other six followed, running now, and Renno heard Beth's bow begin to sing at his back. He killed, then reloaded as the men drew nearer, nearer, and Beth's bow continued its work behind him. He missed with his reloaded musket and laid it aside to seize his pistols. Musket balls plowed the sand in front of his face. He waited until the men were within range of his pistols and fired. He dropped one man but missed another, for just before he fired, that man jerked to a halt, then turned and ran.

"Two here," Renno reported.

In front of Beth lay one body. "One was hit in the leg," she said. "He crawled back into the dunes."

Now there were four, one of them with an arrow in him. All was quiet.

"Lemaître very conveniently fell down before he was clear of the dunes," Beth remarked.

The sun was low. Long shadows covered the positions of Lemaître and the other three survivors of the attack.

Renno cast a glance toward the sea. At last he saw the
Glory's sail to the north. The sloop was hugging the coast,
moving southward. He nudged Beth and pointed. She
grinned and said, "Well, bless Adan and Nate."

The sloop would be directly offshore in half an hour,
Renno estimated. It would still be light. Since there was
no time to build a fire for a signal—and if he had tried he
was sure Lemaître and his men would have had some
slight objections—he would have to rely on the good eyes
of Nate and Adan to spot them on the beach. But that,
too, presented a problem: He could hardly stand up and
wave his shirt while Lemaître and three armed men lay
concealed in the dunes.

He took the longbow from Beth's hand and gave her
the musket. "Try to lower the odds by one with this," he
told her.

She put a hand on his arm to stop him, but he was
gone, running across the sand toward the dune line and
his enemies. Two muskets fired. One ball kicked up sand
just behind Renno as he zigzagged. Another snipped at his
hair, making a little smacking sound. He dived and rolled
and came up with his tomahawk in hand. One Frenchman
behind the dune, desperately trying to reload his musket,
lifted it and pointed it at Renno with the ramrod still in
the barrel. The ramrod could be a deadly missile at close
range, so Renno did not give the man time to pull the
trigger. The white Indian released his tomahawk with all
his strength, rolled to one side, and came up on his hands
and knees after hearing a solid thud—his throw had been
accurate. The tomahawk didn't want to come out of the
Frenchman's forehead, but Renno yanked hard and freed
it.

He heard Beth's musket bark and glanced quickly
behind him to see another Frenchman fall. The musket
that dropped from the dead man's hands had been aimed
at Renno's back.

The wounded Spaniard had pulled Beth's arrow from

his thigh only to cause the wound to bleed profusely. He was scrambling for his musket as Renno approached. He moaned as death came to him with a flick of Renno's wrist.

"You!" Lemaître called from the protection of a dune. "I surrender. Do you hear me? I fight no more."

Renno looked back toward Beth. She had reloaded and had the musket pointed toward the sound of the French captain's voice.

"Come out, then," Renno ordered, moving silently toward the dune, his tomahawk ready.

"I am laying down my rifle," Lemaître called. "I am now going to stand up."

His fine but soiled uniform was sodden, and sand stuck to the wet cloth. He had lost his hat. He extended his left hand toward the white Indian.

"Watch out, Renno!" Beth cried even as she fired, but too quickly. Her shot caused Lemaître to flinch as he pulled a pistol from behind his back and leveled it at Renno. The ball from the Frenchman's weapon and Renno's tomahawk met in midair with a clang of metal on metal. The tomahawk went spinning off, and Renno dove toward the Frenchman as Lemaître pulled another pistol from his sash.

Renno moved with the speed of a striking snake, his hand closing on Lemaître's wrist to send the pistol shot into the air. With his right hand he buried the Spanish stiletto under the arch of the Frenchman's ribs, twisted, and found the heart, then jumped back to avoid the heavy fall of Lemaître's body.

Within minutes Beth and Renno stood together at the edge of the surf. The white Indian waved his shirt, and Beth waved her hand and smiled. The sloop's sails dropped, and she rested on the swells as a boat was launched. Renno and Beth waded to the longboat and climbed in to the excited greetings of Adan. Nate waited on board the sloop. He blushed when Beth hugged him with enthusiasm and kissed him on the cheek.

"That's very nice, Beth," Nate said, "and I appreciate it, but turn me loose so I can get this vessel under way before we have half the Spanish and French navies after us."

The *Seneca Glory* sailed northward in growing darkness. Beth had changed into dry clothing—a seaman's trousers and shirt. Renno had let the balmy air dry him. He stood by the rail with Beth, watching the brave sailors, who had volunteered to make the trip, trim sails for the run toward home. Nate gave over the wheel to a seaman and came to stand with them.

"I will want to hear what happened onshore," he said. "Adan, it seems, had an exciting time."

Adan, having heard his name, joined the group. "From the bodies scattered on that beach, I think that these two enjoyed an even more interesting interlude."

Renno was silent. While it was the Indian way to boast of victories, he did not feel like counting coup for the death of men who may have been formidable at sea, in their own element, but who were fairly easy victims ashore. "Beth fought well," he said simply.

"Renno," Adan ventured, "I've been doing some thinking. The *Huntington Pride* is sitting just inside that inlet, and unless they've changed things, there wasn't one man on her to guard her."

"No," Beth protested.

"It would take at least six men to get her anchor up and raise her sails," Adan continued.

"I will not hear of it," Beth told him forcefully. "It is my ship, and I say let her be. We are safely away. I will not risk lives just to recover a ship."

"We could sneak around the point in a longboat," Adan continued, "and be under way before the Spaniards knew what was happening."

"And the fort?" Nate asked. "Are the gunners going to sit there and watch the ship sail out of the inlet?"

"Well, it seemed like a good idea," Adan said.

"They'd blow the *Pride* out of the water," Nate declared. "Tell the man he's insane, Renno."

Renno pondered for a moment before he spoke. "Yes, they would fire on the *Pride*, but would they fire on the Frenchman?"

"No, Renno," Beth pleaded.

"In God's name, you're right!" Adan cried, fire in his eyes. "They took something from us. Let us take something even more valuable in return." He turned to Beth and grasped her hands. "We can take the *Sans Doute*. I know we can. Then we'd have a ship that could go anywhere without concern. Or we could trade her for a good merchantman when this war with France is over."

"Renno," Beth begged, "please, no."

For a moment Renno envisioned the strong, squat form of Billy the Pequot standing at the bow of the sloop. The Pequot was holding a harpoon at the ready while looking over his shoulder at Renno. Yes, the French had taken something from all of them: Beth's ship, Adan's livelihood, and Renno's friend.

"I will not ask any man to go against his will," Renno said.

Adan whooped with joy and ran to gather the six volunteers who had manned the *Glory*. After Renno told them of the plan, he said, "I will not minimize the danger. As a result of Beth's rescue, the French ship might now be heavily guarded. If we succeed in taking her, the fort might fire on us as we try to leave the harbor."

The crew volunteered enthusiastically. Each of the sailors had lost a ship and shipmates to the French. They were eager to strike a counterblow. Nate, too, said that he wanted to go, and he argued briefly when Renno told him to stay on the *Glory* with Beth and at least one other man to take the sloop home to Wilmington if things went awry in St. Augustine Bay.

There was no time to waste. Renno, Adan, and five

seamen rowed around the northern point into the bay and, with silenced oars, slipped past the silent *Huntington Pride*.

"Everyone's asleep," Adan whispered. "If we had more men, we could take both ships."

Night lights burned on both vessels. As they approached the *Sans Doute*, her gunports seemed to be evil, alert eyes, watching the longboat come near enough to be destroyed. A watchman stood at the ship's bow. Renno pointed him out to Adan.

"He's mine," Adan whispered.

"Quietly," Renno told him. "Wait until I have had time to board amidships."

A boarding ladder hung limply down the side of the ship near the bow. After the longboat was eased in, Adan climbed across and onto the ladder and clung there while the boat moved to a point where the ship's rail was lowest. Renno whispered final instructions to the men, who had learned to regard him with a kind of reverence, then climbed up and over the rail, moving silently in his moccasins. He found the other watchman dozing on a hatch cover and made the man's sleep permanent.

Next he ran to the lighted quarters and slipped in. Two other men were asleep in a cabin that housed ship's officers, and they quickly joined the watchman in death. Four men in all, and then the ship was theirs. Renno called the seamen up from the waiting longboat, which was lashed at the stern to be towed. Men scampered aloft, and soon the sails began to unfurl. Others worked the capstan so that as the sails caught the light breath of night air, the anchor was lifted from the sandy bottom and the ship began to move on the smooth water.

To their left lay the huge, menacing fort. Its big guns were capable of demolishing the ship before she could round the point and make it safely to sea.

"I had more difficulty stealing my first ship," Adan

said as the *Doute*'s sails billowed in a little gust and the ship seemed to surge forward.

"Reserve your judgment," Renno advised just as a voice hailed them in Spanish, demanding to know why the ship was under way. Adan started to answer, but Renno hushed him quickly and responded in French. Precious moments were thus gained as the shore watch explained that he did not speak French. Renno bawled out that he, Jean Claude Lemaître, who was going in pursuit of the dastards who had stolen the Englishwoman, could not speak Spanish. Then, at Renno's cue, Adan called out in Spanish the same explanation that Renno had given in French. For long, agonizing minutes they stared at the guns of the Castillo de San Marcos, expecting at any moment to see them belch fire; but then the ship was rounding the point and beginning to respond to the swells, the breathing of the ocean. The gentle night wind carried them into darkness toward the one light on the waiting *Glory*. Soon the sloop was tied behind the large man-of-war, and a freshening morning breeze sent them romping northward.

Renno was at the wheel steering, for the big French ship required every man of the small crew to keep her sails trimmed, so that Nate and Adan were working with the seamen. Beth had found the galley and came up with a cup of hot tea for Renno.

"I'll have food for the rest of them shortly," she said.

"You are a lady of many talents," Renno said.

"Renno?"

"Yes."

"I died a little when you insisted on going after this ship."

He considered his answer. "I will change that which I can change for you."

"I think I understand. I can expect you to continue to fight the fights of others. Good heavens, are you a knight of old, reincarnated? I have plenty of money. I did not need this ship."

"Adan did."

"Yes," she relented, moving to put her arm around his waist. "I ask you to change nothing, my love. Only to be with me."

"Not even those things that need changing?"

"Such as?"

"I would exchange this hunger I have for a bed and my arms around you."

"Yes, gladly," she said.

But with the afternoon came a storm that served to keep all hands busy far into the night. When it was over and Adan had taken Renno's place at the wheel, the sachem did manage to find his way to the captain's cabin, where Beth was sleeping. He took one look at her, removed his wet clothing, dried himself, and fell in exhausted slumber at her side.

When he awoke, she was not in the bed. He sat up. She was bending over the captain's little table. He walked silently to stand behind her. On the table was a pile of gold coins. She looked up and smiled delightedly. "See what I've found?"

"Since we took this ship to replace your losses, it is yours," he said.

"No." Her voice was firm. "Each man shall share in the reward. There is a standard formula for distributing prize money. Each will have his fair share, including you."

"No matter," he said.

"You found good use for the Spanish gold from Devil's Mountain," she reminded.

"Yes." He was thinking that he had used most of the Spanish gold to purchase weapons and necessities for his tribe, that he'd spent almost the last of the sum that he had withheld for himself during the trip to Philadelphia and thence to Wilmington.

"Although, as my husband, you shall never lack for money."

"So."

She stood and came into his arms. "Don't go all stoic and Indian on me," she said. "I love you, and what's mine is yours."

"I accept that gladly, but at the moment your money is the furthermost thing from my mind."

She knew exactly what he meant.

El-i-chi, traveling lightly, left the army camp in western Virginia. He carried only his musket with shot and powder, his tomahawk and knife, and a blanket for the cold nights in the mountains. He had considered taking the horse that was assigned to him by the army but decided that he would not add horse stealing to what amounted to an act of desertion. He rode a coach for three days, and then, as he directed his steps toward the mountains, he was on his own, first moving at the warrior's ground-covering pace, then walking to slow his pounding heart.

Roy Johnson helped a grief-stricken Ah-wa-o to pack the things that she wanted to take back to Tennessee with her, then assisted in getting the boys ready. Finally he went to the commanding officer's orderly room, dressed in his uniform as a general of the Tennessee militia. "Sir," he said, "I have had an urgent summons to return to my post in Knoxville."

"Sorry to see you go, Johnson," the commander told him.

"There is something else, Colonel," Roy said. "I needed one of your men, the Seneca lieutenant called El-i-chi."

"I don't understand."

"I'm saying, Colonel, that I sent El-i-chi on ahead of me with urgent messages to Governor Sevier."

"You're saying that you encouraged one of my officers to leave this camp without orders or my permission?"

"He had orders," Roy said. "From me in my capacity as a general of the Tennessee militia. If that gives you any problem, Colonel, I can have that order confirmed in writing from Governor Sevier as soon as I get to Knoxville."

"Just what occasioned this urgent call?" the colonel asked, his face turning red with anger.

Roy lied with a straight face. "Guess you've heard about that senator of ours, William Blount?"

"I have."

"Well, it seems that old Blount has raised himself an army and is about ready to start a war with the Spanish. John Sevier wants me back to stop it. Now, if you have any trouble with that, I can have it put into writing—"

"Never mind," the colonel grumbled. "When you get to Knoxville, *General* Johnson, you might send me a letter confirming the fact that the Tennessee militia has accepted this lieutenant, uh, El-i-chi, on detached service." He thought for a minute. "Or, to save paperwork, it might be best if I just write out a discharge paper now."

"Whatever you think is best . . ." Roy said nonchalantly, crossing his fingers behind his back.

The colonel reached for his pen. Roy left the orderly room, whistling and holding El-i-chi's official discharge. El-i-chi's departure had been unwise, for the charge of desertion could have followed him forever. Roy had not even hoped that things would turn out so well. He returned to the cabin to get Ah-wa-o and the boys and start for home.

Chapter XIV

A long the frontier of the United States in those last
years of the eighteenth century, when one could look
ahead to a centennial year, a date ending with double
zeros, it was not unusual to encounter curious visitors
from the old countries of Europe. Englishmen with titles
came from a nation in dire straits, a beleaguered island
country beset by drought, hunger, worrisome naval muti-
nies in the pattern of the French Revolution, riots and
looting in the streets, and continual financial crises. The
English visitors wore odd clothing and professed to be not

at all concerned about that fellow Napoléon, who had
conquered Italy and the Low Countries and had brought
England's last ally, the once mighty Austria, to her knees.
Had not England been saved once more by an act of God,
as she had been saved from the Spanish Armada? After all,
Napoléon's invasion force, turned back from Ireland by
violent storms, had not been nearly as imposing as the
fleet that the Spaniards had sent against Elizabeth.

In the cities of the eastern United States, including
the capital, these visiting titled Englishmen praised the
friendship between old England and the former colonies.
But it was not only Englishmen who wanted to see the
young nation that had defeated mighty England. Germans
came, as did monacled, spade-bearded Prussian barons.
And all wanted to see, in addition to New York and
Philadelphia, the fabled American wilderness and experience for themselves the American frontier—without, of
course, actually having to face any of the bloodthirsty,
red-skinned savages, whose fierce resistance to white settlement had made the saga of the westering United States
so exciting for Europeans. The moneyed visitors cheer-
fully endured primitive conditions in their camps in order
to aim their rifle barrels at a buffalo, a deer, or in a few
lucky cases a mountain lion.

One of the more notable visitors traveling through
America was already known to Renno, Little Hawk, and
Renna, having been introduced the year before in Philadelphia, at William Blount's home. He was Louis Philippe,
the duc d'Orléans, the twenty-four-year-old son of Louis
Philippe Joseph de Bourbon-Orléans. On the surface, the
young man who would one day be king of France was just
another titled traveler who, tiring of the wars and alarms
of Europe, sought amusement and edification in a study of
conditions in a wild and daunting country. As Louis Philippe
was feted and honored in the East by those who had not
turned totally against the French Revolution, he acted as

an ambassador of goodwill even while French ships were
seizing American merchantmen.

He was a charming fellow and, because of his unusual
background, fascinating to the wealthy merchants and politicians of the Eastern Seaboard. In 1790, as a very young
man, he had sided with the Revolutionaries by joining the
Jacobin Club, to become known as one of the most pro-
gressive members of the nobility. He pleased the sansculotte
lotte masses by resigning his royal command of an infantry
regiment to join the Revolutionary Army of the North, in
which he was quickly awarded the command of a brigade.
In his opinion, he won his place in the new France by
leading his brigade in several revolutionary battles.

Perhaps Louis Philippe had taken his guidance from
his father, who had changed his own name to Louis Egalité
and had voted for the execution of Louis XVI in 1793. And
perhaps, like the self-styled Egalité, the young duke was
surprised when he, like his father, was still considered
suspect by the more radical Revolutionaries who loved no
spectacle more than the flow of bright, red, royal blood
from a severed royal neck.

At any rate, Louis Philippe proved to be either more
swift of foot or more intelligent than his unsuccessfully
converted commoner father, Louis Egalité, for the younger Louis saw the drift of things and realized that the
Revolution was stubbornly intent on exterminating every
vestige of the old ruling class, regardless of one's service
to its cause.

Sure enough, the elder Louis came to know the hate-
ful kiss of the iron lady of the Revolution, but Louis
Philippe was in Switzerland, teaching at the College of
Reichenau under an assumed name. The guillotine that
had deprived his father of his head in Paris had made
Louis Philippe the duc d'Orléans and put him in direct
line for, considering the times, a thing of doubtful value—
the throne of France.

He was approached by royal intriguers who begged him to style himself as the king of France in exile. The young man refused. Some very few said he refused because he believed in the Revolution, even if it had killed his father and numerous friends, associates, and relatives. Others said that he was a wise young fellow and knew that the time was not right to claim the throne. Only a very, very few knew the real reason why he scorned his former peers and refused to stand actively against the Revolution. Among those who knew was a cocky little general named Napoléon Bonaparte, who had sent discreet messengers to Louis Philippe over the Alps from his campaign headquarters in Italy. In an uncertain world, Louis Philippe sensed that opportunity had come to him, that the little general was a friend worth having. After all, his family's lands had long since been confiscated and were being enjoyed by a few high-ranking Revolutionaries in the name of "the people." Revolution, Louis had wisely noted, merely meant exchanging one set of privileged few for another set who learned quite quickly to appreciate the finer things of life. Because Louis was now a penniless refugee who had to teach for a living, he would do nothing to jeopardize his life.

So it was that when the man who was first in the line of succession to the throne of France sailed for the United States in 1797, he was no idle tourist, despite his efforts to make it seem so.

After his visit to Philadelphia, Louis Philippe traveled throughout the eastern part of the United States, where he learned that the bloody excesses in his homeland had begun to turn public opinion against the Revolutionaries.

"Monsewer," a grizzled veteran of Wayne's American Legion told him, "it just ain't fittin' to go around cuttin' the heads off purty girls like that there Marie whatever her name was."

Louis didn't bother to explain that Marie Antoinette

had, in fact, been a rather ugly lady who stank. He did allow himself the satisfaction of regaling his audience of congressmen and wealthy Philadelphia merchants—the ex-soldier having become one of the latter—with the story of a ball that Marie Antoinette had held in the Palais Royal, where she had lit the ballroom with thousands of tallow candles . . . on a warm night, in a time when it was considered deleterious to one's health to wash all over . . . when ladies as well as gentlemen used perfumes instead of soap . . . when the fashionably ornate gowns could not be washed and were merely brushed . . .

He felt that he learned a lot about the American character when not one person in his audience understood the meaning of his subtly expressed repugnance. In fact, especially when he traveled beyond the mountains into Tennessee, he found that most Americans still believed that bathing all over happened only when one fell into a creek and that most homes smelled like a bear's den.

The veteran-businessman who had been concerned about cutting the heads off "purty" girls seemed to be more typical of eastern-establishment opinion than Thomas Jefferson, who, although he disapproved of some of the excess carnage of the revolution in France, still propounded the virtues of liberty for all men. And so Louis limited himself to listening whenever he could and to being gallant and entertaining. When he heard or saw something interesting or unusual, he recorded the event in his ever-present journal.

Being broke, Louis Philippe often had to sing for his supper by speaking of conditions in France. He was dependent upon rich friends who, impressed by foreign titles, financed his travels. Fortunately, there were enough Americans who honored the old, continental ideals about royalty to make his stay and his travels, for the main part, comfortable.

At any rate, it was the frontier that interested him

both from a personal viewpoint and from the perspective of his mission.

France was well on the way toward a return to greatness, thanks largely to his friend Napoléon Bonaparte. But France could not be truly great until she regained her foreign colonies. The first step was to force the sick man of Europe, old Spain, to return to France the territory at the mouth of the Mississippi. And since the American frontier seemed to be in flux, with resentment toward the federal government being constantly exhibited by westerners, perhaps he could promote an alliance with the frontiersmen, with the objective of making their homes a part of French America in the future.

Many men had written and said that there was nothing new under the sun. Louis Philippe's mission into the land of the Cherokee was illustrative of that fact. The earliest Frenchmen in America had practiced the same techniques that were in Louis Philippe's plans: He was unofficially empowered to promise total autonomy to any Indian tribe that would ally itself with France once Spain had been expelled from the Mississippi region. Such an arrangement would, as it had in the past, set Indian against Indian; but that problem was not worthy of consideration in view of the cosmic importance of making France the most powerful nation in the world—with a place in the new order for at least three members of the former ruling class: Louis and his brothers.

Knoxville entertained the visiting Frenchman, if not royally, at least with enthusiasm and good, solid, frontier food. He found that admiration for the Revolution had not altogether faded among the rugged individualists who had made a place for themselves in the wilderness, and John Sevier's agreement that it would be desirous to oust Spain from the Mississippi *and* from Florida made Louis think that here, at least, was one potential ally.

Louis's party left Knoxville in midafternoon, took a

erry across the Holston River, and halted for the night at
town named after William Blount's wife, Mary. Maryville
vas a young town amid farmlands recently cleared and
mmature fruit trees newly planted. It lay between the
Little River and the Tennessee and was a point of conflict
n the current treaty negotiations between the U.S. government and the Cherokee Nation.

"Well, it's this way, monsewer," a salty frontiersman
explained to Louis. "When it's time to git more land,
we'uns jest start negotiating a new treaty with the Injuns.
We picks ourselves a few prosperous-lookin' commission-
ers, and we sics 'em on a few of the Injun chiefs with a
couple of gallons of good moonshine and maybe a little bit
of money."

Under the terms of the new treaty, any white settler's
dwelling that had been erected on Indian territory would
be evacuated one month after the setting of the final
boundaries.

"Don't you believe for one minute," Louis was told,
"that we're going to evacuate Maryville and give it to the
Cherokee."

At Fort Wilkinson, known on the frontier as Tellico
Bloc House, Louis spoke with army officers and Indian
agents, gaining much knowledge about the four major
tribes of the south: the Cherokee, Chickasaw, Choctaw,
and Creek. Louis spoke English well, with a charming
accent, so he had no difficulty in communicating. He was
fascinated by frontier types and made it a habit to strike
up a conversation with any buckskinned, bearded fellow
he encountered. As a rule he was met with an attitude of
amused curiosity, which he decided was the characteristic
friendliness of the westerner.

"Funny thing, friend," said one lanky, bearded trap-
per after being questioned at length about Indians he had
encountered in his work, "Injuns don't rot as quick as a
white man when they's kilt."

"Amazing," Louis said. "What is the reason for that, do you think?"

"Don't rightly know," the old-timer replied. "Maybe 'cause them Injuns eat better'n us'ens. Maybe 'cause they don't drink as much whiskey. They's some say it's the white man's gulping of whiskey that sets up the putrefaction."

With dutiful zeal, Louis Philippe set down that interesting bit of information in his diary, along with the other gems of wisdom that he acquired. Being a lusty young man and having a gentleman's appreciation of feminine beauty, he took an interest in Indian morals and recorded, wrongly of course, that marriage was unknown among Indians: "An Indian may take as many wives as he can feed," he wrote. "He takes them on and turns them away like servants."

He might have learned more about Cherokee women, for he wrote in his diary: "All Cherokee women are public women in the full meaning of the phrase."

But it was not for his astuteness as an observer that Louis had come to the frontier. He was slowly wending his way toward the man whom he had been told was the most influential leader among the Cherokee, a chief named Rusog. He had requested to be taken by his Tennessee guides to the land of the most belligerent of the Cherokee, the Chickamauga, but the agents of the state, not wanting it said that a friendly French nobleman had been scalped while on a tour of the Southwest Territory, very carefully kept him among the friendly villages.

"Today," Louis wrote, "I was served a very good corn bread with beans cooked into it. It was called *gato*."

"Do you, Renno, take this woman, Beth, to be your lawful wedded wife?"

They stood before the altar of St. Phillips Church. Beth was in pastel blue. Renno wore a formal suit. His hair had been trimmed. At Beth's side stood Renna, radiant in blue to match Beth's gown, holding a bouquet of chrysanthemums and Queen Anne's lace. Adan was acting as best man. Giving the bride away was Nate Ridley, with his wife serving as matron of honor.

Renno's voice was strong as he said, "I do."

Beth looked up into his face with a faint smile as she made her vows in return. He touched his lips lightly to hers when told by the minister that he might kiss the bride, and then they were walking among well-wishers, with the traditional rice getting down the neck of Renno's shirt, Beth smiling, and Renna laughing as Adan, Moses Tarpley, and Nate demanded their right to kiss the bride.

The wedding feast was at the Ridleys', and it was a festive occasion, made poignant for good friends and cousins by the knowledge that a coach had been purchased and was being refurbished in readiness to take Renno, his bride, and his daughter from Wilmington. The route would lead west, for upon the return from Florida a letter had awaited Renno—a letter from his new friend Thomas Jefferson—informing him that the sachem's son, Hawk Harper, after a not fully explained incident of violence, had left Philadelphia to return to his home in the Cherokee Nation.

Jefferson's letter expressed concern for the safety of a boy who had set out alone on such a journey, and Beth voiced her own fears; but Renno took the news with outward calm. He knew that Little Hawk was capable of making the long trek—if he were not set upon by footpads, or one of the wild bears of the mountains, or by renegade Indians. He would not allow his concern for his son to eat away at him, impair his own effectiveness, or cause him to act precipitously—Beth had business affairs that had to be seen to before they could leave Wilmington—but until he reached his home village and looked into his son's face, there would be a deep black void of secret fear inside him.

The *Sans Doute* had become a U.S. warship in exchange for a tall French West Indian merchantman that
had been taken as a prize in the undeclared war that
continued at sea. Renamed after the first Huntington ship,
the *Seneca Warrior,* she was left in the charge of Adan,
with Moses to captain her while Adan tended the business
on shore. The little *Glory* was plying busily between
coastal ports, staying close enough to shore to be reasonably safe from the French picaroons. Beth invited Adan to
buy his way into her firm as a full partner. He had accepted with alacrity, and Renno teasingly told Beth that
she had become a true aristocrat, earning money from
another man's labors.

"That, dear heart," she said, "is the nature of the
world, and the most desirable state of affairs—to have
money working for one instead of depending totally upon
the labor of one's own back."

"I think it is nice to be rich," Renna remarked, for
the coach's baggage rack was filled with things that Beth
had called "necessities" for living on the western frontier.
Renno had groaned with each purchase and had stated
that it would take at least a dozen packhorses to move
Beth's and Renna's "necessities" across the mountains.

Then, with tears and fond good-byes and handshakes
and good wishes, they were under way. And so it was that
several members of Renno's family were on the way home
at the same time near the end of 1797.

Little Hawk had made a trek that many grown men
would not have attempted. He had traveled from the
Eastern Seaboard of the United States through Pennsylvania and Kentucky and into the new state of Tennessee.
Once he was west of the mountains and south of Kentucky
he felt that he was at home, even though there was still a
long trail ahead of him.

On the frontier, people knew the real meaning of

hospitality. Many farmers welcomed Little Hawk for a meal or for a warm place to sleep in the hay barn or gave him a bag of corn for the horse. These settlers had known a time when company was as scarce as hen's teeth, and if a stranger did show up on a man's place, he might very well have been a war-painted Indian or a hoot-owl white renegade.

More than once Little Hawk spent the night with Tennesseeans who had daughters who, by frontier standards, were nubile, and his bronzed good looks caused much batting of feminine eyelashes and open hints by a loving father that there just might be a place on the farm for a bright, hardworking young lad who wanted to build a future for himself. Closer to fourteen than thirteen, his voice—most of the time—a resonant baritone, his frame large for his age and honed to litheness, he was a good catch for a frontier maiden.

Although his experience with girls was limited to the casual contacts of childhood, he was not totally immune to feminine wiles. He gave his first real kiss to a taffy-haired lass named Naomi Burns when, with the contrivance of Naomi's mother, he accompanied the freckled-faced, budding fourteen-year-old to the spring to fetch water. Their kiss was a thoroughly interesting experience, which he wanted to repeat immediately. As it happened, Naomi desired the same, and there was an extra thirty minutes involved in fetching the water, during which Little Hawk learned that girls blossoming into womanhood have areas of rounded softnesses that, apparently, generate a warmth of their own. He returned to the house feeling slightly out of breath, and it was not entirely because he was carrying two buckets of fresh water.

With the morning he looked at the taffy-haired girl, felt a pang of genuine sorrow, and considered accepting her father's offer to stay and help clear another acre of forest during the winter for room and board and a total of five dollars in the spring.

"I ain't gonna beg ye to stay," Naomi said.

"I can't, really," Little Hawk told her.

She turned and stalked away from him, her shoulders straight, her pigtails bouncing on her back. He started to follow her.

"Well, son," Frank Burns said, "it's sorry I am that you cain't stay and hep me out with the clearing."

"I wish I could, Mr. Burns," Little Hawk said, watching Naomi as she disappeared around the corner of the barn. "But I haven't been home in a long time."

"Reckon I kin understand that," Burns allowed.

"Well, thanks very much," Little Hawk said.

"Reckon ye might come back this here way again?" Burns asked.

Little Hawk was watching the corner of the barn, and sure enough, Naomi peered around, saw that he was watching, and jerked back out of sight. "I'd sure like to, Mr. Burns."

Burns laughed. "Reckon my daughter'd like that, too."

The boy pulled the gray horse toward him and started to mount.

"Meant to tell you," Burns said. "Be best if you ride east into Knoxville 'stead of goin' on south. They's some bad'uns out there in them hills to the south. Name of Harp. Two of 'em. Calls themselfs Micajah and Wiley, and they got two women both already dropped one chile each since they come here this year. But you won't see any younguns around them Harps—folks say that soon as them women drop the chiles, them Harps bash out their brains agin a tree, just like the wild Injuns used to do to white babies."

"I don't think I'd like to meet up with them," Little Hawk said.

"No, sir. They makes their livin' by stealin' hogs. Now, folks thought that was bad enough, but maybe they felt a little sorry for them women, so they didn't do much till them Harps started stealin' horses. A hog's one thing; a horse is another. Got a posse up and went after 'em, and them Harps went off into them hills there, livin' like animals. Few people have seen 'em in there and lived to tell the story. Ain't got sense enough to live good in the woods, like an Injun. Live like animals. Now and agin someone'll go missing, and rightly or wrongly it's said that it's them Harps what done it. I knowed for sure they kilt one man for a sack of corn. Gutted him and filt his belly with rocks and tossed him in the river."

"Well, Mr. Burns, I'll be on the lookout for anyone who looks odd. I think me and Gray, here, can outrun them."

"Don't be too brave, boy," Burns warned. "I'd like to see you come back and visit us again." He grinned. "But not, I 'spect, as much as my Naomi would like it."

Little Hawk stepped up into the saddle. Burns seized the halter and held the horse's head. "I reckon you ain't takin' me serious about them Harps."

"Yes, I am," Little Hawk said.

"You say you can outrun 'em. Well, they kilt another man by runnin' him and his horse over a bluff. They was seen doin' that. And people say they was the ones kilt a woman over beyond the ridge. Cut her throat with a butcher knife and kilt her baby. I'm tellin' you, you'd best ride easy into Knoxville. They stays away from anywhere they's law."

Little Hawk didn't consider it dishonest to ride east toward Knoxville until he was out of sight of the Burns cabin. He looked back as he was about to enter the forest past the Burnses' small area of cleared farmland to see Naomi standing near the barn. She was waving. He stood tall in the stirrups and waved back.

He camped that night in a little glen near a gurgling stream. Mrs. Burns had prepared a sack of food for him. He ate cold chicken and pone and washed them down with the cool, fresh water from the stream. Gray had his corn, too, and found a few blades of dried grass to eat along the stream.

Little Hawk slept to the music of a hoot owl who, having hunted and eaten, serenaded his ladylove from a cottonwood tree as a half-moon lit the night.

He was on his way shortly after dawn. He crossed the invisible boundary between Tennessee and the Cherokee Nation just after noon, and before it was time to start looking for a place to camp and for a rabbit to roast for the evening meal, he joined the trail of a group of about ten men. He got down from the gray and walked the spoor for a time. In damp soil near a stream he saw that two of the men wore down-at-the-heels boots, and about eight others wore moccasins. They were traveling along his route, southward. The tracks were no more than a couple of hours old. He would not have been too concerned about a Cherokee hunting party—although he would not want to come upon them by surprise—but the presence of two men who wore boots gave him pause. In general, men who wore boots were white men, and in general, white men who traveled with Indians were up to no good. It was an unfortunate fact of life that some Cherokee, such as John Watts's Chickamauga, welcomed white renegades among them.

Little Hawk slept lightly with no fire, after chewing on dry corn for his evening meal. He dreamed of huge, wild-eyed men who bashed babies against trees and gutted men to fill their stomach cavities with rocks. He slept until well after sunrise because his dreams had afforded him little sound rest. He freshened himself in the stream with the warm sun on his back, had his fill of water, chewed more corn, and was prepared to move southward with some care, checking the trail of the party ahead of him, when he heard the sounds of several horsemen moving toward him on the back trail. He led Gray into a clump of trees and waited, holding the animal's nose to prevent him from sending equine greetings to the approaching horses.

The entourage that rode into the little glen beside the stream presented a splendid sight. Little Hawk guessed by the fancy riding costumes that at least three of the party were European, but it wasn't until the group had ridden closer that he noticed a certain familiarity about two of the men and remembered that he had met them in Philadelphia at the Blount house. Frenchmen of royal blood. One of them was named Louis Philippe or something like that.

Accompanying the European gentlemen were three other men, apparently Americans, one in partial uniform of the Tennessee militia, the other two in buckskins. The frontiersmen looked capable of protecting the well-dressed foreigners. Little Hawk didn't think that it would be any safer to surprise them than it would be to come upon the Cherokee hunting party without warning.

It was obvious that the two Americans in buckskins had seen the trail of the Indian hunting party with two men in worn boots. Nonetheless, they led their group southward on the trail that would eventually lead to Rusog's village and Little Hawk's home. They moved at a leisurely pace.

Gray was full of corn and acting frisky, and Little Hawk was eager, now that he was in the Cherokee Nation, to get home. He considered circling around, but the trail led up a little valley between two hogback ridges. So it was that he slowly overtook the party. He hailed them when he was within earshot, although he felt sure that the guards—for that was what the militiaman and the men in buckskins seemed to be—had seen him. One man pulled his horse to a halt and waited beside the trail. He had his hand on his musket as Little Hawk approached.

"Good day," Little Hawk said in Philadelphia fashion. "Are you going to Rusog's village?"

The frontiersman, seeing that the newcomer was just a bronzed-skinned white boy, seemed to relax. "So we be," he said. "You?"

"Yes," Little Hawk said. "I intend to move just a bit faster than you."

"Safer riding with us." The man extended his hand. "Name's Luke Long. Knoxville."

"I am Little Hawk."

The man asked no questions. He fell in beside Little Hawk and paced him as they overtook the main party.

"I believe I know the Europeans with you," Little Hawk said.

"The Frenchies?"

"Yes."

"Small world, ain't it? They be royalty, or so I'm told, dukes and the like." He laughed. "So it is obvious that them Revolutionaries didn't cut off every royal head."

Louis Philippe, who had been trailing, fell back to ride alongside Little Hawk and looked at him with evident curiosity. "I know you."

"Yes, sir, we met at Senator Blount's house. I am Little Hawk, son of Renno."

"Of course!" Louis Philippe said. "What a wonderful coincidence. We're planning to visit your father's village, just as he suggested."

"I'm sure that you will be welcomed," Little Hawk said.

"Aren't you too young to be traveling alone?" the Frenchman asked.

"Not really."

"Have you ridden far?"

"From Philadelphia," Little Hawk replied.

"Remarkable," Louis Philippe said. "Well, it will be good to have one with us who knows the country intimately. Have we far to go?"

"Not far. We will first come to the Cherokee village of my uncle Rusog."

Little Hawk could see that Louis Philippe was burning to ask questions of him—for example, why was his skin—and his father's and his sister's—not the coppery red of the other Indians? Why were their features more finely molded than those of most redmen? Were all of the Seneca bronzed-white like this boy? But Little Hawk knew that the duke would be too polite to ask such personal questions, and the sachem's son believed that all such information would be revealed in time.

"You will camp two nights," Little Hawk continued, "and arrive by midday after the second night."

"Excellent," Louis Philippe said. "The fates have intended for us to meet again."

The frontiersman rode forward to inform his mates of Little Hawk's identity. Louis Philippe asked question after question and was impressed by the Seneca boy's ready answers.

Out of curiosity Little Hawk delayed moving ahead of Louis Philippe's party. He liked listening to the Frenchman talk, and he wanted a chance to ask him if the revolution in France had actually been as cruel as some said. Meanwhile, he had been watching the signs left by the group that had traveled ahead of Louis Philippe's party. Moccasin tracks were mixed and mostly obliterated by the tracks of the horses ahead of him, but he noted immediately when the spoor of the hunting party disappeared. He pulled Gray to a halt and dismounted. Louis Philippe momentarily glanced over his shoulder but rode on. Little Hawk doubled back and found the spot where the two men in boots and their Indian companions had left the trail. He followed the tracks a few paces into the forest. They had turned to travel parallel to the trail. He mounted Gray and spurred him into a run, causing looks of surprise to cross the faces of Louis's brothers as he rode past them to rein in beside Luke Long.

"I saw the tracks," Luke said before Little Hawk could speak. "How many, you make it?"

"Eight Cherokee, two men in boots, perhaps white men."

"Saw you follow the tracks into the woods."

"They turned south again about fifty feet into the trees."

"Well," the frontiersman said, "we're a long ways from Chickamauga country, and I ain't heard of no white renegades working with Injuns anywhere near here."

"They were no more than an hour ahead of us when they left the trail," Little Hawk told him.

Louis Philippe had spurred his horse into a trot to overtake Little Hawk and the guide. "You gentlemen seem to be concerned about something," he said.

"Not really," the guide responded. "Cherokee hunting party crossed our trail, that's all."

"Surely there's no danger. We are in friendly territory, are we not?"

"Reckon so," Luke answered, but when Louis Philippe fell back to join his brothers, the militiaman checked the priming on his fine musket.

At the midday stop one of Louis Philippe's brothers opened a huge picnic hamper to a bounty of cold fried chicken, crusty bread, and sharp yellow cheese. Little Hawk accepted the invitation to join the others. He found the chicken to be a bit greasy, but he enjoyed the bread and cheese. As the Frenchmen engaged their frontier companions in conversation by asking endless questions, Little Hawk's attentions were directed elsewhere. There was nothing in particular he could isolate, but something was causing him to feel uneasy. Now and then he could feel the atavistic tingle of rising hackles on his neck.

They had found a pleasant spot beside a little stream for the noontime meal. It flowed smoothly over a sandy, rockless bottom, making only small gurgling noises. A mockingbird protested their presence by warbling his claim

to that section of the forest from a tree on the other side of
the creek. Other birds continued their search for food,
chirping as they flitted through the boughs. All seemed
normal. And then, out over the forest to the south, a crow
cried out a warning. Little Hawk looked up and caught a
glimpse of the crow winging toward their position. The
bird was directly overhead before it screeched again, and
its startled cry was the same warning that it had given a
few hundred yards to the south.

Little Hawk set aside his bread and cheese and stood,
motioning the Luke Long. The Tennessean joined him by
the horses. "If you want to keep them here for a few
minutes, Mr. Long, I'll take a look ahead."

Long had not missed the warning call of the scouting
crow. From the man's hesitation, Little Hawk knew that
the guide was about to say that it was not a boy's place to
look out for a man's own responsibilities; but evidently
there was something in Little Hawk's face that kept him
silent. When Long nodded, the sachem's son went to the
creek, smeared mud on his forehead and cheeks, then
melted into the trees.

His bow rested over his shoulder, within easy reach,
and his feet moved quickly, finding the spot where no
twig would snap, no grass or leaves rustle. He circled to
the east, his ears taking in the sounds of the forest birds,
which went silent in the area directly around him in spite
of his care. Soon he believed he was a few hundred yards
east of the point where the crow had seen something that
caused it to call a warning to other crows.

Little Hawk, more cautious now, eased ahead like a
shadow, using the trees for cover. He went forward on his
knees or his belly. He heard the men who were waiting in
ambush before he saw them. Had it been only Cherokee
lying there, he would have had to get much closer to
detect them. It was a white man's gruff voice that he
heard in a hoarse whisper.

"Shut up," another white man said. "They's comin' when they's comin'."

"I says we'uns goes and gits 'em, Micajah," whispered the first man.

"You aim to hush, Wiley, or do I hush you with the stock of my rifle?"

Little Hawk crawled a few more yards and spotted one of the white men. He was scruffy, dressed in the rags of a pair of homespun trousers and an Indianmade deerskin tunic. He was heavily bearded, broadly built, and his hair was long and matted. The other white man was nearby but could not be seen clearly. The Indians were almost invisible, but after studying the scene carefully, Little Hawk could spot five of them. He saw the markings of the Chickamauga on one face. They were hidden among brush on both sides of the trail. Their intentions were obvious.

Chapter XV

Louis Philippe continued talking with his brothers as he watched Little Hawk go into the forest alone. He thought little of it until a few minutes later when he noted that his frontiersmen guards and guides were acting nervous and checking their weapons. He approached Luke Long and asked, "Why has the boy gone on ahead without his horse?"

"Doin' a little scoutin'," Luke answered.

"Scouting? Why?"

"Well, we didn't like the way that group of Indians

ahead of us was actin' when they left the trail." He wasn't
going to mention the cry of the crow that had alerted both
Little Hawk and him. He doubted that the Frenchman
would credit the ability of a mere crow to spot peril for
man.

"Do you think there's some danger, Monsieur Long?"

"Probably not."

"But perhaps?"

"Maybe."

"And you sent a boy into possible danger alone?"

"That boy is the son of the best Indian scout George
Washington ever had," Luke said. "Don't you worry none
about him. He knows his way around the woods."

"I am going to mount my horse," Louis announced,
"and go after that boy."

"That won't be too smart," Luke warned, but the
Frenchman was running toward his horse and calling out
to his brothers to follow him.

"Damn all foreigners," Luke muttered, motioning to
the others to mount up.

By getting onto the trail ahead of the Frenchmen,
Luke and the other two men managed to keep Louis from
riding into an ambush at a trot. Luke led the way, motioning to everyone to be quiet. He didn't see anything, but
then if Indians had chosen to ambush the party, he
wouldn't—not until the muskets starting smoking and the
arrows began to fly.

Little Hawk had started to back away, preparing to
return and warn Long and the others of the ambush, when
one of the Cherokee hissed at the two white men to be
silent. Hearing the sound of the approaching horses, Little
Hawk was reminded of something his grandfather Johnson
had said once in exasperation: "Never underestimate the
stupidity of your fellow man."

He had choices. He could cry out a warning and then
run like a deer. He did not, unfortunately, have time to

make a silent retreat, circle around the ambush, and head off the advancing party. Since doing nothing was not a viable option, Little Hawk took his only other alternative: He positioned himself behind a tree where he had a good field of fire, drew his bow, and killed. He aimed for the throat of a Cherokee warrior, and the gurgle of death testified to his accuracy. His second arrow had found its target, but not fatally, he feared, for a Cherokee warbled a warning cry and turned to face this unexpected enemy. One of the white men fired in Little Hawk's direction. The boy dropped a Cherokee warrior who, too eager to count coup, had charged into Little Hawk's arrow. And then the young Seneca was running for his life with several fully armed warriors on his trail, whooping as they ran. He paused as an arrow zinged past his head and made it four victims for his bow before resuming his flight.

He ran in a tight circle, praying that the Cherokee would not anticipate his strategy. When he came to the trail, he saw Luke Long astride his horse about fifty yards away. Little Hawk yelled out a warning and dove into the trees on the other side of the trail just as his pursuers burst into the open long enough for the three frontiersmen to take a running shot from each of their muskets. Two Cherokee went down, and the others, still whooping, dashed back into cover. Little Hawk sent an arrow winging after them, but he missed.

Luke Long's horse thundered down the trail and jerked to a halt. The Tennesseean fired a pistol into the trees after the departed Cherokee and then got down to examine the two fallen warriors. "Chickamauga," he said, looking up at Little Hawk. "How many?"

"No more than eight, and the two white men," the boy answered.

"White men?"

"One has a black, tangled beard, a big man with long hair. The man with him called him Micajah."

"Harps." Long spat. "May God see them burn in hell. You do any damage in there?"

"Some," Little Hawk said.

Louis Philippe had ridden up in some agitation. *"Mon Dieu! Mon Dieu!* Have we really encountered hostile Indians?"

" 'Bout as hostile as I want," Long told him. "Now we had best make some tracks, before they decide to try again."

"Merde," cursed one of the younger Frenchmen. "I didn't even have a chance to get in a shot."

"Count your blessin's," Luke said. "These are not your typical gentlemanly British soldiers, my friend. These savages were goin' to shoot us from ambush."

"How common," said the comte.

Luke led the group to the edge of the forest, about half a mile, and left them there with an open meadow leading down to a little lake at their backs. Then he and Little Hawk rode back into the woods to find the scene of the ambush. Three dead Cherokee plus the two shot at the enemies' camp made a total of five dead, and there was blood at the position of the man whom Little Hawk had wounded.

"Anything you want to do before we go back?" Luke asked.

"No."

"No scalps?"

"I don't count coup on brothers. Wrong as they are, they are Cherokee."

"Makes sense. I guess," Luke allowed.

They re-joined the party. Luke pushed them hard for the rest of the day. There was no further sign of the ambushers. Then, as they came nearer to Rusog's village, they began to pass scattered Cherokee lodges and log cabins. Because the inquisitive Frenchmen wanted to chat and visit with every Cherokee they encountered, Little

Hawk, eager to be home, rode on alone, camped for the night, and then pushed Gray hard.

Although Toshabe's official period of mourning was over, her heart was heavy. Her sorrow was made more intense with each passing day by the knowledge that the murderer of her husband went unpunished and was, in fact, unknown. If Ha-ace had died in honorable battle, she would have wept for him and keened her loss in the traditional songs for the dead; she would have had consolation in knowing that he had died for something worthwhile. Her grief, however, was compounded because Ha-ace's life was ended by some petty rivalry within the tribe. Twice now she had been widowed, and both times her husband had been killed without having had a chance to fight back. The white renegade Ben Whipple had killed the great Ghonkaba in a cowardly way. Ha-ace the Panther had been shot from ambush in the supposedly peaceful surroundings of his own village.

Age had dulled Toshabe's shining long hair, but it had not dimmed the spark in her dark, vivid eyes. While she had inherited her hair texture and coloration from her Erie mother, her still-supple dusky skin had been lightened by the blood of her French father. She was a handsome, dignified presence in the Seneca village—the chief matron, wife and mother of sachems—but now her longhouse was empty save when her daughter, Ena, and the lively twins were visiting. At night her bed was empty . . . at night she would awaken at odd intervals and listen for hours to the plaintive call of a whippoorwill, the lonely drip of rain on the roof, the moan of a wind, before she could fall back asleep.

At such times, as she lay in the dark, she would say a prayer to the Master of Life for her two absent sons. It was often difficult for her to remember that life was good. She almost wished that it was her own time to cross to the Place across the River, for when she was lying awake, the

nearly physical pain of loneliness made it easy for Toshabe
to indulge in self-pity. She felt that she had been a good
mother to her three children. In giving birth three times
she had contributed more to her tribe than had most
women. She had been a good wife to her two husbands.
She had conducted herself with dignity and wisdom and
had always been respectful of the Master of Life and the
manitous. Why, then, did it seem that the spirits of evil
were to be triumphant?

The troublemaker O-gas-ah, the woman of the big
mouth, had polarized the matrons of the tribe by insisting
that it was time to choose a new sachem. Renno, O-gas-ah
had said, had deserted his people and was reverting to his
own, for he was, she accused, more white than Seneca. As
for O-o-za, her husband, he said little that was inflammatory but did nothing to stop O-gas-ah's campaign to make
him sachem.

Those who had come to the south with Toshabe and
Ghonkaba were arrayed against O-gas-ah and her core of
supporters, most of whom had come in the second group
led by the dead, disgraced war chief, Tor-yo-ne, whose
spiritual weakness had cost the life of his sister, An-da. A
few of the senior warriors had stated that before they
would see O-o-za named sachem, blood would flow. With
Ha-ace murdered, with both Renno and El-i-chi far from
home, each passing day brought more immediate danger
of an armed clash among brothers, a consummation de-
voutly to be dreaded. In the dim days of the past, before
the prophet Dekanawidah envisioned the great tree whose
top reached to the sky, the tree that represented the
alliance of the five Iroquois tribes and under which burned
the eternal Fire of Great Peace, brothers had often turned
their weapons against each other. To think that it would
happen again was a burden that made Toshabe feel her
years and dread the mornings.

So it was on a dawn of low-hanging clouds and a mist
that was almost as fine as fog. She forced herself to push

aside her blankets and arise. She dressed quickly and
kindled a fire from the embers to break the damp chill
that had penetrated the longhouse. She was heating water
for her morning tea when life, as represented by Ena's
twins, Ho-ya and We-yo, burst in through the front door.

"Grandmother, Grandmother," eight-year-old We-yo
trilled. "You must come quickly." We-yo, looking very
much like her mother, was dancing around excitedly while
her brother tried to remember that he was, after all, the
son of a chief and, therefore, dignified.

"What is it?" Toshabe asked. From We-yo's excitement it wasn't anything terrible, so she was eager to finish
brewing her tea.

"A surprise, Grandmother," Ho-ya said. "I think you
should come along if you want to find out what it is."

Toshabe sighed. "Oh, well."

Smoke was spiraling upward from the smoke hole in
Renno's longhouse directly across the central square.
Toshabe's heart lifted. "Renno?" she whispered. The years
had thickened her figure, and on damp mornings her
joints were stiff, but she showed none of her age as she
ran lightly to the door of Renno's longhouse and threw it
open.

"Mother," said El-i-chi, "I thank thee that thou art
well."

Sudden tears came to her eyes. Her younger son sat
cross-legged on a deerskin beside the fire. He held a
mirror in his left hand, and with his right hand he had
been painting his face in the patterns and colors of death.
He made one last sweep with his forefinger, put down the
mirror, wiped his hands, then rose to kneel before Toshabe.
"Forgive me, Mother, for not being here when you needed
me most."

"There is no need for forgiveness."

"Now I am here."

"Yes, but painted for killing."

"If it comes to that."

She nodded. Perhaps it had come to that. Perhaps there was no other cure for the sickness that had eaten its way into the heart of the tribe.

"You are alone?" she asked.

"I traveled swiftly. My Rose and the young ones follow with Roy Johnson."

"And your brother?"

"I know not."

"So," she said, and the way she said the word made El-i-chi's heart ache, for he had heard his brother express acceptance with that same syllable so many times.

He walked into the misty morning at the side of his mother, placed his hand on Ho-ya's head, and bent to kiss little We-yo on the forehead. The twins ran off to tell their mother and father of the great return.

In Toshabe's longhouse, over tea and reheated corn cakes, El-i-chi listened grimly as his mother recounted the events since Renno and he had left the village. A Cherokee arrow had killed Ha-ace, but no Cherokee stood to gain from the murder.

"Only O-o-za stood to gain," El-i-chi said severely.

"There is no proof," Toshabe reminded.

"Yet it is logical that I accuse him."

Toshabe nodded. Tradition provided for such a situation. El-i-chi would bring the charge of murder against the warrior O-o-za. O-o-za, in spite of the fact that he was blind to the ambition and the faults of his wife, would, being Seneca, see the accusation as a challenge, and in the battle to the death that followed, the Master of Life would decide O-o-za's guilt or innocence. If El-i-chi lived, O-o-za was guilty—dead and guilty. If O-o-za lived, then he was not guilty of the murder of Ha-ace, El-i-chi had been punished for his false accusation, and—this was the hitch in the system—Ha-ace's murderer was still alive. The bloodshed, however, would be limited to the death of one warrior if El-i-chi called for trial by combat—at least for the time being.

The political morass had been caused by Renno's departure. There were simply no rules of tradition to cover a situation in which a sachem just left his tribe, as Renno had done. It would have been a far more manageable situation had Renno been dead. When a sachem died, the chief matron, the senior woman of the sachem's lineage, selected a successor from the old sachem's lineage and announced her choice to the other women of the family and then to the clan. Once the choice of the chief matron was made public, it was accepted automatically, and after a suitable period of mourning, the new sachem was given the deer horns, his badge of office.

It didn't take long for word of El-i-chi's presence in the village to become known to all. In O-o-za's longhouse the news brought a frown to the face of O-gas-ah. She looked at her husband quickly, wishing that she could give him some of her courage, for it was obvious that O-o-za was discomfited by the news. She could not speak, however, for there was another man at their fire. Life would be simpler, she thought, if only her spirit resided in her man's body.

Reverend Waith Pennywhistle, too, noted the impact of El-i-chi's return on O-o-za. "So he defies the wisdom of the entire tribe," Pennywhistle said. "He has come back in defiance of the order of exile."

"He has come because of the murder of his father," O-o-za explained. "The need to avenge that death overrides all."

"The matter will be handled easily," O-gas-ah said. "The matrons who voted in favor of exile will speak, and it will be the duty of the warriors of this clan to drive him away or, if he refuses to go, to kill him."

"After all," Pennywhistle exhorted, "there must be law and order. There must be respect for the will of the majority. The intruder must be killed as soon as possible, for our plans have been moving along nicely. You, O-o-za, will have your wealth and power in return for leading the

Seneca against the Spanish forts on the Mississippi. All that remains to be done is for the council of matrons to name you sachem. If El-i-chi upsets our plans, everything that I have promised you may come to naught."

Pennywhistle followed a glum O-o-za into the street. Small groups of people were congregated here and there, talking with great animation. He watched the reaction of the people as O-gas-ah began her campaign to rouse the tribe against El-i-chi. There would be a sharp division, however, an approximately equal polarization into two violently opposed factions.

The entire population of the village lined the central area toward which the longhouses of Renno and Toshabe faced. When El-i-chi stepped out of Toshabe's house a staccato of talk rose, then disappeared into silence as the tall, bronzed warrior in the paint of death walked purposefully to the center of the clearing and looked around. He carried only a tomahawk and knife. He lifted his blade. The sun had burned through the mist and sparkled off the well-honed weapon.

"I, El-i-chi, shaman of the Seneca, speak."

The hearts of many were gladdened to see the seed of the great Renno, of Ghonkaba, and of Ja-gonh standing so proudly among his own. Even those who sided with O-o-za, those who wanted to go adventuring in war against the Spanish, could not help but be impressed and, perhaps, a bit disturbed to think that they might have to face the wrath and blade of that warrior.

"I, El-i-chi, shaman of the Seneca, son of Ghonkaba, brother of Renno, sachem of the Seneca, say this: Murder has been done in dishonor, and of that deed I accuse—"

O-o-za held his breath. He knew what was coming. He held himself to his greatest height, chest outthrust, chin up. He heard his name.

"—O-o-za."

There was a collective gasp, then silence. O-o-za took

three steps forward and folded his arms over his chest. "So be it," he agreed. He could do nothing else; his destiny had been decided for him in the days long before he was born. "I deny your accusation and say it is the prattle of a liar."

"Then this is a matter to be decided by the Master of Life," El-i-chi said.

A reedy, stooped old senior warrior stepped between the two combatants. His voice quavered with age. "I ask you, young El-i-chi, to withdraw your accusation."

"That I cannot do," El-i-chi responded.

"Then I ask you, O-o-za, to deny or confirm the accusation," the old warrior said, his last words almost lost in a sudden fit of coughing.

"I say that El-i-chi lies!" O-o-za said strongly.

"Then, O-o-za," the old warrior wheezed, "it is for you to choose weapons."

"The weapons of the Seneca," O-o-za declared. Although he knew full well that he could not match El-i-chi's skill with firearms, he believed he was stronger than the young warrior. His best chance would be with tomahawk and knife.

"And the time," the old warrior said.

"Now," said O-o-za, for in his heart he knew that delay would only build the dread he felt at the thought of facing the powerful shaman.

"So be it," El-i-chi agreed, lifting his blade.

"They're going to fight right now?" Waith Pennywhistle asked O-gas-ah.

"Yes," O-gas-ah said, her heart pounding. "I had not expected this. They have not given me any time to incite the matrons against El-i-chi's defiance of our will. I fear for my husband."

"You fear for your plans to be first matron and to have the wealth of the Spanish towns, O-gas-ah," Pennywhistle said knowingly. "You want to know the power of being the wife of a great war leader."

The woman looked at the white man with anger in
her eyes but could not deny that he had spoken the truth.

"Can O-o-za best this fellow?" Pennywhistle asked
nervously, for his own plans for wealth and power depended upon O-o-za's prevailing.

"I pray so," O-gas-ah replied.

El-i-chi and O-o-za faced each other from a distance
of thirty feet. Simultaneously they stepped forward. They
halted again at about five paces, and O-o-za spoke so softly
that only El-i-chi could hear. "I did not kill Ha-ace," he
said.

"The manitous will decide," El-i-chi told him.

He lunged forward, his tomahawk at the ready, but
O-o-za sidestepped skillfully. The man had, after all, killed
his dozens and fought both white and Indian foes in the
past. He made an attempt to end it quickly by going in
low, swinging his tomahawk up toward El-i-chi's groin.
The shaman danced back.

Steel rang on steel as O-o-za parried El-i-chi's coun-
terthrust with his blade while striking out to land a solid
blow on El-i-chi's chest with his left fist. El-i-chi leaped
away. He knew from O-o-za's initial moves that he faced a
worthy opponent.

Now the fight became a slow, careful minuet of death,
with each man testing the other, looking for an opening,
waiting for a fatal misstep on the part of his opponent.

Pennywhistle had backed away from the gathering,
slipped behind a longhouse, and run from the village and
into the forest. He made his way to a large tree that had a
hollow next to the ground, knelt, and reached up inside
the hole. He felt around until his fingers came in contact
with the rough burlap wrapped around his bow and arrows.

Grasping the concealed weapon under his coat and
breathing hard from his run, he returned to the village
clearing and sought a vantage point where he could see

the opponents clearly. He looked around; no one seemed to have noticed his brief absence. With the entire population lined up around the central square, he could not find a clear shot. He backed away several feet and clambered into the low limbs of an oak tree, then positioned himself and waited. What he planned to do was risky and, if O-o-za could handle the shaman, was best left undone. Seeing that O-o-za was holding his own, Pennywhistle waited.

For some time the bout proceeded equally, with O-o-za and El-i-chi alternately taking the offensive, having the advantage. More than once their blades clashed. Sweat flew from their naked torsos at each sudden maneuver.

O-o-za was breathing hard. It had been a long time since he had fought, and he was feeling his forty-two years. He knew that he had to finish the combat quickly or lose through exhaustion. He launched a fierce attack, causing El-i-chi to back away, purely on the defensive, catching each blow of O-o-za's tomahawk with his own blade. Then, when O-o-za's left hand was filled with a deadly, thick-bladed knife, El-i-chi drew his own knife. Now it was necessary not only to parry O-o-za's tomahawk but to watch out for a belly blow from the knife. When the fury of O-o-za's attack began to fade, the shaman began an attack of his own. El-i-chi's tomahawk glanced off O-o-za's blade and slashed a deep cut across O-o-za's left breast.

The wound on O-o-za's chest sapped his strength quickly. The man fought on valiantly, but he was as good as dead. El-i-chi moved in. Now the decision was made; the Master of Life had decreed O-o-za's guilt. But even as El-i-chi passed up one opening and then another for a killing blow, he knew doubt. O-o-za had fought so bravely. And yet what was to be was to be. The shaman glided to a new position and aimed the final blow that would go under O-o-za's guard and slash his throat.

*   *   *

Pennywhistle could see that O-o-za was laboring, his chest heaving as he gasped for breath. Blood flowed in amounts that told Pennywhistle that the fight was as good as lost for O-o-za. Exhaustion and blood loss would make him an easy victim for El-i-chi's weapons.

Pennywhistle looked around carefully. He was fairly well hidden among the leaves of the oak, and the attention of the tribe was on the fighters. He notched an arrow to his Cherokee bow and drew it, waited for the proper moment, and loosed the arrow.

Leading his tired horse, Little Hawk approached the Seneca village from the swimming stream and caught glimpses of many people congregated in the square. He had left his horse to graze and was running forward, skirting several longhouses, when he saw something move in an oak tree ahead of him. At the same time he caught a glimpse of his uncle El-i-chi in combat. Then, to his shock, he heard the *zing* of a released bowstring and saw the arrow strike El-i-chi in the back.

Set to launch the kill, El-i-chi stumbled, halted, and threw back his head in sudden shock and pain. He fell heavily onto his face at the feet of the exhausted, bleeding O-o-za.

Dazed, weak, and resigned to his own death, O-o-za stood stunned for a moment, then lifted his tomahawk to take advantage of the miracle. He was weak, and the loss of blood was making him dizzy, but the Master of Life had sent him a miracle that was to allow him to prove his innocence and live. But then he heard voices crying out and saw warriors running toward him. He started a death-blow aimed toward the head of the fallen enemy, putting all his remaining strength behind it as El-i-chi tried to climb to his knees. Just before the sharp blade split El-i-chi's skull, O-o-za noticed the arrow protruding from the shaman's back. He tried to stay his tomahawk's blow but managed only to turn the blade so that the flat of the blade struck El-i-chi's skull and glanced off. The stroke still retained enough power to send El-i-chi down into blackness.

Little Hawk was behind the man who had shot his uncle and had a clear shot at the man's back. The boy loosed his tomahawk with all his strength. It struck squarely on the spine of the man in the tree, and with a swishing of branches he fell, landing with a great thump at Little Hawk's feet. The young Seneca, recognizing the preacher, turned the head with the toe of his moccasin to be sure the man was dead. A Cherokee bow had fallen beside Pennywhistle. Little Hawk picked it up with an arrow and pushed his way through the crowd to find his grandmother kneeling at El-i-chi's side.

"Grandmother!" he cried.

Toshabe looked up, startled, and mouthed his name. Tears streamed down her face.

"Is he dead?" Little Hawk whispered.

"Thanks to the manitous, no," she said.

"The man who shot him is," Little Hawk said. "Reverend Pennywhistle. He used this."

O-o-za, holding a cloth to the cut on his chest, said, "A Cherokee bow. This is the same type of Cherokee arrow that killed Ha-ace the Panther." He glared at his wife. "Did you know?" His voice was harsh with anger.

"How could I know?" O-gas-ah asked innocently. "Come, let me see to your wound."

The ancient senior warrior who had supervised the fight took the bow from Little Hawk. "A Cherokee bow. A Cherokee arrow killed Ha-ace. The white man, then, is the murderer."

"The Master of Life has not spoken," a matron pointed out. "Both warriors live."

As warriors came forward to carry El-i-chi to Toshabe's longhouse, the chief matron faced the gathering and said,

"The Master of Life has taken this way to declare the innocence of both, while dealing out his punishment. He has
punished O-o-za for listening to bad counsel from the
white preacher and from his wife. He has punished my
son for accusing an innocent man. Now listen to me, all of
you. It is over. My son is back, and he will stay. When his
wife and the boys come, they will be welcomed, and they
will be treated as full members of this tribe. Is it so?"

"This blade says it is so," Little Hawk said, lifting his
tomahawk. It was red with Pennywhistle's blood.

"And this," said a senior warrior, lifting his own
weapon. "Seneca blood dampens the earth in our own
village. This blood is the result of an unwise decision by
our matrons. I say that our shaman is back, and he is
welcome. He who speaks nay threatens a repetition of this
bloodletting of brothers."

"Our shaman is home," said a matron gladly. Words
of agreement spread. No one spoke nay.

A young man came running to hand Little Hawk the
bloody scalp of Waith Pennywhistle. Little Hawk accepted
the trophy, lifted it high on his tomahawk, and cried out,
"This is the fate of the false preacher who cried peace
while tempting our men to war. Let us remember, and let
us, in the future, take our counsel from our own people."

The barbed head of the iron Cherokee arrow had
buried itself in the muscle atop El-i-chi's shoulder. He
was breathing shallowly but regularly. Ena heated a knife
in the fire while Toshabe took advantage of her son's
unconsciousness to make neat incisions at each side of the
arrowhead and withdraw the barbs. Ena pressed the white-
hot knife onto the open wound. Little Hawk's gorge rose
at the smell of burning flesh, but now the wound was
cauterized and sealed.

When El-i-chi began to move his head, Toshabe directed Little Hawk to restrain his uncle. Then El-i-chi's
blue eyes were open, and he was looking around dazedly.

"Renno?" he mumbled. "But why are you so young?"

Little Hawk could not keep from laughing. "It is I, Uncle," he said. "Little Hawk."

"So," El-i-chi said, putting a hand to his head to feel the swelling knot. He closed his eyes and slept. It was dark when he awoke and saw his mother's face hovering over him. "I was dead," he said, "and saw my brother as a boy."

"You live," she assured him.

"How can that be? If O-o-za lives, then I am dead."

He listened with astonishment as Toshabe told the tale. Then she reached out to clasp her grandson's arm and said, "Now you are a warrior. No longer a boy. From now on we will call you Hawk."

French royalty arrived at Rusog's village and was greeted with courtesy. Louis Philippe and his two brothers were invited by Se-quo-i to sleep in his log cabin, since he lived there alone.

In the days that followed, Hawk divided his time between listening to the sometimes puzzling conversation of the learned Cherokee and the Frenchmen and in tending his uncle El-i-chi.

Louis Philippe was totally charmed with Toshabe, who spoke French with the accent of the early French traders and trappers and knew tales from her French father that kept the Frenchmen fascinated long into the night. Ena regaled him with stories of her warrior adventures. Luke Long vied with the Frenchmen in telling of Hawk's feat of saving the entire party from ambush. El-i-chi managed to chant songs of old and hint at many secrets when the Europeans visited him in Toshabe's longhouse. The Frenchmen, with Toshabe translating for those who spoke neither English nor French, described the splendor of old Europe, the grandeur of the French Nation, and the astounding military success of the rising leader Napoléon,

who would be a friend of all Indians once he regained
French possessions in the New World.

The women's harvest had been excellent that year.
There were rich, ripe squash and golden, sweet, yellow
concoctions from pumpkins, dried beans, and fresh, late-
growing greens. New ham shared the menu with venison,
rabbit, squirrel, and fish. Luke and the other two frontiersmen
were content to stay as long as the royalties wanted to
visit, for the food was good, the stories at night interesting, and the people friendly.

El-i-chi's arrow wound healed quickly, and his head-
aches were gone within three days. During that time he
tried to rise from his bed, only to give in to bouts of
dizziness. Another three days saw him walking the streets
with Hawk, listening to his people welcome him home,
and answering their inquiries about Renno by telling them,
"The manitous only know where he is or what he is doing,
but is there any doubt that he is our sachem?"

He walked with Hawk to see O-o-za, who was healing
but very weak. "Forgive me, Shaman," O-o-za requested.

"My head still aches, but for your quick reaction it
would be split," El-i-chi said good-naturedly. Then, with
seriousness, "Forgive *me*, Senior Warrior O-o-za, for accusing you falsely."

Two weeks later El-i-chi was as good as new and was
watching the trail leading to Knoxville when he saw Roy
Johnson, Ah-wa-o, and the two boys emerge from the
forest. He raced to meet them, held his little Rose in his
arms, tossed the boys high, and pounded Roy on the back
until Roy protested his enthusiasm.

Toshabe and Ah-wa-o mourned their loss of Ha-ace.
The family took quiet pride and great pleasure in being
together, while paying homage to the memory of those
who had gone to the west. Toshabe was dealing better
with her grief now that the murderer had been discovered

and took comfort in knowing that Ha-ace had now taken his place with Ghonkaba and other men of great honor.

Only two were now missing from the family circle—Renno and Renna.

Although he had killed more of the enemy than many adult warriors, Hawk was not yet a man. He hunted with the other young ones, played children's games without shame, climbed trees, and practiced with his weapons. Now and then he tired of the other boys' constant movement and went off by himself, sometimes to think of Naomi Burns, whom he had kissed and whose soft, warm places he had discovered with awe and wonder. At such times he would feel strange, oddly uneasy, and there was only one cure for it—to run, to move through the woodlands with the wind and to cover ground with his arms and legs and lungs pumping.

On a beautiful autumn day that was a great credit to the Master of Life, he chose the Knoxville trail and ran for approximately two miles at a swift clip before slowing to the warrior's flowing, energy-conserving, ground-covering pace. He had been thinking of Naomi and seriously considering a visit to the Burnses' farm at Christmastime, since the Americans put such stock in Christmas. He ran thoughts of her out of his system, and then he was thinking of all those he loved—of his grandmother and his aunts and uncles and all his cousins and of his sister and brother and father.

Around him the wilderness lived. Redbirds cried out at his approach. A fearless skunk ambled across the trail, forcing him to stop and wait while the best-protected animal of the woods moved slowly on. The forest was far from silent, but he was so accustomed to its sounds that it seemed silent to him until he heard a faraway noise that he could not, at first, define. He ran on toward the disturbance, which repeated itself with monotonous regularity. He heard the slobbering neigh of a horse before he identified the odd screech as the protest of a dry wheel bearing.

Hawk left the trail, found a hiding place, and waited. When the wagon came around the bend, his heart thudded. He hooted and ran onto the trail, his legs carrying him at top speed to meet the wagon, each footfall accompanied by a whoop of joy.

He saw his father pull the wagon reins, bring the horses to a halt, then jump down and run to meet him. He threw himself toward Renno and knocked his father off balance. They rolled happily together on the sandy trail, whooping and pounding each other on the back.

Renna came to stand beside them and said, "Brother, I shall ask for a slightly less exuberant greeting, if you don't mind."

He jumped up and lifted his sister from her feet, whirling her around. She squealed in protest, but she was laughing, and then she laughed more when he protested her wet kisses.

His world was now complete—or so he thought. Then he looked up and saw a beautiful woman whom he remembered well.

"Brother," Renna said, grinning widely, "we have a mother now."

"How tall you've grown," Beth said. She took Hawk into her arms. She was warm and soft, and for a moment Hawk could remember, or fancy he remembered, his own mother, who had died at Renna's birth. His eyes were wet.

"It is good to see you, Miss Huntington," he said.

"Not Huntington," she corrected, smiling. "I am Mrs. Harper."

He understood. Renno was grinning at him. They would have had to have a surname for the marriage ceremony in order to be married in a white man's church. Harper was the surname of the white family of the original Renno, the same name Hawk had used in Philadelphia.

"I know we haven't seen each other for a long time, but you used to call me Beth, and I wish you would again."

"Thank you," he said. "Beth. And I am now called Hawk."

Renno had a thousand questions for his son: What had happened in Philadelphia? Had the long journey from Pennsylvania to the Cherokee Nation been uneventful? But such questions would wait. There would be good times now, regardless of the political situation in the tribe, of which Renno was still ignorant. He had made his decision during the slow trip across North Carolina and the mountains: The world was changing, but he was Seneca, and he was sachem.

He decided that it was no longer practical to have judgments that affected the welfare of the entire tribe be dependent on ancient traditions made obsolete by events. He would send for his brother and his brother's family, and if anyone stood against El-i-chi and his little Rose, then it would be they who went into exile—or who faced his own tomahawk. His father, Ghonkaba, had not led the Seneca who had been loyal to the United States into the South to see them dissolve into petty factions and, eventually, be submerged and lost forever in the great lake of Cherokee blood.

Deep in his thoughts, he saw Hawk, eyebrows raised in question, looking at the well-loaded wagon and the string of packhorses behind it. Renno spread his hands.

Renna answered Hawk's unspoken query. "Just wait until you see all the nice things we've brought," she said. "Miss Beth is going to have a house built. Not just a log cabin, mind you, but a real house." She put her arm around Hawk's waist and squeezed. "We're going to be so happy."

Chapter XVI

Wiley and Micajah Harp had promised each other that they would take their revenge on the boy who had deprived them of the rich spoils carried by the party from Knoxville. The Harps had run away with their Cherokee friends, but they had not run far.

The Chickamauga had taken the defeat in stride. Sometimes one won a battle, they said, shrugging philosophically, and sometimes one ran away from superior firepower to live to fight again. Not so the Harps. They tracked Louis Philippe's party to Chief Rusog's Cherokee village and spied on them from a safe distance. Sooner or later the foreigners would leave, and next time the outcome would be different. Both feral brothers hoped that the blasted boy who had spoiled things for them before would be with the fancy Frenchies when they left the protection of the Indian village.

Had he been asked, Louis Philippe would have explained that he had extended his stay in Rusog's village because he was learning so much about the Cherokee and the very interesting transplanted Seneca. That would have been the partial truth. He was absolutely fascinated by the events that had taken place: the murder of a Seneca senior warrior, the death of a white preacher, the way the entire matter of justice was handled. Federal Indian agents came from Tellico Bloc House, heard witnesses recount the events, listened with some awe to the testimony of a thirteen-year-old boy, and then declared the matter closed. Justice had been served. Waith Pennywhistle had murdered and had been attempting to kill again when he, in turn, had forfeited his own life.

When the sachem of the Seneca, Renno, returned to his people unexpectedly to be greeted with genuine warmth by almost everyone, Louis Philippe understood the hunch that had kept him in this camp. He had been hopeful of again meeting with the bronzed sachem who spoke flawless French and aristocratic English and who brought with him two marvelously alluring women—or, rather, one magnificent woman and a beautiful, budding girl. Louis was smitten by Beth, a situation that she found to be a bit embarrassing. Renno considered it to be amusing. Nor was Beth's the only conquest.

The youngest member of the future king's party, the comte de Beaujolais, had been christened Beau by the frontiersmen who accompanied the party. The comte had come to be fond of the nickname and introduced himself to Renno, Beth, and the radiant Renna by saying, "Please

call me Beau." Of the three brothers, Beau was, perhaps,
the most handsome. His brothers tended to appear a bit
delicate, whereas he, being an active lad, was solidly
built. He had adapted a frontier buckskin jacket to wear
over his European shirt and trousers and looked less the
dandy for it. His face was open and pleasant, his smile
brilliant, and his eyes a lively walnut brown.

He was very familiar to Renna, for he was the same
handsome lad she'd admired in Philadelphia. She smiled
when she and Beau were introduced. It was a measure of
her own self-esteem when she did not remind Beau that
they had met before.

That divinely designed, miraculous alteration that oc-
curs in girls of Renna's age had nearly completed itself.
Her hips had begun to take on feminine contours. Her
breasts were small, shapely, pert under the dresses that
had been chosen for her in Wilmington by Beth. Her pale
hair—Emily's hair—glowed with life and framed a face
that could only have been described as vivid, for she was
an expressive girl, not in the slightest the stoic-looking
Indian. Her one-quarter of Seneca blood served to make
her skin romantically dusky, a splendid contrast to her
hair.

The comte took her to be older, but he was not
dismayed when he learned that she was still very young.
It was obvious that she had become a woman, and that, to
a Frenchman of Beaujolais's age—still in his teens—was
the final consideration when it came to feminine beauty.

So it was that in addition to Louis Philippe's respectful admiration for Beth—he was not stupid enough to
express anything other than admiration for the wife of a so
obviously capable man—there was a flurry of open court-
ship on the part of young Beau.

At first Renna found his attentions to be disconcert-
ing. Somehow he always managed to find a place beside
her. He took every occasion to "kiss" her hand, although
his lips did not actually touch her skin. She could feel his

breath on her hand, could look down at the top of his
dark, curly head, and could smell that he was clean, with
only a hint of a manly perfume about him.

His compliments caused her to blush: "Ah, that such
beauty languishes unseen in the wilderness."

"Hardly unseen," she said, using the upper-class British accent modeled after Beth's. She, like her father, had
an ear for languages and accents.

"But such exquisite femininity deserves to be feted,
to be seen whirling at the center of a gigantic ballroom
while all others stand and watch in awe."

Becoming a woman, Renna decided, had its pitfalls.
Seneca and Cherokee boys with whom she had run and
whooped and played games looked at her differently now.
They blushed and spoke to her in respectful tones and
turned their heads to watch as she walked by. And now
the intimidating Frenchman seemed determined to be in
her company every minute of the day and evening.

"Enjoy, darling," Beth advised her. "This is your
time, now and in the years to come. There is no hurry,
you know."

Indian girls were marriageable as soon as they passed
into puberty. Renna knew that; Beth knew it.

"No hurry," Beth repeated. "I know you are Seneca,
but you are also my daughter, and *my* daughter will not
become the cook and housekeeper for some warrior until
she has had an opportunity to enjoy her girlhood."

Renna gave no thought to marriage. Romance did not
appeal to her, although she remembered with great fondness the way Philip Woods's hair grew close to his head in
tight little curls and how his dark eyes seemed capable of
looking deep into her as they ice skated together. After
some intimidation, she began to treat the comte de
Beaujolais as she would have treated a Seneca boy who
had become too forward.

"Beau, really," she said, "you are going to turn my
head completely with your flattery." And, "Beau, I'm

quite sure that you must pay the same compliments to all
the girls you meet in your travels."

It was a pleasant time for all. To Beth's pleasure, she
had been welcomed with open arms by both Toshabe and
Ena. She quickly became a favorite of the young ones,
Ena's twins and Ta-na and Gao. Beth had been fond of
Ah-wa-o from the time when the Rose was in Wilmington.
Ah-wa-o very quickly became her best friend and companion.

Renno and El-i-chi, needing an excuse to get out into
the wilderness, took Louis Philippe on a hunt, put him
into position to bag a deer with a nice shot, and laughed as
El-i-chi smeared the blood of the young buck on the
duke's cheeks.

When Louis Philippe expressed an interest in seeing
the country along the Tennessee River in that area known
as Muscle Shoals, Luke Long told him that it was time for
them to head back for Knoxville if the duke expected to
get across the mountains before late-winter's heavy snow
closed the passes. At that time Louis was actually contem-
plating spending the whole winter in Tennessee, for he
had hopes of making Renno and his Seneca allies as well as
friends. Now that he knew the relationship between Renno
and the principal Cherokee chief, Rusog, he believed that
if he could convince Renno that the future of the Seneca
lay with France, Rusog and the Cherokee would follow
Renno's lead.

"Perhaps, Monsieur Long," Louis suggested, "you
and your men might want to return to Knoxville. My good
friend Hawk has offered to bring us into the town at a later
time."

Long turned to Renno. "Sachem," he said, "Governor
Sevier thinks it would be very bad for all of us if any harm
came to these Frenchies. Bad news travels and could scare
off potential settlers, you know. Now, the boys and me,
we have to get back to Knoxville. We got families. So if
you would tell Louis Philippe that it's time for him to
leave, I'd appreciate it."

"Mr. Long, why don't you go, if you must?" Beth asked. "I assure you that the duke and his brothers will be in good hands."

"We'll look after 'em, Luke," Roy offered.

"Well," Long said, "I reckon if you say it's all right, General—"

So it was that in the clear days of an unusually mild winter, a festive mixed group set out from the Seneca village toward the south, to show the visitors Muscle Shoals. Renno, eager to be in the forests, on the move, was easily convinced. He had agreed to show the Frenchmen the Tennessee and the shoals, and then to escort them into Knoxville.

Beth had said, "Don't even consider leaving me behind."

Renna, now making the most of being courted by a genteel member of a royal European family, asked, "If Beth goes, why can't I?"

Hawk went because Louis Philippe wanted his company and because the boy wanted to be with his father.

Roy Johnson went because he, like Renno, was tired of sleeping indoors and missing out on the extraordinary mild temperatures.

The group of eight was small enough to move quickly. The horses were rested and eager. They made good time the first day. Hawk acted as scout, moving ahead of the others, although he knew they were in friendly lands, where the only other people around were Cherokee under Rusog's influence. Still, it didn't pay to be careless. It was after they had passed through the areas of Cherokee population that Hawk sat Gray at the top of a ridge, looking back at a view of a valley and their trail. Renna was leading the main party, with Beau just behind her. Roy Johnson was riding with the duke, the duke's other brother, and Beth. Renno brought up the rear, some distance back.

Hawk's was a good vantage point. He could see for

several miles down the valley. There were clumps of trees along the stream, and marshy glades beside it, where waterfowl fed. Some miles back was a rise to a grassy bald meadow leading upward to a tree-covered ridge. A hawk soared over the valley, passing directly over Hawk's head with a cry that he took as a greeting, for the bird was one of his clan's totems. He watched the bird as it grew tiny with distance. It was only a dark speck in the sky when it dived toward the distant ridge. As Hawk's eyes followed its downward swoop, he saw a flash of light—sunlight reflecting off metal just at the edge of the trees. He stiffened, shaded his eyes with his hand, and waited for the flash to be repeated. It wasn't. He told himself that it had been just a trick of the light or the sun bouncing off leaves, but he was not convinced. He rode down the ridge, met the group, then passed them to pull up beside Renno.

"I am going to circle back a few miles," he said.

Renno waited.

"I saw something at the other end of the valley at the tree line. A flash."

Renno nodded. "But I will go," he said. "You stay with Beth and Renna. Make camp at the foot of the rise, on the eastern bank of the stream."

"I will go," Hawk insisted.

Renno put his hand on his son's shoulder. "I know you are a warrior. But would you retire me to my long-house and my warm bed so soon?"

Hawk laughed. Renno leaped down lightly from his horse, took his musket, longbow, and arrows, then gave Hawk the reins of the horse. He stepped into the forest and disappeared. Hawk rode forward and led the party to the place indicated by his father. He chose a spot with good trees but with open areas around it so it could be guarded easily. The two younger Frenchmen insisted upon helping Beth and Renna with the fire and with beginning the preparation of the evening meal.

*   *   *

Renno ran lightly, his feet making small sounds that would not have been heard from more than a few yards away. He ran parallel to the trail, came to the rise, and continued his pace as he experienced once again that good feeling of second strength. He had to circle to the east in order to reach the trees at the ridge top without having to cross the open, grassy areas. Then he was moving along the crest of the ridge carefully, taking advantage of every tree and every bush for cover.

He smelled the men before he heard them—tobacco and sour sweat. He had to duck for cover when two Chickamauga Cherokee came through the trees, heading for the smokeless camp where two white men talked in low voices.

The sun went down behind the trees to the west. Twilight came quickly. Renno snaked forward until he could see the clearing in which the white men sat. He counted six Chickamauga Cherokee in addition to the two white men. From Hawk's description they were the same white men who had lain in ambush for Louis Philippe's party on a previous occasion.

Renno was tempted to kill a few of them before total darkness came, but the odds were formidable. His better judgment convinced him to back away quietly and start down the ridge toward his own camp. He met two more Chickamauga warriors on the way down the ridge but avoided discovery. That made eight Cherokee and two white men.

At a safe distance from the fireless camp he found the trail and began to run. He had traveled no more than half a mile when he was alerted by a slight movement in the brush just ahead, a rustling sound that could have been made by some small animal startled by his approach. Renno darted into the darkness of the forest and waited, listening carefully. After a long time he heard the sound of movement again. He crept to the trail and by the light of a full moon saw a man in buckskin emerge from the brush, look up and down the trail carefully, then set off toward the end of the valley where Renno's party was camped.

It was a simple matter for Renno to outdistance the man and wait for him. He leaped out and immobilized the stranger with one arm around his throat, his knife gleaming in front of the startled man's eyes.

"Easy," the white Indian whispered. "Who are you?"

"You know blasted well, you murderin' animal." The man suddenly lifted his feet off the ground in an effort to pull Renno forward. It was a reckless move, for Renno could easily have sliced the man's throat on the way down. Instead, he released his hold, let the man fall, and stepped back, tomahawk at the ready. When the man rolled and started to lift his musket, Renno kicked the weapon out of his hands and stood over him.

"I asked you a question," he said.

"You ain't—" The man lifted one hand, palm out. "Listen, friend, I thought you was someone else."

"I am Renno of the Seneca."

"Heard of you. Name's Jed Batten. Live over west of Knoxville."

"Why did you try to waylay me?"

"Didn't. Heard you comin'. Thought you might be one of them murderin' Chickamauga or one of them devil-inspired Harps."

"There's a group of Chickamauga and two white men in a fireless camp at the top of the ridge."

"Big man, woolly, tangled black beard?"

"Yes."

"Harps. I reckon they's followin' you, friend."

"And whom are you following?" Renno asked.

"Them Harps come to my house when I was gone," Jed Batten said between clenched teeth. "I come home to find my wife cut to pieces, my baby's head smashed agin the wall. They was soiled plates on the table. I reckoned them Harps made my Sally cook for 'em, and then they kilt her and my little boy. I been after 'em ever since. Tracked 'em into old John Watts's country but couldn't go in after 'em because they's too many of them Chickamauga. Them Harps teamed up with the worst of the Chickamauga to rob and kill. I reckon they's after you now."

"Come," Renno said. He led Batten to the camp, announcing his coming by signaling Hawk with the call of a whippoorwill. Batten ate hungrily, then told his story again for the benefit of all. Hawk, hearing that the Harps were about, checked the priming of his musket.

"Should we go back to the village?" Beth asked.

"They're between us and the village," Hawk told her.

"My brothers and I are crack shots," Louis Philippe offered.

"Your skill may be required," Roy Johnson responded dryly.

"They won't come in the night," Jed Batten said. "Them Harps ain't woodsmen. They's more like animals. They'll come first light. If they's no objections, I'm goin' to get some sleep."

Renno motioned to Roy and took him aside. "If they attack at all, they'll come from the woods, there." He pointed. "We'll keep the creek at our back. Just before dawn we'll move everyone down to the creek, where they'll be protected by the bank. We'll see then if the Frenchmen can shoot. Hawk will anchor the southern end of the line. Beth will be in the middle with the longbow."

"And where are you going to be?" Roy asked.

"You and I are going to be out there," Renno said, nodding toward the woods.

"Yep," Roy approved. "Good idea. Let 'em think it's easy pickings, then you and I hit 'em where it hurts."

"So," Renno said.

"In the meantime," Roy suggested, "we might as well follow Batten's suggestion and get some sleep."

Roy was snoring within minutes. Renno briefed the others, pointing out the positions he wanted them to take

before dawn. After they had their instructions, he told
them to try to sleep. Hawk quickly followed Roy's example. The Frenchmen were restless, whispering among themselves. Beth and Renna lay down together.

Renna's eyes were wide as she looked at her father in
the flickering glow of the fire. "I have no weapon," she
whispered.

"Nor will you have," Renno said.

"I want to help."

Renno knelt beside her and put his hand on her pale
hair. "You are the daughter of my beloved Emily," he
whispered, "and although she was a good Seneca wife, she
did not believe in killing. She bore no arms. Nor will
you."

"All right, then," Renna said, lifting her head to kiss
her father. "But I don't think I can sleep."

Her gentle, regular breathing minutes later put the
lie to her statement. Renno sat beside Beth. The fire had
died to glowing embers.

"I can't sleep," Beth said. "Here, put your head down
and close your eyes. I will watch."

"There will be time tomorrow for sleeping," Renno
said.

Soon he was the only one awake. Around him the
nocturnal life of the wilderness went on. While a fitful
night wind gusted, a hunting owl swooped through the
trees with a whirr of wings. A rodent scampered over dry
leaves, seeking the crumbs of their evening meal. A mockingbird that had not yet gone south serenaded the full
moon from the top of a cottonwood. And a twig snapped
on the other side of the creek.

Renno slid out of the camp on his belly, crossed the
creek below the camp, and came through the trees as
silently as a hunting fox. He spotted the dark shadow of a
man kneeling behind the brush opposite camp. The white
Indian asked no questions this time. He closed the distance but allowed himself to be heard at the last minute so

that the Chickamauga warrior saw death slash toward him in the form of a Spanish stiletto.

Renno knew then that it was the intention of the group of Chickamauga to attack with the morning. He left the corpse where it had fallen and circled the camp carefully. The Harps had sent only one warrior to keep watch on their quarry, and now that warrior would see no more.

In the chill of predawn Renno woke Roy, Batten, and Hawk. As Renno told Batten the plan, Hawk wakened the others and got them into position. Next Renno melted into the forest with Roy at his back. The pair found a position where they could watch the camp and the approaches at the same time and waited.

The first of the Chickamauga came with the dimness of false dawn, waited until the eastern sky was pale, and crept forward past the well-concealed Renno and Roy. The two Harps were not in evidence.

Renno counted silently. Other warriors had joined the group, for now there were eleven Chickamauga. He made it ten by taking the last man of the group, the rear guard, with a quick slash across the throat. The Chickamauga died with only a small gurgle and a tiny thrashing of limbs as Renno lowered him to the ground.

Roy put his hand over the mouth of another unsuspecting warrior and drew his razor-sharp knife quickly across the exposed throat, lowered the body, and jumped back to avoid the pumping blood.

Hawk noticed movement in the brush beyond the abandoned camp. He lay flat on his stomach behind a sandy bank cut by the stream in flood. He hissed, and Beth looked his way. He pointed. She squinted and nodded, for she, too, had seen the movement. As she readied her bow, Louis Philippe looked at his brothers and forced a smile. When Beth saw copper skin through evergreen leaves, she drew her bow and let the arrow fly. There was an immediate cry of agony and surprise, and a Chickamauga warrior shot up to his feet, tugging at the arrow that was

lodged in his throat before he ultimately fell. Fierce war
cries broke out, and the Chickamauga charged into the
clearing. A musket blasted, but the shot went wide.

Hawk dropped the warrior at the far right of the line
of attackers and reloaded. The three Frenchmen fired
almost as one, and two more of the enemy pitched forward. Jed Batten kept looking for the Harps but finally
used his shot to kill a Chickamauga. Louis Philippe's pistols spoke, and Beth was sending arrows faster than the
muskets could be reloaded.

From the rear Roy and Renno took their toll with
muskets and pistols, and then there was an odd hush. One
solitary Chickamauga warrior halted his rush, having seen
all of his companions go down. He cried out his anguish
and, with pride driving him, continued the charge only to
take a deadly, stinging, barbed arrow in his solar plexus.

Renno stepped out from the trees, tomahawk in hand.
A wounded man stumbled to his feet, cried out his defiance, and hurled his tomahawk at Renno. The sachem
ducked and with a skillful throw split the Chickamauga's
forehead with his blade. He went to retrieve the tomahawk as Jed Batten walked among the fallen. Two men
moved feebly. Jed saw that one would soon die, so he
dispatched the other with a blow.

"Not very sporting," remarked the duc de Montpensier.

"He was shot in the stomach," Roy Johnson explained.
"Better a quick blade than to die like a dog in agony."

The fight had lasted no more than two minutes. Dead
Indians littered the ground, but still there was no sign of
the Harps. And then one shot rang out. Jed Batten yelled,
grabbed his left arm, and fell. Renno, ordering the others
to get down, darted into the trees in the direction of the
shot. After finding the place where the sniper had stood to
fire at Batten, Renno followed the clumsy trail made by
worn boots. He heard sounds behind him and turned to
see Roy and Jed following.

Renno could hear two men crashing through the brush

ahead of him. He increased his speed, leaving Roy and Jed behind. He burst out into a clearing and threw himself to one side, rolling, as a musket blasted from close range and the ball hummed close by his head. The man who had fired was big and had a tangled black beard. He was reaching for a pistol when Renno jumped to his feet and swung the butt of his musket to connect with the side of the big man's head. Roy and Jed came rushing into the clearing as the smaller man, who had been trying to reload his musket, gave up the fight and fled.

"Wiley Harp's gettin' away!" Jed shouted. He was bleeding near his shoulder, and when he tried to follow the white renegade, he stumbled and fell. Roy ran out of the clearing and after the fleeing man. Jed crawled to sit beside the unconscious Micajah Harp. He pulled a kitchen butcher knife from his belt and used it to cut Harp's shirt for thongs to tie the big man's hands. Harp began to moan and opened his eyes.

"You're gonna pay for what you done to my family, Micajah," Jed said.

"Go to hell, Batten," Micajah Harp shot back.

"You wide awake now?" Jed asked. "I don't want you to miss anything."

Harp glared.

Renno made a move to prevent what happened then, but he stopped. He had been moved by Jed Batten's tragedy. Jed, using the kitchen knife almost lovingly, slashed a long, raw wound on Harp's cheek. Blood began to flow.

"Did you cut up her face while she was still alive, Harp?" Jed asked. He slashed again. Harp flinched but did not cry out. "Did she beg you for mercy, Harp? You didn't seem to have any with you that day, did you?"

The kitchen knife sliced through buckskin into the flesh of Harp's chest. Incredibly, the big man who stank of filth and acrid sweat and chewed tobacco laughed. "I did a better job on your old lady, Batten. You're a poor butcher. Cut and be damned."

Something like a sob escaped from Batten's throat as he ended Harp's life.

Renno turned away and quickened his pace to put the little clearing far behind him. He met Roy after following the trail for a half mile. Roy was walking slowly and breathing hard.

"Well," Roy said, "I reckon we could catch that fellow if we wanted to make a month's work of it. He's right spry on his feet, that boy."

They walked back to the camp together. Hawk had packed the horses and moved away from the scene of death. Renna, looking pale, smiled wanly at her father while clinging to Beth's hand. The Frenchmen were subdued, but as the day went on and Renno continued toward the Tennessee, Beau regained his ebullience and, in an area of open meadow, challenged Renna to a race.

They camped that night on the bank of the Tennessee, and Renno was reminded that from a point not too many miles away he had once begun a journey that had taken him all the way down the Mississippi and across the Gulf of Mexico to the Yucatán Peninsula. He had not told Beth about that trip, not yet. He wanted to be alone with her, to talk and touch and look into the depths of her sea-green eyes; but he was the center of attention for the three Frenchmen, who were questioning him as to why the Chickamauga Cherokee were warlike while the rest of the tribe was at peace with their white neighbors.

"I have found that man—man of any color—is a creature of great variety," Renno explained. "While it is true that the Chickamauga have grievances—they were dispossessed of their lands—they also have much for which to be thankful. Why they choose to let the past color their actions is beyond my ability to comprehend."

"In a way," Roy said, "you have to admire 'em. They don't give up the fight."

"The greed of those of English blood for land is prodigious," Louis said. "And yet you, Renno, have cast your lot with the United States, which, as I understand it, is agonizing over whether or not to break off their treaty with France in view of the sea war that France is waging. They say it's because the French government has yet to abrogate a treaty, and yet one only has to read and listen to realize that many treaties with various Indian nations have been broken by the United States government."

"Things change," Renno said, "but they remain the same, after all. For centuries the Indian lived on this land. He lived in the forests that stretched from the Atlantic to the far Pacific and on the windy plains where there are many buffalo. Some say that those were the times of plenty, but even then there was change. The Cherokee Nation was expanding, driving neighboring tribes off the land, and again the Iroquois were in the process of building their great league. Indian fought Indian, and people— men, women, and children—died, just as they have died fighting the Europeans. To a dead child it matters little whether he was killed by a Shawnee tomahawk or an Englishman's pistol."

"But there could be peace!" Louis said with great feeling. "Renno, my friend, I know a man who could make a real difference. He is small of stature, but his soul, his courage are those of a giant. And he has the ability to inspire men to do impossible things. He has conquered almost all of Europe. Soon he will defeat England, and he has plans for portions of your great land that were once French and are now Spanish and English. Although this man is a master of war, he desires peace. I have heard you say that in order to survive, the Indian must conform to the white man's way of thinking."

Renno started to protest, but Louis held up his hand and said, "Perhaps I misquote you, but my point is this: You do not have to change your traditional way of living. When France is on the continent again, when my friend has taken the land from the Spanish and the English, we will grant you your hunting grounds forever."

Renno smiled. He had heard this all before and now gave his standard response. "As long as rivers run and the grass grows?"

Louis Philippe smiled and spread his hands. "Or words to that effect."

"And what would France want in return for this guarantee?" Renno asked.

"Friendship, alliance against potential enemies."

"Such as the United States?" Renno asked.

"If it came to that," Louis told him. "The Indian would also find that France can be generous. Our factories turn out excellent weapons, cooking utensils that would make the work of the Indian woman easier, and tools for the cultivation of your fields."

"But now and then," Renno said, "our great friend France might ask us to take up our arms in some common cause?"

"That is the purpose of an alliance," Louis said. "To ensure the common safety of those who participate."

"My lord duke," Renno said, very formal, his voice rising to make interruption inadvisable, "when Hernando de Soto landed on the shores of Florida, he must have used approximately the same words in his efforts to get the Choctaw to do his bidding. When the French and English came into North America, they asked for an alliance with those tribes who lived on the shores of the great sea. And from the earliest times when Spain, France, and Great Britain were fighting each other to keep their foothold on this continent, first one and then the other came to the Indian with his promises. 'Fight our battles, and we will give you the land that has always been yours forever. Be the pawns in our plans for colonial empire, and we will give you trinkets and a few guns so that you can better serve us as cannon fodder.' Every colonial nation, from the Dutch to the British, has tried the same tactics. France, in the Southeast, practiced a policy of divide and conquer, fomenting wars among the southern tribes to make them weak so that the forces of France could move in."

Now it was Renno's turn to hold up his hand to keep Louis Philippe from interrupting. "Only this year death came to my own village, to the husband of my mother, only this year because the white man was looking for Indian foot soldiers to fight his wars." He made an abrupt motion with his hand. "No more. We will fight perhaps, but only when it serves our cause or the cause of a friend who delivers more than trinkets, a few long rifles, and promises. My lord duke, you may tell your great man that his plans to regain a foothold on this continent will go a-glimmering if he depends upon recruiting the Indians of the Southwest to fight for him."

"I don't think you understand," Louis Philippe said.

"Perhaps not," Renno told him. "But I understand this: Forces that neither you nor I can stop are shaping this continent, and it is my belief that one day the flag of the United States will fly from the Atlantic to the Pacific. I can only pray that our people will have a place in that great nation. But I can promise you this—no European colonial nation will."

The remainder of the trip was pleasant enough, although Louis could not help but be disappointed. He contented himself with learning as much as he could about the country and its people, in chatting pleasantly with the charming Beth, in being amused at how thoroughly his younger brother had fallen under the spell of a part-Indian girl. Farewells were said on a chill day with lowering clouds. El-i-chi would take the Frenchmen into Knoxville.

Beau, the comte, had asked Renna to walk with him. Renna, realizing that she was truly going to miss the young Frenchman's presence, his constant attentions, and his compliments, led him down the trail to the swimming creek. A family of otters was at play. They would clamber onto the bank and slide down the little ledge of skim ice along the edge of the creek.

"I would that I could take you with me," Beau said.

"Assuming, that is, that I would agree to go," she replied with a smile.

"Would you?"

She played her large, green eyes over his face. "I'm not sure. If I were older, perhaps. If you could go back to France and I with you, it would be interesting to see the countryside you describe so well, the fine palaces, and Paris. But I'm not old enough, and you are an exile."

"With no money," Beau added, laughing, "dependent on the hospitality of friendly Americans." He sobered. "It will not always be thus. Sanity will return to my country. Even in upheaval we have proven to the world that we are great, and Napoléon—" He paused. He was not supposed to know anything about Napoléon, who was nothing more than a general, a tool of the Directory that ruled France. But Renna was only a girl, and she lived so far from France, and he was smitten with her. "Napoléon will change France and the world. He is a wise man and will stop the foolish squandering of the best minds of France through the murder of the guillotine. Then we will be able to go home, and—"

"I hope so, Beau," Renna said fervently. "I wish you very good luck."

"A kiss, then, for luck?" he requested. She looked up at him, felt his lips on hers, and knew, during the next few minutes, that she was being kissed by a man and that her response was not that of a child. She pushed him away, breathless.

"Soon you'll be living in a new house with your father and your stepmother," he said.

"Yes."

"Will you take your schooling here or go to the East?"

"Here," she said. "Beth will teach me, and perhaps I will go into Knoxville."

"I'll write."

"You have written down how to send letters to Knoxville, in care of my grandfather?"

"Yes." He leaned toward her, kissed her once more, and then led her back to the village with her hand in his.

William Blount's health had failed him. He suffered fevers and ague and lost weight. His plans for an empire in the Southeast were not dead, he felt—only postponed. In the meantime there were millions of acres of western land open for speculation. And he was still an active participant in the Yazoo scheme, which envisioned a vast new area of settlement reaching northward all the way to the big bend of the Tennessee. With his friend John Sevier, Blount began to agitate for a new treaty with the Indians, a treaty that would deliver all of southern Tennessee—the land of Rusog and the Cherokee—to the Yazoo Company with its vast purchasing power.

Even while the Senate in Philadelphia was debating his impeachment, Blount made plans for his political comeback in Tennessee state politics, for he had found that an officeholder's powers cannot be matched by a private citizen.

Blount's agents had once been numerous. One by one they had withered away. John Chisholm had gone to England to work there for the cause and had faded into limbo. Waith Pennywhistle was dead. But there were always men to do errands if the stakes were high enough. Blount and Sevier sent a settler named James Ore to call on the various Cherokee chiefs and to tell them to prepare their own minds and their people for a sweeping change, for a cession of Indian lands.

A new year began, and in the Seneca village it was once again time for the feast of the new beginning, but Blount and Sevier's agent had not yet made his appearance in Rusog's lodge.

It got to the point where Roy Johnson was going to hang around just to see what Beth was going to do next.

After the first of the year, following a trip by Beth and Renno into Knoxville, wagons began to arrive to deliver materials for Beth's house. She had chosen a hillside near the village. The clearing had been done. Skilled carpenters and masons from Knoxville came with the wagons. A stone foundation was laid.

"Well, Beth," Roy Johnson asked, "what are you building, a New World Huntington Manor?"

Roy was not the first to call Beth's attentions to the size of the house, which was, after all, rather modest by the Englishwoman's standards, having only fourteen rooms.

"Call it what you like," she said, somewhat sharply. "Call it Huntington Castle, if that pleases you."

"Sorry, honey," Roy apologized. "Didn't mean to lick the red off your candy."

Napoléon did not invade England. In 1798 his armies were defeated by Lord Nelson in Egypt. On the waters of the Atlantic, the U.S.S. *Delaware* took the French ship *Croyable*. The *Constellation* demolished the warships *Insurgente* and *Vengeance*. The young American navy was flexing its muscles.

In September of 1800 the undeclared war ended with the termination of the old treaty of friendship and alliance between France and the United States. A portion of the duc d'Orléans's prophecy had come true, for Napoléon had taken a giant step toward being ruler of France by becoming first consul. The little general's plans, however, concerned Europe, not faraway America.

Renno and his family observed the coming of 1800 in peace and happiness. Renna's sadness at Beau's leaving lessened with time. Beth, working with Se-quo-i, was earning a reputation among certain young members of the family of being a stern schoolmistress. With a need to educate not only Hawk and Renna but Ena's twins and El-i-chi's two ruffians, life was seldom dull for Beth as she watched her new abode take shape ever so slowly. She had come to accept the local name for her house, a name that had been good-naturedly spread by Roy Johnson: Huntington Castle.

Renno would remember those few years with ever-lasting fondness, and as the longest period of time that he had ever spent at home. He was sachem to his people, son to his aging mother, father to his children, and husband to a woman of unceasing appeal. No letters came from the East as they once had come bearing the signature of George Washington and containing a summons to a doubtful duty. And, although there were times when he left Huntington Castle and ran far, feeling the wind in his face and looking wistfully at the crest of the next ridge, for the most part the white Indian was very content.

Here is an exciting preview of Volume XXI in the
WHITE INDIAN series:

RENNA

Coming in June 1991, wherever Bantam Books
are sold.

Prologue

Othon Hugues, envoy of the ruling body of revolutionary France, rode through a dense forest of firs, pines, and birches toward a pretty little town lying under the slopes of Segovia's Pico de Peñalara. There, in the comely resort of San Ildefonso, seven miles southeast of the city of Segovia, France had once before dictated terms to Charles IV of Spain.

Although it was midday and although Hugues was surrounded by an honor guard consisting of twelve brightly uniformed French dragoons, he was sensitive to the gloom cast by the overlapping branches of the trees. The impenetrable shadows reminded him of the darkness of the woodlands near his home and sent him seeking moodily into his past, to a time when, to escape the jibes, laughter, and cruelty of his half brothers, he sought sanctuary in the forest.

Hugues wore the plain black garb of the Revolution. His hat, not at all stylish, was pulled low over his brow to protect his unusually pale eyes from the occasional dazzling rays of October sun, which penetrated the canopy of the trees. They were the light of ice, his eyes, and men who were seeing him for the first time were often led to mistakenly believe that the irises' lack of pigment connoted weakness. His face was deeply marked by the same pox that had killed his mother when he was eight years old. His shoulders were broad and his torso long, making him half a head taller in the saddle than any of the soldiers who rode on the jangling, leather-creaking escort.

San Ildefonso, where Spanish kings had summered

since before the reign of Philip V, boasted gardens designed by the famous Frenchman E. Boutelou, with twenty-six fountains by R. Fremin and J. Thierri. Philip V and his wife, Isabella Farnese, were buried in the palace chapel.

The loveliness of the town was lost on Othon Hugues, a man who, as chief executioner of Paris, had risen to sanguine prominence during the early stage of the Revolution and, it was whispered, now had the ear of Napoleon himself. Only a certain kind of beauty moved him; to him the spurt of blood from the severed necks of men and women like those who had lorded over him in his early life was true loveliness. The elegant neck of Marie Antoinette herself had provided him with one of the more satisfying moments of his life. He had stood for long, long minutes, his hand on the trip cord of the guillotine, savoring the thrill before letting the heavy blade fall. That particular gushing fountain of red had soothed his bitterness for a time.

It was true that Hugues had the ear of the first consul, the man who had restored France to glory. Before his stint as executioner, he had earned his reputation as a soldier in many battles early in the Revolution, then as a representative of the Directorate with the general during the Egyptian campaign. Hugues had made himself useful while proving that his loyalties lay with Napoleon Bonaparte, not with the political fools back in Paris. He would balk at nothing in carrying out his general's requests, so no one had been surprised when the first consul chose Hugues to journey to the little Spanish resort to represent the consulate in the continuation of Napoleon's plan to seize new colonies abroad to provide food for the French armies during the struggle for dominance in Europe.

Hugues's dark, pitted face was expressionless as his host, the king of Spain, accompanied by his top advisers, took him on a tour of the royal apartments. There the envoy saw Flemish tapestries from the era when Spain had been a power in Europe, cartoons by Goya, and a grotesque golden statuette from Peru.

"Shamefully," Charles said, "many such works of árt were melted down and have long since been dispersed as coin around the world. For a time, my friend, the gold of Spain enriched all of Europe."

Hugues made no comment. His predetermined opinion of the King of Spain had not been altered by the man's polite hospitality nor by his garrulous comments on the riches displayed in the royal apartments. It was well known that the power in Spain was in the soft hands of Maria Luisa of Palma, the queen, and her lover, Manuel de Godoy, a government minister who had been appointed by Charles himself. And certainly it was Charles who had allowed Spain to become a vassal of the French and to be forced into France's wars as nothing more than a satellite, a poor relation.

Hugues remained silent until the tour of the apartments had ended. He declined a glass of wine, waited for the king to seat himself, and, standing, delivered the message from Napoleon. He was not a diplomat. He was a soldier. The only softness in him was hidden deeply, in the form of his attachment to a woman years his senior—an odd, unearthly creature whom he had first met when he was an unhappy ten-year-old hiding in the dark shadows of the dense Pyrenean forest. Melisande . . . no matter how often circumstances forced him to leave her, he never ceased to be surprised by the intensity of his longing for her.

Even as he stood delivering Napoleon's message in a low, roughened voice, his thoughts were never far from Melisande's little house in the forest near the chateau where he had been born. Hugues was the bastard son of a milkmaid and the master of the estate, a man who boasted of his noble blood until Othon Hugues, as an adult, returned to the place where he had been exposed daily to the arrogance of his rich, spoiled half brothers. On that day his father made no boasts. Instead, the man who had never acknowledged Othon as his son screamed in agony. The master's noble blood flowed down the sharp blade of Othon's sword, which pierced his bloated, aristocratic belly.

And the half brothers? They had no laughter, no harsh words, no orders for him—only frightened pleas for mercy and screams of fading mortality as Othon killed them slowly, one by one.

Now, as he stood uncomfortably in the presence of an aristocrat, moments from the past flowed back to him. He lost patience with diplomatic talk.

"The first consul thinks that the time has come to rectify the mistakes of 1763," Othon said in his deep, gravelly voice.

"I must confess," said Charles, "that I sometimes have difficulty remembering dates."

"Sire," said an adviser, speaking in Spanish, "I think the ambassador is referring to the time when France turned over to Spain her holdings in the New World, specifically the areas west of the Mississippi River."

"Ah," Charles said, his face clouding.

"The first consul is prepared, of course, to return value for value," Hugues said. "Even though he doubts Spain's ability to maintain herself in her American possessions for any length of time."

"See here, sir—" said an adviser, rising to the insult.

Charles waved the adviser into silence. "Has the first consul noted my request that my son-in-law be given the throne of Tuscany?" Charles asked.

"He has," Othon replied.

Charles turned to his advisers. "There is no gold in Louisiana. For Tuscany we exchange deserts and wilderness inhabited by wild Indians. You will draw up the agreement immediately."

Never had a decision that would affect the lives of so many been concluded more quickly. Othon Hugues departed San Ildefonso on the day of his arrival. To the chagrin of his escort he rode hard and long, making camp only after darkness had fallen. Now that he had concluded his business for the general, his only desire was to be at home, with *her*.

He dismissed his honor guard after crossing through

the Basque Provinces in northern Spain. The young officer in charge had served with Othon in Egypt and could be trusted not to open the sealed pouch that contained the Agreement of San Ildefonso. As Napoleon had instructed, the negotiations with Charles of Spain would be kept secret—at least while the agreement was in the care of Othon Hugues or his men. What would happen once the agreement reached Paris was not Othon's responsibility. Knowing Paris and the consulate as he did, Othon believed there was little likelihood of any secret being kept for long.

Soon he was galloping through country that he knew well. As he rode he could see Melisande's face, could hear the sound of her voice. Was the awareness of her that hovered over and around him a manifestation of her odd powers? Had she sensed his nearness? He had long since ceased trying to answer such questions.

When he had first met her, he had given in to her blandishments and placed his ten-year-old cheek against her prim, adolescent bosom. He reveled in the tenderness of her touch, the musky-warm smell of her, the delightful taste of her. She was living in a hut that, in winter, admitted the frigid winds from the mountains. Over the years he had improved her dwelling place: Rooms had been added, a fire sizzled in the stone fireplace, and the house hidden away in the shadows of the forest was snug and warm. She was expecting him. She had dressed in a lacy, frilly black gown. Through the cut lace he could see the pale glow of her skin. The flickering fire cast moving shadows on her cheek. She had matured over the years into a creature of lush and splendid softness. The small, hard breasts of her youth were now enticing mounds. He never tired of her beauty. "You have done well."

"I saw," she told him, as he stood just inside the door.

"Yes," he said.

She smiled as she loosed her hair. It cascaded over her shoulders in an ebony mass. He could anticipate its clean fragrance, the pleasant tickling sensation even before he moved to press his face into it and inhale deeply. The goodness of her in his arms caused him to shiver uncontrollably.

"I know, I know," she whispered. She took his hand and led him to a wide down cushion, sat, pulled him down, and opened her loose garment with one hand while pulling his head into the softness of her breasts with the other. She inhaled through her teeth in quick ecstasy as his lips closed over one swollen nipple.

The warm flow of her milk into his mouth soothed away the tiredness of his body and obliterated all concern from his mind. He felt like a child again, and the nourishing, pungent stream strengthened him. He did not question the perpetual abundance. He accepted it as he had of old until, sated with the rich warmth of it, he let his hands search down and away from the fullness of her breasts. As she removed his clothing, he let himself drift into lazy sensuality.

He had seen many naked women. He had seen nude women consumed with emotions that ranged from sexual passion to the anguish of dying, but he had never seen a woman who was as soft, as smooth, as beautiful as she, his Melisande. She prepared him and, with deep-throated croonings, mounted him. She rode him with passion, and he quickly spent himself.

Long after she had drained him of all desire, he lingered with her, touching, clinging, sipping her substance from her fecund breasts.

It was she who broke the comfortable silence.

"You will travel far," she whispered.

"I must go to Paris."

"No . . . beyond Paris, beyond France."

He pulled away and sat with his strongly muscled legs folded under him. "Tell me what you perceive."

"The sea. A far land of moist heat and a polyglot people."

"America?" he asked.

She nodded. Her eyes, tilted in exotic loveliness, were as black as the night, sparkling ebony orbs flirting from behind long lashes.

"Then you must leave this house and the forest, for I will not go without you."

"Yes," she assented, and from that he knew that her prediction was true, for she had never consented to leave her home before, not even when he had gone with Napoleon to Egypt.

"And what else do you see?" he asked.

"An opportunity to serve the master."

He felt his pulse increase. "Tell me," he said hoarsely.

"In the American wilderness you will be your own law," she whispered. Her teeth were bizarre. They were round and strong, but they were dark, an irridescent black. It was as if the arcane and ancient quality of her talents gleamed there, hidden except when she smiled. But her breath had the freshness of a forest fern, and her lips were full and soft. "There you will have the pleasure of serving him. You will praise his greatness with the blood of many."

He was breathing rapidly and the thought of such opportunity had sexually aroused him. "Many?"

"The red Indians of the wilderness," she confirmed. "And those who oppose the will of the general."

"You know the content of the Agreement of San Ildefonso?" He asked. "You know what I accomplished in Spain?"

"Yes," she said, nodding, showing her dark teeth. "Those who resent the return of France to the North American continent will speak out against her, and it will be your *duty*"—she put a certain amount of irony into the word—"to educate them."

"More slowly this time," he whispered, reaching for her.

And this time, imagining rivers of blood and remembering past displays of pleasurable agony, he was the aggressor.

Chapter One

To the residents of the Cherokee and Seneca villages it seemed as if Flame Hair, wife of the Seneca sachem, Renno, was always entertaining company. Citizens of the new state of Tennessee came from Knoxville and Nashville to see the house that had become known as one of the man-made wonders of the Southwest Territory. Roy Johnson, the sachem's father-by-marriage, had once jokingly called it "Huntington Castle." Solemn Indians traveled from the western reaches of the Cherokee nation, from Chickasaw Bluffs on the distant Mississippi River, and from Creek and Choctaw lands to the south to see the Lodge as Big as a Hill.

Not everyone who appeared before the whitewashed gate of Huntington Castle came merely to see the house. Some came partly to see the house and partly to see Beth herself. The Englishwoman's beauty was as much a topic of conversation in some quarters as was the house.

Beth Huntington Harper, whose Seneca name was chosen because of the autumn-leaf tint of her hair, genuinely liked people and possessed considerable political astuteness. Thus, she made everyone welcome. Even before the house was finished, Beth had realized that the future of both her husband's small tribe of Seneca and the great Cherokee Nation depended upon the friendship of men who wielded power in the states adjoining the Indian lands. On behalf of her adopted people she had appointed herself goodwill ambassador for the new state of Tennessee. She was less in evidence when the visitors were chiefs or senior warriors from the various tribes of the Southwest Territory, who had signed his name RENNO HARPER on the marriage certificate at St. Philip's Church in Wilmington, North Carolina.

All visitors, Indian and white, were offered sustenance that included produce from the garden of the Cherokee women—that tribe's principal chief was Rusog, who was Flame Hair's brother-in-law—and from the plantings of the Seneca women, who allegiance was to Beth's husband, the sachem Renno.

Beth called her home "The House." Once or twice she had tried to explain that the residence was not nearly as grand as the name that Roy Johnson had thrust upon it. To Beth, accustomed to the great manorial halls of old England, hers was just a *T*-shaped two-story frame house with a colonnaded veranda rising in front to the full height of the roof. From front to back the main wing was two spacious rooms deep and extended north-south for just over one hundred twenty-five feet. The rear of the house greeted the morning sun. Each room of the main wing had either a western or an eastern exposure, planned to catch the breezes of summer and to escape the icy northern blasts of winter. A dogtrot extension from the dining room, at the center back of the house, led to the kitchen and servants' quarters. That wing formed the base of the *T*.

The furnishings of The House—or Huntington Castle, as some visitors preferred to call it—were still arriving by wagon from Knoxville, some items having made the long Atlantic crossing on one of Beth's merchant ships. Each arrival was the cause of intense celebration for the flame-haired, mature mistress of the house and her petite, shapely stepdaughter, whose name, Renna, was a variation of her father's.

Roy Johnson might grumble "Where in tarnation is she *putting* all of it?" and Renno might shake his head in bemusement, but Beth ignored their teasing. She simply directed the black servants in trying each new item in as many as half a dozen rooms and dozens of individual locations until Renna and she were satisfied—at least temporarily.

The servants—like the furniture, the linens, the sets of fine English china, and the racks of ringing crystal goblets—had arrived by wagon from Knoxville. They had been purchased just as the furniture and goods had been purchased, and their arrival had sparked a disagreement between Renno and his wife. The dispute was short lived.

"I do not keep slaves," Renno said quietly. The glint in his blue eyes told Beth that no discussion would be allowed. "My wife does not keep slaves."

Beth solved the matter by drawing up papers of manumission for the servants while continuing to treat them as they expected to be treated, as valued workers who received remuneration in the form of ample food, adequate clothing, and a place to call home. Once the former slaves viewed their cozy quarters, they chose to remain in Flame Hair's employ.

Huntington Castle had another name also. To many, especially the Cherokee and Seneca warriors, it was "Renno's House." Such men knew the white Indian as a great sachem, a stalwart warrior, and a leader dedicated to the welfare of the Cherokee Nation as well as that of his smaller group of displaced Seneca. It did not matter to them that payment for building materials, workmen, artisans, and furniture came out of Beth Huntington's cache of gold. In the Indian society men had their place and women theirs.

Perhaps the most inquisitive Seneca wondered why their friend and sachem seemed attracted to women of the white face, but they did not voice such questions. Renno was Renno, and it was his business that he had married a daughter of the settlers Nora and Roy Johnson, to give her two children, a boy and a girl. To Renno's credit, after the death of his first wife he had married a Seneca maiden. Together they had one son. But the sachem lost her, too, before bringing the flame-haired Englishwoman to the land of the Cherokee for the second time.

The Cherokee Nation was at the very center of a titanic collision between cultures. Violence, blood, and death were its product since shortly after the white man's arrival on the shores of the North American continent. For two years, however, Renno's family had enjoyed peace and togetherness. For the boy called Os-sweh-ga-da-ga-ah Ne-wa-ah, or Little Hawk, there was sometimes entirely too much togetherness. On evenings when his stepmother read aloud or tinkled odd, minor melodies on the harpsichord that had come all the way from England, Little Hawk longed for the freedom to go "torching" opossums in the woods—spotting the reflecting eyes of the taciturn little beasts by the light of a blazing brand.

Unfortunately, Flame Hair did not cook opossum. When Little Hawk did manage to sneak away from all that family cohesion into the nighttime forest, he took his catch to his grandmother Toshabe, probably the finest baker of opossum east or west of the Mississippi. Toshabe knew from her own experience of raising two sons the appetite of a growing boy.

On balmy afternoons, when other lads of his own age were splashing and playing chase in the swimming creek beyond the village, Little Hawk was imprisoned in the classroom. There, with his sister, Renna; his half brother, Ta-na; his cousin Gao, son of his uncle El-i-chi and Ah-wa-o the Rose; and his aunt Ena's twins, Rusog Ho-ya and We-yo; Little Hawk was exposed to the writings of men with names like Plato and Josephus, to the mystery of numbers, and to the oddities of the spelling of the English language. Little Hawk, who had inherited his father's sense of responsibility, understood that his education in the lore of the white man fulfilled a promise made by his father to his dead mother. But there were times when he longed for the old days, before he became a junior warrior, when he could spend a whole day in the woods without attracting the attention of an adult.

On this evening in May when the breezes were cool and the moon was due to come up full, Little Hawk felt no desire to sneak away into the woods, for Beth's visitors included his rangy, ruggedly handsome grandfather Roy Johnson and a gaunt, leonine man who had greeted Renno by name and with a firm handshake.

Andrew Jackson was thirty-three years old, three years younger than Renno. With Roy Johnson as his guide he had ridden out from Knoxville on a handsome stallion to confer with the white Indian.

Renno and Jackson had first met when Jackson, along with Roy, was a member of the convention drafting a constitution for the new state of Tennessee. Renno had been in Nashville to present the views of the Cherokee and the Seneca. The last time Andrew Jackson and Renno had seen each other was in Philadelphia, during the last days of George Washington's presidency. Jackson, a member of the House of Representatives at the time, had been elected to the Senate shortly afterward, only to resign in 1798, swearing that he was finished with public life. He was currently serving as judge of the Superior Court of Tennessee. Upon his arrival Jackson greeted the sachem in Cherokee and was answered in the accents of the British upper class, an affectation that Renno reserved for certain types of white men. He was not fond of Jackson, for the politician-judge had never been a friend to the Indian.

Jackson then turned to the son of the house and held out his hand. "And you, Hawk?" he asked.

"I am fine, sir," Little Hawk said, taking Jackson's hand.

Jackson's eyes crinkled with amusement. "I hear, young man, that you left Philadelphia in a hurry."

Little Hawk squirmed uneasily. His hasty departure from the nation's capital, where he had been a Senate page, was still a touchy subject in The House. "I think one could safely say, sir, that I did not tarry for too many good-byes," he said in an accent much like his father's.

Jackson laughed. "Well, every now and then we have to show those dag-blamed Easterners what's what, don't we?"

It was a small dinner party for The House, only the family, which consisted of Renno, Beth, Renna, and Little Hawk, and the two guests from Knoxville. Jackson was dressed for dinner in fashionable black evening wear, slightly the worse from having been carried in his saddlebag. In spite of the wrinkles in his trousers and coat, the white of his collar and a touch of lace at his throat gave him a dapper appearance. The judge seemed most interested in Beth's reaction to life on the frontier.

"Although," he said with a chuckle and a wave of one graceful hand, "one can hardly think of this excellent house as being an isolated oasis of civilization three days' ride from anywhere."

"But, Mr. Jackson," Beth said with her best smile, "we're only a stone's throw from two well-populated towns."

"Yes," Jackson responded. "I see." He obviously did not believe that an Indian village scarcely qualified as being somewhere.

Beth, having landed her little barb, changed the subject. "Speaking of civilization, Mr. Jackson, I am surprised that you did not take to life in the nation's capital."

Jackson snorted. "My dear, I did not like being separated from my family. Morever, the hypocrisy of national politics makes my stomach queasy."

"You'd never know it by your actions, Andy," Roy remarked. "You were one of the very few who had the guts to tell George Washington that he was wrong to support the Jay Treaty."

"Yes, that," Jackson mused. "Well, the general *was* wrong. Only twelve of us out of the whole House of Representatives spoke out. All the others voted to reply cordially to his Farewell Address. I still say that the Jay Treaty gave too much to Great Britain, and, mark my words, we'll pay for it in the end. We haven't heard the last of good King George the Third. We keep flip-flopping on what some folks in Philadelphia call our foreign policy. One minute we're scared out of our wits by Napoleon's France and the next we're talking turkey with him. But our main enemy is still the nation with whom we share a common language. England."

"Mr. Jackson," Renno said, "I pray that you are wrong but I fear that you are not."

"In a year, two years, perhaps five, we will begin to see our recent allies showing their true colors again," Jackson said.

When the meal was finished and topped off by an excellent after-dinner sherry, the men retired to the front veranda. Jackson puffed life into a battered corncob pipe. It soon became apparent that Jackson was slowly leading up to the purpose for his visit to the Seneca sachem. He spoke of hunting and horses and the vast, undeveloped lands of the frontier. At last he turned the conversation to the unrest in the Indiana Territory.

"I have heard of your contributions at Fallen Timbers," Jackson told Renno.

"If you heard of them from a certain ex–father-in-law of mine, you might have to pick and choose to find the truth," Renno remarked with a chuckle.

"All I told him was that you not only scouted the field but drew up and directed Anthony Wayne's battle plan," Roy protested. "Now if that isn't the truth—"

"I suppose," Jackson said, also chuckling, "that I'll have to accept it as fact, Roy, since General Wayne, rest his soul, isn't around to deny it." As he turned to face Renno, his eyes gleamed in the glow of lamplight from an open window. "Let me say only that I've known your father-in-law for a very long time. The slaughter at Fallen Timbers was a sad affair, my friend, but there are those among the Indians who are not content to confine such tragedies to the past. Even in these times of peace, isolated instances of violence are erupting all along the frontier. And up north there's a chief who is showing every sign of trying to follow in Little Turtle's footsteps."

"If you're referring to the Shawnee Tecumseh," Renno said, "oddly enough, he is not a chief."

"So I have been told," Jackson responded. "Nevertheless, he has sworn to unite all the Indian tribes for one final campaign against white penetration of Indian lands. Now it's none of my affair—not yet, at least, although I do have connections with the Tennessee militia—but I'd be curious to know if the sachem of the Southern Seneca still believes that the future of the Indian rests with the United States."

"So I have stated," Renno confirmed.

"And the Cherokee?" Jackson asked.

"I speak only for myself," Renno replied, "but I know my brother Rusog and his people. The Cherokees have stood at the side of their white neighbors in the past. They will do so again should the need arise."

"I have been told that you are wise," Jackson said, nodding in satisfaction. "Now I believe that is true. Interesting times are on the horizon. Interesting times indeed."

★ WAGONS WEST ★

This continuing, magnificent saga recounts the adventures of a brave band of settlers, all of different backgrounds, all sharing one dream— to find a new and better life.

☐	26822	**INDEPENDENCE! #1**	$4.50
☐	26162	**NEBRASKA! #2**	$4.50
☐	26242	**WYOMING! #3**	$4.50
☐	26072	**OREGON! #4**	$4.50
☐	26070	**TEXAS! #5**	$4.50
☐	26377	**CALIFORNIA! #6**	$4.50
☐	26546	**COLORADO! #7**	$4.95
☐	26069	**NEVADA! #8**	$4.50
☐	26163	**WASHINGTON! #9**	$4.50
☐	26073	**MONTANA! #10**	$4.50
☐	26184	**DAKOTA! #11**	$4.50
☐	26521	**UTAH! #12**	$4.50
☐	26071	**IDAHO! #13**	$4.50
☐	26367	**MISSOURI! #14**	$4.50
☐	27141	**MISSISSIPPI! #15**	$4.50
☐	25247	**LOUISIANA! #16**	$4.50
☐	25622	**TENNESSEE! #17**	$4.50
☐	26022	**ILLINOIS! #18**	$4.50
☐	26533	**WISCONSIN! #19**	$4.50
☐	26849	**KENTUCKY! #20**	$4.50
☐	27065	**ARIZONA! #21**	$4.50
☐	27458	**NEW MEXICO! #22**	$4.95
☐	27703	**OKLAHOMA! #23**	$4.50
☐	28180	**CELEBRATION! #24**	$4.50